BRUTAL OBSESSION

S. MASSERY

Edited by Studio ENP

Proofread by Paige Sayer Proofreading

Cover photo by Michelle Lancaster (www.michellelancaster.com)

Cover design by Qamber Design

To the dark ones who make our fantasies come to life

INTRODUCTION

Hello dear reader!

Brutal Obsession is my darkest book to date.

Please be aware if you have triggers that are common to dark romance/bully romance, this story checks quite a few of those boxes! (Including: blood/knife play, dubious consent, breath play, consensual non-consent, primal play, and mental/physical/emotional bullying.)

Greyson wanted me to inform you that he does not grovel. Under any circumstances.

Thank you and happy reading!

xoxo,
      Sara

GREYSON

The cash slides from my palm into the valet's. His fingers curl around the wad of bills as he pulls back, and he looks away.

Aw, he's embarrassed.

The girl on my arm giggles and leans into me.

Money and good looks will help people get away with just about anything. I learned that at the tender age of five from my father, thank you very much. He toted me around and flashed his smile or his wealth, and doors opened for us.

Sometimes literally.

Sometimes figuratively.

We were invincible.

Look at that sentence. Then read it again. *We. Were. Invincible.*

Back when I was a kid, my father and I wore gilded armor. He was a king, and I was a prince. We floated above the rest of society, and nothing was out of our reach.

I experienced the world through my father's view of

getting everything he fucking wanted. It's only natural that I became him.

Look, I'm not saying it's right. I'm just saying this is how it works. People are sheep, all too eager to be sacrificed to the wolves. And the wolves... well, they only survived if they were willing to get a little dirty.

The girl releases me long enough to stumble around the hood of my car. She practically falls into the passenger seat, her dress shifting to give me—and the valet—an eyeful of her tits.

That right there is the only reason she's here.

Paparazzi cameras flash from across the street, and I turn on my brilliant smile. The one that worked on the girl at the bar. And the waitress. And the cop who pulled me over a few hours ago for speeding. He let me off with just a warning.

I raise my hand as someone calls my name. Trying to get me to make eye contact, to get the perfect photo. Everyone wants something but fuck them if they think they can *get* it. They get the bare minimum of my acknowledgement, and it probably gives them a hard-on.

The passenger door shuts. I take one more look at the valet, making sure he knows. I see him. I saw him put the cash into his pocket. I want him to know that the money doesn't buy speedy service—it buys his silence.

He nods once, then averts his eyes again.

I slip into my car and leave the restaurant parking lot with a screech of tires. The familiar, intoxicating smell of burning rubber follows me. I love it—it means I'm making an exit. One that people will notice—and remember.

The nameless girl leans over and licks my cheek. I'm undecided if it's hot or gross, so I ignore it. She whispers something that I also ignore, and I press my foot harder on the gas pedal. I don't care about her right now.

Only two more streets before we hit the highway, and I can push this baby to a hundred. She has a certain purr when she gets that quick. The steering wheel almost vibrates in my hands.

It's an adrenaline rush I never pass up.

Later, when the girl is sucking my cock and moaning my name, I might pretend to give a shit about her.

I shift her away and readjust my grip.

We skid around a corner, our light green. I hit the gas, and we fly down the darkened street. Ahead of me, the stretch of road is empty—until it isn't.

The car comes out of nowhere. My headlights illuminate the driver's pale face seconds before I smash into her vehicle.

My airbags explode, and only my seatbelt, which I don't remember putting on, keeps me from rocketing through the windshield. My passenger's head slams into her airbag, and she falls back against the seat. Blood drips down her face from her nose.

I struggle to inhale. The seatbelt is too fucking tight, and smoke fills my car.

I unbuckle and shove my door open, falling out.

Fuck.

The asphalt bites into my palms. Miraculously, though, I'm unhurt. I pat myself down just for the hell of it, but besides what I can imagine will be a pretty nasty bruise across my chest, I'm okay.

The girl in my car seems to be okay, too. She regains consciousness, blinking slowly and touching her upper lip.

I stumble around to the front of my car, which is currently smashed up against the other one. A silver compact car, one of those old ones from a decade ago. I hit the driver's side, but ahead of the seat. It almost appears like I was aiming for the front tire—in an effort to avoid her entirely, I guess, and I just miscalculated. That's how it could be argued, one way or another. *If* it's going to be argued.

"Help." Her voice is soft, hoarse. Like she screamed before impact, and her throat shredded.

I wince.

She has blood streaked down her face, and I can't tell if her eyes are open or not. Her airbags didn't deploy, but her window is broken. Glass cuts, then. And even though I didn't hit it, her door is dented inward.

The street is empty. No cars, no people. When does *that* ever happen in a city like this? A city that usually buzzes with nightlife—in fact, it *is* probably buzzing with people only a few blocks away.

I nod to myself, calculating. Always calculating.

Another gift from Daddy Dearest.

I go back to my car and open the passenger door. I pull the girl out and lead her around, sitting her in the driver's seat. I fold her into it, even as she stares at me. Confusion mars her face, turning it ugly.

Confusion is akin to stupidity. If you can't understand something, you're just not thinking about it hard enough.

"Where's your phone, baby?"

Bless her soul, she perks up when I call her that. It's not her fault she doesn't know it's my cover, because I don't have a clue what her name is. She points to the floor of the passenger seat. To her purse.

"You were driving," I tell her. I lean into her, cupping the back of her neck. "I need you to tell them that, okay?"

Her brow furrows. "Why?"

"Because I'll make sure your wildest dreams come true if you do this for me." I meet her eyes, my thumb rubbing a soft spot on her neck just under her ear. She leans into it, barely, and sucks her lower lip into her mouth. "You borrowed my car for the night. You were going to return it to me tomorrow."

"Tomorrow," she repeats.

I nod once and release her, closing her back into the door. I dial nine-one-one on her phone and hand it to her, then take a step back. Once I'm halfway down the block, I call my father.

I thought that would be the end of the story. He wouldn't blame me for leaving the scene. It isn't just about getting our way. It's about preserving his image. *Our* image.

Exactly as I predict, he doesn't say a word about my bad luck. Or who I was with. I send him the address of the house I'm sitting in front of, and he sends a car for me.

I arrive home thirty minutes later, and he doesn't ask what happened. He's like a lawyer, unwilling to incriminate himself in the fine print. If anything comes up, he'll expect me to smooth it over. If I can't, he will.

Two hours later, the cop cars come screaming into our driveway. I'm arrested on the spot.

SIX MONTHS LATER

1

VIOLET

A widely known fact about me: I don't like surprises. I'm jumpy. I make unholy noises. My face gets beet red, and my body gets hot and tingly, and sometimes I feel like I've run out of air. Unfortunately, that combination is the perfect reaction for people who *do* like surprises.

Which is why I've spent my life being surprised. Birthday parties, jump-scares, visitors I wasn't expecting... People *love* to see the dramatic reaction, and I seem unable to help but give it to them.

And, naïve me, I keep expecting people will remember I loathe them.

Not today.

I've barely pushed open the apartment door when the lights come on and a dozen people scream, "WELCOME BACK!"

I scream right along with them. My coffee goes everywhere, and my feet go out from under me. Only quick hands grasping my arms keeps me upright.

And falling would probably suck a lot under my conditions.

After my heart stops trying to escape from my tight chest, I find my darling roommate-slash-best friend at the center of the group, grinning wickedly. Willow knows my feelings on surprises and gleefully continues. I shake my head at her and laugh. If she had such reactions to surprises, I'd spring them on her, too.

With a wide smile, I glance around the room. Familiar faces that I've *missed* in the last six months fill the space. If anyone was here to surprise me, I'd want it to be them. Willow knows. Sometimes she knows what I want before I do.

I finally realize that someone is still holding my arms. I look over my shoulder, already sheepish, and meet Jack's gaze. It takes me a second to register that it's actually him, and my stomach knots.

"You okay, Violet?" His lips twist, him trying not to laugh at me. His eyes still crinkle, though. And damn, does he look as good as I remember.

I stabilize my feet under me before gently pulling away. "I'm good. Thanks."

Not good. Not by a long shot. But I'm definitely not going to be spilling my heart out to my *ex*-boyfriend. Guess I forgot to mention that to Willow...

"I'm surprised you're here," I say.

He shifts and rubs the back of his neck. It's his turn to be sheepish. We met here, at Crown Point University, our freshman year, and it was lust at first sight. I was on the dance team, and he was a football player. We would perform during half-time, and it didn't take long for us to notice each other.

And why wouldn't I have noticed him? He's gorgeous.

Wavy dark hair that he keeps a little longer than most guys, warm honey eyes. A square jaw, strong nose. He towers over me, too. People always said we looked good together.

We were opposites in appearance. He has the muscle mass, and I'm lean. The classic blonde hair and blue eye combination my mother always made a fuss about. Maybe that's why my skin crawled every time someone commented on how attractive a couple we were. It was more a reflection on me than *us*.

He lifts his hand and moves my hair off my forehead. The gesture is intimate, but I'm too stunned to stop him. He brushes his thumb over the scar on my temple. "I was worried about you. You wouldn't let me see you in the hospital. Or after?"

A sigh escapes before I can school my features into something a little more... regretful. "Well, I was embarrassed."

That's a lie. I just didn't want to face whatever the fuck emotional roller coaster I was riding the last six months. Seriously. My life went from normal to shit in a split second. Adding Jack—and the life that I thought I had, the one that seemed to go up in a puff of smoke when I woke up in the hospital—would've been more pain than I was ready to accept.

"Violet!"

I step away from Jack, ignoring his wounded expression, and turn to my other friends. Half the dance team is here, and they all crowd around me. Someone pulls at my coffee-stained blouse, and another swoops in to clean the floor where my cup dropped. I had forgotten, in my Jack-shock.

"Lucky it wasn't hot." Willow nudges me.

"Luck and I aren't on speaking terms."

She visited faithfully every day while I was stuck in the hospital. Kept me sane, kept me looped in to the gossip. She's the only one who knows what I went through, and I'm keeping it that way. I'm not in the habit of airing my dirty laundry—or my newfound nightmares. I've been plagued by bright lights, crunching metal, and snapping bones.

She rolls her eyes at my luck comment. "You need to change. We're taking you out."

Oh boy. My first instinct is to say no, but honestly? I could use a bit of normalcy. My therapist—the talk one, not the physical one—said something about getting back into a routine. Well, for the last two years, I've gone out with my girls on Friday nights. There's nothing more *normal* than that.

I'm actually looking forward to it.

She leads the way to the bedroom I haven't been in since... *before*. She steps aside and lets me do the honors. Opening the door is like cracking into a time capsule.

Fucking devastating.

Willow stands behind me, her hand on my shoulder, as I stare around at the remnants of the person I used to be. If I wasn't aware of how different I was after six months away, I am now. Mentally, physically.

There are still clothes that I left on the floor. My chair is pulled out and covered in clothes. There's a pile of books that I had planned to conquer over the summer in the center of the desk. My bed is made.

"I kept the door open sometimes," Willow says. "Especially in the last week. So it shouldn't smell too stale... Also, I changed your sheets. You're welcome."

I crack a smile. "Thanks."

The luggage that I dragged inside earlier today is now at the foot of my bed—courtesy of Willow, I presume.

I step inside and go straight to the wall of pictures. Dance team competitions, selfies with my girls, photos of Jack and me at nearly every event you can think of—concerts and football games and the beach and house parties. Bonfires on the lake.

"You know I love surprises. So, *thanks* for that."

Willow snorts. She and I met in high school, and we've been through thick and thin together. We've seen each other at our best... and worst. Evidently.

"The team wanted to be here when you got back." She smirks. "Well, most of them."

There are some girls on the dance team that Willow and I never vibed with. They've just got sticks up their asses, so why would we be friends with them? They only cared about chasing whatever team was doing well. Football, hockey, lacrosse.

Boring.

I go to my closet. "Jack and I broke up."

"I know."

"Of course you know," I grumble. "You still invited him." I yank it open and flip through clothes. I lost weight while I was away—but most of it was muscle mass. My body is soft where I used to be strong. Physical therapy helped, but not nearly enough. Not enough to give me back the muscles I had before.

"He begged. And he does look cute when he's on his knees..."

I glare at her. "Seriously?"

She shrugs, still smiling. "I think he missed you. He made a point that you like to isolate when you stress, which is *true*. You can't deny it. We're just trying to prevent that from happening, is all."

Freaking hell. I can't explain the knotting high in my chest, but I need to explain it to her. "He missed the dance team, peppy version of me. I've been doused in..." I struggle to find the right way to explain, finally settling on, "gray."

"Violet's gone to the dark side, then? Well, to keep up with that thinking, how about this?" She plucks out a black sequined dress.

I've only worn that one a handful of times. It's short and sexy, and immediately bile rises up my throat. I swallow hard.

"No." My voice is flat.

She raises an eyebrow. "Is it because—"

"I'm not going to show off my leg on my first day back. Or ever." My leg. I really don't want to talk about my leg. "My days of shorts and skirts are over."

I pick out black leather pants and a pink sweater. Compromise. There's snow on the ground, after all, and if we're going out, I don't want to freeze to death.

Willow closes my door and leans against it, filling me in on the latest drama while I change. She doesn't flinch when I pull off my pants and reveal the thick scar on my lower leg. The surgeons did their best, but they had to cut me open. My tibia and fibula were both broken—snapped nearly clean through.

My leg took the direct impact of the accident.

I was lucky they didn't use hardware to keep me together when they reset the bone. After surgery, I had physical therapy in the hospital. Then crutches for weeks while it healed, with strict orders that I couldn't put any weight on my leg. After that, physical therapy to slowly help my muscles get used to walking, bending... functioning.

Crown Point University let me take a medical leave of absence for the fall semester. I've had to add an extra class to my schedule this semester, plus both semesters next year, to graduate on time.

That's the only silver lining.

"You look good," Willow tells me. She extends a tube of lipstick toward me.

I finger-comb my blonde hair into somewhat respectable curls and then swipe on the dark-red color. It's bolder than what I would've normally gone for, but I trust my best friend's judgment. It gives my pink sweater a bit of an edgier vibe.

Probably.

Maybe it's wishful thinking.

She loops her arm in mine. In the living room, our friends are spread out on the couches and the floor. Now that I look closer at them, they do seem ready to go out. Flawless makeup, nice clothes. Dresses, heeled boots.

"Where are we going?" I ask.

"Haven. There's a game tonight, but it should be okay if we get there before it ends. Should we call a cab, or are you good to walk?"

Haven is a local bar that's almost always overrun by CPU students.

"Walking is fine." I'll pay for it tomorrow, but my blood runs cold at the thought of getting into a car. It was a struggle to sit in the passenger seat of mom's car on the way here. Our silence was tense. My leg constantly jigged until she pulled over and let me out in front of my apartment building this morning.

Since then, I walked to campus to register for classes

and confirm my financial aid, applied for three jobs near school, and got myself a congratulatory coffee. I missed Willow when I dropped my stuff off earlier, and I definitely didn't venture farther into our space. I didn't want to walk down memory lane too soon.

My leg already aches, but I ignore it. Spring semester starts on Monday. I've got the weekend to rest and recuperate.

This is my college experience.

So, no, I'm not getting in a car. I smile at my friends and lie. "I could use the exercise."

Willow scoffs. "Whatever you say, Batman."

The ten of us gear up for the weather—snow or not, it's actually still rather mild—and walk two blocks to the bar near campus. It's a regular hangout known for being lax on IDing college kids, and they have a five-dollar margarita night which usually draws a big crowd.

The oval-shaped bar in the center has a million bar stools. There are televisions mounted on almost every wall, showcasing the pro athlete games. There's not a bad seat in the house. And after a CPU game finishes—especially if we win? Standing room only.

I considered applying for a job there, but I don't think I could do it. Serve my friends, I mean. Even if they tip well, some students get weird when they're drunk.

It's relatively quiet when we arrive. We stamp our feet in the small vestibule, knocking off loose snow and salt. I blow into my hands, laughing at how ridiculous we are. The others shake their heads and chuckle along with me. Yeah, the lighthearted blame rests on my shoulders. So much for it being mild outside. That was before the sun set, and now it's colder than a witch's tit.

We claim a U-shaped booth, everyone climbing in and

pressing close. I end up across the table from Jack—luckily —and beside Willow. On my other side is a fellow junior, Jess, who joined the dance team last year.

"Paris just texted," Amanda says, tapping on her phone. She glances up and leans forward. "Says the team is heading here."

Willow rolls her eyes. "Place will be flooded with puck bunnies in a matter of minutes."

"Hockey team?" I clarify. I feel like I've lost my sense of time since I've been gone. Everyone has moved forward except for me.

Hockey starts sometime in October, and their season goes through the winter and into spring—especially if they're on a winning streak and make it into the national tournament. We never went to many hockey games in the past because it usually conflicted with the dance team competitions or basketball games.

If there's one thing CPU has going for it, it's the D1 sports.

"There's a new hotshot on the team," Amanda says. She blushes. "We've only lost one game. Some of the girls even started a petition to move our Friday practice so they can go to the home games. They're probably going to get their way."

My eyebrows hike. Puck bunnies—the girls who fawn over hockey players—or not, I doubt our coach would let that slide. Perhaps if enough of them protested...

"There's talk of them being selected to participate in the Nationals tournament," Jack adds. "Whole school's been talking about it. They just have to win a few more games."

CPU hasn't won a title in almost a decade—not in hockey, anyway. Jack's team made it to the Rose Bowl last year, but they lost by a field goal. And this year, they didn't even make it to the playoffs.

That's a sore subject.

"Well, let's get drunk before they show up and make us all miserable," Willow says. She flags down a waitress and orders us a round of tequila shots.

Yep, definitely going to be paying for this tomorrow.

Still, it's nice to be back. The conversation shifts from hockey to the dramatics on the dance team, and I smile and pick at my sweater as I listen. I'm familiar with most of the names, but a few times I glance questioningly at Willow. She provides context. A freshman, a new transfer, an older girl who finally made it through tryouts.

We get our tequila shots, plus wedges of lime and a salt shaker passed around. I lick the back of my hand and pour the salt onto it, then hold my wedge and shot glass until they're all ready.

"To Violet's return," Willow says.

They raise their glasses and clink them together in the middle of the table. As a unit, we lick the salt, tap the shot glasses to the table, and toss the liquid back. The taste of it is familiar, searing down my throat. I bite down on the lime, and the citrus explodes across my tongue. It mixes with the tequila and makes it actually enjoyable.

"That never gets old," I giggle, leaning into Willow.

She hugs me. "I missed you."

"Missed you, too."

"Good. Another round!" She slides out of the booth and knocks on the table. "I've got this one, then you sorry lot are buying next."

Jack takes Willow's place beside me. He puts his arm around my shoulders and pulls me into him. His warmth is familiar. The weight of his arm is comforting. "Have I told you I missed you?"

"Once or twice." I roll my eyes, but I don't straighten up. I should, because my behavior toward him over the past six months has been nothing short of atrocious. I don't even know why he still cares.

He *couldn't* see me. Not how I was... and how I might still be. I wasn't lying when I told Willow I was different. I feel like an uglier version of myself. Not as nice, not as bubbly, not as optimistic. Literally *darker*. Something broke inside me after the accident.

The dance team was just a hobby. A way to stay in shape and make friends. Willow was the one who begged me to audition with her our freshman year. She loves to dance, just as I did, but was terrified of doing The Big Brave Thing by herself. I went, but I didn't expect to love it. My true passion was bigger than that. *Deeper* than that.

Ballet.

My heart hurts just thinking about it.

There should've been no room in my life for the dance team. No room in my life for friends. Not with my mother choreographing my schedule like a complicated piece, weaving appointments and training and rehearsals.

My whole college schedule was arranged around five-hour dance training, and I'd be a liar if I said I didn't love every second of it. The long days, the sore muscles, the relief of finally nailing a piece of choreography.

The dance team was a compromise to my career. One I insisted on along with college. I missed more than a few dance team days for ballet—and the coach accepted it from the start. From everyone else, she demanded perfect attendance. But she had to admit, I had skill. I had *talent*, the sort of natural movement my ballet master always praised me for. The natural grace and intuition on top of training.

The dance team's different style gave me a mental break —and a physical challenge.

As for ballet, I was going places. First as a soloist in the company's productions, then I became a principal—one of the leads. I dreamed of bigger shows. Bigger companies and productions after I graduated CPU. *The Nutcracker* or *Sleeping Beauty* in New York City or San Francisco. The sort of principal roles that make a ballerina in the industry.

And then that dream shattered along with the bones in my leg.

Willow comes back with a tray, her eyebrow raising at the position Jack and I are in. He just grins at her and plucks one of the glasses from the tray. He sets it down in front of me.

"They're here," Amanda says, her voice high.

I glance around. The bar has been filling up, sure, but now the noise climbs. A new energy rushes through the room. My stomach knots for some reason. I can't explain it. It's like anticipation but worse.

I'm surprised to recognize the first pair of guys through the door. Knox Whiteshaw is legendary, even at a school like CPU that doesn't usually get national recognition. He's accompanied by the goalie, Miles. No surprise there. They're brothers and thick as thieves.

Knox is a junior, like Willow and me, and Miles is a sophomore. Even so, he rose to meet the expectations set by his brother. On the medium-sized college campus, everyone tends to know each other. And when you're in sports? You're *definitely* known.

More players follow in behind them, and I catch a glimpse of another starter on the defensive line.

"Violet," Jack says in my ear. "You okay?"

I glance at him, and my face gets hot. "Perfectly fine."

My confidence took a hit when I missed a semester. Which is why my cheeks stay hot while girls come up to us. Some grin at Jack, congratulating him on a good season—as if this is the first time they've talked to him in months—but more welcome me back. I'm actually surprised at how many people notice us. Notice *me*.

Willow nudges my leg under the table. "See? They missed you."

Jess laughs. "Yeah, the dance team sucked without you. I mean, we did okay. But we just missed the positive energy you always brought. We're so glad you're back."

I pause. Willow's smile drops off. I give her a look, but she can't meet my eyes. So, she didn't have the courage to tell them—I don't blame her, I wouldn't want to be the messenger of bad news. Coach knows, but I doubt they've seen her since we had a phone chat with my doctor two weeks ago.

The basics?

While my bones healed—and they're still technically healing, the ligaments and tendons strengthening by the day—my nerves didn't. Over the last six months, I've experienced incredible pain that comes out of nowhere. Not to mention my muscles are weak.

I'll never be on the dance team again, and I'll never be a ballerina.

Goodbye, dreams.

"Violet?" Jess leans into me. "What's wrong?"

I realize I have a tear rolling down my cheek. I quickly brush it away and take a deep breath. "Sorry, guys. Didn't mean to..." I gesture to my face. "I'm not able to come back to the dance team. Doctor's orders."

"But, Coach—"

"Talked to my doctors and agreed," I finish quietly.

Their stares are heavy. Sad.

I shake my head and force a smile. "It's okay. I'll cheer you on from the sidelines. Yeah?"

Amanda scowls. Her gaze lifts, and she tosses back her shot. "They're coming over here."

I take a second to rein in my emotions. Not easy when I suddenly feel like I've let everyone down... again. I stare at the table until I'm sure my eyes aren't burning.

"Hey, Steele," Amanda sings. She's in the middle of the table, perfectly poised to be the center of attention. Her cheeks are pink from the tequila, and her smile widens.

"Amanda," he greets her, then turns to Jack. "Hey, buddy. Have you met our newest left wing?"

He and Jack slap hands and bump fists.

I finally glance up and realize that Steele isn't alone. The blood drains out of my face.

He stands beside Steele, looking like... like nothing ever happened? *Impossible.*

The man who hit my car and ruined my life.

Greyson Devereux.

2

GREYSON

My teammate nods to the guy sitting at a table full of girls. "Jack, Greyson. Jack is the quarterback on the football team."

I quirk my lips. The football team lost spectacularly this year, no thanks to *Jack* here. It's a good thing the hockey team is picking up the slack and bringing some attention back to this school.

That's where I shine.

In the spotlight.

Well, correction: that's where I used to shine.

My gaze goes to the girl beside Jack, who seems like she's about to be violently sick. She looks familiar in the way most girls do. Like I might've had a chance encounter with her at some point in my life but nothing worthy of me remembering.

Maybe we ran into each other here, at Haven. After a game.

I smirk at her, and she flinches. Not the usual reaction.

Interesting.

Steele is going around the table, introducing the dance

team. I register it faintly, still trying to figure out the girl under Jack's arm. She's watching me, too. Her blue eyes on mine are like daggers. I'm intrigued.

"And Violet," Steele finishes. "Back from…"

"Hiatus," she says faintly.

She has an unusual name. I've only heard of one other…

"Violet Reece," Steele continues. "Best damn dancer on the team—no offense, ladies." He winks at the other girls.

Violet Reece.

I clench my jaw to keep from saying anything. My expression smooths, although what I really want to do is ask why the *fuck* she's in my town. I've been here since the start of the fall semester, and I haven't seen or heard of her. Not even a fucking whisper.

Best damn dancer on the team. Back from hiatus. So, what, this is a massive coincidence? My luck. No, *her* luck. I'm glaring holes in her skull, I think, but she makes a point to not look away.

Challenge accepted.

"So, how are you liking playing with the Hawks, Greyson?" one of the girls asks.

I tear my gaze off Violet and try to find who asked. The girl in the center, with perky breasts peeking out from a low-cut shirt, leans forward. It seems to be a tactic girls employ to drive attention down to them.

So I go with what she wants and let my eyes fall to the swells, then back up to her face. She's flushed from whatever they've been drinking. I've seen her with some of the other girls who always shadow the team. We're regulars at Haven—the owner has a soft spot for the team, especially after a win—and she just has the look.

A puck bunny in hiding. They're usually not so subtle.

Although I'm not sure what she's doing is *subtle*. Maybe she's just in denial.

"It's a good change," I finally reply. "Much better than where I was."

Violet lifts the shot glass in front of her, slamming it back. My attention is pulled back to her. It's unnerving. She swallows delicately, her throat moving. She's stopped staring at me and has chosen to go with ignoring my existence.

But it's subtle enough that I don't think many other people pick up on her snub.

Maybe she's regularly like this.

Cold.

It's all the more intriguing, because I realize that I don't actually know her. I've only heard her name in association with my future being choked to death.

"We'll see you ladies around," Steele says. He pulls at my sleeve. "Come on, man."

"You look like you have room for two more," I say.

The girls giggle. Except the one on the end, across from Violet.

A best friend? She seemed to catch whatever was going through Violet's mind.

"No," whoever she is says. "We're celebrating—no boys allowed."

I raise my eyebrow. "Oh? Hear that, Jack?"

He flushes. "She meant no *hockey* boys allowed."

I sneer. "Right. Well, catch you later." I stick my hands in my pockets and follow Steele back to the bar. More dance girls—the ones I'm more familiar with—are waiting for us with my buddies, Knox and Jacob. The right wing, Erik, leans against the bar, as well. He and I don't get along as well as Coach hoped.

Not my fault he's a fucking dumbass. He's graduating this year, though. Good riddance. Next year, when Knox, Steele, and I are seniors... we'll take the hockey world by storm. More than we already are. Then we'll take on the NHL.

"You meet the rest of the dance team, Greyson?" Paris puts her hand on my arm.

I let her. Why the fuck not? She's pretty, too. And she sucks dick well enough. Found that out last month, before we all split for winter break. The hockey team came back a week ago to get back into practice, and now everyone has returned to Crown Point. School starts back up on Monday, and this is the last weekend hurrah.

There's a new reverence around me. My old school didn't have that, although I sure as fuck made the title for myself. Everyone knew who I was at Brickell University because of my last name. Money can open a lot of doors— but charm *keeps* them open.

Good old Dad taught me that one.

It worked, too, until everything blew up in my face.

I order a beer and rest my elbows against the bar, sandwiched between Paris and another girl. Paris has her long blonde hair loose, fanned out across her shoulders. Despite the fact that it's January—and fucking cold out—she only wears an off-the-shoulder black blouse and tight jeans. She's still running her hand up and down my bicep, stroking me like a fucking dog.

"Grey?"

My brow lowers. "It's Greyson or nothing at all, Paris."

She flushes. "Sorry."

"Steele introduced me to the rest of your team. What's up with the moody one?" I tip my head back to the table we just left.

Paris scoffs and glances over. "I don't know. Everyone's hung up on Violet not coming back to the team."

I rotate a bit and study Violet. Her hair is ashy, and the bangs that sweep to either side of her face hide half her forehead. In a split second, I can see her clear as day with blood running down her temple. The way she was after the crash.

Did she get that haircut to hide a scar?

Even now that I'm gone, she still seems stiff. She drums her fingers on the table and doesn't seem to care much when Jack leans into her. He whispers something in her ear and doesn't get a reaction.

My blood boils.

Instantly.

I clench my jaw and force my reaction to be minimal. So slight, the girl in front of me doesn't notice until I ask, "You friends with her?"

"Violet?" Shock colors her tone. "We're friendly, sure."

"But not best friends."

She wrinkles her nose. "No. She was Coach's favorite."

Was. I read between the lines—now that Violet's gone, the top dog spot is open for Paris to take. For a second, I'm impressed with the level of ruthlessness girls like Paris possess. But then I remember that, if not for me, Paris would probably still be seething in silence. She wouldn't have done anything to unseat Violet.

That's fucking cowardly.

Jack stands, and Violet slips from the booth. She hurries to the bathroom, still so stiff. Her outfit is drastically different from the girls I'm used to seeing here. Even from her teammates at her table. *Friends.* They wear dresses, the skirts short enough to leave almost nothing to the imagination.

I gulp my beer and wait a second, then follow her.

It isn't anything I consciously decide—I want to, so I do.

I push into the women's restroom and duck down to check the stalls. They're all open except one. A thrill goes through me, and I flip the lock on the exit door. I lean against it and wait.

Maybe she heard me enter, because she doesn't seem particularly surprised to find me. She's shorter than I would've guessed. Her pink sweater hides her body, the leather pants only giving away muscular thighs and calves that must've come from years of dancing.

Did she pick pink to look innocent? If she did, her red lipstick throws it off.

She goes still, her hand gripping the edge of the stall. Her chin lifts. "What do you want?"

I laugh.

What the fuck do I want?

I shake my head slowly and step toward her.

She steps back.

Mistake.

I've never quite felt such an awakening to my anger like this. Like... like I can get my revenge and actually satiate that part of me. The craving for retribution.

After I was arrested, a local news outlet picked up the story. They smeared my name across the state, and the effect on my life was immediate.

The Brickell hockey coach called and said I was off the team. *Bad publicity.* Even though the article was only live for a few days, the damage was done.

Then the college dean called and strongly advised me not to return.

I couldn't go any-fucking-where without people staring. For the *wrong* reasons. Because they thought I was a shitty person who drove drunk, who crashed their car and framed an innocent girl. Beyond that, they made all sorts of assumptions and accusations. That my life was gilded because of my last name. They wondered how many other offenses I ducked.

And my father...

Not going there.

"Tell me what you think I want," I say. "Let's see how close you are."

Her brows draw together. "I don't know."

"You recognize me."

I'm still getting closer, and she's still retreating. She bumps into the trying-to-be-cool spray-painted wall and stops, but I keep approaching. Right until I'm inches away. Heat pours off her body.

Or maybe it's my imagination.

Either way, I'm enjoying this much more than I should be. This close, she feels electric. I know, it sounds insane. But there's something immensely satisfying about it. About *her*.

"I don't think I could ever forget your face," she admits. "Now get the fuck away from me."

I reach forward and touch her chin. My fingers wander up the side of her face, and I push aside her hair. She doesn't stop me. Doesn't hide from me when my fingertips brush the ugly scar on her temple. It snakes into her hairline, silver against her red face. The only part of her that isn't burning hot, I imagine.

Oh, I think I like touching this girl. She shivers, glowering at me like her expression will get me to back off. It's a nice try—it might work on lesser men.

Even through that, I register that I can't be attracted to

her. I'm suddenly furious at myself, too. It's her fault. She cracked the gilded mirage I've been living in. She hurt my relationship with my father, jeopardized my future. All because she couldn't keep her mouth shut.

"You ruined a whole lot for me." I lean in closer, like I'm telling her a secret. When really, I want to know how she'll react to me. "So how about I do the same to you?"

She flinches.

I see it, I catch it. I savor it. Her immediate blast of fear is what I've been waiting for, and something in me knots with anticipation. Her fear is so like the fear I felt sitting in that jail cell, even if I only had to suffer for hours. She'll suffer for a lot longer.

Oh, yes.

This is going to be fun.

"When I'm done with you, your precious little dance team won't be the only thing I take from you," I promise.

I withdraw. She's stuck against the wall, her chest heaving. I didn't even touch her that much, but she looks at me like I just stuck a knife into her and twisted the blade.

I can't wait to see how she looks when she breaks.

3

VIOLET

Sunlight slants across my face, and I groan. I block it with my hand, but then my overhead light flicks on.

"Rise and shine, Sleeping Beauty. It's almost one o'clock." Willow climbs onto my bed, flopping beside me. "How are you feeling?"

I squint at the ceiling. "Like my head is an anvil and it's being struck by a hammer over and over. Undecided on my leg. Or the rest of me." That's a lie. As soon as I focus on my lower leg, pain shoots up into my hip in waves. I grit my teeth.

"Well, you went a little hardcore..."

Yeah, that's true. I couldn't bear to look at Greyson at the bar. He completely ignored me after accosting me in the bathroom. Instead, he flirted with Paris and one of her friends. And meanwhile, I kept freaking out.

Why the hell is he *here*? Did he know I went here? Crown Point University is so far removed from our home-town, Rose Hill. Different state. Hours away. This small town was *my* reprieve, and now it's becoming my nightmare.

He's the hotshot no one can shut up about.

My friends are obsessed with hockey.

And, admittedly, I'm friendly with them, too. The team. At least, I was. I now have the urge to avoid all of them.

Am I going to run into him on campus on Monday? Am I going to have to avoid him like the plague?

If only I could just *leave*. Go back to Rose Hill, climb into the narrow daybed my mom shoved into the corner of her living room while I recovered, and hide under the covers. But with dance gone, and the money for college slowly dwindling, I don't think I have much of a choice but to persevere.

"What happened with Jack?" Willow asks.

I grunt. "He's a sloppy kisser when he's drunk."

Another mistake. Willow refused to let him back into our apartment, even though he pleaded. Which is probably a good thing. No doubt he would've climaxed in less than ten minutes—or taken an hour. No in between. Meanwhile, I would've been left to live with the ache between my legs or take care of myself.

It's his toxic trait. Leaving me hanging when he's blasted.

"What do you want to do today?" She picks up my hand and threads our fingers together. "I'm thinking a movie. A matinee? Then we can just relax."

"Sure." Really, anything dark sounds good. The light is still burning into my eyes, and I roll onto my side to face Willow. "Has Greyson been big on campus the whole time I've been gone?"

She narrows her eyes. "I thought I saw something on your face when Steele introduced you two. What happened?"

"Um..." I swallow. A lump forms in my throat. If I tell

Willow, she'll go protective mama bear on my ass. Or worse. Potentially way worse. I've just got to blurt it out. So I do, in a rush. The words mash together on their way past my lips. "He's the one who hit me."

She pauses a beat. Then, "Bullshit."

I wince.

She stares at me and rises on her elbow. "Violet Marie Reece, you've got to be KIDDING me right now. He hit you? He's the one who did..." She waves vaguely at my leg.

"Greyson Devereux." I exhale sharply. "I can't make this shit up, Willow. The asshole hit me with his car. But—" I reach out and grab her hand. "You can't tell anyone."

"Why not?"

Because I signed a nondisclosure agreement. It was part of the reason why I dropped the charges. My mom didn't want to let go. She wanted to wring out every last penny from the Devereuxes. Wanted them to cover the medical expenses, wanted Greyson to serve jail time.

Of course, he was out in less than four hours. Too much time elapsed between the cops interviewing me at the hospital, before I was rushed into surgery, and them arriving at Greyson's house. They told my mom that they couldn't administer a breathalyzer test, even though I swore he was drunk. He got away with it.

As the story goes, his dad made some phone calls and nudged the police chief to drop the charges. Greyson walked—quickly and quietly. I don't know if they even took his fingerprints.

But there was still a civil suit to deal with. Mom threatened it. Loudly. Greyson's father came and appealed to my mom's sensible nature. He pointed at me and asked her if she was willing to drag me through a trial.

I would be questioned.

Why I was out.

What I was doing.

What made me pull into the street then.

Did I check both ways?

Did I try to avoid the car?

Questions I can't answer. The day leading up to the accident is a blank. Like the slate in my mind wiped it clean. I don't know where I was or how fast I was going, or if I was even wearing my damn seatbelt. If I didn't see pictures of my car after the wreck, I wouldn't have believed it.

And after seeing them, I don't know how I survived. The front, the driver's-side door, was all crumpled in. It didn't look so much like metal but shredded paper. The passenger door of my car was open. The first responders pulled me out that way, my neck braced and head supported. That part is blurry, too.

My memory of that entire day starts with pain and Greyson and blood. I might've passed out after that, because it seemed like only seconds later the EMTs were helping a girl out of his car and working to extract me.

And I just remember how *wrong* that felt. To see her stumble between them, apologizing over and over. He didn't just ruin me—he almost ruined her, too.

"I signed an NDA," I tell her quietly. Like the walls are going to lean in and steal my secrets. "So even telling you that he was involved could get me in trouble. If I even so much as admit out loud that Greyson had anything to do with a car crash, or my injury, I'm done."

Devereux. A powerful name in Rose Hill. And their attorney, Josh Black, is an influential man in the community, too. He has friends in high places—and by high, I mean rich. Infamous. They've carved out their spots in Rose

Hill, been there for decades. Everyone in the county knows their last names—they're *that* sort.

It's Greyson who hit me, but somehow, I was paying the price.

And then the media got wind of the story. Suddenly, they had something to use against me. The defamation countersuit would've buried my family.

I signed the NDA so I wouldn't have to deal with any of it. Signing it meant my mother couldn't keep pushing. It meant that I could sleep without guilt. Yeah, because I was guilty. Somehow. Mr. Devereux painted it as my fault, and I let myself believe it.

It was a mistake. I should've tried harder. Should've refuted the defamation suit, should've sued Greyson for personal injury. Insurance only goes so far.

"Oh, Violet," Willow whispers. She closes her eyes. "Fuck."

"It could be worse," I offer.

That's a lie. And even worse, Greyson isn't going to let this go.

That means I can't either.

"What are you going to do?" Willow asks. "What do you need?"

I sit up and brush my hair out of my face. I look down at my best friend. She's willing to go to bat for me. She's willing to put everything on the line for me. I know that as surely as she knows I'd do the same for her. We're more than best friends. More like sisters.

"I'm going to ignore it." I nod. Yeah, it's a great idea. Ignore Greyson Devereux. No problem. "It's a big enough campus."

She snorts. "You sound like you're trying to convince

yourself more than me. But okay. Fine. We'll play it your way, Reece."

I grimace when I stand. Today is a bad leg day, I can already tell. I put my knee on the bed and rub my hand down the back of my calf. The scar is neat and precise down the front, starting a few inches under my knee and ending above my ankle. A plastic surgeon had a hand in it, making sure it was the least ugly thing I'd be walking away from the accident with. (Or, in this case, wheeling away from it.) It almost blends into my shin bone.

There was a time when my calf muscles were strong. When I could rotate on a pointe shoe, and my leg would hold me.

Not anymore.

My muscles have gotten weak. It would take a lot of work to get the strength back, if the pain wasn't a factor.

My mother came to one of my physical therapy appointments. She sat in a metal chair in the corner and watched, and at the end, she said, "You still move like a dancer."

It wasn't the compliment she thought it would be. On the inside, I still felt like a dancer, too. I still had a phantom sensation of spinning, leaning, curving my body in specific ways. Rotating my hips, my feet, my knees. My toenails are all but destroyed from years of training. Walking like a ballerina is a hell of a lot different than walking like someone with a broken leg.

"I'm thinking a thriller," Willow says, drawing me back to the present.

"I'm thinking I need water and Tylenol," I mutter.

She laughs and hops up. "Did you want me to cut off your drinking?"

Trick question. When has either of us ever listened to

the other when we're in that sort of mood? When Willow broke up with her boyfriend, we went to Haven and got plastered. I got us home and held her hair while she puked all night.

It's that sort of purge that tends to be necessary.

She gets me the Tylenol while I slowly get dressed. I brush out my hair and pull it up. My bangs, which Greyson oh-so-rudely pushed aside to gawk at the scar, stay down. I've got a limp in my walk today, but Willow doesn't comment on it when we head to the theater.

Willow buys the tickets on her phone. Some thriller, but I couldn't tell you the name. It sounds up my best friend's alley... something with one of the Chrises as a lead, and a train.

We stand in line to buy our popcorn.

"Willow!"

She glances back, then tenses. Her back goes rigid, and she makes a face. Just a subtle one, her lips flattening and her brows drawing down. And then her eyes move to me, and she lets out a quiet, "Uh-oh."

"What?"

She grips my arm before I can turn around. "Um, sorry in advance for not telling you that I slept with Knox while you were gone. A few times."

My eyes bug out of my head. Willow and *Knox*? I make a mental note to interrogate her about that. But it's too late now because someone steps up beside us.

"Hey." Knox's dark hair curls down, almost long enough to get in his eyes. He pushes it back and grins at Willow. He looks at her like he's ready to devour her. Makes sense, since he's seen her naked. He steps close, tilting his head down to meet Willow's gaze. "Thought I recognized you."

"By the back of my head?"

Seeing my best friend flirt is nothing new—but it is surreal to see her flirt with *Knox Whiteshaw*. Her fascination with him isn't a big deal, but it is surprising that she acted on it. We used to whisper about him. Gossip, try vague moves to catch his attention. As previously discussed, he's one of the all-stars on the hockey team.

One of the guys who easily rules the school, just by existing.

Still, one-night stands haven't been her thing. Historically.

"By your ass." He chuckles. "You disappeared last night."

"We were there for a few hours." She shrugs and steps up in line, towing me with her.

Knox comes with us, a smile still on his lips. "Well, not long enough."

"I was drunk," I say. "She was being a good friend."

"Jack Michaels seemed to be intent on getting you home, Violet." Knox winks at me. "Good to have you back, by the way. The dance team has been lacking."

I bite my tongue. I guess people will find out I'm not back when they make their first appearance at a competition in a few weeks. Or when they perform to send off the hockey team for an away game. Whichever comes first.

"Pretty sure she won't be competing."

My spine snaps straight, and I slowly face Greyson. He has on a black CPU Hockey sweatshirt and gray sweats. And a cocky grin. His hair is actually dark blond. It's easier to see now that we're not in a dim bar. And those eyes... angry eyes.

For a second, I think he might spill *why* he knows I won't be dancing.

"She's scared."

I narrow my eyes. Wishful thinking on my part, to believe he'd tell the truth. "Like you know anything about me?"

He shrugs. "Not yet. But I do know that you use too much tongue when you kiss."

I jerk back.

He grins and pulls out his phone, flashing me a video.

Of Jack and I... making out. Last night. In it, my ex tugs at my pink sweater. His hands slip under the fabric, palming my breasts. I don't seem to have much to do with it. I hold on to his waist, my back pressed against the wall outside Haven.

"Where did you get that?" I hiss.

Willow makes a noise in the back of her throat.

Greyson raises his eyebrows. "If you don't want people to see your awful kissing skills, you probably should stick to doing it in private. Or forget lips altogether and keep your mouth on a cock. Judging from the rest of the video, you do *that* well..."

Shock hits me first.

Did he just say what I thought he said?

Did I do that? In *public*? I barely remember last night, but the vague memory of Jack guiding me to my knees is there.

Fucking fuck.

Greyson winks and motions to Knox. He tucks his phone away, smiling at me like he just won. And maybe he did.

"See ya, babe," Knox says to Willow.

"Maybe in your dreams," Willow scoffs.

They both head into the theater. No popcorn or anything, just shit-eating grins. We watch them join more of the hockey team—they're like a cult, only friends with each other for the most part—and give their tickets to the worker at the entrance.

Shit.

"This feels like the start of war," Willow says quietly. "Did you really suck Jack off outside Haven? I left you alone for five minutes."

I sigh and rub my eyes. "Yeah, I don't know. I guess I did. It's kind of a blur."

"No wonder he wanted to come inside so bad. Maybe Greyson is just..." She lifts her shoulder, mystified. "Maybe he's jealous?"

"Next in line," the guy behind the counter calls.

I sigh. "I'm not even hungry anymore."

She nods, and we step aside and just go to our theater. The guy at the top of the hallway scans our tickets and waves us through.

My leg still hurts, although it's reduced to a dull throb that shoots upward with every step. Better than how it was, I guess?

We push through the door into the darkened theater, and both of us stop dead.

"Of course they pick the thriller," I whisper, eyeing Greyson, Knox, and some other guys sprawled out in one of the middle rows.

"Let's just get out of here," Willow answers.

She's hurt for me, I know. Because I did something stupid, and she couldn't prevent it. Being mad at them won't change it. Certainly won't get them to delete it.

She doesn't wait for an answer and tows me to the exit.

4

VIOLET

I've been getting strange looks all day. And, stupid me, I write it off as being back after a semester away. It wasn't like I was unpopular. People liked me. I had a good amount of friends, including a lot of the athletes. That was the circle I ran in, being on the dance team. But now, there's a weird hush that precedes me. I've been in a quiet bubble, unable to break through it.

Until Amanda finds me.

She skids to a stop in front of me in the hallway outside my third and last class of the day. I created my schedule so the majority of my classes were on Mondays and Wednesdays, and I'm paying the price for it now.

But besides that, Amanda seems stressed. Or nervous?

"What's wrong?"

She bites her lip and releases it. "Willow's been yelling in the IT department's office for an hour." She unlocks her phone and shoves it at me.

I shake my head slowly, not taking the phone. But my stomach twists, because I have an idea of what might've happened. It could be worst-case scenario. Right? Maybe it's nothing. "I'm not following."

"Just, please look." Amanda pushes her phone under my nose.

This time I do take it and glance down. I'm not surprised that the video of Jack and I making out is playing on her screen—but I am surprised that it's on the front page of the school's website. And there's now text slapped on it. Commentary.

She's off the dance team, but she'll still horizontal tango if you give her the time of day... Or maybe if you pay enough.

I shut it down. They're branding me as a slut? Worse— someone who would do those things for *money*. Fury and embarrassment race through me, heating my skin. I suddenly understand why I've been getting looks all damn day. When did Greyson post it? And *how*?

I eye the video again. I've lowered myself to my knees at this point, my hands gripping Jack's waist. I don't seem steady, and my eyes are half closed... and then Jack moves a little, giving the camera his back. I quickly close out of it and hand her phone back.

My stomach turns. Did Jack know they were there?

I'm going to be sick. "And Willow is trying to get it taken down?"

She could've texted me and warned me. But... nope. I've been going through the day ignorant. It makes sense why I'm getting stares. Everyone thinks I'm that girl now.

I take a deep breath and close my eyes. I need to find Jack. If he didn't know, he's going to be pissed. If he *did* know someone was filming... why didn't he stop me?

How the hell am I going to ask that?

"Slut," someone coughs, knocking into me.

I stumble sideways, and Amanda grabs my arms.

Her eyes are wide. "Who'd you piss off? I'm just asking so I can avoid them." She forces a laugh, but it dies off quickly. "Seriously, though. Are you okay?"

I pull away and shake my head. Does that really matter? Although it's clear that I've pissed off the one person who already had a vendetta against me. I grimace and check my watch. I've never been more relieved to take a step back and point vaguely to my wrist.

"Running late for my class. Um, we'll talk later."

I hurry to class and slip inside. I'm on the cusp of being late, which means most of the seats are taken—except for two. One is in the front. And as much as I try to be a good student, I've never been a great student. My focus has remained steadfast on ballet. Sitting in the front is practically asking to participate.

The other one is in front of Greyson Devereux.

He's already spotted me, and his brows lift.

A silent dare?

Fuck, no.

I take a step toward the seat in the front, but I'm too slow. Someone walks around me and sinks into the chair, their head buried in their phone.

Ugh. What are the chances I can drop this class?

But I can't do it right now.

I steel myself and walk down the row to the empty desk. I sit gingerly, expecting Greyson to say something. A barb, or gloating.

Instead, he's silent. I feel his stare burning the back of my head.

The professor arrives and smiles at us. "If you're not here for Environmental Economics, you're in the wrong class." Her gaze sweeps over us, and she nods to herself. "Okay, good. Let's begin..."

I can barely pay attention. I flip my notebook open and jot down what she writes on the board, but it goes in one ear and out the other. I've never done especially well in economics. Or any of the math-focused business classes required for my degree.

But it's more than that. It's that I can hear Greyson behind me, and I'm hyper-aware of him. Every breath he takes, every shift. The scratch of his pencil against the paper. It grates in my ears, and I grip my pen hard enough that my knuckles turn white. Before long, my hand cramps.

She concludes her lesson, basically the broad scopes of what we'll be covering, and opens the door. A clear dismissal.

Greyson stands. His notebook and pencil are the only things he brought with him. No backpack, no jacket. Just a tight gray sweater that flatters him way too well. He pauses beside my desk and taps my half-filled page.

"This is going to be fun," he says.

I watch him head to the front. He introduces himself to the professor. Shakes her hand. And then he's on his way out, his gait graceful for a stupid moron.

I want to kill him.

But... he didn't rub it in my face. He didn't say anything about the video today.

Did he even post it? Did he send it to someone else who posted it?

I heave a sigh and hurry to collect my things.

"Violet," the professor calls. "Good to have you back."

I meet her at the whiteboard. "It's good to be back."

"How's your leg? The dean shared with a few of us that had you in our classes regularly that you were out because of an injury." She shakes her head. "It can be tough to get back in the swing of things."

"It's okay. There was some nerve damage, so I deal with that... but otherwise, I'm feeling fine."

She smiles. "I won't hold you up. But I'm glad you've returned."

"Thank you, Professor."

I hurry outside and lean against the wall. I pull my phone out and ignore the million messages, going straight to the school website. There's just a huge error sign on the main page. Willow must've at least been partially successful.

From there, I check my message thread with her. There's eight from the last hour.

Willow: I got that godforsaken video taken down.

Willow: Bullshit IT guys pretend they know how to do something, then they can't figure out a password reset to get into THEIR WEBSITE?

Willow: It's fine. I'm going to murder Devereux when I see him, though. Fair warning.

Willow: We're setting some hard rules next time we get drunk in public.

Willow: Number one: no Jack. No boys. NO DICKS.

I chuckle. Those are good rules.

Willow: Number two: No boys. Wait, I said that already. But I really mean it.

Willow: Knox is friends with that asshat. I'm never fucking him again.

Willow: But, bitch, your drunk BJ game is strong.

Great. A blow job I don't really remember. Video evidence. And a guy who apparently wants to make me... as infamous as him?

I push off the wall and walk slowly back toward the student center. I don't particularly feel hungry, but it's almost an acceptable time to have dinner. If anything else,

I'm not going to slink away and let Greyson think he's won.

My phone buzzes, and I check the screen. I expect it to be Jack. Maybe he missed the excitement. Somehow, I doubt that. Which means he's not reaching out on purpose. It's Willow, though, telling me she's outside the student center.

Right on time.

I find her with Jess and a few other dance team girls. They all eye me with mixtures of sympathy and pity.

"Hey, Violet," Paris says. She wraps her arms around me. "I'm so sorry for what you're going through. God, I can't even imagine."

Right. Like she doesn't have a JustFans account. But it's different when it's posted against your will... publicly. She has paying customers, and I just have humiliation.

A lump forms in my throat, and I gently extricate myself from her grip. I can't quite get the image of her and Greyson out of my head. Not that anything is going on there, but obviously he had something to do with it. He filmed it. And whether he shared it or posted it himself, he's at fault.

"Hey, Violet!" A guy waves at me. "I've got a twenty. Wanna suck me off in the bathroom?"

I grimace and turn away. His friends burst into laughter, and they all sweep past us into the student center.

"Ignore them," Willow says. "It'll blow over in a few days."

I nod and follow her inside. We swipe in and get food, then all get a table off to the side. That bubble of quiet from earlier has indeed popped—but now I can hear the snide laughter and questioning gazes. My face gets red and stays that way.

"My parents are flying in from Atlanta next month," Paris says. "They want to meet Greyson."

Willow flinches.

"Why would they want to meet him?" Willow snaps at her.

Paris tosses her hair over her shoulder. "Because his father is a senator, and Dad wants to run for office next election. Plus, I have a feeling we'll be dating by the end of the week."

Willow's eyes bug out of her head. I'm not sure about my own reaction, but my face gets hotter. My whole body gets warm, too. There's a raging inferno under my skin, and I scratch at my wrist. I hope my expression remains somewhat neutral.

Everyone knows Greyson's dad is a senator in New York. He's been here a semester, after all. Not much stays secret on a campus this size. But still, putting that fact next to what I told Willow this morning? She's now seeing the scope of the situation.

"Oh?" My best friend's voice is strangled.

Paris rolls her eyes, misreading the situation. "Did you think he was a different Devereux? Everyone's been talking about it."

Ugh. Willow still has a sour look on her face when she stands abruptly. Her gaze falls to me, and I know what she's thinking.

That I'm in deeper shit than she figured.

"Why are you looking at Violet?" Paris asks.

Willow can't even answer. She shakes her head and grabs her plate, stalking away. Should I have mentioned that? Maybe. Probably. I mean, it's just a little, messy detail.

"I've got to go," I mutter. I take my plate of food to the trash and scrape off what I didn't eat. I'm nauseated.

How many people saw me blow Jack?

I touch my lips on my way out. A dirty feeling washes over me. I've never let myself feel this way before. Shameful almost. I guess I never had a reason to feel it.

On my way out, I catch sight of Jack.

"Hey!" I call.

He glances at me, then away.

The tips of his ears are red.

"Jack?"

He turns to me, and his lips press together. His brows draw down. I've never seen him angrier, and I almost take a step back. Something holds me firm, though. Whether that be my own stubbornness or fury at this situation, which we should be in together, I couldn't say.

"What do you want, Violet?" There's real venom in his voice.

"I—"

"You're an embarrassment." He steps closer, and he ducks his head so we're practically eye to eye. "I don't know what the fuck sort of game this is, but—"

"Game?" I choke. "Are you kidding me? You think I wanted everyone to see me—"

"That video painted you as a slut." He lifts his shoulder and lets it fall. The anger is melting into indifference. "And how should I know? You were someone else over the summer. The girl I used to know. And now..." He shakes his head. "You're doing to me what you did to Greyson."

I rear back. He's got to be fucking kidding me. "You're blaming *me* for... ruining your football career? I drank too much and someone took advantage of us in a vulnerable spot. That's not my fault."

It's violating. That's it.

I let myself feel it for a moment. Simmer in the raw vulnerability of it.

And then I shut it off.

"Well, you know what, Jack? Fuck you, and fuck all your buddies who have been whispering about me behind my back." I shake my head. "I'm done."

Ridiculous to think he might've been upset *with* me. With me, not at me.

I'm tired.

The video is down.

Jack is an asshole.

Greyson is a monster.

It's fine. Everything is fine.

But... it is until it isn't.

Until I get home, and the front door is ajar.

I push the door open carefully, and it swings inward on silent hinges. I bite my tongue to keep from calling out to Willow. I just left her in the dining hall—there's no way she'd have beaten me back. I creep inside, my phone clenched in my fist. I dial a nine and a one, ready to hit the last one and call for help. The living room and kitchen are untouched. Same with Willow's room. Her door is open, the bed neatly made.

It's my room that's been affected.

Demolished.

The mattress has been stripped and yanked from the frame. Slices cut into it, rendering it useless. Pieces of foam and fluff litter the floor. The frame is cracked. All my clothes have been ripped out of my closet, the dresser, and spread around. Even the dresser is broken.

I step farther inside and rotate slowly.

The picture wall has been slapped with paint. Just one word. And not one that should even hurt that much, given the discussion my class just had. But it does hurt. It pricks my eyes like little needles. The red paint has dripped down, dotting the pieces of foam and carpet against the wall. None of the photos seem salvageable.

I force myself to read it again. To actually look at the word, the way the letters were formed. I let out a sigh and shake my head. I'm not what they think I am. I'm not anything, at the moment. I'm free-floating.

But to them? I'm a...

Whore.

5

GREYSON

I pop the puck into the air with the blade of my stick, passing it to Knox. He catches it on his, letting it sit for a moment, before sending it flying across the room to Steele.

Erik sits in the corner, his head bent as he works on... something.

Fuck if I know.

We're all two beers in and getting restless.

It's been a hell of a week. Practice every night has been kicking my ass more than usual, and Coach has repeatedly yelled at us to get our heads in the game. He blew his whistle tonight until he was purple, then finally ordered us to run two miles in the gym and get the fuck out of his sight.

Besides that, I've been watching Violet.

She walks to school with Willow Reed. Sometimes they drive if the weather is particularly poor. On occasion, Violet takes her time and pauses often to rub down her thigh or massage her calf. If it's cold enough, she walks with a limp. Just slight enough for me to notice.

I hate that I want to watch her.

I've mapped out her schedule. The psychotic Monday and Wednesday classes. I switched into two of her classes on Tuesdays and Thursdays. She seems to not have anything on Friday. Not that I can suss out. But it doesn't stop her from going to campus with Willow and taking a seat in the library.

Her friends didn't abandon her after the video.

It was taken down too soon, I think. I didn't admit to anyone that I was the one who posted it. As far as Knox knows, I shared it with someone who took it too far. And for his sake, I pretend to feel guilty about it.

There was a little argument between Jack and her. Jack didn't bear the brunt of it—far from it. As these things go, he got accolades from his teammates. His anger isn't justified, but it satiates the desire to grind Violet further into the mud. For a moment.

The school has moved on to the next big thing. A freshman caught kissing one of the residence hall directors, I guess. Erik briefly mentioned it yesterday. The director was fired, and the girl withdrew from school.

Fine.

I need to take it a step further. Or five steps further.

Violet cares about Willow. She cares about school... barely. Enough to graduate. She cared about dance, but that's gone.

I could press on that wound. Make it bleed.

The puck comes sailing back at my face, and I snatch it before it can give me a black eye. Miles laughs at my glower.

"What's up with Paris?" Erik suddenly asks. "She's been blowing up your phone, Devereux."

I already know what's up with Paris. Small-minded girl with big dreams of marrying rich.

Miles scoffs. "She's already talking about marrying the senator's son."

I raise my eyebrow. "Yeah?"

That's me, obviously, although she hasn't mentioned anything about marriage. I hope she goes down on one knee... or maybe two. Although when I think of a blonde on her knees in front of me, it isn't Paris who I picture.

That's how I know I'm in trouble.

"Didn't take you for a guy to settle down, Devereux," Erik says from his corner.

I glance at him. "I'll tell them exactly how it is. It's not my fault girls don't believe me when I say I only fuck."

Knox snickers. "Good luck shaking Paris. She's a leech."

I shrug and lean back. "That's what makes her good at head."

"Like Violet?"

I crane around and glare at Erik. "What?"

He smiles. "She's gives good blow jobs. Surely you saw the video? I might just ask her, myself. If the rumors are true."

This is what I wanted. But the thought of Erik putting his hands on her—or worse, talking to her? No fucking way.

I don't realize I've shot out of my seat until Miles steps in front of me. He's a few inches shorter than me, which doesn't help cut off my line of vision from Erik. Who, unerringly, seems unperturbed by me.

Maybe that's what bothers me about him. Why we don't get along. Steele, Knox, Miles. Hell, even Jacob—the last of the starting lineup—seem to understand me without saying much. They have an aggression in them, too, that comes from somewhere deep. It's not out all the time. Mine brims under the surface constantly, but they've figured out ways to keep it hidden.

Erik just glides through life like he doesn't give a shit. And then he says something like *that*, and I want to tear his fucking eyes out.

Miles tugs my hockey stick out of my grip. He has to jerk it, because I have a death grip on the thing. And the puck in my other hand. I imagine smashing it into the side of Erik's face over and over again...

"Take a walk," Miles suggests.

Knox sighs and sets his stick aside. "Come on, Devereux. I'll buy you a beer at Haven. And Erik? Stay the fuck away."

Erik chuckles under his breath, but I'm already turning away. I shouldn't have had such a visceral reaction to him talking about Violet Reece like that. Deep down, I'm mulling over what to do about it.

Turning the school against her is just a step. But I need to make her Public Enemy Number One, not the girl everyone wants to fuck. Right now, all the guys at school are picturing her blowing *them*, and that's fucking infuriating.

Again, I see her with the blood on her head, trapped in that car. I can't get that image out of my mind. It floats in front of me when I sleep, just flashes that interrupt regular dreams. Reminding me of what we did to each other.

I sigh and follow Knox outside. A few guys on the hockey team share a house. Fortunately, Erik's room is in the basement. Knox, Steele, Miles, and I have the upstairs bedrooms. Jacob used to live with them until I came along, but he decided to live with others. Maybe to give me a spot, maybe because being around these assholes twenty-four seven can be annoying as fuck.

But it does help us play better. After only a few months, I'm able to read my teammates better than any Brickell team. Crown Point fosters a sort of brotherhood—and I have to imagine the dance coach tries to do the same with her girls.

How would I break us apart?

"You have a scheming face." Knox nudges me. "You gonna talk out loud or are we going to walk in silence to the bar?"

"Violet and I are acquainted."

"Shocker." He raises his eyebrow. "Steele mentioned you got weird when he introduced you on Friday."

I snort. "It's a long story."

Knox shrugs. "We can walk slower."

"You're a jackass."

"I could be worse." He grins. "Coach is going to kick our ass this week if you're distracted. Which you are, so don't try to give me some bullshit answer."

Bonding. That's what I wanted, wasn't it? Guys I can't charm. Who see through my shit. And he does. So do the other guys. Including Erik, unfortunately.

"How loved is she?"

He tilts his head. "At school? Probably less now that she's not on the dance team. But she's got the whole sympathy going for her now. It wasn't exactly quiet that she was on *hiatus* for a semester."

I grunt.

"You want her miserable?"

"I want her alone."

His eyes go dark. "Well, good fucking luck getting between her and Willow. They're glued together. Have been since high school. Maybe middle school, I don't fucking know. Reed and Reece—alphabetically, they'll almost always be together."

Huh. I knew they were close, but that makes a lot more

sense. I look at him. "Maybe my problem isn't that they're close. It's just that Willow and Violet are too focused on each other."

He nods along to my words. "True enough."

"So... we need to give Willow a distraction." I glance at him out of the corner of my eye. I don't normally do this. I operate alone. At Brickell, I didn't have a lot of friends. I had a team that grudgingly admitted I was better than them. But here, I actually feel like I'm making the team better, and vice versa. That's largely due to Knox and Steele welcoming me into the fold.

They might not if they knew who I was before—but that makes me all the more determined to push him toward Willow. Give him someone to focus on instead of me and Violet.

"I can do that," he eventually says. "But how about we make it a bet?"

Things just got more interesting.

I grin. "First to fall wins?"

He extends his hand, and I slap my palm into his. Violet's affection isn't my goal. I don't want her to love me. I don't want her to like me. But it'll keep Knox busy. He's a competitive son of a bitch.

Love is overrated. I want to torment her until she breaks.

6

VIOLET

It takes me three hours to put my room back together, sans mattress and box spring. In fact, my room looks a whole lot bigger without the bulky furniture. My pictures are all gone.

When I first discovered it on Monday, I did three loads of laundry to get rid of the paint on my underwear, and I had to toss all the clothes that were ripped to shreds. But I didn't want to deal with the furniture. I didn't want to take down the photos. So I hid it from Willow for four days.

Now it's Friday, a quiet day with no classes, and I have the mental capacity to deal with it.

Whoever did this had a lot of anger, which makes me think of Greyson.

And trust me, I don't want to be thinking about *him*.

Willow gets home on the tail end of my cleaning spree, when I'm struggling to push my red-stained, gouged dresser out the front door. The only thing making me feel less guilty about putting it outside with a *free* sign on it is the fact that I picked it up at a secondhand store for twenty bucks.

She watches me struggle for a moment, then comes and helps me lift it over the threshold. We carry it to the street, and I lean against it.

She waits, clearly ready for me to spill.

I just shrug and turn around, knowing she'll follow me all the way back to my room. And she does. She gasps softly when she steps inside.

My room is *bare*. Like, to the bone. The walls are blank, scrubbed paint-free. There's a few pieces of clothing still in my closet. My backpack that I had with me hangs in the closet. Otherwise, nothing.

"What the fuck?"

"Someone broke in and destroyed everything. On Monday." I don't tell her that they wrote whore across my wall, and that all my memories are gone. I mean, they still live in my head. But beyond that...

"MONDAY?" she shrieks. She smacks my arm. "Why the hell didn't you tell me?"

"Because..." I don't know. I haven't cried this whole time. Not when I found it, not when I started to tear down the pictures. Or when I discovered my journal missing. I told myself that tears were useless and action could fix this. Make it better.

But now, with Willow witnessing the aftermath, the backs of my eyes burn. And they fill with tears. I blink rapidly, trying to keep the liquid from spilling out. But my shoulders hunch, and my chest gets tight, and the floodgates open.

I break down in the middle of the room, slowly sinking to my knees. I let it go, and the shuddering mess of emotions comes pouring out.

Willow sits beside me, her arm coming down around my shoulder. "I'm sorry," she whispers.

"It's not your fault," I respond. My voice is hoarse. I wish it was for a good reason, but I'm just exhausted.

"You can sleep in my room until we get you a new bed. Like a sleepover."

I choke on my laugh and wipe under my nose. "Thanks. Just like old times."

She nods emphatically. "Right? It'll be great. Or we'll get sick of each other in the middle of the night and one of us will move to the couch."

"That only happened once." I rub at my eyes and clear my throat. "Mexican food just does something to me."

She snorts. "Trust me, I remember."

Then she rises and holds out her hands. "Come on, you deserve a drink after dealing with this shit."

I let her help me up. "I'm going to need to get new clothes, too."

"Those fuckers," she breathes. "What didn't they touch?"

"The rest of the apartment." I can't even feel particularly bad about that—I'm glad they only targeted me. For whatever I did. I think, on some level, I might deserve it.

"Did you take photos?"

I nod and pull them up. She takes my phone and swipes through, her face getting more and more pinched as she goes. I wanted evidence, but now all I want is to forget it happened.

Fat chance of that.

"Definitely time for a drink," she mutters. "Not that I'm a proponent of drowning our problems in alcohol. But the game is tomorrow, so it should be relatively tame."

I nod along.

And then we get to Haven, and we both swear.

Five-dollar Margarita night.

"Well, at least we like margaritas," I say.

She laughs. "Yep. Jess is on her way, too."

We find two stools at the bar, and the bartender arrives shortly after. He's a senior at CPU, but he doesn't comment on the video. He just gives us a broad smile and takes our orders without comment.

Willow glances around. There's a lot of underclassmen here today, which normally isn't a problem. I don't mind them here, being loud and distracting. It helps. I focus on the television hanging on the wall over the glass shelves of liquor bottles instead.

"Did you talk to your mom about him?" Willow asks.

I shake my head. "Haven't heard from her since she dropped me off last week."

She grunts. Willow knows my mother's antics. Knows what to expect from her and what she's become.

And what she's become is a flake.

It's okay, though. Once my dreams went down the toilet, I understood that her dreams went along with them. She spent a lot of time carting me to dance classes, recitals, buying pointe shoes and tutus and the outfits I had to have as a kid and teenager.

She wanted to see me succeed, too.

"My parents and sister are coming up next week," Willow says. "I guess my sister wants to apply here and follow in my footsteps."

I raise my eyebrow. Willow's sister, Indie, is a wilder version of my best friend. At sixteen, she already has a reputation of dating too much, of sneaking out, drinking when her parents aren't home. She smokes weed, too. Something Willow and I tried exactly once before my mother forcibly smacked some sense into me.

I still can't smell it without my ass cheeks hurting.

"I think they want me to take her around to my classes and shit."

I grin. "Good luck."

Indie and Willow are almost too similar. Headstrong, chaotic. They argue and fight, and that's their love language.

I don't get it. I'm an only child from a single mother. It was just the two of us when I was growing up. We lived in an old Victorian house in a sprawling neighborhood. One of the last that didn't actually have congested traffic or a commute.

We went to the best school in the county. We got a solid education. But besides Willow, I didn't walk away with more friends.

Which is fine. It just means we're close. I spent weekends at her house when my mom needed a break from me. Her parents fed me dinner, helped with my homework on occasion—her mom is a mathematician, and her dad is an engineer. They're like-minded and whip-smart.

Willow gets that from them. It's why she's majoring in computer science. She's going to take the tech world by storm when she graduates.

I picked business because I thought it would be easy. And then I missed a semester.

The bartender returns with our drinks. I take a sip of my watermelon margarita, and the sugar on the rim adds an extra sweetness. Willow clinks her glass against mine and winks.

On the other side of the bar, I catch sight of Greyson and Knox. My stomach knots.

I think of my trashed room, and I can't shake the feeling that he would do something like that just to mess with me. But, he didn't say a word about it in any of the classes we're in—and we're in a few together, unfortunately. In my environmental economics class, I can't seem to get away from him.

I'm probably going to fail it because he keeps messing with me. Not that he does anything, but I can feel his stare on my back the whole time. It's like my body is hyper aware and I can't turn it off.

"Earth to Violet," Willow says.

I jerk, spinning to face her. She squints at me, her expression etched with concern.

"I'll be right back." I slide off my stool, take another hefty gulp of my drink, and circle the bar. I don't have a plan. All I know is that I'm pissed about the video and I'm upset about my room. I had true memories on that wall of my past life. Photos of me and Jack, sure, and the dance team. But I had prints of my ballet recitals, too. Things I'll never get back.

Not Jack, not the dance team, and certainly not ballet.

My muscles ache for it.

And that just makes me angrier.

Greyson spots me coming. He's running his own version of court, Knox and him acting like royalty around a gaggle of impressed underclassmen. His lips keep moving, something about their upcoming game against the Pac North Wolves. He sips a beer between sentences.

I stop at the periphery of his circle.

"Violet," he calls.

They part for me, suddenly realizing I'm there. Some girls, some guys. Seems no one is safe from the Devereux charm.

I scowl at him and step forward. "I know you did it," I accuse.

His lip curls. "You're going to have to be more specific."

I make my way closer, determined not to show him fear. I'm not afraid of him. I just need to remind myself of that... "The video," I hiss. "And my room."

He leans in. "Listen, gimp. Only in your wildest dreams would I be anywhere near your room. Is that what you want? Someone to fuck your mouth? Maybe a bit better than Jackie boy did, hmm?"

Gimp. That stings.

The people around us laugh, and that fuels him. I force myself to lift my chin and face him head-on. No use shrinking now, even though I'm woefully unprepared. I didn't expect the barbs to come out so soon, so viciously. After all, I left *this* bar, drunk, with Jack, and blew him. It's not a secret, thanks to him.

"How about this? You can go back to your seat with your little friend over there and drink your cheap margarita, and you fantasize about what I'd do to you... if you were worth my time. Or better yet? Just get out of my fucking sight." He sneers. "You gave up your spot on the dance team. You're essentially useless to this school, aren't you? No more accolades, no more recognition. Soon enough, you'll be invisible."

I flinch.

His eyes light up, like he's finally found something that scares me.

"Poor little gimp." His voice is low and cruel. He's found a wound and he's going to press on it, drawing out the pain. "Can't make it as a dancer, probably won't get a job in whatever fucking career path you chose as a plan B. You'll go back to living on your mommy's couch and working twelve-hour shifts at a gas station until you rot of old age."

"No." I'm shaking. Trembling with anger. How dare he talk to me like that? "No, I'm going to succeed. And your demons are going to drag you back to Hell where you belong."

He smiles. "If I belong in Hell, so do you."

He takes his drink and sips it, then extends his arm. I watch his hand, watch the glass. Watch it happen in slow motion, but I can't fucking do anything as he tips it over my head.

Beer hits me. It drenches my hair in an instant, soaks my shirt, and makes it stick to my chest. I take a quick step back, then another. The people part for me, not wanting to get splashed. It's cold. My skin pricks, every part of me on *fire* at the humiliation. And the echoing laughs. There's a *whoosh*ing sound in my ears that muffles everything.

I brush my hair out of my eyes, trying to hide my tremors. "This isn't over."

He nods slowly. "I hope not."

I turn around and head back to Willow, then stop short. Knox is on my stool, giving her all his attention. There's a chance she completely missed what just happened... and I don't want to ruin her night. I've been doing that a lot lately. Ruining things.

The beer has traveled to my jeans, dampening the waistband. My skin is sticky, my hair gross. I want to scream. That verbal spar didn't go as planned. Didn't happen the way I wanted it to at all. And if I want to retaliate, I'm going to need to take another look at that fucking nondisclosure agreement.

For the first time, I feel utterly silenced. I feel *small*. Unable to respond in the way I want to, knowing that if I insinuate anything about the accident, he could take everything from me.

I spin on my heel and march right past Greyson and his cronies, heading for the exit.

7
VIOLET

I make it halfway home when someone grabs me. Their hands wrap around my mouth and waist, yanking me backwards. They pinch my nose closed. I suddenly can't take a breath.

I thrash and kick wildly, but my attacker doesn't care.

On some level, I know it's Greyson. The neighborhood on this side of the university has always been quiet, almost sleepy at night. Willow and I have been living here for three years without incident.

My chest aches the longer I go without oxygen. My throat screams. Black spots flicker in my peripherals, and it only takes another few seconds for my vision to dim.

It's only when I sag that he releases my face.

I suck in a deep, hiccupping breath.

He spins me around and puts me against the wall. The rough brick of the apartment building rubs into my back, catching on my hair. He has his hood pulled up, and there's a wild look in his eye.

Without warning, he covers my mouth and nose again.

His other hand presses down on my chest, keeping me pinned. Tears burn my eyes. My body is on fire, and all I want to do is fight my way out of this.

I scratch his skin. Pull at his wrists. For the first time, I *am* afraid of what he'll do. And he sees it the moment it registers in my eyes.

He releases my nose, keeping my mouth covered, and leans in close. I suck in as much air as I can get. His lips touch his knuckles, the only barrier between us. His fingers dig into my cheek. His gaze moves all over my face.

"This is what I want," he breathes. "I didn't know it until just now. But your fear is better than any drug. I thought I wanted to torment you. But now I just want this. Over and over again."

I shudder.

He's a fucking lunatic.

And then his hand on my chest inches lower. He cups my breast through my wet shirt, squeezing roughly before moving down.

I swallow, and he catches the movement.

He's breathing heavy, too.

When his fingers slide under the waistband of my pants, a new fight emerges. I buck and jerk my head to the side. I need to dislodge him.

"Do you fight me and make this worse for you?" he muses. "Or better?"

A rhetorical question, seeing as how I haven't been able to get him to release my mouth.

"One day I'll want your fight," he decides. "Right now, I want your silence."

He pushes past the hem of my panties, and I close my eyes. I have to fight my own groan. No one's touched me there in months. I haven't wanted anyone near me after the crash—especially not Jack. Evident by the sloppy blow job I gave him without asking for anything in return.

Greyson doesn't have that problem. And even if I were able to voice my opinion—that he should get the fuck away from me—I have a feeling he wouldn't listen.

He runs his finger down, and my eyes flutter open again. He pins me against the wall better, his leg keeping mine open. And when his finger moves across my clit, I can't hold back my groan.

"Fascinating," he murmurs.

I don't want to know what he means.

His finger dips inside me, and he exhales harshly. I let out a low moan. It feels good, even when it really shouldn't. He strokes me until I squirm, then keeps going. I fight it, my eyes narrowing. I clench my abs and ignore the intense feeling at my center.

I will not come because of him.

But it seems he won't take no for an answer. He shifts, pressing against my clit with his thumb and pushing two fingers inside me. He finger-fucks me and watches my face. His tongue darts out, licking his lips, and he readjusts his grip on my mouth.

It's a good thing, too, because his palm catches the obscene noise that bubbles out of me.

The orgasm crashes through me out of nowhere, and I'm suddenly grateful for the wall to keep me standing. He absorbs it all. My cunt clenches around his fingers. His hand slides out, and he brings his wet fingers up to his mouth.

He tastes me, and I freeze. I don't know what to make of this—any of it. My skin is feverish, my core still tingling in the aftermath. And he licks his fingers, cleaning them and seeming to enjoy it. He finally releases my mouth and steps back.

"I take what I want, Violet. Remember that."

8

GREYSON

I skate out onto the ice, contemplating my next move
with Violet.

My obsession with her is getting worse. I can't
stop thinking about her. Bloody. Bruised. Brutalized. I want
to push my limits, yes, but I want to push her limits. See
how far I can take things until we both crumble.

Part of me looks forward to that.

I had a phone call with my father this morning. He
wanted to know how Crown Point is treating me.

The two months leading up to the start of my junior
year were volatile. Both in how my father and I reacted to
what happened, but also in Rose Hill. Our attorney, Josh
Black, was by almost every day to advise us on the best
legal action with Violet Reece. The civil suit haunted us
through August, until she dropped the charges.

I wonder about that now as I pass the puck across the
ice to Erik.

Why did she drop it?

We never saw each other in court. Never had to face
each other in person. Except for the night of the crash, we

didn't interact. It was run through our lawyers. Everything from Mr. Black escorting me out of the police station a few hours after I was arrested, all the way up to the news of Violet's personal injury suit being dropped.

Now, my father is the sort of man who will do anything to get his way. What lengths did he have to go to in order to manipulate Violet?

And a better question: how can I exploit that?

Where is the weak point?

Her leg. Her dance career.

Finances, family, her future.

Take your pick. She seemed well-rounded. Friendly. Happy.

I want to press on her bruises. I want her to squirm under me until she can't breathe. Because taking her breath away has been the most exciting thing to happen to either of us all year—I can feel it. I can sense it. She let her fear in for a second, and then it was gone. The tears in her eyes were a show.

She's just as angry as me, but she won't let it out.

Come play with me, Violet.

She doesn't want to. She wants to remain safe. She wants everything to go back to how it was. The dance team, school, friends. It's not possible for her, and I doubt it's possible for me either.

How many ways can a person break before they can be reshaped into something new?

"Devereux! You're skating like your blades are coated in molasses."

I heave a sigh and move faster, trying to anticipate the pass from Knox. Erik and I skate up opposite sides, racing toward Miles in the goal. He taps his stick against the ice, his face a mask of concentration.

Knox passes to me. The puck glides across the ice, and I cradle it. One of our younger players, a defensemen who just started this year, comes out to intercept me.

I dart around him, leaping over his stick as it swipes at me. If we had the wrong ref, we'd get shot down for him trying to trip another player. No matter, though. It doesn't stop me. I aim for the top corner of the net.

Miles catches it. Barely.

Erik and I pass each other behind the net, and he gives me the finger. "Better luck next time."

I growl and keep moving. Miles sends the puck back out, and another trio takes their turn charging for the goal. I skid to a stop beside our bench and snag my water bottle. I squirt it through the cage of my mask and toss it back.

Coach comes over and slaps my shoulder. "You're off today."

I look out toward where Miles and Knox are facing off. "Sorry, Coach."

He makes a noise of disgust. "I expect my starting line to bring their A game. You've got eight hours to pull yourself together."

I scowl. I always play best under the stadium lights, with a crowd screaming in the stands. With strangers staring at me like they're going to eat me for lunch, only to be surprised when we outskate them at every turn.

My team is agile. We race each other just for the hell of it, working on our footwork and maneuvers. It gives us a slight edge, but we can't rely on it. The plays Coach has been drilling into us all month are next level.

We had a slight break from games, and he took full advantage.

"Get back out there."

I nod and shove off. I'm happier when I'm focusing on

what I can control. How fast I move, the way my skates cut into the ice. The stick in my hand, the puck. It all blends into a harmony unlike any other.

"Watch it!" someone yells.

Someone bulldozes into me from the side, and we both go down in a tangle of limbs. He lands on top of me, and it only takes his disgusting grunts for me to realize it's Erik. Fucking twat. I shove him off and push up, then circle him.

"What the fuck was that?"

He clamors to his feet, leering at me. "You should really watch where you're fucking going."

I brush off ice shavings. "You could've avoided me. You hunting for a fight, Smith? You want me to beat some sense back into you?"

"Okay, okay," Coach hollers. He reaches us and looks between the two of us. He seems to be contemplating who was at fault and what to do about it. It only takes him a moment to decide. "Erik, get out of my fucking sight."

"Coach—"

"OUT," he roars. "And come back when you know how to skate."

I wink at him on his way past. He rams his shoulder into mine, but I shake it off. He can be as disgruntled as he wants—for now, he's gone.

Coach just shakes his head at me. "Sometimes you're more trouble than you're worth."

I shrug at him and retrieve my stick. "Sorry, Coach."

The rest of practice passes relatively quickly. We shower off and grab a bite to eat back on campus, then all stomp to the library. I've got a test coming up in environmental economics. That class is kicking my ass. As much as I enjoy making Violet uncomfortable, I really need to get a better handle on it.

So we bury our heads in our textbooks for the next few hours. Erik comes in with some of his buddies and takes a seat at a far table.

Someone catches my attention. Just a flash of blonde out of the corner of my eye.

Violet.

She's been wearing the strangest outfits lately. Baggy sweatshirts with Crown Point University across the front, or the dance team t-shirts that must be free. Black leggings and boots or sneakers. Nothing crazy or outrageous. Nothing that shows off her shape. Just like the pink sweater the first night I saw her at Haven, or the shirt she wore when I dumped beer over her head and then chased her out of the bar like a lunatic.

I don't regret what happened after I caught her, though...

I shift in my seat.

"Be right back," Knox says. He pushes back and goes over to where Willow and Violet are sitting. He joins them with an ease that picks at my jealous nature.

That has to do with my upbringing, no doubt.

Raised to have the best things, immediately, I don't quite understand the mechanics of getting something I can't have.

Like Violet.

No, brain. I don't want Violet.

I grit my teeth and turn away abruptly. It's either that or go and rip her book to shreds—and there are more subtle ways to undermine her. And lead her in my direction...

Knox comes back and falls into his chair. He winks at me. "Girls are coming to the game tonight. In case you were wondering."

"I wasn't."

He shrugs. "Okay."

Something else catches my eye. Jack, coming into the library and joining Violet and Willow. He leans into Violet, whispering something to her. I clench my teeth so hard, my jaw aches. Why the fuck is he still talking to her? I thought that was over and done with.

Apparently not enough.

Still, I force myself to ignore it. There's nothing between Violet and me. No spark, no attraction. Animosity, sure. Anger, yes.

I need more than that.

I stand abruptly and cross the room. I ignore Jack completely and grab Violet's arm. She lets out a squeak of protest, but I don't give her much choice. She can either stand and come with me or she can be dragged.

Lucky for her, she chooses to come—albeit not as quietly as a library would usually dictate. I pull her down one of the aisles, between the stacks, and find an abandoned corner. I box her against the shelves and brace my hands on either side of her.

"What do you want?" she snaps.

So fearless... until she's not.

"I'm craving another taste of your pussy," I tell her.

Not particularly true, but whatever. Now that I think about it, blood rushes to my cock. I don't have a public sex kink. But by the way Violet's gaze drops to my pants, then back up, I think this girl might be darker than she lets on.

Interesting.

I add that to my mental file about her.

"Or maybe I just wanted to see what you'd do if I interrupted you and what's his face."

"Jack," she replies hotly. "Which, if you'll excuse me..."

I tsk, not moving. "Not how this works."

"How does it work?"

I look her up and down, frowning. "I want to see it."

"See what?"

"What I did to you. The damage." *The reason she limps.*

Her gaze goes frigid. "So you admit it?"

I lift one shoulder. "Admit what?"

"That you hit me." She's too pale. "And then will you admit that you snuck into my room?"

This is the second time she's mentioned it, and I haven't gone near her fucking room. It's on my to-do list to find out where she lives, but I've been a little preoccupied trying *not* to obsess over her. Clearly, my plan is going so well.

I sneer. "If I wanted to sneak into your room, I'd do it when you were asleep. I'd put my hands around your pretty little throat and squeeze until you woke up, and then I'd squeeze some more…" I can imagine the flush of her cheeks, how her whole face would slowly turn redder. How she'd gasp and gape like a fish out of water. How pretty she'd look, struggling for breath. "Something tells me you'd be into that, though."

"Not quite."

"Okay." I look away, then back to her. "Tell you what. I'll say whatever the fuck you want me to if you meet me after the game. You're coming, aren't you?"

Her eyes narrow. I'm just now realizing they're so blue, they're almost violet. Like her.

And I'm all shades of gray. No color, no personality except what I want people to see. I wonder how she'd react if she realizes every smile, every laugh line and crease in my eyes, the things people search for to indicate genuine happiness, is all fake.

If she'd run from me.

I hope she'll run.

"Tonight," I prod.

She glowers at me, considering. I see the thought process. I see her weighing the pros and cons.

"I suppose I'll go to the game. But I'll only meet you after if you win," she says.

I smile, and I run my hand down her side. She immediately tenses, but I find what I'm looking for in her back pocket. Her cell phone. I swipe it open, mildly irritated to discover it isn't even password protected. I shoot myself a text, then close out of it and tuck it back into her pocket. She doesn't try to stop me.

Choosing her battles?

I step back, ignoring the urge to carry her away now. That caveman instinct is going to get me in trouble. I've got to be patient.

"We'll win," I promise.

"Otherwise, you leave me alone."

I'm already turning away, walking back to my table, when her last condition reaches me. But I don't pause. I don't even fucking acknowledge it, because there's no way we're losing. Not with what I have planned riding on it.

I always do better under pressure.

9

VIOLET

We're going all out for this. The whole dance team is going to the game, and half of them are in our apartment. While Greyson was whispering in my ear to come to the game, Knox was inviting the whole damn team via Willow. What started as Knox innocently asking if Willow and I were interested—which she responded, *maybe*—turned into him trying harder. More persuasive of an argument, I would assume. Based on Willow's pink cheeks anyway.

Amanda and Jess are in Willow's room, applying their makeup on the floor using one of those cheap wall mirrors. Paris has planted herself beside me in the bathroom, using our curling iron. The rest of the girls are in the living room.

"You're wearing that?" Paris asks, wrinkling her nose.

I look down at my blue tank top. It has the Hawks mascot in white across the chest. Underneath it, I have a lacy black bra that's visible on the sides. I fully plan on layering it with a black jacket and scarf, because the stadium will be cold. And in that case, it's the thought that counts when it comes to school spirit.

"Um... yes." I lean closer to the mirror and run my nail under my lower lip to perfect the line of dark-blue lipstick. My eyeliner is blue, and so is the obnoxious eye shadow. It's a remnant from our dance team competitions and performances during the football and basketball halftimes.

She's got similar makeup anyway. Her winged eyeliner is sharper, and she went with a red lip instead of the blue. But that's fine. She's a good three inches taller than me.

"It's cute," she offers.

I don't know why she came. She doesn't like me and has never made that a secret.

"Thanks." I can't help how flat my voice is. "When do your parents come into town?"

She smiles. "In two weeks. They're actually attending a charity event with Senator Devereux, so it might turn into a whole thing."

A whole thing? I nod dumbly, not sure what she means. It doesn't really matter anyway. The last thing I need is to get caught up in Greyson's web. I don't need to be his victim again.

And yet, I've been pondering what the fuck he wants with me. Why he made me come on his fingers... on the street, no less. Where anyone could've seen us.

I get the uncomfortable feeling that he did it on purpose. *There.* For an audience.

I let out a sigh and cap my lipstick, tucking it into the little clutch I'm taking with me. "We need to leave soon."

She twirls a lock of hair around her finger, posing in the mirror for a moment. "I'm done anyway."

She stalks out and almost crashes into Willow in the hallway. My best friend wears a white long-sleeved shirt with the Hawks logo in dark blue. It was a craft project last year, where she carefully cut the sides and retied them. It looks like ribbons up either side, exposing slices of her tanned skin. Her hair is up in a crown braid with a few loose curls.

"Cute," I say, and unlike Paris, I mean it.

She grins. "You're going to be freezing."

I shrug. "Layers."

"Let's go round up the cats," she says. In the living room, she pulls on her jacket. She claps to get everyone's attention. "We're leaving in two minutes. Y'all ready?"

She's greeted by a chorus of yeses, and I smile. Willow should've been the captain of the dance team. All the girls respect and listen to her. But instead, Paris won out. She's a senior, after all.

I let out a minuscule sigh.

"The Wolves won't know what hit them," Jess says in my ear. "When's the last time you went to a Hawks hockey game?"

"Last year." I roll my eyes.

She grins. "Just wait until you see Greyson skate. He's so freaking fast. And he clicked with the other guys instantly."

"We don't know what kind of work went into it." Paris breezes past us. "He's talented, of course, but he's also hardworking. They probably all took a lot of shit from their coach. Like us."

I snort. "When's the last time you took shit from our coach?"

"She's not yours anymore, Reece." Paris levels me with a look. "Or did you forget?"

Ouch.

Willow grabs my hand and squeezes. "You don't need to rub it in her face like a bitch, Paris." And to me, under her breath, "I brought a flask. We can drown her out if necessary."

"Or we can get her drunk enough to shut up," I whisper back. It took way too long in the shower to get the smell of beer off me. I'm not sure I want to dull my senses before meeting Greyson—if they win—and I'd rather watch Paris make a mess of herself.

The rest of the way to the stadium is relatively painless. Paris complains a few times about the cold and the walk from our apartment—without ever offering her place to get ready. Truth is, she lives farther away than us. We live in prime real estate, and we got it by pure luck. And then we refused to let the lease go at the end of our freshman year.

Our student IDs get scanned on the way into the stadium, and we join a horde of similarly dressed students. We find the section we usually sit in and take our seats. I end up between Willow and Amanda.

The energy thrums throughout the stadium. We're on one of the corners, closest to the blue-and-silver painted goal and a good view of the rink. The student section fills quickly, and the ticket holders fill in more gradually. But soon enough, the whole lower level of the stadium is full.

Diagonal to us, the students who traveled with the Wolves sit in black-and-lime-green attire. They have banners and tassels, and one occasionally sets off an air horn. It's followed by cheers and screams from their section.

The lights dim, and an announcer's voice booms over the speakers. "Introducing... the Pac North University Wolves."

The crowd in their section goes nuts, jumping up and waving their flags. The skaters slip out and race around their half of the rink, quickly moving into formation. Their uniforms are all-black with neon-green numbers, and their names printed in brick letters across their shoulder blades.

"And for our home crowd," the announcer continues, "the Crown Point University Hawks!"

A door opens across from us, and white-and-blue-clad hockey players burst onto the ice. My heart jumps into my throat as they split apart and zoom close to the glass. I catch a flash of what I think is Greyson, his head angled toward the crowd.

And I swear he spots me, but then he's past. His stick is loose in his grip. A spotlight appears in the center, and the announcer calls out the starting lineup for the Wolves. Then the Hawks. First Knox, team captain and center. Then Erik Smith. Greyson Devereux. I lean forward as he lifts his hand and acknowledges the crowd.

They scream and cheer for him, and my stomach somersaults.

How did he rise so quickly?

We climb to our feet as the last few names are called. They skate around, doing quick drills on their respective sides.

"What's up with you and Knox?" I ask Willow.

To my astonishment, she blushes. "Not much. I mean, we hooked up. I told you that."

"Yeah..." I follow him on the ice. "But he's flirting."

"Right?" Willow immediately turns toward me, her expression pained. "I don't know what to make of it. Is he just trying to sleep with me again? Because he doesn't need to try so hard. I've got nothing against a fling. But when he talks all nice, I don't know what to think."

I think he's trouble.

I wouldn't have thought that last year. But now, he's friends with Greyson. And if Greyson is anything, he's a dangerous influence. So... yeah, I'm worried.

"Just don't let your heart get involved," I warn her. "I'm all for a fling, too."

"Especially now that you're free of Jack." Amanda chuckles. "No offense, Violet, but he's been holding you back."

I grimace. "He's..."

"Comfortable," both girls say.

I smack my forehead. I can see the truth in their words. I can see it, but I didn't see it back then. I was so in love and so obsessed with the idea of being the perfect couple. It wasn't until the "perfect" part fell through that I realized we didn't have anything else between us.

I had dance. He has football.

When we couldn't be the college versions of prom king and queen, we were just... drifting away.

"Now you get to try something new," Amanda says. "Preferably someone more exciting. Greyson was eyeing you last week at Haven."

I snort. "Did you miss the part where Paris laid claim to him?"

And she definitely missed the part where he dumped beer over my head.

I shouldn't want Greyson, of all people. He's vile and twisted and probably a psychopath. My lungs ache just from remembering our last encounter.

And... ugh. I've been turned on by thinking about it, too.

"We've only got a finite amount of time left," Willow says. "We should be adventurous before the rest of the adulting shit has to happen."

I grunt my acknowledgement. The problem is, I'm not sure if I want my adventures to begin—and most likely end—with Greyson. If that's a battle I want to engage in.

A whistle shrills, and the nonstarters leave the ice. A

referee in black and white meets the two opposing centers in the middle circle.

He says something to the players. Both Knox and the Wolves guy give a brief nod. We stand as soon as the ref drops the puck. Knox gets control over it and snaps it over to Greyson. He immediately takes off, and my attention stays on him. Even when he sends the puck soaring across the ice to Erik. He skates easily, like the blades are an extension of him. Easier than walking.

I envy that.

Dancing was like that for me, except it was just my body that I had supreme control over. Every little muscle, every expression. Down to my fingertips and my toes. It was a way to express myself, yes, but it was more than that.

It was more beautiful than that.

I see it in Greyson. In the way he skates.

And I've never wanted to break his legs more than I do right now.

"I need a drink," Willow informs me after Knox is slammed into the glass, fifteen minutes into the first period.

Greyson passes by us with a scowl, his head on a swivel. For a moment, I'm afraid he's going to start a fight. Avenge his friend. But he lets it go, and the game continues. Back and forth. I love the rapid speed of motion, the adrenaline rush from just watching.

Willow squeezes past us. The game has my rapt attention. Some of the other girls have started a chant. Something basic. *Let's go Hawks*, and *Defense! Defense!* I keep my mouth shut. It's dry anyway. Greyson checks one of the Wolves into the glass, and I smile at the retribution.

Hockey is brutal.

It suits him.

It suits all of them, really.

Miles, their goalie, is put to the test when the Wolves bring it back to our section. Greyson and Erik move on their line, and eventually Steele gets the puck back to Greyson. We burst into cheers, and Steele winks at our section as he coasts past.

He knows how to play the crowd.

And off they go again.

Back and forth. Back and forth.

Willow returns with two beers, and I gulp one down. It doesn't quite quench my thirst or hose down my nerves, but it helps. A little.

She pulls her flask and takes a swig from the metal mouth, then chases it with the beer. I stare at her, but she just shrugs. "Liquid courage."

"To do what?"

She winks. "Approach Knox, of course. Why do you think all the puck bunnies go to the bar and drape themselves across the players? Because they have all that excess energy…"

"And you're trying to get to him before someone else picks him up?" Amanda asks.

Willow nods emphatically.

"Who would you get with?" I ask Amanda. "If you have a preference."

She shrugs and looks out on the ice. "I don't know. Steele, maybe. Miles and I had a fling last year, so I don't think I'd go near that again. Too messy."

I scoff. "You two dated for two weeks."

"Yeah. We were seen in public together." She eyes me. "People remember that kind of thing."

"Noted," I mutter. My mind goes back to Jack. When we went out after his games, I was always on his arm. And if I wasn't, no one else approached me. I was untouchable in that regard.

But now I'm... not. Protected anyway.

And it feels good.

In the strangest way, it's scary, too. The door to my cage has been left open, and I didn't even realize I was living in a prison. It didn't feel like one. It didn't feel like I was trapped or contained. It was just safe and easy and comfortable.

Exactly what the girls said my relationship was. They spotted it before I did.

I heave a sigh.

It's not like Jack was abusive, or manipulative, or controlling. He was cautious. Protective of what other guys might do or say to me. He often said he knew what went on in locker rooms and he didn't want any of that to touch me.

Whatever that meant.

The ref blows the whistle, signaling the end of the first period. The players go back to their locker rooms, leaving the ice empty.

Immediately, my phone buzzes.

A text from a number I don't have saved. I click on it, and it opens to a preexisting message thread. Just one word sent from my phone: *Vi*

Ah. Greyson.

Greyson: Saw you wince for Knox. You got feelings for him?

I roll my eyes.

Me: Did you see me smile when you knocked the other player into the glass? Don't judge.

Greyson: Didn't take you for one to be bloodthirsty.

I smile, despite myself.

Me: Some things can't be helped

Greyson: I certainly hope not.

My stomach flips, and my phone goes off one last time.

Greyson: Remember our deal.

Why does he go from somewhat charming to irritating in a split second? I glance at the scoreboard, which still rests at zero-zero.

Me: You haven't won anything yet.

An hour later, they win. Two to nothing.

10

VIOLET

"Are you sure?" Willow is skeptical.

I don't blame her. I'm asking her to leave me at the stadium, downstairs on the lower level where the team locker rooms are. She walked down with me and a few other girls, and most of the guys have come out. As she watches me, Knox and Miles leave the locker room and stride toward us.

Since this is our home stadium, there's no bus waiting to take them home. They're done and free to go.

"You waiting for us?" Knox asks. His gaze is on Willow.

"Maybe," she replies. "Anyone left in there?"

He glances over his shoulder. "Just Greyson and Steele."

"I'm fine," I repeat.

Knox grins at Willow and offers his arm. "Violet seems good here. Let me buy you a drink? Then maybe we can find somewhere to chat..."

My phone buzzes again.

Greyson: Come in.

I wait until Willow, Knox, and Miles are out of sight. My

chest is tight, but I force my legs to carry me to the locker room. I push the door open slowly, surprised that the room isn't brightly lit. There's just a single row of fluorescent lights on down the center of the room, and the rest is in shadow.

Against my better judgment, I go inside. The door swings shut behind me, and I go down the aisle to the main part of the room. Greyson leans against a row of lockers against the far wall, his arms over his chest.

"Violet."

I jump a little and meet his gaze. "Why are we here?"

He lifts a shoulder. "I had some questions for you."

I narrow my eyes. "Oh?"

"First question. Do you feel hopeless?"

I tilt my head. "I don't understand."

He pushes off the lockers, straightening to his full height, but he doesn't come any closer. He's changed out of his hockey uniform into a black t-shirt and dark-wash jeans. "Do you feel hopeless? About your situation?"

Awareness prickles along my spine. Like this is a trap.

"What situation?" I ask carefully.

"The one where you can't dance anymore." He steps closer. "The one where your leg is trash."

"Because you hit me—" I clamp my mouth shut.

He smiles. "Ah, I see you realized your mistake." His gaze lifts, moving to our left.

Only then, belatedly, do I realize Steele has been here the whole time. Leaning against a wall almost entirely in the shadows, blending in with his dark clothes. He stands and tosses Greyson a phone. The screen flashes, enough for me to realize what the fuck just happened.

Did I just break the NDA on video?

I try to think about what it said. The terminology.

Can he sue me for simply saying that he hit me?

He can't do that.

The words ring in my head.

"Here's what's going to happen, Violet," Greyson says quietly. He approaches, stopping just in front of me. "You're in trouble for what you just said. You know it, I know it. And you're going to help me out by taking care of my friend here."

My stomach turns. "No."

"Yep. You blew Jack, the worthless sack of a football player, where anyone could see you. If you get Steele off with your mouth like the good slut you are, I'll delete my evidence." His gaze hardens. "Or I'll send that little clip to my father, and we can see what he does with it."

I look at Steele. Then Greyson.

I'm going to be sick, but I'm not going to let him steam-roll me.

"Absolutely not."

Consequences be damned. He can't just blackmail me into it.

He gets even closer. I tip my head back to keep my eyes on his face, on his twisted expression.

"You suck him, or I hit send." He shows me his screen. There's a message already typed, the video loaded. Ready to blast off to his father.

He's not kidding, and I feel trapped against Greyson and a hard place that I fought to escape. I glance at Steele again, who doesn't make a fucking move to stop his friend. He seems fascinated... and confused by the situation.

"Eyes on me," Greyson orders. He touches my chin, turning my face forward again. "Fair's fair, don't you think? I made you come... now it's your turn."

"This isn't funny." I hate the way my voice shakes. I

don't want to show him fear—that's what set him off last time. I eye Steele. "Are you okay with this?"

He lifts his shoulder. "I'm fine with whatever you want to suck, Violet."

I shiver. I didn't expect that. I didn't expect a guy I've known for three years to have the dark edge... to be okay with this. Maybe Greyson has convinced Steele that I do want this and I'm just playing hard to get. That this is some sick game between us.

Can I convince myself of that, too?

"On your knees," Greyson says in my ear. "Or shall we run through what might happen after I hit send? I don't mind giving you a play-by-play."

I glower at him, crossing my arms over my chest. I refuse to answer, although my stomach feels like it's full of snakes.

He pretends to contemplate it, but I know better. He's already six steps ahead. "I hit send. Daddy Dearest sees the video, knows you broke your NDA, and now you're in the shit position of wondering what the fuck he's going to do. What did he do to get you to drop the suit in the first place, I wonder?"

Does he not know what his father did for him? None of the details? Just that one day I was pressing charges, taking him to court for a personal injury suit, and the next there was a nondisclosure agreement with my signature on his father's desk.

And he was off the hook.

I almost laugh. "I'm not sure who the bigger asshole in the family is, Grey. You or your father."

"I'll let you in on a secret," he says, as if I hadn't spoken. "We'll take everything from you. But not only you. Your pathetic little family. Your father's name will be ruined. Your mother will have to leave Rose Hill just like you did. Retreat to a new city and hope that it doesn't haunt her there. She'll have no money, no friends, no future. Sound familiar?"

My dad. How dare he bring him into this? I'm so pissed, I don't know how to answer him. I don't know how to defend myself against this without making it worse. There's not a single part of me that thinks he's joking.

Then his gaze moves down to my leg, hidden by fabric. It always hurts, but the attention he gives it brings the pain to the forefront of my mind.

"Maybe, eventually, someone won't be so nice. They won't give you the choice I'm giving you. They'll trip you or push you down a flight of stairs. Those bones will break again. You're as fragile as those bones."

He's not wrong. One of my fears is that they'll break again. That I'll have to endure the last six months over again, only it'll be worse. Because there are some wounds you can't heal from. Some pain that never goes away.

"So?" Greyson steps back.

I can breathe again, barely. Just a little space between us eases the squeezing pressure in my chest. It doesn't negate that I've already decided on my path. That he's given me the hard and the easy way out of this room, and I'm not an idiot.

I'll choose the path of least resistance... this time.

Next time, I'll be better prepared.

I won't fuck up.

So I don't look at Steele at all when I nod slowly. My gaze stays trained on Greyson's face. On the expressions he'll try so hard to hide in the next few seconds. Because

I've got a feeling Greyson is doing this to test both of us—
and I'm not going to be the first one to cave. Or regret this.

"Okay," I say simply. "I'll do it."

11

GREYSON

My grip on my phone is hard enough to crack the screen. I get rid of the text to my father and shove it back in my pocket.

The princess gives me one last look, then walks over to Steele. He's still half in the shadows, but he straightens up when he realizes it's actually happening. His lips part, like he's going to back out. But we talked about this—I need to test her. To see how far she'll go to save her own skin.

And he agreed. Quiet, stick-to-the-peripherals Steele, who has a small group of friends and likes it that way, agreed to help me. In a perverted, twisted way.

My gut clenches, but I follow her toward him. It's like she's got me on a leash, trailing me along behind her. I watch her sink to her knees in front of him.

This is a test for me as much as it is for her. I need to withstand this, because the alternative is too devastating to comprehend. I've never been possessive over someone before—certainly not a girl. Certainly not one like Violet.

She reaches out and unbuckles Steele's pants, then reaches in and frees his cock. Her movements are quick and sure, but she's not rushing. The asshole is already hard, not that I can blame him. I ball my hands into fists and keep them by my side, then force myself to take a seat near the lockers on the far wall. I have a view of her. I'm almost level with her face when I sit.

She licks her lips, casting a quick glance in my direction. "You having regrets, Devereux?" she asks.

I narrow my eyes.

She inches forward, wrapping her hand around the base of him. He lets out a groan, his head tilting back. She takes him in her mouth, tasting first, and then she lets out a noise of her own. A whimper. Like he tastes... *good*.

White-hot fury goes through me in waves. A pulse that rocks my whole body.

Violet moves forward, her eyes closing for the barest moment as she takes him deeper. She sucks, and her cheeks hollow with the action. She pulls back and looks up at Steele.

"You like that, baby?" She licks him from base to tip, then swallows him whole again. It's so fucking erotic, like she's trying to win a blow job contest.

This is better—and infinitely worse—than any grainy video on my phone.

Steele groans again, and his fingers fist in her hair. He lets her control the pace for all of two seconds, then takes over. He thrusts into her mouth, and she makes a gagging noise. Tears spill down her cheeks.

It's fucking beautiful. It makes me rock-hard in a split second.

Steele ignores it and keeps pushing into her mouth. He's big, and I'm sure the head of his cock is going down her throat. She gags again, and her wet eyes flutter open.

She grips his thighs, trying to push away, but he's got her in an iron hold.

Her helplessness turns me on even more, even as the anger drives me higher. I hate the sight of one of my best friends face fucking her. I hate that he's the one touching her hair, that her mouth is closed around him.

I thought I could stand it, but I can't.

Her eyes roll to me. The tears mix with the drool spilling from her lips. The noise is toxic. Grating. I'm going to hit Steele in the fucking balls.

I rise and go toward them before I can help myself.

Steele doesn't notice me in front of him until it's too late—but I'm too late. He comes in her mouth, and I see red.

I yank her away from him. My grip on her hair and arm is too strong, and Steele's fingers slide away. He's still coming, a low hiss slipping from his mouth as his cock jerks in the air. His cum hits her in the side of the face, her neck. Ropes of it.

She leans to the side and spits his cum on the floor, and satisfaction fills me. It eases some of the brutality that's coursing through my veins. But not enough to stop me from what I want to do next.

"Get out," I bark at Steele.

He lets out a breath and shakes his head, staring down at Violet. "That video didn't do that fucking justice. Holy shit."

"Get. Out," I roar.

He chuckles and tucks his dick back into his pants. He takes his time with it, and I clench and unclench my fists. Violet kneels between us, her head bowed. He adjusts himself, wearing a knowing smirk. And he nods at me on his way out.

I look down at Violet. She's an absolute fucking mess. Her mascara is streaked down her face, the blue eye makeup mixing with the black. It gives her a bruised appearance. Her lipstick has smeared. Who the fuck wears blue lipstick?

Like a knockoff version of a Goth girl. Before anyway.

She's got his cum on her face, and she makes no move to wipe it away. She makes no move to do anything at all, actually. She just kneels in front of me, glaring at the floor like she doesn't know who to blame more—me or herself.

It's my fault—but not the way she thinks.

I slowly undo my pants and shove them down. She sucks her lower lip between her teeth and bites down. She draws blood. It bubbles up on her lower lip, staining her front teeth.

Good. In the most fucked-up way possible, I'm looking forward to her blood on my dick. I step forward, and she leans back. Her head tips back, too, and she keeps her gaze locked on me.

"Delete the video," she says. "I did what you fucking wanted—"

"I want a whole lot more than that."

She stays still when I grip my length and pump it once, twice. I don't need it, but I want her to look down and see what I'm stroking. To know that, as impressive as Steele's dick might be, he's got nothing on me.

I smirk when her gaze does drop, and her eyes go wide. She releases her bloody lip from her teeth. I run the tip over her lips, then up her cheek. She doesn't move, and I have to wonder why she doesn't shove me away.

Maybe because she's finally realizing she's the prey and I'm the predator. And even though I promised to cut her free, beasts like me don't tell the truth.

She walked into my trap, and now she's mine.

Fuck it.

My reaction confirms it.

I run my dick across her lips for a second time, and then I lean down and grip her chin. I pull down until her mouth opens, revealing her pink tongue and white teeth. The red of the back of her throat, looking sore from Steele. I get her lipstick on my fingers, a streak of blood. Her tears, too.

I don't give a shit if she cries, but I do want to drill into her in more than one way. Her mouth, yes. Her mind? Abso-fucking-lutely.

"That was the last dick you're ever going to touch that isn't mine," I inform her.

I've never had to think about the consequences of my actions. Not really. I've never had regret. And I don't plan on regretting my actions now. It's a side effect of being the son of my defective father. The one who can charm anyone, who flashes money when charisma doesn't work. Because doors have always opened, and panties have always dropped, and things have always been given, I don't think anything about what I do next.

The taking.

Because maybe she'll forgive me for this, or maybe she won't.

But it only registers in the back of my mind that she might not—and that part of me doesn't even care enough to stop.

I thrust into her mouth in one motion, filling her so thoroughly that I cut off her air. I stay there and wait, looking down at her. It feels too fucking good. Her throat pulses around the tip as she gags and works to try and breathe.

Her face gets redder.

I pull out, and she gasps sharply around me. Her teeth touch me, and I glare at her.

"Bite me, and I'll choke you to death right here."

Her eyes widen, but her jaw drops, too.

I take my time thrusting into her mouth. I can feel myself about to blow—I don't know what it is about her, about the crying and anger, that puts me so on edge. But I'm about to fall off the ledge, and I'm not ready to finish savoring this.

When I hit the back of her throat, then deeper, she scrambles at my thighs. I grip the back of her head and keep her immobile until her eyes roll back and her body goes slack. Then I give her her breath back.

Over and over, until she's losing her mind on my cock. She sucks, she swirls her tongue when I give her the chance. She wants me to come so this is done faster.

She thinks this will be the end of it.

Not even close.

I meant what I said: she's never going to know another cock.

She reaches up and cups my balls, and I groan. Fuck, that feels good. She massages them, squeezes gently, and lifts them away from my body. Her hands feel too good. I pick up my pace, driven on by need. I'm just chasing a high now, and my knees are weak when I finally feel myself go.

I pull out of her mouth and grip my cock, pumping myself once, twice. Cum explodes out and splashes across her face and chest. And when I finally step back, she sags to the side. Barely catching herself.

I turn away abruptly, going to snag a towel from my bag. I dampen it and wipe my dick off, then yank my pants back into place. My thoughts are going a mile a minute.

She's mine. That's what plays on repeat, underneath the current of how I can keep her bound to me.

She coughs weakly, and I turn back around. I toss her the used towel, and it lands in her lap. It takes her a second to pick it up and wipe at her face.

"Until we meet again," I tell her. Then I leave her there.

12

VIOLET

I pull myself together and go home. It isn't lost on me that Greyson didn't delete the video—so now he has another thing to hang over my head. My lips are swollen and chapped, and my throat hurts. My eyes sting.

I don't know how to feel. My emotions are all over the place, and it takes the whole walk home to wrangle some control over myself. I sniffle and swipe the back of my hand under my nose, collecting snot and tears.

Ugh.

When did I become this person?

My phone vibrates.

Mom: Got a call from Mia Germain. She wants to talk to you.

Then her contact information below it. A phone number sits glaringly in the gray text bubble. Ignoring the fact that my mom is texting me—something strange all in itself—my heart does a funny skip at what she said.

Mia Germain is the director of the Crown Point Ballet, the company I danced with up until my injury. I had left rather suddenly, of course, after my broken leg led to ongoing nerve pain complications.

I had to give up my spot as the lead for *Swan Lake*.

I had just been home for the weekend, visiting my mother, when Greyson hit me. Stupid twist of fate and bad fucking timing.

I contemplate reaching out to Mia now, but it's approaching midnight on a Friday. I'm not sure why my mother is awake, unless she's just getting in from a night out herself. I sigh and unlock my apartment door. It's silent and dark, an indication that Willow isn't home yet. And who knows if she'll be home tonight with the way Knox was looking at her.

Besides, I don't want to get my hopes up that Mia would have some solution to my impossible problem. Something that would give me back the months that I wasted eating real food for the first time in my life, putting on more than just muscle. I'm what most people would consider healthy, but in the ballet world? I'm far away from the size I maintained.

That hurts to admit. That I didn't develop a healthier relationship with food until I started going to therapy—not just physical but talk. And a nutritionist was added to my team, coming to chat with me while I worked on flexibility and strength training with the physical therapist.

There are limits to how far we can push the human body.

I let out a sigh and drop my phone on the nightstand, then strip out of my clothes. I toss them in the hamper and pull on an oversized shirt. In the dark, I go into my bathroom and flick the light on. I don't want to see my reflection, but I force myself to look. To take in the black and blue streaks down my cheeks and mouth. My bloodshot, stinging eyes. My lips are swollen. My hair, even, is a mess. First Steele gripping it, using me the way he wanted, and then Greyson.

A shudder works its way up my spine, and my stomach churns. I'm going to puke.

I lunge for the toilet and barely make it in time. I fall to my knees and vomit, sour bile burning my throat and mouth. When my stomach finally stops rolling and my throat stops convulsing, I sit back on my heels.

I let two guys fuck my mouth, and I don't know if I can forgive myself for giving in to Greyson like that. The more he pushes, the more I want to stab his eyes out—but in that, I caved.

He's learning how to manipulate me.

I turn on the shower, the skin-crawling feeling kicking up.

It seems to be coming in waves, like flashbacks of what just happened in the locker room.

And his words.

The expression on his face.

He was a man possessed...

And I have a feeling it's my fault. Somehow, I intrigue him. I caught the attention of whatever demons lurk under Greyson's skin.

I step under the cool water and tip my head back. I can't do hot. Not when I'm burning from the inside out. I brush my teeth and rinse out my mouth until I have no evidence of my physical reaction to my horror. I spit and dunk my face under the stream. And then I scrub. My face, the makeup coming off on my washcloth, my neck, my chest. Every inch of my skin, leaving it pink and tingling.

Finally, I feel a little bit more human. I dry off and slip back into the shirt, then go into my room.

I stop dead.

Someone stands in the middle of my room.

Tall. Black outfit. Hood. Mask.

Good guys don't wear masks.

I open my mouth to scream, and the guy rushes past me. He's around the corner and down the hall before I can so much as let out a peep, and my fucking instinct is to chase after him. I make it two steps before I realize what a dumb idea that is, and I skid to a stop.

But I do make sure he's gone, and then I lock the door. I contemplate sliding a chair under it for good measure, but I don't want to lock Willow out. My heart pounds, and I press my palm to my chest.

I turn on every light in the apartment and check the windows. Even in Willow's room. Everything is locked. He must've come in behind me... I shiver and go back to my room. I should call Willow. Tell her to be on guard in case she comes home drunk and unaware.

Our safe neighborhood is deteriorating.

Back in my room, I hit the switch for the overhead light and scour my space. It feels colder, but maybe that's just my imagination. I check my window, and it's cracked.

A more violent shiver racks through me.

He came through *my* window.

I slam it closed and lock it, then look at the space again. It still seems untouched, but I can't be certain. Not at a glance. My desk has always been a mess. It's just part of my chaotic organization—papers everywhere, a splayed textbook, the chair pulled out and half-covered in almost dirty clothes.

Part of me, the part that reads thrillers and romantic suspense novels, suspects it could be Greyson trying to mess with me further. Drive me into a tailspin or closer to insanity. It would benefit him—probably for no other reason than to feel satisfaction.

I grunt and sweep everything off my desk. The books crash to the floor. My computer bounces once, the charging cable snagging. The papers are slower to float to the carpet, and they go farther. They scatter.

I go to my dresser and touch everything on it. Taking mental inventory. Baubles, trinkets, a sticky note from Willow. A lamp for when I'm feeling like the world is too bright to deal with the overhead light.

My fingers land on a little glass globe, and it reminds me of my mother. And the text she sent out of the blue.

She always left pieces of herself behind for others to find.

A scarf, an earring, a belt. Her engagement ring, once. A trail of personal breadcrumbs that always led back to her.

As a child, I would go around behind her and keep track. I'd harbor them to return to her. Like I was trying to keep her together. She would take the item after a moment of silence, staring at it like she'd never seen it before.

"Easy come, easy go," she'd say, smiling. "Thank you, sweetheart."

Then she'd set it down, and I'd find something else the next day.

Lipstick. A hair clip. Her phone.

I should've realized that easy come, easy go was a motto imprinted on her heart. She accepted things into and out of her life with the sort of grace I never understood. Friends. Men. They took up space in our apartment and in our lives until one day she'd lose them.

It was only a matter of time before she shook me loose, too.

When I became the one who felt untethered from her in

a way I never had before, I began to collect the things she left. I kept them close, stored them in a box or on my nightstand. I didn't give them back. I willed her to come in and recognize the pieces of herself that I'd saved. I wanted her to see herself in me.

The globe is one of those things. The paint has worn off, so much so that flecks of blue ocean come off on the pad of my finger. I spin it and watch chips of paint flutter down, collecting on the top of the dresser.

For the first time, I start to resent her. I want to call her and tell her that there was someone in my room, that I'm afraid to stay here. But my call would undoubtedly go to voicemail. When she doesn't need me to rely on her, she isn't there.

My leg was the exception.

My career would've been the exception.

But all good things come to an end.

The anger bubbles up out of nowhere again, and I pick up the glass globe. It fits in the palm of my hand, just big enough that it's hard to wrap my fingers all the way around it. The stand is glass, all the pieces are delicate and ornate.

Where did she get it?

Why did she leave it behind?

I chuck it at my wall, and it doesn't explode into shards like I expect—like I hope. All it does is separate from the stand with a tiny crack, and the world rolls under my bed.

I take a deep breath and go back to the window. There are scrape marks in the paint on the sill. Evidence that someone gouged into the wood in order to unlock it. Whoever did it could come back, and that makes me act.

I call Willow.

She answers on the third ring. The noises behind her

almost drown out her voice, but she yells at me to hold on, and then the voices fade.

"Hey, where are you?"

I dig my nails into my palm. "Um, home."

I explain the situation quickly. That I got home and took a shower, and when I came out there was someone in my room. They came in through my window. That I don't think she should come home tonight—either that, or she should come home immediately and save me from going absolutely insane.

"Oh my god," she gasps. "Are you okay?"

"Fine," I lie.

"Oh, wait—"

"Violet?"

I grimace at the new voice. Knox, I think. I've never spoken to him on the phone, and it gives his voice a different quality. Willow's in the background. Saying something to him.

"Someone broke in?"

"Yeah. I just—"

"Who the fuck would do that?" He pauses. "I'll take care of it."

It? What it?

Is Willow the it?

"Thanks," I say, instead of asking the questions I want to ask. "Can I talk to Willow again?"

He grunts, and then her voice is in my ear.

"He looks mad," she whispers, breaking off to giggle. "You good?"

"Yeah. Is... um, is Greyson there?"

If rolling eyes had a sound, that's what would be coming through the phone right now. I can practically feel her judgment—and her curiosity. I told her what I could, but beyond admitting that he was the one who hit me and broke my leg, there's not much I could say without incriminating her.

I still want her to be able to look him in the eye. Because if she can't, then I'm fucked. He's smart. He'd be able to tell why my best friend is suddenly icing him out... and then other people might pick up on it, too.

She doesn't have a good poker face. Not enough to save either of us.

"He got here about an hour ago," she says. "I mean, we're at his house. So."

My eyebrow lifts. "Oh?"

"Yep. The whole team is here celebrating their win. I thought they were going to go to Haven, but apparently that's out for now... Change of scenery, Knox said."

I sigh.

"Oh." Her voice pitches lower. "Knox is talking to Greyson."

"Stop it."

"Well, I don't know what he's saying." She breaks into more giggles—of the nervous variety. "You don't think he's going to send Greyson to get you, do you? That would be..."

"Terrible," I finish. "I hope not."

But I don't have to worry. An hour later, it isn't Greyson who comes to get me—it's Steele.

13

GREYSON

"What do you mean, someone broke into her apartment?" I glare at Knox. On one hand, I shouldn't fucking care. But that persistent side of me that wants to claim her—publicly—rears its ugly head again.

He lifts one shoulder. "She called and seemed pretty upset. She wanted Willow to find somewhere else to stay..."

"Because her being alone in that apartment is a good idea." Sarcasm is my default when I'm trying to hide my real feelings. It's not a great sign that it's choosing to come out now.

"Listen, man. Steele offered to go pick her up and bring her here. It isn't ideal, seeing as how we're in party mode..." He gestures to the beer bottle in my hand. "But whatever. She can hang out in one of the rooms upstairs if she wants."

Violet didn't call the police.

Which probably means she thinks I'm behind it.

I frown and shake my head. Then the first part registers. Steele went to get her? Steele offered?

I didn't think I'd have to knock his teeth in, but I will if I have to. Happily.

Jesus, when the fuck did I get like this? All twisted up on the inside?

"When did he leave?" I bark.

Knox shrugs, but there's something else there. A glimmer of triumph.

"You ass," I groan. "You did it on purpose? Because of the bet."

He snickers. "I can't give you a leg up in this competition."

No doubt he doesn't care that Violet sucked Steele off at the stadium. If Steele opened his mouth anyway. I push my bottle into his hand and storm toward the door. I don't really care what Steele wants—I need control over this situation.

I need to kick the shit out of Steele and remind him that there's only one reason why Violet went down on her knees for him. Because I allowed it.

I get as far as the foyer, and then the front door opens, and Steele and Violet enter. She looks around and finds me almost immediately, then her gaze shifts away. Black leggings, and white sneakers. Under her unzipped coat, she wears an oversized blue Hawks shirt that hides her curves. Her hair is damp and braided, hanging over her shoulder. Not a speck of makeup, and definitely no hint of what happened between us not too long ago.

"You can stay in my room if you don't want to hang out with us," Steele offers.

"Thanks," she murmurs, shedding her coat. "But I think I want something to relax."

"I've got what you need," I interject.

Her gaze flicks to me, eyes widening in surprise. I pull

her jacket from her grip and tip my head, indicating that she should follow me. She does without a word. Her attention is fixated on my back. Her focus makes me feel like I'm stepping into a warm bath.

I lead her to the stairs and up, then down the hall to my bedroom. Knox has the largest, with its own bathroom. Steele, Miles, and I all share the one in the hall. I guess she'll just have to deal with that.

She follows me like a lamb to slaughter, all the way into my room. She lets me close the door behind her and toss her jacket onto the bed.

"Sit," I order.

She doesn't. She stays in the center of the room, looking around like she's never seen a guy's room before. Maybe Jack was a different breed and never let her go over to the house he shares with some of his football buddies.

My room is neat and organized. It reflects my mind. I don't like chaos, I don't like uncertainty. And Violet is the biggest uncertainty I've faced. She's unpredictable.

In here, I know where everything is. My desk is clear of papers, notebooks, and textbooks. The pens and pencils sit in a mug that says *Number One Hockey Babe* that was a gift from a nameless puck bunny. A thank you for an orgasm, probably.

The walls are cream, my bedspread quilted, dark-gray and soft. White sheets—I'm not a monster, and I'm not sixteen anymore. Black sheets are a red flag... and I go out of my way to eliminate all the red flags that might make someone run.

Well, not Violet. She had the chance to run because she's seen past the veneer, and she knows what my family is capable of. When it comes to Devereuxes, you're either in our good graces, not worth our time, or you're our enemy.

Violet seems to have the uncanny ability to waver between all of those things. Exiled but worth my time. An irresistible enemy.

"You don't have any artwork," she says. "No pictures, even..."

I consider what I know of Violet Reece. I did some digging this week, just simple internet searches that gave me a variety of information. An article in the *Times* had a few quotes from her after a performance of *Don Quixote* with the Crown Point Ballet. She was raised by a single mom who sang her praises in public. Dad wasn't on the scene, although another search turned up an obituary for him.

Violet was seven when he died.

She grew up in Rose Hill, New York. The same town I grew up in, although we went to different high schools— her the public one a town over, me to an elite private school. She lived in a house that would sell for a fraction of the price of my dad's in the current market. It's not a particularly bad neighborhood, but it's isolated. The homes are old. I took a tour of it on a real estate website, clicking through staged photos. Still, even the real estate company couldn't completely erase Violet.

She had a purple room with a waterfall mural on one wall. Her two dressers were white with sky-blue tops, the paint chipped and worn. The drawers looked like they had seen better days. Her twin bed was made, the white-and-purple comforter tucked tight enough to satisfy a military drill sergeant.

Where her mother and her went after that is a mystery. But her childhood was in that old house.

I wonder what year she met Willow Reed. Knox thought it was in high school, but I crave to know the details that I can't get from a search. The first public photo of the two of them wasn't posted until their junior year. And then there was a slew of them shortly after that, from summer at a pool party, their arms looped around each other's waists, all the way to starting at CPU together.

Violet was thinner then. Her neck seemed longer, more slender. More breakable. She stood with the same grace that she does now, but there was more self-assurance.

I took that from her. I ground her down into whatever she is now.

And right now, she's moving toward the one thing I actually care about: a family photo album.

It's pure sentiment that made me keep it. That made me haul it all the way from New York to Crown Point. There are photos of my mother in there, smiling into the camera. Her on her wedding day, her expression happy and content next to my tall, brooding, asshole father. Her pregnant. Her with me as a baby.

After the wedding day, I couldn't find another picture of my parents together.

She picks up the leather-bound book and runs her palm over the front. It's stamped with Devereux on the front, in simple, slanted font. A gift from my cousin on my mother's side on my sixteenth birthday.

That was the last time I saw anyone from her family.

"Put that down," I snap.

She doesn't. She flips it open to the first page, and a photo of my mother and me—one at a water park, if I remember correctly—stares back at her.

Her eyes move as she takes in every single detail, and I'm stuck in the middle of the room. Unable to snatch it out of her hand, unable to order her to drop it again.

She flips the page, and I catch a glimpse of a wedding

photo. The cake-smashing one. Candid's that my cousin printed. I don't have any professional photos. Nothing father-approved. I can imagine her standing off to the side, raising the disposable camera to her eye. The scrape of the dial, loading the film into place, and the click-and-flash.

The noise rings in my ears, and when she turns the next page, my muscles unlock.

I stride forward and grab it, slamming it shut and dropping it back to its spot on the low bookcase. I grab her by her throat and walk her backward, until she hits the wall. Her eyes widen, and her lips part.

"Don't touch that," I hiss.

The breath goes out of her in a quick exhale, and she lifts her hand to hold my wrist.

"What's wrong with a few memories between friends?"

I curl my lips into a sneer. "I know my friends. You're certainly not one of them."

"Am I your enemy?"

"You very well may be," I retort. I haven't decided yet—but I don't tell her that. Instead, I increase the pressure. Her pulse jumps under my fingers, but her expression doesn't change. "You went with Steele."

Her eyes narrow. My grip isn't so tight that she can't speak. Not yet.

"What was I supposed to do?"

"Call *me*," I growl.

"You don't even like—"

I squeeze, cutting off her words. Her lips move soundlessly. I live for this control over her, and I wait for the spark of fear to come. Because I want to keep pushing her, even when she's trying to drive me away. Someone broke into her house, but that won't fly.

I'll make sure the whole fucking world knows Violet belongs to me.

"There is no like." I lean in and brush my lips along her cheek, sweeping back toward her ear. My tongue flicks out, tasting her skin. She smells like wildflowers. "I don't have to fucking like you to own you. There's no affection between us. You're mine. Your mouth is mine. Your cunt is mine. Every fucking thought that runs through your head belongs to me."

She shudders, and I let up long enough for her to breathe. I miss her expression, because I bite her ear and she shivers again. I press my body to hers, pinning her with more than just my hand at her throat, and let her feel how hard she makes me. How her helplessness turns me on.

I bite her ear again, rougher, and then move to her lips. Her lower lip was bleeding earlier, but there's no sign of it now. I take it between my teeth and tug, and she gasps. Her pulse is a hummingbird's wings beating against her skin. It singes my fingertips. I bite until the metallic taste seeps across my tongue, and then I bite harder.

She whimpers.

The sound drives me fucking wild.

I release her throat and attack her clothes. I shove her leggings down and her shirt up, exposing her breasts.

No bra.

My mind blanks for a second. Her breasts are perky, smooth and pale. Her nipples pebble. I stare and lick my lips, tasting her blood again. My cock is so hard, I might explode on first contact. But there's urgency, too, and it seems to infect her as much as me.

She unbuttons my pants and pushes them off my hips. I step out of them and look down. Her panties are white. The picture of innocence. For a split second, I wonder if she's a virgin. I dismiss it almost immediately. Her ex-boyfriend wouldn't have let that pussy remain untouched for two fucking years.

I tear her panties off. The material rips easily, and I lift the fabric to my nose. I let her see my expression when I inhale her scent, and my cock twitches.

"Mine," I repeat, dropping the material to the floor and hoisting her up.

She locks her legs around me, and I slide into her with one thrust.

God, she feels like heaven. She's wet and ready, and her head falls back against the wall when I pull almost all the way out. I force myself back inside her. Her cunt clenches at me, tight and hot. Perfect. Fucking perfect.

I fuck her like a madman. Her spine hits the wall with every movement. Her breasts bob. I lean down and bite her skin, leaving a trail of wet marks as I home in on her nipple. When I have it between my teeth, she shrieks.

If that isn't the best sound I've heard. I could live for those screams, tinged with pain and pleasure. A combination.

I release her thighs to slip my hand between us. I pinch her clit, twisting it and tugging. I play with her harder than I've ever fucked a girl before, and I still feel deranged. Like this is only the tip of the iceberg.

Her nails rake down my back, and I shudder when she grips my hair and forces my head up. We lock eyes. I see everything she wants me to see and more. How every stroke deep inside her is hitting a special place that makes her eyelids flutter. How the pressure is something new, something twisted.

I ease up on her clit and rub fast, shallow circles. My balls tighten, and I pound into her faster. Harder. She lets her head fall back when I pinch her clit again, and her cunt clenches around me as she comes.

Her mouth opens and closes, but she doesn't give me that scream. She doesn't say my fucking name, but she shakes and trembles and grips my biceps so tight, I think I'll have half-moon cuts in my skin when we're done.

Sweat rolls down my back. Between her breasts. We're both panting.

I bury myself inside her and go still, ecstasy sweeping down my cock and exploding inside her. I grip her to me as I come, knowing full well that there's no barrier between us. I didn't give her a choice—and she's not going to get one.

There's no going back.

14

VIOLET

Greyson kneels in front of me. I feel strange, like I don't fit inside my skin anymore. I've been stretched and snapped back into place, and everything is just... off. He runs his hands down my leg and lifts my left one. I don't realize until it's too late.

He touches the scar running down my calf and stares at it.

Then, without warning, he digs his thumbs into my skin. I hiss, the shock worse than the pain, and jerk my leg out of his grasp. He lets me inch around him and go to the door. He knows before I do that I'm not going outside. Not when I'm naked, with cum dripping down the inside of my thighs. The party downstairs is still raging.

I turn back around and find my shirt. He sits on the edge of his bed and watches me with dark eyes. He's dangerous. I need to repeat that. *Danger, danger.* A warning siren flashes red in my mind, twisting behind my vision.

There's no way I'm calling it quits tonight. He offered me a way to relax—and I'm not sure that sex was on the agenda. Not at first.

I go to my leggings next, ignoring that I don't have panties. They're torn and forgotten on his floor, so fuck it. I'll go without. I shimmy in front of him, barely keeping my balance to yank them on. I'm better than that—my balance is usually solid.

He's shaken me more than I thought.

I picture the woman in the photo album. It must be special to him—it was front and center, practically displayed. The only thing on that bookcase that seemed to hold any value. And the photos themselves. Worn around the edges, like they've been touched countless times.

Maybe he hurts like I do. Maybe he dreams about the parent he doesn't have, but he won't admit it. He shouldn't have a soft side. He shouldn't be appealing.

He follows me into the hallway. I twist the knob to go into the bathroom, and he blocks me.

I raise my eyebrow. "What are you doing?"

"If you're going downstairs, you're fine as you are."

I glare at him. "Excuse me?"

"You're excused." He leans against the bathroom door. "If you're going downstairs, I want everyone to know that you were just thoroughly fucked. I want them to smell it on your skin and see it in the flush in your cheeks. I want them to know my cum is seeping out of your cunt."

He can't be serious.

"It's healthier to pee after sex. It prevents UTIs."

He shrugs. "Fine, then you're not going downstairs."

His indifference is infuriating. Seems like he doesn't care one way or another, so I shake my head and go for the stairs. I've never been afraid of people looking at me. I survived the aftermath of Greyson sharing the video of my drunk blow job, I can survive a few people knowing I had sex.

When we get downstairs, he becomes my shadow. He follows me into the living room, where the party has evolved into couples paired off on the couches and chairs. Willow and Knox sit in a loveseat opposite the large, L-shaped couch. Steele found himself a girl, and so did Erik. Miles sits beside Amanda, close but not quite touching. Jacob and another dance team girl, Madison, are making out in the corner—but they're the only ones not paying attention to the conversation.

"They just need a better goalie," Miles argues. "The rest is fine."

"Well, their forwards were shit," Steele says. "Not that I'm mad about that."

"I'm just saying, if they want to get ahead, they've got to up the ante. Stop more shots."

"They should just stop..." Steele pauses, attention bouncing from me to Greyson. "Hey, Violet."

My face flames, and I step over Erik's legs to get to the empty spot in the center of the couch. Greyson disappears into the kitchen, and I sink into the cushions. Realistically, I wish I had thought better of my plan. I should've just gone to sleep to pretend that this never happened.

But... nope.

Steele leans over the girl beside him. "You okay?"

I stare at him. "Don't I look okay?"

"You look satisfied," the girl says. She twists to glance over her shoulder back the way Greyson had gone. "He doesn't strike me as the giving type."

"Just because he didn't make you orgasm doesn't mean he's incapable." Erik snorts. "Unless you had to finish the job yourself, Violet?"

I shake my head slowly. Of course she's slept with Greyson before. At this rate, I'm not surprised. Paris is probably on that list, too. And half of the other hockey-player-chasing girls I know.

"I just blew him," the girl mumbles. She folds her arms over her chest.

Steele laughs. "Low standards, sweetheart. Stick with me."

I quirk my lips. "You don't seem like the giving type either."

A hand lands on my shoulder, and I jump. A second later, Greyson is leaning over the couch and forcing my head around to look at him. He stares into my eyes, letting me and only me see his anger.

I raise my eyebrows. If he didn't want me to insinuate that I gave Steele a blow job—which I did because Greyson *made* me—then he shouldn't have put the dick in my mouth.

I think I communicate that just fine, because Greyson's lips twitch. And then he vaults over the back of the couch, landing beside me. He grabs my hips and hauls me onto his lap. I don't miss that he's growing hard under my ass, and I try to get off him.

He bands his arm around my waist, keeping me still.

Well.

I finally take a breath and relax against him, and he relaxes, too. Like he's content now that he knows I'm not going anywhere.

But I can't look my best friend in the eye. She'd know something is up. And Greyson was right—I think they can literally smell the sex on me.

"So, um..." I swallow. "Maybe I should head back to the apartment. Or get a hotel."

"Nonsense," Greyson answers. "You can't go back tonight. Not until we can check it out."

I frown. "We?"

He pats my thigh. "If you want to sleep, I have a bed."

"You're going soft on me."

He leans forward, teeth against my neck. "Never." His breath fans across my skin, raising goosebumps.

Willow shakes her head and glares at Knox. "You told her you'd take care of it—not that she needs to stay here. We're going home."

She stands and holds her hand out to me, wobbling slightly.

I hesitate.

I love my best friend. I do. I love that she always wants to keep me safe, and that she tries to do what's best for us. I love that she's fierce and loyal and smart. But I'm afraid that the man in the mask might return, knowing we'll be there—or, worse, we'll go back and he'll have ransacked the place again.

Everything was locked when I left, but I don't know if that's enough to stop him. If he's determined enough, he could break down our door, or jimmy open another window.

"You want to put your best friend in danger?" Greyson whispers in my ear.

I shake my head sharply and ignore him.

"Violet," Willow says. "Come with me. Don't worry, caveman, we won't leave. Yet."

His grip on me eases slightly. I take her hand and let her pull me out of his lap, and she drags me into the kitchen.

Immediately, she seems more sober.

Maybe there's a difference between her being happy-go-lucky buzzed and drunk, and she was just riding that line. But now it's clear that she hasn't been overdoing it, because her expression is clear. And accusatory.

She narrows her eyes. "You went upstairs with him. Alone."

I lift one shoulder and glance away. "I..."

"Are you okay?" She steps closer. "No offense, but you look like he twisted you like a pretzel... and that you enjoyed it. You have bite marks..."

I slap my palm over my neck. I knew I should've just stayed upstairs. Freaking hell.

"Everything is fine," I assure her. I'm not quite sure that's true, though, but I won't be bursting her bubble. Or, even worse, worrying her. "Yes, we had a little thing. It was consensual. And hot. So, we're good."

"And you want to stay here?"

I bite my lower lip, running my tongue over it. I don't want to stay, but as Greyson said: I don't want to put her in danger.

I say as much, and she nods.

Concern creases her eyes. "That guy... he didn't do anything, right?"

"He saw me and ran." I grab a cup and pour myself a glass of water, chugging it down.

I refill it in the sink and hand it to her, then tip my head. We go through the kitchen and down a short hall to a bathroom.

She locks it behind us, and I take the much-needed opportunity to pee. She fidgets with her fingernails. "I just don't get what someone wants with you, in particular."

"I was sure it was Greyson." I pull up my leggings and wash my hands, then follow her out.

"But you called right after it happened?" She glances through the doorway to the living room, pausing again in the kitchen. It seems safe enough to talk in here without them overhearing. "He was here. The whole hockey team was, actually."

I grimace. "Yeah."

"So, ruling him and the team out... was it someone else we know?" She rubs her forehead. "You know what? Maybe this is a conversation we'd have easier when I'm not tipsy."

"Tomorrow? Brunch." We're obsessed with brunch. I'm not sure why. It's always been a Sunday treat.

"Deal."

She finishes the water and sets the cup in the sink. When we reenter the living room, the lights are dimmer. Someone has put a movie on, and everyone has adjusted to watch it. Greyson's gaze on me is a weighty thing, and I sense him watching me as I pick my way toward him.

I try to sit beside him, but he redirects me again. I land on his lap, and he wastes no time rearranging my limbs to suit him. He shifts me so I'm cradled sideways, my legs up on the couch and extended toward Steele and his girl. Greyson wraps a blanket around both of us, but I know it's not a comfort thing. It's a possessive thing.

I don't know how I know, until his hand goes into my leggings.

"Thought I told you to keep me between your legs," he says in my ear.

I shake my head. "You can't just stop bodily functions."

He grunts, and his fingers move. I let out a breath when I realize what his intention is. My clit is sore from the earlier abuse, but he's gentler now. My pussy pulses with need, reawakening, and I put my hand on his wrist.

He tsks. "Watch the movie, Vi."

Vi. He called me that in his text to himself from my phone, too. No one calls me that, not even Willow. As a kid, I was very against nicknames. I hated that my name could be shortened. Unlike Willow, whose only real option is Will, there are too many ways to chop mine up.

Violet can turn into so many terrible things to creative kids. Vile was common for the bullies. Lettie by my well-meaning mother, although she dropped that by the time I turned twelve. When I met Willow, I was sick of people asking what I'd rather go by, that I ranted to her about ending all nicknames. Outlawing them.

But, damn it, I've got to admit that I like the sound of it coming out of his mouth.

I shift, rotating in his direction. I let my head rest against his shoulder and make myself a promise.

Tomorrow, we will go back to hating each other. Tomorrow, all the bad things can sweep back into my brain. Tomorrow, tomorrow, tomorrow.

Right now, I close my eyes and enjoy the slow strokes of his finger on my clit and the way his cheek feels against the top of my head. And the sounds of the movie and the people around us. I should be wary, or afraid, or just altogether unwilling to orgasm in front of people.

But when it sneaks up on me, I turn my face into Greyson's neck and bite. Hard.

His fingers push into me, and I clench around him. I try not to make a single noise with my teeth locked on his skin. My tongue flicks out, automatically soothing the area. His cock stiffens, pressing against my hip.

Why do girls always go for the bad guy?

I don't think I can change him. I don't think I want to—in fact, I'd be happy if I never had anything to do with him ever again. If we walked away right now, I'd accept it.

No, Violet. That's a fucking lie.

Girls like me need guys like him to spar with, to fight.

To hurl the miseries and the anger at someone who can handle it.

He withdraws his fingers and puts them to my lips. I clench my teeth and ignore it. There's no fucking way I'm sucking on his fingers that were just in me. Nope.

His breathy laugh is the only warning I get before he pinches my jaw with his free hand. He grips my cheeks so hard, my mouth opens to avoid the pain. And then his fingers slip into my mouth, pressing down on my tongue, and he waits.

Mortification floods through me at the taste, and the position, and the power of him. I loathe it, but he's more stubborn than me. He rubs his fingers back and forth across my tongue until I close my lips around his two fingers and tentatively suck at them. He releases my jaw, and that hand slides down my back.

He lets my tongue explore his fingers, the edge of his nails. The texture of his knuckles. When I've done what he wants, he pulls them from my mouth. I lick my lips and lift my head to glare at him, but he's uninterested in my reaction.

It isn't the aftermath that he cares about—it's the act. And since he got what he wanted, he's ready to focus on the movie.

I let out a sigh and put my head back down on his shoulder.

I'm so fucking tired. I don't give a shit that my eyes close. That anyone could've seen what just happened. Instead, I fall asleep.

15

VIOLET

Willow and I follow Knox, Jacob, and Greyson into our apartment. Jacob has a metal baseball bat in his grip, just in case there's someone still lingering. Knox and Greyson walk in empty-handed.

They split up and search our apartment, checking over every square inch. Willow and I ignore their orders to wait outside and go with them. I follow Greyson down the hall to my room. He finds it with unerring accuracy, which makes me wonder if he was behind that first time it was destroyed.

"See anything familiar?" I lean against the doorjamb.

He moves in a small circle, taking everything in like I did to him.

This morning, I woke up alone in Greyson's bed. I don't think anything happened, but I don't remember the rest of the night. One minute, I was coming on his fingers and then falling asleep... and the next, I woke up in his bed, with sunlight streaming in through the window.

He sees things I don't want him to, of course. The things

I swept off my desk. The glass stand for the globe on the floor. He goes to that and lifts it, hefting it in his palm before setting it on my dresser. He rights the papers, flipping through them before shuffling them into a neat stack and leaving them on the edge of my desk.

"I don't think your burglar did this." He continues straightening, so much so that I wonder if he has a compulsion to do so. He puts my texts in a pile from largest to smallest and adds it to my desk. Then he gets on his knees and reaches under my bed.

When he rises, he tosses me the ball of glass that rolled away last night.

The miniature globe.

I catch it and look down. More blue has come off, revealing murky, raised lines meant to be valleys and peaks. The world in three dimensions. She used to spin it idly at night. She said she didn't think she'd ever get the opportunity to see the world, and this was as good as it was going to get for her.

"Something important to you?"

I shake my head and set it down beside the stand. I intentionally step away from it—and, in fact, him. No need to give him any more ideas about me.

What I do want to do is ask him where he slept. Why he didn't push the issue.

My throat is sore, and my body aches. Too much excitement, too much strain. My leg hurts worse today, too. The temperature has dropped further, necessitating jackets and hats and gloves. More snow is in our near future.

I find Knox, Jacob, and Willow in the living room.

Knox looks at me and shrugs. "We didn't see anything of use," he says apologetically. "I'm sorry."

"What should we do?" Willow asks. "Is it too late to call the police?"

Jacob shifts. "I mean... Violet should've called them last night."

I wince.

"My dad's a police chief. It's just, the sort of after-the-fact thing is hard, because leads go cold. We've already trampled over most of the house, you know?"

"He wore gloves." I sigh. "But I get what you mean."

"Next time," he says helpfully.

Greyson strides out and shakes his head. "Nothing unusual in her room."

Willow makes the decision for us. "We're fine," she says to them. Mainly Knox.

I don't think *he* was gallant enough to sleep on the couch... just saying. She's got the same just-fucked look that I sported last night. Part of me is proud of her. She deserves to have a fling. Some fun. She's never been that type. She's always wanted commitment.

And most guys in college are hesitant to, in their words, tie themselves down.

She used to say I got lucky with Jack, but now I'm not so sure luck had anything to do with it. We both got comfortable.

"Okay," he acquiesces. "But if you need anything, you call the police and us."

Greyson grunts his agreement.

And then they leave, and Willow locks the door behind them.

I go into my room and flop on the bed. I'm tired and vaguely hungry and in desperate need of another shower, but I just want to sleep for a million years.

Willow joins me. She crawls up next to me and lies on her side, facing me.

"Spill," she says.

I open my mouth to deny everything, but I end up telling her the whole story. Even the most embarrassing parts about Steele and Greyson in the locker room. I leave out the gritty details, like them both coming on my face...

"Jeez," Willow whispers. "No wonder you're tired."

"Yep," I agree.

We both doze after that and wake up when her phone goes off. She blindly reaches for it behind her, finally finding it and bringing it in front of her face. She swipes it open, reads something, then tosses it facedown between us.

"Now you've got me curious." I snag it before she can stop me.

I scan the text from Madison—she's on the dance team, the one who was playing tonsil hockey with Jacob last night. She's also the best friend of Paris.

Madison: Paris is rioting. She says she's pissed at Violet because she called dibs on Greyson first. I'm not sure what to do. She's normally on pretty good terms with Violet, but I guess she feels insulted since Greyson and Paris have been a thing for the last few weeks.

I drop the phone, and Willow cringes.

"I didn't know," she says. "I just saw them together that one time, the first night you got back."

"It's fine. It's not like I'm on the dance team anymore." Oh, fuck. I bolt upright and grab at Willow's hand. "My mother texted me last night. She said Mia Germain, the director of the Crown Point Ballet, contacted her."

"Bitch!" Willow squeals. She sits up, too. "What the hell? You waited until right now to tell me?"

"I'm sorry, I forgot! A lot went on last night." I laugh and grab my phone, scooting back to sit against my headboard.

Willow sits up, too, and hunches toward me.

I dial Mia's number, and I hold my breath. I put it on speaker to put Willow out of her misery. Otherwise, I'd just have to repeat the whole conversation back to her.

It rings twice, then clicks as it's picked up. "Ms. Germain's line, this is Sylvie. Can I help you?"

"Hi, Sylvie," I say. God, my palms are sweating. "This is Violet Reece. My mother contacted me saying Mia reached out..."

"Oh, hi, Violet." Sylvie's voice turns cheerful. "Let me patch you through. One moment."

There's a dial tone, and then it rings again. Willow grips my hand hard.

She knows how much this could mean. I don't have any hope of them taking me back—I mean, not like I am. But maybe there's a chance. Or... an opportunity to work with her in another manner. Or something.

"Good morning, Violet!" Mia's warm voice comes through my phone. "I tried your old number, but it seemed you changed it. I apologize that I had to go through your mother. How are you doing?"

I had to change my number after the crash. I kept getting weird texts and calls from random numbers, making it impossible to block them all. Not to mention I lost my phone in the accident—it was smashed beyond repair. The phone company was able to transfer some of my old pictures and contacts, but I lost at least a week of data. So changing my number a week or so after that didn't seem like that big of a deal. In the grand scheme of things.

"I'm good, thank you. How are you?" I always feel formal around her, even when she told me last year to call her Mia instead of Ms. Germain—what I'd called her for the past five years previous to that. It's not stiffness in my voice, exactly. More like... I respect her too much to be casual.

"Good, good. Listen, your mother explained the situation with the doctor." Her voice drops, and a door in the background closes. "I'm so sorry to hear about your leg. However, I have a relationship with some of our own physicians, and I was wondering if you'd like them to take a look? They know the particular strain a dancer puts on her legs."

My heart leaps into my throat. "Oh, I'd—"

"I'm in New York for the next week to secure sponsors. We're finishing with *Swan Lake* next month and opening auditions for *Sleeping Beauty* a few months after that." She pauses. "If you're able and cleared by our doctors, I'd like to see you audition. To see if we have a role for you."

"Wow. Honestly, I didn't expect..." A lump forms in my throat. "Sorry. Thank you."

It's my turn to grip Willow's hand like my life depends on it. She leans into me, silent support, as my eyes burn with tears.

I can't lose it now. "They told me it was impossible with the pain."

Mia exhales. "I'll be honest with you, Violet. It very well could be. However, your mother mentioned that the orthopedic surgeon you saw was one of the best in the country, but the doctors on your team weren't versed in dancers. Do you want to hang up your pointe shoes on one opinion?"

"I don't," I answer. In a fucking heartbeat.

"Good. Dr. Michaels practices in Vermont. Let's meet with him in two weeks and go from there. Okay?"

"Okay. Thank you." I hang up and drop my phone, then promptly burst into tears.

Holy shit.

I'm not ready—and I need to be. I need to prove that, in a month, I can get back into some semblance of fitness. I have a feeling they'd be a little generous, coming off an injury, but not *that* much.

And everything rides on this.

Willow throws her arms around my shoulders, squeezing me tight. "You can do this," she whispers in my ear. Just a secret passing between us. "I'll help you. Whatever you need to chase your dream."

I hug her back and close my eyes. There's a weird giddiness in my chest, separate from the emotions I've been holding on to for the last six months. The grief of losing dance isn't gone, per se. But maybe it doesn't have to be forever.

"Call your mom," Willow urges. "She's going to have something bratty to say, but she'll be happy for you."

I hesitate. "Yeah, but then she'll want to come up here. You know, visit. Or worse, try to attend the appointment and taint it. Or she'll try to make sure I'm eating well."

I give her a look. Not too long ago—I think it was our freshman year—my mom noticed I had put on a little weight on a video chat. Nothing crazy. In her words, my face seemed wider. So she rushed up and got rid of all the sugar in our apartment.

Even Willow's stash of chocolates.

She threw out the salt, too, citing the fact that salt can make your body hold on to water weight. Instead, she filled our fridge with greens, plain chicken, fish. So many salads. Enough that I thought I might turn into a rabbit and take Willow right along with me.

"Good point." She sighs and crawls out of bed. "Okay, fine. Maybe only tell her after that appointment."

Unless she ignores my call altogether, which she has been doing since I got back to campus last weekend. Out of sight, out of mind.

Easy come, easy go.

I have the urge to get rid of the globe and delete her number from my phone. But that's dramatic... and overkill.

Drama is Paris and her weird claim on Greyson. I gesture to Willow's phone. "Just tell Madison that Paris can have him. I don't really give a shit what she does."

Another bald-faced lie, but whatever. It's not the first one I've told, and it won't be the last. Willow gives me a look that tells me she knows I'm lying, and she's judging, but she still types it out and hits send.

"How are you going to get to Vermont?"

I grimace.

"We'll cross that bridge when we come to it. What's going on with you and Knox, huh? I thought it was just a little hookup..."

She has the good grace to blush. "I don't know. At least Greyson didn't have him waiting for you in the locker room."

"Ew, no. I would've refused on the grounds that you're my best friend, and we don't do that to each other."

She smirks. "Pretty sure Greyson would've been more than happy to bury you for that."

I shrug. "Worth it."

We go to brunch and talk about normal things. When we return home, the rest of the day is spent on the couch, watching movies and struggling through the homework we've been putting off. In my environmental economics class, we have to pick a project and do a presentation on it at the end of the semester. Some of our homework is leading us in baby steps toward it. Pick something that's impacting the environment—water pollution, for example, or subsidized crops. My mind spins at how little I know about the world and how humans are steadily destroying it.

We make dinner, and I stare at the food. My appetite is nonexistent. It doesn't help that my focus keeps getting yanked back toward ballet like a yo-yo.

Willow gives me a look. "Don't do that."

"Don't do what?" I know what she means, though. And yet... I can't help it. I want to be ready for an audition so fucking bad, I can practically taste my dreams reviving. I have to stop myself from pressing my hand to my stomach.

She shakes her head. "You're going to do what you want no matter what I say."

"You said you'd help."

"Figured you'd go about it in a healthy way, is all," she mumbles.

I nod once and grab a plate. The television fills the silence, but that's it. I sense her wanting to say something else, to try and make it better, but there isn't anything she can do. She's waiting for me to assure her. So I do.

"I just need to make it," I tell her in a low voice. "After that, I'll ease up. Okay?"

She rises abruptly. "I love you, and I want you to chase your dreams. But, Violet? I don't believe you."

I spend the rest of the night watching Mia Germain choreography. Old videos of her teaching open classes, of the ballerinas who excelled under her guidance. They went on to dance for famous companies that toured around the world.

My heart aches with desire.

I hadn't let myself go there, and suddenly it all seems like...

It's there again. It's a possibility.

Hope is this dangerous thing. It's quiet and warm and it stays locked away until we feed it, and then it bursts into flame. It can consume us.

It will very well eat me alive.

16

GREYSON

I have the briefest warning of my father's arrival. My phone chirps with a social media alert that I set up forever ago, which pings when his location changes. Well, when his secretary checks him into specific cities.

It's how I used to keep tabs on him without reaching out. When I was alone in a big, empty house with nothing to do, I could check and see where he was. Nebraska, California, Edinburgh, Dubai. The man traveled overseas a lot —especially for someone who is supposed to be a New York senator.

I'd like to think that it's his fault I turned out the way I did. Because I was rotting of boredom as a teenager, I sought out my own thrills. I found parties, and if there weren't any? I created them.

He always gave me access to a credit card that he paid monthly without blinking, as long as I didn't surpass the high limit, and I knew the combination to the safe where he kept an array of valuables: cash and firearm included.

Anyway, it pings that his private jet just landed in Crown Point, and I scramble to make my room presentable.

I hide the photo album in with my textbooks, run downstairs, and shove dishes and cups into the dishwasher. I even get through sweeping half of the lower level when my phone goes off again.

This time with a phone call.

"Hello?"

"Greyson? It's Martha."

Dad's long-time, aforementioned secretary. I didn't mention that she's only recently crossed the line into lover. His excuse? We can't all be saints.

I let the silence fill the call.

She clears her throat. "Your father is in town. He's meeting with the university president and the mayor, and then he wants to see you for dinner."

I open my mouth to answer, then close it. It's not a request, that's for fucking sure. He didn't even have the nerve to call and tell me himself.

This is a publicity stunt.

Dinner with the rising hockey star—never mind that I already *was* a hockey star at Brickell. People tend to gloss over that when my past is littered with slander. And trust me, those articles still exist. They're buried, and they don't come up on regular searches. My father pulled way too many fucking strings to give the illusion that scandal didn't rock our family.

"A car will pick you up at six," she finally says.

"Okay."

She makes a noise, like she fucking won something. And maybe she did by getting me to answer. I don't know what she thinks of me, and I don't really give a shit. Who knows what my father told her, or the opinions she formed on her own.

I've only met her a handful of times.

I gather my swept pile and throw it out, then head back upstairs to make myself presentable. Erik is making noise in the basement—a loud, violent video game, judging by the sounds drifting up—and the other guys aren't home. As soon as I close my door, the noise fades.

Once I'm clean, I text Violet.

Me: I want to see you later

My phone stays silent for too long. The seconds tick past, and I stare down at the screen. I haven't seen her in two days—too long. Sundays are our only day without practice, which means most of the hockey team does absolutely nothing. I spent the morning at the gym, then I lounged around and caught up on homework.

But I want to know what Violet is doing.

I want to know what she's thinking and wearing and where she is.

Finally, the bubble pops up that she's typing.

Vi: I'm busy later.

That's not acceptable.

Me: Make time.

Me: I'll make it worth your while.

I drop my phone on the bed and finish getting dressed. A button-down shirt that my dad expects, the silver chain he got me when I turned twenty. Black slacks and dress shoes—it's an outfit I'd wear to go to a game. They always demand a certain way of presenting ourselves. The professional vibe.

You never know when a recruiter is watching.

Vi: Fine. If you can find me, you can see me.

I perk up at the text. Immediately, blood rushes to my cock. It stiffens against my zipper. There's a certain thrill that comes with a hunt. And that's exactly what this feels like: she's the prey and I'm the predator, forever trying to get her ensnared.

Eventually, she won't be able to run from me.

The urge to track her down right now is strong. I force myself to remain in my room, to lie back and go still. It's an exercise in patience that I usually don't excel in. The quiet is too much of a reminder of my childhood.

As a compromise, I open my Instagram and search her name. It doesn't take too long to find her account. There's one photo of her standing in front of the Beacon Hill hospital, her left leg encased in a black walking boot. Her dress hangs over it, stopping at her knees. A woman who looks startlingly similar to her, with more creases around her eyes and mouth. There's a garish smear of red across her lips, and her hair seems more expensive than Violet's wardrobe.

For the first time, it occurs to me that she might be poor. Even though her mom tends to be made of flashy things—or maybe she does that in spite of their financial situation. Because Violet drove a shitty car, and she's lived in the same apartment with a roommate for years, and she never seems to wear anything new or crazy.

Maybe she's chosen this lifestyle because there were no other options. Because of a selfish mother?

Whatever it is, I want to know every little thing about her.

The thought irritates me.

I keep scrolling.

There's a video of her and Willow at a dance team competition. I pull the screen closer, searching for her in the throng of girls. They all wear the same thing: royal-blue tank tops, black booty shorts, blue-and-white knee-high socks under white sneakers. Their hair is all in high ponytails, slicked back and tied with blue-and-white ribbons.

It doesn't take me too long to find her—she's front and center, after all. The girls move around her, letting her take the lead. My mouth waters. She flips and twirls, then scoots backward to let other girls take the spotlight.

I scroll to the next one. A professional photo of her in a ballet leotard, mid-leap. The sort of image that could easily be in a magazine. Her muscles all stand in perfect relief, her limbs extended so it looks like she's floating. Her expression is peaceful.

No sign of the physical strain that must take.

Not even her eyes show it. I zoom in to make sure, studying her relaxed lips, her jawline.

My erection comes roaring back. What is it about Violet Reece that makes me so fucking hard? Paris certainly didn't get that response from me, and her mouth was on my cock. No other girl at CPU has so much as put a dent in my fixation on Violet.

If only I'd known about her sooner.

She was in my hometown. We might've even crossed paths.

I keep scrolling, trying to figure out where she went. I would've noticed a girl like her, wouldn't I?

I didn't, though. That's the thing. But now that I have, I can't get her out of my fucking mind. The slope of her nose and curve of her cheeks, her blue eyes, her blonde hair. She has curves now, more than when she danced. Her hips are padded, her belly soft. It's fucking attractive.

The next few are photo dumps of her and her friends over the school year. Her and Willow with their cheeks pressed together, grinning at the camera. Her and Jack, his arm looped over her shoulder. I swipe past that one angrily.

And even worse when I get to the last one in that group-ing. His lips are pressed to hers.

Besides that, there are only a few other recent posts. I get so far back, I watch a video of her and Willow opening their acceptance letters to CPU at the same time. There's hesitation when they both unfold the paper and scan it, their anticipation and nerves visible even to me. Then the realization that they both got in.

I let out a sharp exhale. I was happy to go to Brickell, sure. It was a good school, and the hockey coach had come to watch me play a few games for Emery-Rose Elite. But I didn't have that jump-for-joy excitement that Violet has with her best friend. I thought I'd made it in terms of success, but... now I'm questioning it.

And then my success turned out to be an epic failure.

My alarm goes off, and I splash water on my face, then head downstairs. Right on time, the doorbell rings.

"Who's that?" Erik asks, coming around the corner. He sees what I'm wearing, and his brows hike. "Now I'm more intrigued."

I roll my eyes and smooth my shirt. "I'm being summoned."

He grunts, and jealousy flares in his eyes. "By Coach?"

"By my miserable fuck of a father," I reply. I yank the door open.

The driver my father's skank sent smiles at me. "Mr. Devereux—"

I stalk past him, down the concrete steps and walkway. He scurries after me, leaving the house door open, and makes it to the car just a moment before I do. I climb into the back seat, right where he probably wants me, and give him a bland expression when he drops his arms to his sides.

Poor guy. He's probably been catering to my father—or

politicians like him—his whole career. The car is nice and clean. There are mini water bottles in a polished black cup holder in the center armrest. I take one and crack it open, bringing it to my lips. The driver finally shuts my door and returns to his seat.

I smirk to myself and tip my head back.

We go past the campus, to an upscale restaurant on the water. Crown Point got its name for the *point* it comes to, like the centerpiece of an actual crown. A lake spreads out below it, but it's the cliff that's truly impressive.

Perfect for jumping—which is exactly what the hockey team did as a sort of initiation and bonding experience at the beginning of the year.

Swimming back to a spot where we could easily climb out was a bitch, and hiking back to our clothes was even worse. But, whatever. The drop was exhilarating.

Now it's cold. An icy wind travels off the water and up.

The car rolls to a stop outside the restaurant, and I spot my father through the glass. His secretary isn't with him.

He probably wants to have a little *chat* about how things are going, and as much as he likes her, he doesn't trust anyone except himself.

I get that from him.

The driver opens my door, and I blink. Shocked that I actually let myself get so focused on him that I forgot to get out.

"Thanks." I slide a twenty-dollar bill into his palm, then stride inside with my game face in place.

Smile. Charm.

Everything a politician's son needs.

The host takes me to my father's table, and the latter rises on my approach. I hesitate, unsure what he wants. A handshake? A hug? In a split second, I understand. The latter—all for the show. I should've known.

His arms wrap around my shoulders, and he pats my back hard enough to leave prints on my skin. He smiles widely and gestures for me to take a seat. He's all show, and I'm hyperaware that we're in the center of a well-lit room. There's an awareness here that sticks to my skin, like eyes on us for the wrong reasons.

I don't know why he's in town. His true motivation, I mean, beyond meeting with the president of the school and whoever else the secretary mentioned. There's always an ulterior motive when it comes to my father.

"How has Crown Point University been treating you?" he asks.

I tilt my head. "Fine..."

I didn't see him over winter break. He was in California, schmoozing with the governor and his wife, while I was here. A world away. Training and pretending it didn't matter that I was celebrating Christmas alone.

"The president says you're an excellent addition to the hockey team." He appraises me, steepling his fingers in front of him. His elbows on the table. "I have to wonder if that's all you do."

I bristle. "It's one of my main areas of focus, yes."

"Because...?"

"I'd like to play for the NHL." I narrow my eyes. "Why?"

He looks a bit like me. Gray hair, because polls say that people trust men more when they show their age in their hair. Smooth skin from routine Botox appointments— because polls say that people don't actually want their politicians to *look* old—and manicured eyebrows. Every-thing is a fabrication, right down to his spray-tanned skin.

It's like leather against his white shirt.

Still, there are hints of similarity. The color of our eyes, for example. The square jaw. Even our noses. I pulled some features from my mother, like her dark-blonde hair, her fair skin, her smile. Maybe that's why Dad wrinkles his nose in disgust whenever I show happiness.

"You need to set more reasonable expectations," he says. "There are a lot of eyes on us. Voters haven't quite forgiven us for your mess-up."

Ah. I knew he'd cut to the chase sooner or later, but I am surprised it's this. His own stupid political campaign.

"What are you saying?" I ask.

He shakes his head. "There's a reporter sniffing around. Picked up the story by dogging the local police for a scoop, and some rookie gave him a soundbite to run with. Pointed him in the direction of the junkyard that took the cars." He waves his hand, then busies himself with the silverware.

I watch, dumbfounded, as he shakes out his napkin. The fabric snaps before billowing down to his lap. He straightens his wine glass, the water glass.

"I'm taking care of it," he adds.

An afterthought.

"What does that mean?"

I bite the inside of my cheek to keep from fidgeting. He's always hated my desire to move. *Still waters run deep*, he used to tell me. As if to insinuate that if I move too quickly, I can't have a single complex thought or emotion.

"The reporter won't find anything." Dad smiles at me. "Your grades are good?"

Another question to tick off his checklist.

I nod along. "Yep. Straight A's last semester."

"And this one?"

"Should maintain the four-point-zero just fine." Probably.

I lean back and kick my legs out, taking another look around the room. I clock a journalist—probably one hired by my father to document the father-son bonding time—and Dad's security at a separate table. Their gazes are alert, too, as they scout for signs of trouble.

"Good, good." Dad checks his phone, then looks up.

A waiter approaches with food, quickly setting it down in front of us. Food I didn't order. Grilled salmon, asparagus, coconut rice. I lean down and sniff it, my stomach already turning. I haven't eaten fish since I was seven. Coconut irritates my skin, makes me break out in hives. The smell does something to me, too, because the churning in my gut doesn't ease.

Dad has steak and mashed potatoes, broccoli covered in a glazed sauce and sesame seeds. He glances over at me and frowns. "I ordered for us. Hope you don't mind, it seemed you were running late."

I wasn't, but I don't bother arguing. Or pointing out his failure to know my food preferences.

He'd have to actually share more than five meals with me over the last year for that to happen.

I pick at the salmon and cut the asparagus carefully, avoiding the coconut rice. I divide the green stalks into small, manageable pieces, and shove them into my mouth one at a time. I watch Dad devour his steak like he's never had anything better, while I take gulps of water between each small bite of salmon.

Finally, our meal comes to an end. My father finishes his wine and food, and I've messed my plate up enough to look like I put a dent in all of it. He pats his mouth with his napkin and slips the waiter his card.

Once the receipt comes back, he signs it with a flourish. He rises, and I mirror him. We walk to the door together, and he hugs me again. It's one of those things that I wish I could duck out of, because he doesn't deserve this publicity. Maybe he sees it on my face because he grips me harder.

Out of the corner of my eye, a camera flash *pops*. Capturing our engineered moment.

His mouth presses against my ear. "You fucking owe me, kid. The least you can do is look happy to see your old man once a quarter. Now smile."

I smile on autopilot as we step back. I offer my hand, and he shakes it once. His fingers are cool and dry, not a callous on him, and he squeezes once. There's another flash of a camera. Then, I'm free.

I take a step back and watch him get into the car. I catch a blur of pink fabric and know Martha's already inside, waiting out of sight. The driver closes them in, encasing them in a tinted glass bubble, and I remain on the sidewalk. I slip my hands into my pockets, and I watch them pull away from the curb. I ignore the reporter who lingers in my peripheral.

No part of me wishes tonight had ended differently, because my thoughts are already turning to Violet. Where would she be?

The better question: where would she think I wouldn't find her?

I mull that over and start walking. I unbutton the top of my shirt and crack my neck. Already, I can see Crown Point in my mind and start to piece together more of what I know about Violet. Anticipation licks at my skin. I'm eager to begin the hunt.

She doesn't know it yet, but this is my favorite sport.

17

VIOLET

The gym on campus is in the basement of one of the residence halls. After signing in, I go quietly down the stairs and into the dark room. There's a wall of mirrors, exercise machines, weights.

It's as familiar as it is foreign.

I bypass the weights and go to the elliptical. In theory, this should be easier on my leg. Less impact. I say a quick thank you to my body that nine times out of ten, I land jumps on my right leg. It was always stronger, holding me upright through all the grueling exercises and rehearsals.

Dancing again still seems like a dream. I consider that as I climb onto the machine and turn it on. I program my height and weight, then set it to a weight-loss program. It climbs in resistance quickly. Within five minutes, I'm drenched in sweat.

I tear off my sweatshirt and drape it across the machine beside me. My t-shirt sticks to my skin, and my lungs sear with how little exertion I've put them through in so long. I'm ready to quit immediately, but I don't. I keep pushing until my thighs tremble and I'm heaving so hard I might puke.

The time ticks down, and I stumble off the machine. I stand in the middle of the room, trying to regain my breath, then gulp water from the fountain. The nausea eases slightly, and when I straighten, I start. A person stands in the shadows of the alcove entrance. I back away and bump into the mirrors, until they step into the light.

Greyson. In black slacks and white collared shirt, a black puffer jacket unzipped over it. I tilt my head, wondering why he's standing in a random basement gym. Dressed like that.

Then I realize what I stupidly texted him earlier.

A dare to find me.

"How did you know where I was?"

He smirks and takes another step toward me. "Lucky guess."

I shiver, but he doesn't stop. He comes right up next to me and leans in. His tongue flicks out at my temple, no doubt tasting my sweat. Goosebumps rise on my arms.

"Here's the thing," he says quietly. "I liked finding you —but it was too easy."

"Too easy," I repeat, my voice faint. "You found me in the basement of a dorm I don't live in..."

"You're going to run." His arms rise, caging me in. The opposite of his orders. "Run and don't let me catch you. Because wherever I *do* catch you, I'm going to tear your leggings down and fuck you until I come inside your cunt. If it's in public, if it's in front of your best friend, or your fucking dance team, or your precious ex—I don't give a shit."

My mouth gapes open. "I don't—"

"You want this to stop, and you say *stop*. Anything other

than that word, I don't care. If I catch you, I'm fucking you."
He trails a finger down my chest, between my breasts.
"How much you fight determines if you get to come or not.
But understand this, Violet. I'm always going to be the
monster hunting you down. I'm always going to be right
behind you wherever you go."

Oh, great.

"And if I don't?" I lift my chin. "If I just stay?"

The finger he ran down my chest now hooks the bottom
hem of my shirt. He balls it into a fist and pulls me closer.
His gaze turns to ice. "You can chance it..."

My body clenches, and my mind immediately goes to
the video he has. The fucking blackmail. He doesn't say it,
doesn't even hint, but I'm not an idiot. I have a good imagination, too. There are other ways he could get back at me.

This shouldn't sound like something I'd be into, but my
heart racing belies my nerves. The fact that I don't just
scream *stop* right now and end it means I've officially lost
my mind.

Running seems like the better choice. He knows it and I
know it.

He steps back, dropping his arms, and I bolt. It's a split-
second decision. Fight or flight. Run or... something worse.
No fucking way is that video getting out.

I leave my sweatshirt behind and dash up the stairs,
bursting through the doors. I take half a second to choose a
direction, even with the girl at the desk yelling after me
about my student ID. His threat of fucking me wherever he
catches me rings in my ears. I can't stick to public roads—
not when he's bound to be eager to hunt me down.

The woods.

I glance behind me and see him striding out the door.
Not in a hurry. Not at all perturbed. He looks every inch the

composed predator, and I'm turning into the scared prey. He says something to the girl at the desk, and she hands him my ID. His lips keep moving, the smile in place, but the glass blocks me from hearing the lies he tells her.

His gaze shifts to me, and I gasp at how hot it is. If it had any weight, I'd combust on the spot. But it also holds more malice than I expected, and that forces me to move.

I burst into a sprint, heading away from campus. I don't want him to catch me, but perhaps I can lose him on one of the many trails that winds through the park a block away. It's parallel to my neighborhood, so if I get far enough, I can cut across and lock him out of my apartment.

My breath comes in ragged gasps by the time I get to the trail head. It's nothing more than a break in a two-post fence line, but the wide, wood chip path is easy to spot. Behind me, my predator has picked up his pace. His footsteps drum steadily against the pavement—and then the noise dampens. He's reached the trail.

I'm swallowed by the forest, where the air is colder. It's lit intermittently by glass lamps on wrought-iron posts. They give off just enough of a glow to illuminate a small circle around each one. It doesn't touch the pockets of darkness in between.

My fear spikes, adrenaline bleeding in with it.

I should be scared—I know what Greyson is capable of. My stride lengthens, but I won't win this race. He's in shape. Tall. Strong.

He draws closer. Relentlessly closer. *Thump, thump, thump.*

I can't tell if that's my heartbeat in my ears or his footsteps.

All I know is that this is worse than walking into the locker room, because I don't know if he's serious. I don't know which version of him I'm going to get when he catches me.

I veer off the path, crashing between two shrubs. The long branches snatch at my clothes and hair, and fallen twigs snap under my sneakers. I push myself faster, weaving between trees. If I can't outpace him, I might be able to outmaneuver him.

But that proves false, too. He tackles me out of nowhere, and we crash to the ground. My hands slide in the dirt and pine needles, my teeth clack with the force of the fall. I dig my nails in, trying to get purchase, but he grips the back of my head and forces my head down. My cheek rubs the dirt. The earthy scent fills my nose.

I scramble, still trying to break free, when something heavy presses into my lower back.

I let out a strangled whimper.

He yanks my leggings down. I'm slick with sweat, collecting pieces of leaves and needles as I squirm on the ground. He pins my legs together, and the sound of his zipper going down is my undoing.

He's going to fuck my ass.

I let out a shriek, doing my best to try and twist around. He grunts, and his fingers dig into my hair. He lifts my head and slams it back down.

Stars burst in front of my vision, sparking in the darkness. The noise in my throat dies to a small cry, and my chest heaves. Simultaneously, I'm surprised by the violence —and not. Heat rushes through me, fire pooling under my skin and between my legs.

I can say stop.

I shift, my mouth opening and closing. I don't want to say it—not yet. I'm running purely on adrenaline and instinct.

He runs his finger through my wetness, shocking me into silence. His throaty chuckle is the only warning before he grips my hips, pulling them up slightly, and slams into me. Not my ass—*thank god*. His thighs bracket mine, keeping my legs pinned together.

The friction of him sliding into me is too much, and I moan. Fucking hell, I shouldn't want this. I push up, but he collects my wrists and pins them behind me. He torques one of my arms up, and I fold back into the ground. Pain travels up my arm, pulsing into my shoulder.

But then he moves faster. He hits a spot deep inside me, drilling into it like a wild animal.

That's what we're reduced to—animals fucking in the forest.

I pitch myself to the side, throwing him off balance, and get free long enough to burst up. My leggings around my knees don't give me much time to move, and Greyson is on me in a flash.

His fingers tangle in my hair, and he rips my head back. I crash into his chest, and he walks me forward. Into a tree. The rough bark scratches my cheek, my throat, my chest. And then he yanks my hips back again, and I grip the trunk to keep from falling over. My skin burns.

I close my eyes as pleasure and pain spark and tangle together, until I can't tell which is which. He grunts, not bothering to touch my clit or try to get me off. My orgasm is building slowly with every thrust of his cock against my G-spot, but it isn't enough to tip me over the edge.

He pounds into me with renewed energy, and stills all the way inside me. He groans and leans forward. His forehead touches my shoulder.

Without speaking, he pulls out and steps back.

Immediately, I feel the wetness between my legs. He came in me without a condom.

Again.

I say a quick thank you to my mother, who forced me to start taking birth control when I turned seventeen. She didn't want any grandchildren. Said I was still a child myself, and she'd end up doing all the raising.

Greyson's knuckles ghost along my chin when I finally push myself upright. He's lost the malice and anger in his expression, so much so that I want to ask him what tonight means to him. It doesn't feel like it has a lot to do with me.

Maybe only a little.

He yanks my leggings up, snapping the waistband into place, and leans forward. I don't expect him to kiss me, but he does. His lips touch mine softly, briefly, before he pulls back.

A silent thank you? Does he even know how that works? My bet would be on no. The rich boy has probably never uttered those words—or *please*—in his life. Because of his personality, for one, and also because he's a dick.

I guess those two might be the same thing.

"Do you get it?" He brushes his thumbs along my hips, just above the waistband of my pants. "Do you understand better now?"

Yes, I think I do. The anger inside him needs an outlet.

My teeth are chattering. His eyes narrow, and it only seems to register with him now that it's the middle of fucking January. He grabs his jacket from the ground and guides my arms through the sleeves. He takes care zipping it up, lingering between my breasts. He must've shed it beforehand. An earthy smell, plus a spice that I've been associating with Greyson, surrounds me. And *warmth*. Here

I was, racing through the woods in a sweat-dampened t-shirt and leggings, like a dumbass.

Being around Greyson inspires dumb decisions.

"Thanks," I whisper.

I eye his arms in his dress shirt. The muscles bulge against the white fabric. I resist the urge to reach out and touch him.

He grunts. His one hand stays pressed between my shoulder blades, and he walks me out of the woods. I let him forcefully guide me all the way to the corner of my street, and then I shake him off.

"I'm fine from here."

He narrows his eyes, then nods. "Go on, then."

I pull the zipper down to give him the jacket back, but he stops me. A clear sign that he wants me to keep it on, at least for now.

I shake my head slightly and walk away from him.

"Oh, and Violet?"

I glance back.

"Don't even think about making yourself come."

My face flames, and I swallow sharply. I don't answer, turning and hurrying away. Putting more and more distance between us, hoping that I'll finally be able to breathe with every step I take.

Spoiler alert: it doesn't work.

His gaze stays on me all the way to my apartment.

Once I'm inside, I lose it. A lump forms in my throat, and my eyes flood with tears. An ugly sob tears out, breaking the silence.

I press the back of my hand to my mouth to try and stem the flow of sound, but it's useless. My leg is on fire, pain lancing up from my shin through to my hip. I massage my thigh hopelessly and make my way to my room.

Willow's door is shut, the light off.

It's late—I made up an excuse about studying at the library and to not wait up, so she should be sleeping. I can lie and tell myself I don't know what I'm doing, or why. But I'm worried that she's going to try and talk me out of getting back into dancing shape.

I catch a glimpse of myself in the mirror. My hair is an absolute mess. My clothes, too. And Greyson has my student ID. I curse, then light up and pat down his pockets. Sure enough, my ID is safely tucked away in the left one.

I peel off his jacket and set it on the back of my desk chair. My phone is still on my charger on my nightstand, because I didn't want Willow to wake up and track my location.

See? Total guilty person behavior.

I exhale and turn on the shower. There's smudges of dirt on my arms, and it's all over my clothes. The bed of pine needles and leaves we rolled around in seem to have all come home with me, too.

It's a slow process to remove my clothing. Another zing of pain travels up my left leg when I try to balance on it, so I lean most of my weight on the counter to peel off my leggings. I touch my clit tentatively and gasp at the sensation. He didn't get me off—didn't want to, from the sound of it.

I consider continuing, taking myself there... but then his warning sounds in my head. And as painful as it is, I pull my hand away. I leave myself breathless and horny. Then I get in the shower and try to erase what happened tonight.

18

VIOLET

I wake up to my phone buzzing next to my face. I lift my head off the pillow and make out my mother's name on the screen. My shock wakes me up a bit, and I swipe to answer it.

"Ah, so you are alive." My voice is hoarse and rasping. About time she decided to check up about Mia Germain—it's unlike her to curb her curiosity.

Well, I suppose it's more like her nowadays, and I just hadn't caught up to the new her. But she's calling now, and that's the important part. Right?

"You signed an NDA," my mother hisses. "What the fuck were you thinking?"

I rear back from my phone. Not quite the response I was expecting.

"Um..." I scramble to catch up. Did Greyson release the video? I thought it was blackmail... I thought I did what he wanted. Panic stabs through me, ice-cold, and I throw the covers off my legs. The scar on my shin stands out in sharp relief against my pale skin. "Can you fill me in?"

"The *Times*. Look at the fucking *Times*." She moans. "Oh, our lives are over. How could you do this to us?"

I don't answer, putting her on speaker while I grab my laptop and type in the newspaper's website. It's a local Crown Point paper that runs print and digital. I think my mom gets their emails just in case I ever did anything impressive enough to warrant a screenshot—or, worse, for her to find a printed copy and carefully cut out the article or photo that mentioned me.

That was a lifetime ago, though.

Now, it's Greyson's picture that's spread across the front page.

I scroll down, my heart in my throat. The headline says: *Crown Point University's rising hockey star has a torrid past.*

I can't breathe. Mom is still talking about how I've ruined us, how they're going to come after both me and her. I tune her out and scan the article. It lays out an accusation without real evidence: that Greyson was involved in an accident, driving drunk, and it was swept under the rug.

"I didn't do this," I say weakly.

"Of course not," Mom snaps. "That's exactly what we're going to say."

The story goes on to talk about what happened to me. They found a photo of me outside the hospital in a walking boot. One I posted to my Instagram, if I'm not mistaken.

A chill goes through me. Did they do their research on me? Did they just look at my social media, or did they actually try to get in contact with me? It doesn't seem like anyone wanted a quote. No missed calls or emails...

Farther down, there's another photo of Greyson on the ice in his CPU jersey, skating along the wall. His expression is serious. The writer goes on to say how all is well in

Crown Point, with his past transgressions seemingly swept under the rug.

It mentions us. Me and him. There's a photo of us together, with Steele blurred out in the background. In his apartment? Who would have taken a picture of that?

I stare at the words on my screen, which go blurry after a minute. *Violet and Greyson seem to have no problem moving on. Perhaps they agree that mutual destruction is the way to go. Either way, Crown Point citizens should know who they're rooting for when Greyson Devereux steps on the ice every weekend.*

"Are you still there?"

I flinch. "Yeah."

"Well?"

"Um, sorry, I didn't..." I clear my throat. "I'm not quoted. There's no proof that I said anything at all—because I didn't."

Mom scoffs. "Of course not. I said, don't talk to anyone. This is libel, and I'll be contacting the newspaper immediately. This is absolutely ridiculous. To think, this piece had to be approved to go to print."

My stomach drops. "It's in print?"

"Front-page news," she says, her tone conveying her continued disgust.

Oh god.

He's going to kill me. He's going to release the video that already proves I broke the NDA, and wrap it up with this article, and deliver both to his father. And then I'll be well and truly fucked.

"Let me know." I hit the end button, not bothering to say goodbye.

She'll either make headway or she won't. Simple as that. And until then, I'm not going to be seen in public. No chance of that. I can afford to miss my Monday classes exactly twice before I fall behind.

I can already picture how pissed Greyson is going to be and what he'll do to retaliate. This was already a game to him, but it's getting worse. The stakes are inching higher and higher, and I'm afraid I'm not going to like where he takes this.

The ball's in his court... Or is it?

What if I act first, for once? What if I set the record straight with him and make him understand that I had nothing to do with this?

Before I can lose my nerve, I text him.

Me: This wasn't me. I promise.

He texts back a second later.

Greyson: I know.

I narrow my eyes. He knows?

Willow bursts into my room, her phone in her hand. "Violet—"

I motion to my computer, open on my lap, and make a face. "I got a call from mother dearest, accusing me of breaking the NDA."

She gasps and comes to sit beside me. "You didn't."

"I know." I narrow my eyes. "But someone obviously found out about it."

She reels back. "You think I had something to do with it?"

Oh god. I grab her hand to keep her from getting too far. "Oh, hell no. Girl, my trust in you is absolute. But I'm wondering if Greyson mentioned anything to... someone else."

Relief flows across her expression, quickly chased by confusion. "I doubt it. The whole point was to pretend it didn't happen, right?"

"No chance of that," I mutter.

Willow checks her phone again. "Wait."

"What?"

"Screenshot the page," she orders. "I think they just pulled it."

I do, making sure to get the headline and all the images, too. I refresh the page, and the headline has been replaced by something else. An abandoned mall being converted into an indoor dog park later this year. I type in Greyson's name into the search bar and get an error.

I meet Willow's gaze. "How many people do you think saw that?"

She winces. "I found it because the headline and first image were in my inbox."

Shit. Fuck.

No doubt that's going to raise questions, whether or not they're able to read the full article. Actually... at least that puts me in the clear. I'm not mentioned until the second half. But Greyson?

"His dad was in town last night," she says.

I pause. "What?"

"His dad. The senator. They were photographed getting dinner together, hugging, the whole thing. The senator's social media was making a big deal about visiting Crown Point to see the mayor and the president of CPU."

"Protecting his investment. Isn't he coming back for some charity thing next month, too?"

Willow grunts her affirmation. Paris had mentioned it —bragged about how her parents are coming in specifically for it.

I pace beside my bed. "Okay, so this article might've been planned for a while, or it could've been a spur-of-the-moment thing. All we know is that I didn't say anything, and I can't imagine Greyson would've either. Obviously."

"Suspicious timing, for sure."

I suck my lower lip between my teeth and think about everything that's happened this semester. It just feels like everything is unraveling. Not just school but my life.

"Do you think it has to do with the break-in?"

Her face brightens, then falls. "What if it does? That's fucking creepy."

I grimace, then grab my phone again. I took a picture of my photo wall as evidence, and now I pull it up. The word whore is still harsh to read, but I block it out and zoom in on the prints.

"What are you looking for?" Willow rises on her knees and peers over my shoulder. "That's awful, by the way. Still."

"Yeah. I'm checking to see if there was a picture of my mom and I outside the hospital. It's kind of like the one I posted on Instagram, but we're both frowning in the one the paper used." I shrug. "It's just a hunch."

"Did you have the frown printed out?"

I sag. "No idea."

She chuckles and shakes her head. "Okay, Detective Reece. Let's just... I mean, if it's taken down, that's not a bad thing. It's actually probably good, they'll just see the headline and the first paragraph in the email and think it's... I don't know, propaganda from a rival team or some shit. You know how everyone gets competitive when it gets close to the end of the regular season."

Right. It's barely seven o'clock in the morning—there's a chance no one saw it.

Against my better judgment, I get ready for school with Willow. My muscles ache, and I find more than one bruise when I get dressed. I don't particularly mind it. In fact, I think I like the reminder. I experiment by pressing on one of the bruises like Greyson probably would.

Never mind the bite marks he left on my neck and breast that have only just begun to fade.

The man is possessive with a capital *P*.

Anyway, we go to school, and all is fine for the first half of the day. Two people ask me about it, but I feign confusion and they leave it alone.

At lunch, Paris marches up to me with a scowl marring her face. She looks like hell—her makeup is full throttle, per usual, but it's smudged. She needs another coat of gloss on her lips, and her hair has been hastily put up in a high ponytail.

Not bad, just not her style.

Clue number one that she's pissed.

Willow makes a noise in the back of her throat.

Clue number two? She has what appears to be the photo they used of Greyson farther down in the article, of him on the ice, on her screen.

"How'd she get that?" I ask Willow out of the corner of my mouth.

We've been sitting at our table with Jess, Amanda, and a few other dance team girls for twenty minutes.

Paris gets closer, and her eyes laser into mine.

Belatedly, I realize she has a blue drink in her hand.

I've never seen her drink anything other than water or vodka—she's on the clear liquid diet, she says—and I gulp.

"You bitch," Paris snarls, stopping at the head of the table.

Then, in a fashion very similar to Greyson, she turns the cup over on my head.

The blue liquid crashes down over my hair, immediately soaking into my white graphic t-shirt. It's ice-cold—actually, she did put ice in it. The cubes slide down my hair and under the collar of my shirt, catching in my bra and lap.

It's so fucking cold, I can't move for a moment.

The dining hall goes from loud to silent in an instant.

I stand slowly, brushing the ice chips and loose liquid off me. The faint plinks of the ice hitting the floor are the only noises.

"Obviously you have a problem with me," I snap.

She sneers. "I wish I had half the balls you do, to be so bold and desperate as to try and hook up with my boyfriend—"

I whip my hand out before my reasoning can take over. My palm cracks against her cheek, and her head snaps to the side. My palm fucking stings, but I mask it. I can't believe I just slapped her, but I'm so annoyed, I don't have time to regret it.

"I'm so sick of your shit," I tell her. "Now get the fuck out of my way."

Paris turns back slowly, her eyes narrowing. I can see the thoughts that run through her head. She's thinking of retaliation. She's thinking through what the worst possible thing she can do to me is. Without another word, she pivots and stalks back the way she came.

She makes a beeline for the far corner of the room, where the hockey table sits.

My stomach knots.

"I didn't see them," Willow says, suddenly at my shoulder.

There's a rustle of movement throughout the dining hall as people shift to watch where Paris is headed. Sure enough, she zeroes in on Greyson the same way she did to me. Minus the blue drink. Instead, she grabs the front of his shirt and slams her lips to his.

From our table, I have the perfect view.

It sears into my mind how he doesn't push her away— he pulls her onto his lap. He kisses her like he should've kissed me last night. Their mouths open, and he dominates her. It's clear in the way he holds her ass and her arm, in the way she gives in to him, even though she's above him.

I'm going to be sick.

"Violet—"

"Don't," I whisper.

I have two options. I could run away, or I could walk out with my head held tall. Always with the dignity, I take my time grabbing my jacket and shrugging it on over my wet shirt. I flip my hair over my collar, ignoring the way the liquid still drips down my back.

I start to take my tray, but Amanda reaches out and covers my wrist.

"We got it," she says.

My gaze lifts again. That's the worst part. I actually look up and over at Greyson and Paris, who are still locked in an embrace.

But his eyes aren't closed, and they're not on her. He's watching me out of the corner of his eye. We don't have a conversation. It's not like the movies where I can know what the fuck he's thinking from his eyes, across the room, while he makes out with another girl.

Fuck no.

All I can hope is that I translate my anger.

This isn't over. I thought I was doing the right thing by telling him I didn't have a part in it. I've been continually pushed into the dirt by him, over and over and over.

No more.

This is the straw that breaks my back.

I won't be that person who caves to pressure. No fucking way. Under the right circumstances, pressure can turn coal into a diamond—and that's exactly what I'll become.

Tougher than he could ever imagine. Stronger, too.

I take one last look at Willow and mouth an apology. My phone is safe in my jacket pocket, and I take a deep breath. No one makes a noise as I stride toward the exit.

I don't know if they can feel my energy. How I've accepted that this is happening, and while it's so far from okay it isn't funny... I can handle it.

But then someone claps. I wonder if it's Willow, spitting mad at Greyson and cheering me on the way she can. It's contagious, though. The whole dining hall just saw a spectacle they weren't expecting, and now they're picking me over him.

They nod at me.

I nod back.

More clapping. It follows me out the door. Not everyone, of course. Not the people who think, for some crazy reason, that I'm the one coming between Greyson and Paris, or Greyson and hockey. It takes me by surprise that people support me at all. He's the hotshot, he's the one who's going to bring the school a hockey championship.

But I'm the one who's been here longer.

Maybe that matters to some of them.

I make it all the way outside before I let my expression drop.

19

GREYSON

I step into my hockey coach's office with Knox at my back. Coach Roake has a newspaper folded on the edge of his desk. My face is creased on the page, my eyes dark on the thin paper. Coach is reclined with his arms folded behind his head. His face is perfectly stoic.

"Sit," he orders.

Knox, as captain, took it upon himself to come with me. But he must see something in our coach's face that I miss, because he hesitates at the door.

I take the chair and twist around, my eyebrow lifting at Knox. I jerk my chin, and he steps back, shutting the door on the way out. When I face forward again, Coach hasn't moved.

"I spoke to your old coach," he says.

My chest tightens, but I try not to let my expression change. So far, we've gotten along. I'm not one to ruffle feathers if the person is useful to me. I keep things smooth with my father, with the school administration, with the man sitting in front of me... they can all do something for me.

They're all relevant to my success.

But now, I wonder if I've made a mistake. If I should've done more to get on his good side instead of just letting my talent pave the way. Buttered him up with the charm that exhausts me.

He sighs and drops his arms, bracing them on the desk. "The Brickell one *and* your high school coach," he clarifies.

Shit.

"And?" I ball my fists, squeezing hard. There's not much I care about, but hockey is absolutely one of them. Plus, I've got no fucking idea what Coach Marzden from Emery-Rose Elite would say. Maybe he'd sing my praises... or he'd throw me under the bus. He's a fickle guy.

My Brickell coach, though? Asshole material. Especially since there were no charges filed, and I got dumped over a newspaper article. He blamed it on the administration in general, but I know better. He preferred a spotless team. The players were angels with clean records, and here I was with the accusation of drunk driving and reckless endangerment hanging over my head.

With a sudden burst of fear, I realize that this could be headed in that direction, too.

And then where would I be?

Roake sighs. "Let me put you out of your misery."

"Please do." I sit back and brace for the worst.

"This is an embarrassment." He picks up the newspaper and tosses it at me.

I don't move to catch it. The newspaper hits my chest, sliding into my lap. I ignore the garish distortion of my face. The online article was pulled, and print copies were retracted—but that did nothing for the people who had already had copies delivered.

And clearly, print newspaper isn't a dying breed.

"You're kicking me off the team." I have to say it before he does, and I rise from my seat. "I understand. This sort of publicity—"

"Get your ass back in that fucking chair," Coach snaps. "I'm not kicking you off the team. But this sort of thing cannot go unchecked. They're accusing you of a lot. Your *only* saving grace is that article is an opinion piece that the paper decided to fucking put in front of everyone's faces."

I shift. "That's—"

"And that Violet girl. Is she involved?"

"If she says she is, she's lying." I shrug. "I don't know where they found her, to be frank, and they've exaggerated our relationship."

"What is your relationship?" Roake narrows his eyes.

"I slept with her once." I shake my head, aiming for rueful. "Maybe she talked to the journalist who came sniffing around, or maybe they paid her. I don't know."

If I keep saying it, I'm going to believe it. There is a small part of me that *does* believe Violet would do something like this. That she'd go to an extreme to get back at me. Another part knows that she's just as caught up in this as I am.

But it still doesn't lessen my anger.

It's why I let Paris maul me in the dining hall. Because my fucking feelings were hurt, and making her hurt eases some of it. Like pushing on a bruise until she cries out, or insulting her, or reminding her that she'll never dance again.

"Well, perhaps that's our solution," my coach says slowly, chewing over his words.

I straighten. "What is?"

He eyes me. "Your father called me, you know. Said that

I'd be blameless to let you go. But to me, that just means you're guilty. Are you?"

"No." Another lie.

They're stacking up, but what the fuck do I care? It's either lie and stay where I am or tell the truth and reinvent myself at a new school. The truth won't get me into the NHL. The *truth* has done nothing for me.

"Okay." Roake nods. "You're going to meet with the hockey team's publicist and put together a statement. I want this handled."

Relief hits me. He's not forcing me out. "Done."

"And we'll need a statement from Violet, too. Just to cover our bases."

I wonder how I'm going to make that happen. Can she lie to a publicist? Would she even? That's not part of the NDA. That's not part of anything except *maybe* her good nature.

But—let's be honest. After my stunt with Paris?

Not fucking likely.

"Thanks, Coach."

"You're welcome. Now get out, I've got work to do."

I finally take the paper and fold it under my arm. I consider the ways I can twist Violet to do my bidding and say what I want her to say.

Pressure. Like lifting her arm behind her back, torquing her shoulder, and getting her to twist the way I wanted.

Just like that... but more.

20

VIOLET

Every day, I keep up the ruse of my routine. I go to class. I eat with Willow and some other girls from the dance team—ones who've sided with me since Paris declared war. I study in the library, watch movies on the couch at night. I dodge questions about the article, doing my best to ignore the accusing glares.

Willow eventually brought to my attention that someone had made copies of the article and posted them on a blog. Everyone wanted to know what Greyson and I were doing together, and they blamed me for the smear campaign.

How does that happen?

How do they see a single photo of us together, not even *together*-together, and pin the blame for his actions on me?

They can't blame their star hockey player. Not when he's going to help carry the team to a championship...

It doesn't matter that they sided with me after the cafeteria incident. It doesn't seem to matter that there's no hard evidence against me either. What Greyson wants, Greyson gets.

And he got the whole school to loathe me.

I don't see Greyson for days.

I don't talk to Paris. She's been absent from campus, eating lunch or dinner at what I have to assume are off hours. Not avoiding me, probably, but planning her next attack. She's always been one to hold grudges. I've seen her lash out at others, but I didn't think I'd be on the receiving end.

After Willow goes to sleep, I sneak away to a local gym. Their monthly membership fee wasn't too hard to swing, and it's better than potentially repeating what happened in the CPU gym. Sneaking out also affords me the ability to not explain myself.

A week passes. My leg constantly aches, but it isn't the muscles. And I can't do anything about nerve pain. Still, I force myself to believe it can be willed away. Mind over matter.

Now, it's Wednesday.

I load ice into the bathtub. Willow is at class, and my body is screaming at me. Muscles I forgot existed now make themselves known. Once the tub is full, I set a five-minute timer and step into it.

The water is cold enough to take my breath away.

I grip the edge of the clawfoot tub and then let it go, putting my arms under the water. I sink down until my chin barely brushes the surface. It takes me a few seconds to regulate my breathing.

"Relax," I say. I close my eyes and remind myself why I'm doing this.

It's a peculiar sort of drive, because I've spent the last six months convincing myself that my future will be different than what I had always dreamed. But suddenly someone has shoved it back in my face, and I'm desperate. I want to take it. I want to hold it to my chest and defend it with every fiber of my being.

Dancing is my life. A broken leg couldn't change that.

My phone chimes, the timer going off. I reach out and tap blindly at the screen until the noise shuts off. I'm not ready to give up, though. I take a deep breath and sink below the surface. Ice chunks bump my face, and I let out a little stream of bubbles.

There are degrees of pain that I got used to as a dancer. I don't want to let myself get soft. With that thought in mind, I remain submerged until my lungs feel ready to burst.

I surge upward and suck in a gasp. My hair sticks to my face, and my fingers are numb. My toes, too. I lift myself out of the water.

My skin is pink and tingling. I shiver and pull the plug. In seconds, a tiny whirlpool whips over the drain. I step out and grab a thick towel. My phone goes off twice in a row, and I frown.

The list of people who have my new number is small. Since I changed it, I made a decision to limit who had access. Willow, of course, and my mother. Greyson—by force—and some of the dance team.

The first text is from Greyson. I ignore it in favor of the second.

Mia: Dr. Michaels can see us on Friday at 4:30 p.m.

She follows it with his address in Vermont.

Okay. Now I just need to *get* to Vermont. My phone's navigation says it's only about two hours away. Not terrible —at least she's not having me fly across country. My mother would almost definitely find out about that one.

I send her a thumbs-up, then switch over to my thread with Willow. I send her a screenshot of my conversation with Mia, followed by the emoji that looks like its head is exploding.

Me: How am I going to get there?

In the past, I might've borrowed a car... or just had my mom take me.

The little typing dots on Willow's end pop up, then disappear. Then again. I stare at it, gnawing on my lip, until her text comes through.

Willow: I have a solution... but you're not going to like it.

Uh-oh.

When she comes home an hour later, she wears a sheepish expression.

"I took care of it already." She's keeping her hands behind her back, too, which is... odd. She sidesteps me into the kitchen and smiles. "See? Everything is fine."

I watch her with suspicion. "You took care of getting me to Vermont?"

She rolls her eyes. "You've had your head stuck in the sand. Guess who's traveling to Vermont for a game on Friday night?"

Oh shit. "No." I immediately step back. "Absolutely not."

She reveals what she's holding. *Yep*, two tickets to the away game.

"It's the only way I could get us a hotel room. And seats on the bus. This was the best solution, and we can totally skip the game. Even if you just want to mope around all evening, then we can catch the bus back in the morning..." She smiles, brightening. "The bus is basically a designated driver anyway."

Yeah, right. The only thing I need more than a panic

attack is to go to an away game. If Greyson has the wrong idea now, he'll *definitely* get the wrong idea then.

"Wait." I grab one of the tickets and scan it. "Did you just say hotel room? And bus?"

"You know that the school likes its section filled." She shrugs. "I just paid for the tickets. We can take a cab to the doc."

I swallow.

She comes forward and takes my hands. "Come on, Violet. You've been sulking since the Paris and Greyson thing. It's starting to freak me out."

I can't exactly say that my sulking is due to my body rebelling against my sudden workout regime. *It's only for a few more weeks.*

"Okay," I agree quietly.

"Great!" She kisses my cheek. "Now, I propose a sleepover."

I blink at her. "Huh?"

"Sleep. Over." She loops her arm through mine. "We're going to Amanda's apartment. It's been literally weeks since you had a social outing."

"Weeks is an exaggeration."

She pouts. "You wouldn't go out last weekend. Even though the hockey team was at an away game."

She has a point.

"Fine." I heave a big sigh. "I need to dry my hair the rest of the way."

We separate, and I stew over what the hell a sleepover entails. Like... a slumber party? As if we're still in high school. I poke my head into the hall. "Are we actually spending the night?"

Willow laughs. "Yes, you dork. We're going to drink

martinis and do our nails and talk shit about Paris and her cronies."

Okay, you know what? I can get behind that.

I finish getting ready, stuffing pajamas and toiletries into my backpack, and meet Willow by the front door. Ever since the guy broke in—and before that, even, to when my room was trashed the first time—the apartment hasn't felt the same.

My skin prickles the whole time I'm outside. So much so that I have to resist the urge to hike my bag up higher, and to lift my shoulders to my ears. Willow doesn't have such a problem. She looks ready to hit the ski slopes with a white-and-pink argyle hat, white puffer jacket, and white leggings. Her pink boots are laced up her calves.

"Really?"

She grins. "You never know, okay?"

Fair enough... but there better not be guys at Amanda's. Or anyone other than the few people Willow promised would be in attendance.

Shit. I get the sinking feeling that I'm walking into something bigger than just an innocent little sleepover.

We walk to Amanda's apartment, which is only a block west. She opens the door as we come up the front walkway, grinning at us with a glass of white wine in her hand. She rents half of a house from an old lady who lives next door, so it's one of the quieter streets.

She usually doesn't host for that reason. Part of her lease is respecting the quiet hours, and I think she's terrified of getting evicted. I don't blame her—she has a good deal.

I glance over my shoulder and scan the street, but it's quiet.

"Come on," Amanda calls, stamping her socked feet. "It's freezing out here."

Willow and I hurry in behind her, and I stop dead.

This is not just a *little* sleepover. There are fifteen girls here. I only recognize some of them from the dance team, but that's not surprising. Amanda does a little bit of everything around campus. Student government, clubs, working in the dean's office part-time. She knows everyone, and everyone knows her.

I nudge Willow, who just grins.

"We just ordered pizza. I'm so glad you could make it!" Amanda plants a kiss on my cheek and slips back into the living room.

It's a good-sized room, but still there aren't enough seats. Many of the girls are sprawled out on the floor. Not that they look put out about it.

"Drink?" Jess asks, coming over with two red cups and a pitcher of pink liquid.

Willow laughs. "What the hell is that?"

"Jungle juice." She leans in and lowers her voice. "I guess the landlord is out of town for the week, so Amanda is taking full advantage. No fucking quiet hours tonight!"

The other girls whoop and cheer behind her.

I extend my hand for one of the cups, and Willow takes the other. Jess pours us a hefty amount, and I don't think before I throw back a big swallow. The flavor is fruity, with a citrus tang. It completely blocks the bite of liquor.

Warmth spreads through me.

Jess snorts and refills my cup. "Off to a good start."

"You've been noticeably absent," another girl calls.

I turn my attention to the group. The one who spoke is a sophomore on the dance team. I think her name is Michelle?

I shift, suddenly uncomfortable with the spotlight.

I shouldn't be. I grew up in the spotlight. I was culti-vated in the spotlight. But somehow, sparring with Greyson has worn away the edges. I've come to learn that it hurts when I'm put to the test and don't pass.

Is that what happened? I didn't pass his test?

My cheeks burn.

Willow grips my free hand. "She's been letting Paris cool off. You know how she gets."

More girls nod, and I relax. We find seats, and the discussion moves from me to Paris. I'm not the only one who's felt her wrath over the years, I guess. Then from Paris to Greyson—and the whole hockey team. They're on a winning streak, demolishing the competition at an away game last weekend.

I smile and drink and nod my way through the evening.

I'm as plastic as my cup—and I hate that I feel like this. The more drunk I get, the more I settle into the floor. I go from sitting next to Willow to leaning on her, to resting my head on her shoulder.

When the pizza comes, I pick at a single piece and blame my churning stomach on the alcohol. I don't want to know how many calories I'm drinking, how much sugar... the hangover will be my punishment.

Tonight I just need to let go.

Before I know it, the pizza is gone and someone puts on music.

I hop to my feet, suddenly invigorated. I haul Willow up with me.

"Dance party!" I yell.

They're with me. The music cranks louder, and I sink into the rhythm. It took too fucking long to learn how to move the way real people do—not just ballerinas. I was flexible, but I didn't know how to use my body.

That's why I joined the dance team.

That, and the Crown Point Ballet has a distinct contemporary flavor. If I wanted to succeed, then I had to incorporate some new theories into my study—a common Mia phrase. She wants the best, but she wants *new*. Eccentric. Beauty that comes in odd shapes.

She has the best choreography because of it.

I twist and whirl, and the drinks did their job—I can't feel the pain in my leg at all. I grab Jess's hand and spin her, pulling her back toward me. I tip my head back and relish moving my body again, until the walls blur and I lose track of myself.

The longer I dance, the more I convince myself that I needed this. I needed to forget for a while. And that's exactly what I'm doing.

Forgetting.

21

VIOLET

I don't know what wakes me up. A noise? A sensation? My eyes open in the darkness, and I blink a few times to try and see more clearly. All around me are the faint snores of the other girls. A sliver of moonlight streams in around the edges of the blinds.

I open my mouth, then realize there's something covering my lips.

What the fuck?

I touch the slightly bumpy texture of tape over my mouth, and then the shadow descends. My hands are yanked over my head and connected to something. There's a soft *click*, and cold metal closes around my wrists.

Fear twists through me.

The shadow returns, and it takes precious seconds to realize it's Greyson.

His face is a mask of ice.

Duct tape.

Handcuffs.

I wriggle, trying to move my body up so my arms aren't useless, but he ignores it and yanks my sleep shorts down.

I go still.

My heart is rioting, slamming against my ribs. My pulse is all I can hear, like rushing water in my ears, and I struggle to calm down.

To breathe through my nose.

He crawls over me, straddling my hips. He bends down and licks the side of my face. His tongue leaves a wet trail up my cheek, over the corner of my eye.

"I love your tears," he confesses, his lips pressed to my ear. "I fucking love your terror."

I shiver. He's said that before—but what lengths will he go to get it?

"What do you think will happen if one of them wakes up?" He turns his head, looking out over the girls spread across the living room.

I don't remember falling asleep. I just remember the dancing, and eventually the exhaustion. Did I decide to lie down? Did we all collectively decide to go to sleep at the same time?

Sleepovers generally don't involve *that* much sleep.

And for Greyson to have gotten in here...

How the fuck did he find me?

I thrash against the handcuffs, trying to dislodge him, and he covers my mouth over the duct tape. It's different, feeling the barrier between his palm and my skin.

His fingers brush my nose, and I twist my face away.

No use.

He pinches my nose shut.

My panic makes it worse. I thrash harder, the handcuffs —which are looped around something, although I have no idea what—clinking together.

Someone rolls over across the room.

Greyson leans down again. "Do you want to wake them up? I won't stop. I'm going to fuck you either way."

My chest burns. I desperately try to open my mouth, but it holds fast.

He releases my nose, and I suck in a noisy breath, gulping down oxygen. I'm so fixated on breathing, on easing the pain in my lungs, that I don't notice his attention move down. He moves my panties aside and runs his finger up my slit.

I groan through the duct tape, then bite my tongue. Whether or not he's serious about being undeterred if one of the girls wakes up, I don't want to test it.

He lifts my leg and slams into me in one go.

I jolt and bite my tongue harder. Blood fills my mouth, the taste sharp. It's all I can do to not let another noise escape me. Fuck if it doesn't feel good. I hadn't even realized he pulled his cock out of his pants, and now he's thrusting into me with powerful strokes.

My cunt clenches around him.

Do I want this?

Do I hate him?

I twist and try to pull myself away. He's got a grip on my hip and under my knee, but I manage to turn my upper body. I press my face into my arm and hold on to the chain between the cuffs. It's looped around the leg of the couch.

He's inside me, invading me, and everyone around me continues to sleep. Even as pleasure rolls through me. We're skating a thin line between consent and something far worse. So I guess I have to decide—is what he's doing okay? Am *I* okay with it? His hand slides down and cradles my calf. He runs his thumb over the surgery scar, again and again. In time with his thrusts.

Both quicken.

He hits a spot deep inside me, but it isn't enough. He doesn't go near my clit.

I let it happen.

I fucking let him do this to me, and a part of me is getting off on this knowledge. If I truly wanted him to stop, I could scream through the tape. I'm in a room full of sleeping girls. I'm staying quiet on purpose.

The rational part of my brain has shut off and checked out. She's long gone. Yet I can't just make it *easy* on him. I rip my leg out of his hold and kick him.

He falls backward with a sharp exhale, catching himself on his hands. My eyes have adjusted to the darkness— enough to see his slow smile.

I pull myself into a sitting position and glower at him.

He just shakes his head, then lunges for me.

It's not soundless. The huff that comes out of me is loud in my ears, as is his grunt of pain when he collides with me. My knee digs into his gut, my elbow catches his throat.

He grips my jaw, turning my head back to meet him, and rips the duct tape off.

"Scream," he orders in my ear. His voice is barely above a whisper. "Scream, Vi. If you're not wet and horny from this, then fucking say *stop*. This is your chance."

I eye him and lick my lips. I don't say stop. I don't speak at all.

He covers my mouth with the tape again. I've curled into a fetal position, but it doesn't matter. He fucks me like that, looming above me. Chasing his release.

It isn't enough for him. Not for me to agree.

So he leans down and cuts off my breath again.

Tears have flooded my eyes, and white spots flicker in my vision, before he releases me again. He repeats it. Over and over, until I'm a quivering mess beneath him.

Only then does he reach down and touch my clit.

It doesn't take long.

How pathetic is that?

I'm strung so tight, he only has to touch me a few times for me to come apart.

He pounds into me as I come. I clench around him, my silent orgasm triggering his own. He grits his teeth and explodes inside me.

We both go still when someone yawns.

In the silence, I strain to hear their slow breaths as they fade back to sleep.

Greyson pulls out of me, and the noise is loud. Slick. His weight covers me. He stretches out on top of me, and he unlocks the handcuffs.

"Next time you don't answer my text, I'm going to repeat this little game... but I might make sure someone else sees. I like this little game of you resisting, Vi." He meets my gaze. Some of the ice has melted, but he's still frigid.

I want to set him on fire.

"You and I have a meeting tomorrow morning. Ten o'clock." He gives me a look. "With a publicist."

I swallow.

"Remember your NDA. Remember what my father can do to you." He analyzes my face.

Does my expression change? Do I show more fear when he mentions the senator? Because it's true—no matter what Greyson does to me, there's always a bigger threat.

Greyson hides behind his father's name. He hides behind the money and the prestige, and even though he's a psychopath... there are worse monsters.

Like his father.

His eyes narrow, but he doesn't push it.

I don't think he wants to know.

He shifts off me and pushes back up. His earlier threat registers, and a thrill goes through me. My mind is fucked if that makes me excited. If *that* is what I'm looking forward to.

So twisted.

I need my head checked.

I stay still until he's gone, then slowly peel the tape off my mouth. I touch my lips. I count to one hundred in my head, then slowly rise. His cum is coated on my thighs, seeping out of me. My muscles ache when I stretch, and the room tilts.

Still buzzed.

And utterly confused.

Greyson is obsessed with me. It came out of nowhere— and I think my reaction to him has put my feelings into perspective, too. I'm not obsessed... but I am curious.

And turned on.

Shit.

Who knew I'd be this depraved? To enjoy when he fucks with my head, when he steals my breath, when he forces himself into me.

Jack was vanilla. Nice. He could make me come, which was a plus, but it wasn't as earth-shattering as Greyson.

So now... I don't know what to think.

Before, vanilla was good. I was content. There were only so many exciting things I could dedicate my time to, and ballet always won. Jack was the same, with football stealing a lot of his attention. He liked me cheering him on at the games, just as I liked it when he came to see the dance team.

Not that he ever came to a ballet...

Besides the point. Ballet was something he just didn't

get, like I didn't understand why the clock had to stop every ten seconds in a football game.

Some things just aren't worth explaining, Jack said on occasion.

I stretch and hunt down my sleep shorts that got tossed. I sneak into the bathroom, and when I come back, one of the girls is sitting up. She squints in the darkness.

"Violet?"

My heart thunders. "Yeah?"

"I thought I heard a noise..."

I swallow, my throat tightening. "I just had to pee. Sorry."

She nods to herself and lies down. I do the same, pulling my forgotten blanket back over me. Amanda keeps her apartment warm, but I think I've caught a chill.

One thought keeps circulating in my head. If I'm becoming something new... where did the real Violet go?

22

GREYSON

Violet and Willow come out of Amanda's apartment an hour before our meeting with the school's publicist. My teeth have been grinding for the last ten minutes, but I refused to go pound on the door —or text her. Not when she couldn't have been bothered to text me back yesterday.

Her indifference in the daylight irritates me. All week, she's been acting like nothing is wrong. Like a former friend didn't dump a drink over her head and then make out with me. Like she wasn't *hurt* by that.

Maybe she wasn't. Maybe Paris has always been the enemy, and she's used to her behavior.

I could dig deeper.

Cut harder.

My cock twitches, and I lean forward. I rest my chin on my forearm, on top of the steering wheel. I can almost see her as I will when I'm finished with her. I can't get the thought of blood out of my head. The little winces of pain, the distrust.

The other day, Knox reminded me of our bet. He said

Willow was coming along, and it didn't seem that I gave a shit about Violet.

That's wrong.

I don't give a shit about the *bet*.

But it keeps him occupied.

I reach down and grab the folding knife from my cup holder. I flip it open and press the point into my thumb, hard enough to sting but not hard enough to draw blood.

Seeing her handcuffed last night just deepened my fascination. She squirmed, she seemed scared, but then a switch flipped.

She wanted me.

Violet and Willow reach the sidewalk.

Her head comes up, and she finds my out-of-place sedan a good ten seconds before Willow has even noticed something is amiss. She stares at me, her brows furrowing.

Hmm.

The windows on my vehicle are tinted, making it impossible to see in unless you're right up against the glass.

I've become a certified stalker.

But we've got limited time, and I need to make sure that she's ready for what I need her to say. Coach Roake wants us to deny anything. The picture was a coincidence, the party was just a hockey house party, and someone else invited her. Her roommate, maybe, or another player.

They begin their walk home, and I drop the knife back to the cupholder. I put my vehicle in drive. I roll behind them, uncaring that I've raised the alarm bells in Violet's head. She seems ready to bolt.

I smirk.

This scared version of her is new.

Is it because of what happened last night?

Willow finally clues in and looks around. She glances at my sedan, then faces forward again. Their pace increases.

Finally, we reach their apartment. I pull over, ready to jump out, but Violet is already stomping toward me.

I open the door and hop out.

She skids to a stop, her mouth dropping open.

Then... relief?

I tilt my head, confused as to why she's relieved to discover me. A question for later, though, because she advances again and whacks my chest. Her pretty face is pale, her blue eyes boring into mine.

"You—" *smack* "asshole—" *smack* "you—" *smack* "make me—" *smack* "CRAZY!"

I have to resist the urge to laugh at her, instead snatching her wrists and pulling her close. Her gaze is wild, and she fights with surprising viciousness. Much better than last night when I caught her unaware.

I drag her with me as I open the back door of my car and force her inside it. I climb in after her and slam the door shut.

"What the fuck?" she demands.

So saucy.

"Say something." She yanks at her wrists, which I have in one of my hands.

She's delicate. I could break her bones if I squeezed hard enough.

I reach forward and grab the knife, flicking it open.

She goes still.

I look from it to her. She's pressed against the far window, her arms extended in front of her. But she's given up on getting her hands back. With my free hand, I drag the knife over her fingers.

Her tell is her shivers. When she's found something that

intrigues her, that scares her, that pushes her out of her comfort zone.

"Did Jack take your virginity?" I ask, still sliding the knife tip up and down. I'm making a little path over her knuckles, down the edge of her thumb, then back up. "Was he the one who fucked you first, or was it a high school boyfriend?"

Violet loves to give me nothing.

I tsk. "Even your silence tells me what you want to hide. I should know."

Her eyes narrow.

I release her wrists and flick the knife down, cutting open her leggings on the inside of her thigh. The move is unexpected, and it nicks her skin, too. She gasps, but there's nowhere for her to go. I'm the fucking wolf, hunting her down. Scenting her blood.

And it wells up so prettily on her pale skin.

"What was that for?" Her voice trembles.

I look up from it. "Not answering my question."

She twists around and yanks at the door handle.

It doesn't budge. That one's tricky. It sticks sometimes. I crawl forward and remove her hand from the door, then kiss her knuckles. I shouldn't. It feels wrong, like I'm plying her with affection. Something that might give her a sense that I care about her.

"Greyson," she whispers. "Let me out."

I shake my head and lean down, licking the strip of exposed skin on her inner thigh. Her blood hits my tongue, and my cock immediately hardens. Fuck. Her blood is warm and metallic, and I suck and bite at the shallow wound.

She groans.

Her hands slide into my hair, tugging me away, but I

ignore it. I drag my teeth along her flesh, then lick. Suck. Repeat.

Her thigh shouldn't be erotic.

Her blood shouldn't make me hornier than a teenager.

I just fucked her last night, and I want to do it all over again. Savagely.

"Grey," she says, louder.

Damn it, I like it when she calls me that.

I slip my hand into the hole in the leggings, up to her panty line. I run my finger along it, over the damp fabric, and rub her clit over the barrier. It's not nearly as satisfying, but she shifts her hips all the same.

"You're a little slut for me," I tell her. "No one else will give you this rush."

"Fuck off," she snaps breathlessly.

No *stop*. I should've picked a more unique word for her. A safe word that won't slip as easily from her lips.

But she hasn't spoken it, even when I gave her the chance last night.

It solidifies a few things in my mind, but the main one is that she *wants* this. She's a glutton. And I can keep pushing her until she breaks, or I do.

"Please," she begs. "Jesus, just fucking touch me."

I take in her pink cheeks, the heat that has flushed her exposed skin across her collarbones.

I look and watch and bring her right up to the edge of ecstasy, and then I withdraw.

It takes every last ounce of willpower to not rip her clothes off.

Instead, I shove the door open and lean back in the seat.

I tilt my head to the street. "Get ready for this interview and try not to look freshly fucked while you're at it."

She rears back.

I'm clearly in her way, and she waits a beat for me to move.

I don't.

It seems to occur to her only seconds later, and she climbs over me. Her pert ass slides across my groin, and she lets out a hiss when she brushes my cock. I don't move to touch her, still practicing that self-control. And then her feet are on the asphalt, and she must feel safe enough to turn back and look at me.

Her gaze drops to my lap.

"Anytime you want to take a ride, sweetheart," I goad.

She narrows her eyes.

"You've got an hour."

That makes pretty Violet pause. "To meet with that publicist?"

I check my watch. "Technically, we meet with her in forty minutes."

"Why should I go with you?"

Oh, a test? I do love these. I pull my phone from my pocket and open the video of her breaking the NDA. Her anger comes off her in waves on my screen, palpable even from here. I let it play, enjoying the theater of it.

When it ends, I watch her. "If you don't talk to me, then this goes to my father. Remember?"

"This is blackmail," she says.

I smile. "Clock's ticking, Vi."

"You're a controlling ass," she murmurs, already heading back to her apartment.

I don't bother refuting that. Therapists have told me I have a controlling nature. It has to do with my parents. My father's blasé child-rearing, my mother's abandonment. Dad only cared about success, prestige, money. *Power.* He raised me to care about those things, too, and only those things.

The therapist said I tried to control people through manipulation to regain power over my environment.

Whatever.

Fifteen minutes later, Violet reemerges from her apartment and climbs into my passenger seat. She adjusts the long charcoal-gray skirt and sweater decorated with oversized opal buttons. The color is fitting, even if she doesn't know it yet.

She gnaws on her lower lip as I take us back to campus. Her fingers dig rhythmically into her left thigh. I keep glancing at her out of the corner of my eye.

She's in my car.

She smells good.

I shouldn't fucking like that she smells like flowers, that her blonde hair is brushed straight and lays over her shoulders, that her makeup is flawless.

It makes me want to fuck her mouth till mascara streams down her cheeks.

If only that was an option...

"Take a picture," she says, not looking at me. "It'll last longer."

I smirk. "Why take a picture when I have a video of you? Two, actually..."

"Wow, just when I was thinking you weren't that terrible." Her gaze is fastened out of her window, and her fingers keep digging into her leg.

I check the clock—we have time to spare—and pull over swiftly. Annoyance surges through me, and I reach out and grab her chin. I pull her back toward me and wait for her eyes to follow. She gives them to me eventually, as the seconds tick by, and they go from my lips to my eyes. Her tongue pokes out, wetting her lips.

"Let's get something straight," I say slowly, my gaze fixed on her lips. It's a real struggle not to kiss her. "I am *that terrible*—and worse. Remember that, sweetheart, when you go to sleep and wish for dreams. Because you'll just get nightmares. And me? I'm the worst fucking nightmare you could imagine."

Her eyes flash, giving me not fear but hurt. Like she has a better picture of me in her head, but I'm ruining it.

Good. It should be ruined.

I release her and pull back out onto the street.

23

VIOLET

He's going to kill me.

I didn't think it before. When we first collided—well, not the *first* time—I thought I was strong enough to endure him. To outlive his anger and his ego.

Now, I'm not so sure.

It's funny how things change when hope enters the picture.

I sparred with him because there was a recklessness inside me that didn't give a shit if I came out unscathed. In fact, I think I expected the barbs to sting, if only to distract from my own pain. The voice in my head that said I'd never dance again. The worry that my mother was done with me. The fear of not knowing what I was going to do after college.

Mia Germain infused hope back into me with one phone call.

I'm less than forty-eight hours away from seeing if my dreams are still possible.

And it. Fucking. Sucks.

I've never been more stressed.

We park outside the stadium, in one of the VIP spots— as if Greyson needs more ego—and go inside. It's cool and dark here, and intensely quiet.

"Do you practice here?"

"Most evenings." He straightens his shirt and glances at me. "Some girls watch."

"Why would they do that?" Seems it would get tedious, watching them do drills over and over again. At the very least, mind-dullingly boring.

He lifts a shoulder. When I glance over at him, he's smirking.

I stop. "They come for you, don't they?"

Greyson's smirk widens into a shit-eating grin. "Me, Knox, Steele..."

I narrow my eyes. "Yeah, I know pretty intimately why they'd show up for Steele."

His gaze turns flinty, the smile sliding right off. He doesn't respond to that—how could he? He's the one who forced me to get on my knees.

In the back of my mind, I know I had a choice. I could've walked away.

But then I would've had to deal with the repercussions —worse ones than these.

He leads me to an elevator and hits the up button. We wait in silence, then step inside. Immediately, it feels like we're in a vacuum. The silence gets louder.

My skin itches with the need to break it. To say something.

I last two floors before I crack. "What are we telling her?"

His cocky, self-assured smile is back. The same one I'm sure he wore when he strolled out of the police precinct after his father got him out. The same one he probably also wore when he left the scene of the crime. He rolls his shoulders back, then cracks his neck. Everything about him relaxes. Even the little muscles around his eyes that, up until this point, held stress.

I look away. This Greyson has been hiding. Shuffled out of sight, because everyone we interact with already knows and loves him. I'm fascinated by it. By the way he just seems to radiate an easy-going confidence. He's brought out this persona for the publicist.

She's going to fall in love with him before our time is up.

Am I going with him to be the scapegoat?

Or his savior?

I eye him again, drawn back to the expression he wears like a mask. Maybe I've been getting it wrong. Backwards. The anger, the way he is around me... maybe that's his true nature, and *this* is the mask. It's easier to believe that than to think he wears his anger as a guard.

No. He's shown me who he really is deep down. Not everyone gets to see that.

My nerves are eating me alive by the time the elevator doors slide open. And he still hasn't answered me about what we're telling her—what he expects me to say, if anything. I mean, I'm assuming that I have to say something. Otherwise, it's pointless that I be here.

We exit into a brightly lit foyer. There are windows to our left, and a set of glass doors to our right. We go through them and stop in front of the wide desk that a receptionist mans.

Greyson smiles and tells her who we're here to see. His gaze flicks up and down the woman's body, and he winks at her.

She blushes.

I silence my disbelief.

She rises and gestures for us to follow her, and Greyson winks at *me*. This is all an elaborate game to him. When we reach a corner office, the receptionist opens the glass door and steps back to let us pass.

"Thank you," he says to her. Then his attention switches to the woman striding toward us from behind her desk, and his smile widens. "Ms. Dumont."

"Mr. Devereux," she answers.

They shake hands.

She's probably a few years younger than my mother. Her hair is white-blonde and pulled back in an elaborate braid. Her makeup is flawless, and her eggplant-purple dress is form-fitting. She has the sort of energy that translates into no bullshit. I imagine she's had to become a shark to survive in a male-dominated sport.

How did she end up a publicist for CPU? With a corner office at the stadium, no less.

"Good game last week," she says to him. "The final few minutes were exciting."

"It was the one time I broke out in a sweat," he responds. "But we managed to put them away."

"That you did." She gestures for us to take a seat. "This year has been great for donors. They particularly like seeing the self-assured nature of the team this year. There's been minimal stress—and minimal sweat, as you said."

"Well, that comes down to our coach." Greyson takes my hand and pulls me with him to the couch against one of the walls. There's a glass coffee table in front of it, and two single chairs beside themselves on the other side. When he sits, he drags me down so I'm almost on top of him. "This is Violet Reece."

The publicist's gaze flips to me. "Ah, yes, I recognize your face from the pictures."

I swallow and slowly extricate my hand from Greyson's grip. "Right. That—"

"Is what we're meeting with you about," Greyson finishes. "Coach's orders to straighten this out and all."

"Of course. Your reputation is our reputation."

He nods along with her words, then leans back. He splays himself out, his arm over the back of the couch behind me, his legs spreading. Taking up space comes easily to him, I think. It's natural. Whereas girls are taught to shrink.

For an insane second, I contemplate mimicking him. Spreading out like him, my legs thrown wide.

Might not endear me to the publicist, who's sitting in the chair like it's stinging her ass. She's perched on the edge, her ankles crossed. She opens her phone and types something, then springs back up and grabs her laptop off her desk.

Once she's reseated, the laptop open on her knees, she looks up and meets his gaze. "So, Greyson. There are some very harmful allegations against you."

He nods once. The movement is jerky, brittle. I wish I had reread the article before I got in his car, just to better familiarize myself with it. It feels like a blur. It's been too long.

"And Violet. The author of the piece seems to insinuate that you're involved."

I glance from her to Greyson, then back again.

Sink or swim time?

"It's a fabrication," I lie. "There's nothing between us. Never has been."

Anger doesn't count. Shame doesn't count. Twisted

hate. His brutal obsession. It's all meaningless, because it won't protect either of us.

"Violet Reece was a ballerina," Greyson says suddenly. "She had supporters, and after she injured her leg and ended her career, I think some people were upset."

I grit my teeth. *Was. Had. Ended her career.* I desperately want to refute it, but I can't. That hope in my chest, that burns so brightly sometimes I can't sleep at night, is just for me.

"Oh, Violet, I'm so sorry to hear that." Her features soften.

I don't remember her name. Isn't that bad? Greyson knows it. I'm sure he probably already said it. Maybe he'll use it again at some point, as part of his charming, schmoozing act.

"What happened? Do you mind if I ask?"

Greyson's hand lands on my thigh, hot over my skirt, and I blink. It's a warning.

"A car accident," I say. "I don't remember much about it. I was rushed into surgery..."

Greyson's fingers skim my head, pushing back my side-swept bangs to reveal the ugly scar across my temple. I avoid looking at that stupid thing as much as possible. I keep my bangs long to hide it. And now he's touching me, and the publicist is staring in horror, and I can't breathe.

I rise. "I'm so sorry. I don't know what else you expect from me... I just need some air."

I rush out the door. They let me go. I don't think they move as I navigate the halls back to the elevator and slam my palm against the button. The doors slide open, and I step inside.

As soon as I start to move downward, I lean back against the wall. I let out a breath.

Everyone thinks ballet has evaporated for me.

I have two days to prove otherwise.

When the doors open on the first floor, I step out and almost crash into Steele.

He grabs my arms, steadying me, and then looks me up and down. I find myself doing the same to him. He's dressed in sweats and sneakers. His dark hair is damp and combed back, and there's a little scruff on his cheeks. It gives him a more rugged appeal.

His lips quirk. "You okay, Violet?"

I shake myself out of it. "Yep, perfectly fine."

His gaze lifts to the elevator doors, now closed. "You meeting with Rebecca?"

I raise my brow. "Who?"

"The school's publicist. Coach said Greyson had to meet with her to clear up that article, and since you're in it..." He shrugs. "Either that, or you're coming to watch our practice... and you're early. Very early."

"Don't you practice in the evenings? Why are you here?"

"The gym." He wiggles his eyebrows. "It's the best one in Crown Point. Of course, most of the athletes at CPU use it, so it has to be the top of the standard."

A gym. I'm getting tired of hiking to the public one—not to mention, there's been a creepy guy there the last few nights. Creepy enough to deter me from going back at that time. He leers at my ass when I run and turns into my shadow when I circulate around the weights area.

"Is it open to anyone?"

Steele smiles. "Anyone? No. But if you want in, I could help you out. Be an escort, you know?"

I smirk at the double meaning. "Didn't take you for an escort, Steele." I shrug. "But either way, our schedules wouldn't align. I work out at night."

"Okay, Violet. I like to work up a sweat at night, too. Here." He pulls out his phone and opens it up to a new contact. "Put your number in, we'll see if we can figure something out."

This is a bad idea, but the thought of getting on Greyson's nerves does give me a certain level of satisfaction. I take Steele's phone and give him my number, then hand it back.

"I'll text you."

"Okay." I sidestep him. "I've got to get to class."

He chuckles. "Okay. Well, don't be a stranger."

I eye him. "Pretty sure that's out of the question. After…"

His chuckle turns into a full-blown laugh. "Yeah. Right. If you ever want a repeat… You know, a different kind of workout? I'd be open to it."

"Oh, um… no, I think I'm good." I shake my head and speed-walk away from him. I only have room for one asshole in my life. Well, maybe that's not even true. Dare I say I don't have room for any, since Greyson takes up my whole capacity for dealing with them.

But if Steele can get me into a nicer gym, he can be useful. And Greyson can just… deal with *that*.

24

VIOLET

I meet Willow in the student center. We're wearing the requisite blue and white, our jackets open to expose the colors—mainly so the coordinator doesn't yell at us. The coordinator, a staff member in Activities, stands at a booth and checks people off.

There's a whole group of us going.

"Heads-up," the coordinator, Lauren, calls. "We've got two buses. The first is the party bus, which will be full. Then we have room on the team bus."

My stomach twists. "We have to get on the party bus."

The doors open, and Paris strolls in with her minions. Dance team girls she won in what Willow calls *the divorce*. I haven't so much as glanced at her since she dumped a drink on my head. Not that I've wanted to. I get the urge to rip her hair out when I think of her.

And, yep, it's worse when I see her in person.

"If looks could kill," Willow murmurs. "Down, girl."

I force myself to turn away. Who would I hate to see more? Greyson or Paris?

"Do you think we'll get lucky and Paris will get on the

team bus?" I ask Willow. "Like, Karma can't really hate me *that* much, right?"

"Right..." My best friend winces. "Yeah, nope. I don't think so."

I glance over my shoulder. Paris has picked up the sign for the party bus. Her golden hair is perfectly curled. Her eyeliner is blue, and the highlighter illuminates her cheekbones when she turns her head.

She's definitely the type of girl who all the guys fall for —it's no wonder she thinks she can just stomp all over me.

"You have a look."

I meet Willow's gaze and shrug. "I don't."

"You do. It's like scheming but worse. What's worse than scheming?" She loops her arm through mine. "Methinks this has to do with Paris. Listen, we're just going to go sit on the team bus with Jess and Amanda, and we'll totally ignore the guys."

I snort. I've ridden on the football team's bus to away games before. They're loud. Rowdy. They sing and argue and generally cause a ruckus. Adrenaline runs high, anticipation runs higher.

Greyson won't just let me sit there. I'm pretty sure it's not in his nature to let me do anything unchecked.

She shoulders her bag. "Come on, we're rolling out."

We head to the two buses that await us. Paris keeps her sign lifted. I notice another girl has the team bus sign in her grip, but she lags behind. She seems put out to be assigned to that one—and who can blame her? She probably wanted to be with the girls. Full of pep and shit.

The hockey team hasn't come out yet. I think we have to go get them from the stadium anyway. It'll be a whole big thing.

Willow takes my arm and pulls me aside. "It's worth it,"

she whispers. "Whatever the hell happens. It's worth going to see the doctor, right?"

I nod vehemently. It *is* worth it.

Yesterday was quiet. I have two classes with Greyson on Thursdays, but I didn't see him in either of them. Unlike him to skip, but I wasn't going to push the issue.

He didn't text either. Or sneak into my room and harass me that way.

Jess and Amanda break away from the throng as soon as Paris has climbed into the party bus with her friends. We cross over to the second bus, accompanied by the sign holder and the coordinator. "There are five more students coming," she tells the driver. "Then head to the stadium to get the team."

We toss our bags into the storage space underneath and climb the steps. It's nicer than a school bus—the seats are individual and cushioned. There's even a tiny bathroom at the very back. Amanda and Jess pick seats, and Willow and I take the row behind them. More people filter on, dressed in blue and silver like us, with *Hawks* or *Crown Point University* splayed across their chests.

Two girls from Amanda's sleepover take the row beside us, across the aisle.

The girl on the window side, Michelle, leans toward us. "We brought face paint if anyone is in the mood to streak their cheeks with blue..."

"Later," Jess decides. "I don't want to sit with it on my face for two hours."

If I show up to my doctor's appointment with blue stripes on my face, I think they'd automatically just stamp me as a failure. So, yeah, that's not happening.

"How are we pulling this off?" I ask Willow quietly. I didn't ask too many questions, and now I'm wishing I had.

"Your appointment is at four-thirty," she says under her breath. "We get there at four to check into the hotel. Game starts at seven. We just sneak out of the hotel and call a car. Should be easy."

I swallow. Okay, yeah, sure. Sounds fine.

Except for the whole cutting-it-close part, but I don't mention that. I just need to not think about the fact that my whole life is riding on this doctor's appointment.

Dramatic?

Maybe.

I feel like I'm entitled to some dramatics.

The bus doors hiss closed, and we pull out of the parking lot. In no time, we're stopped in front of the stadium.

The hockey team comes out with their duffle bags slung over their shoulders. The driver hops out and opens the storage doors, and I watch them each toss their bags in and then climb on the bus. Their coach watches them all carefully.

My focus is drawn toward Greyson. Of course. He's one of the last ones out. He wears black slacks and a maroon sweater that clings to his lithe form. It really accentuates his body, unfortunately.

I think he'd do better wearing a paper bag.

I try not to stare at him too hard, convinced he's going to feel my gaze on him. I force myself to sit back in my seat.

Jess and Amanda are craned around, chatting to Michelle and the girl beside her. Lucy, I think. She has teal hair, pulled back in a bun on top of her head, and wicked eyeliner. She smiles a lot. I don't know her very well, but she seems genuinely *nice*.

Some of the players—skaters who don't get a ton of ice

time, I think—slip past us to sit in the way back. They barely acknowledge us.

More fill in the middle, and then Greyson, Knox, and Steele are coming down the aisle.

Greyson's gaze fixes on me. He doesn't have much of a reaction, except the corners of his lips tip up. Just for a second.

Fucking hell.

I don't really know what I was thinking, subjecting myself to two hours of this. Well, not *this*. But whatever Greyson has in store for me, I know it's not going to be pleasant.

Or it's going to be really fucking pleasant... in a humiliating way.

I gulp, and my stomach knots.

Willow squeezes my hand. Knox has already probably made eyes at her—or she told him she was coming along. I miss his reaction as he slides into one of the seats toward the front.

Steele lifts his eyebrows and grins. "Hey, Violet."

I suppress my cringe.

He drops into the seat behind me, then leans forward. "What a nice surprise."

"Yep. Party bus was full."

He smiles knowingly. "Uh-huh. Hey, you didn't text me back."

Willow chokes behind me.

"I've been busy." I don't bother looking to see that Amanda is glaring holes in my head, too. I can feel it from here. Also, I forgot about her crush on him.

Damn it. That means I take the cake for shittiest friend. I literally didn't think of anything except using him when I put my number into his phone. But I can't very well say that to her, can I?

Not right now.

Miles comes down the aisle and pauses beside Steele. "Hey, man. Greyson wanted to talk to you."

Steele snickers. "Did he?" He leans back in his seat, kicking his legs out. That move shouldn't be sexy, but it is. Every time. Especially on someone attractive like Steele, whose abs could probably have their own zip code.

I mean, Greyson's could, too, but he's not in front of me right now. And when have I paid attention to him shirtless? Never. See? Greyson isn't on my mind. And he's definitely not messing with my head at all. *Not me.*

"I'm comfortable here," Steele continues. "Talking to my friend, Violet."

Willow makes another noise in the back of her throat, and that's the only warning I get before Greyson looms over us.

Miles scrambles out of the way.

Greyson grabs the front of Steele's shirt and lifts him. He doesn't so much as look at me as he drags his housemate toward the front of the bus. He throws him into a seat and marches back to me. His knee comes down on the edge of my seat, and he leans over me.

"Stop playing games," he hisses.

I meet his gaze.

Somehow, that got under his skin worse than anything else. I shift forward, until we're nearly nose to nose. "You don't fucking own me."

He smiles. "No?"

"No."

"We'll see about that." He straightens and backs away.

Just in time for Coach to come barreling down the tight aisle, stopping just before he crashes into Greyson.

"Get back to your seat, Devereux," he snaps. His attention sweeps over us, his face scrunching in disgust. "Fucking party bus. And *you*." He glares at me. "You should know better."

I'm so surprised, I can't say anything. Not until he's turned around and made his way back to the front. He sinks into his seat, and I let out a slow, shaky breath.

What the fuck was that?

Willow makes a face. "And here I thought we could ride under the radar."

"Hate to break it to you, but that was never going to happen."

25

GREYSON

I'm supposed to be preparing for the game. Mentally. The team we're facing is undefeated, which is already a setback. They're coming in confident. If their coach has done their job, the team won't be arrogant. They won't make shit plays. Of course, we'll be on the lookout for weak spots.

We spent the week reviewing tapes, both of our previous games and theirs. Hunting for holes in their armor.

This game is important. Coach warned us at the start of the season that *this* point in our season, if we played smart, would make or break us. And he's right. We're two wins away from qualifying for the national tournament. Two games left to play. If we lose, we're out.

Then the real battle would begin.

Even if we do make it into the tournament, we'll have to face this team again. The Knights have more funding and a larger school than us. They're monsters. Who knew this little Vermont town would be so crazy about hockey?

But instead of mentally preparing, I'm thinking about Violet.

And Steele.

It infuriates me that he thinks he can just slip in and take her away from me. If that's what he's doing, he's going to lose some teeth. I'll beat him bloody, and I don't plan on playing fair. The asshole is two inches taller than me and packed with twenty-five pounds more muscle. It's what makes him a good defenseman. He can check someone into the glass like no one's business.

Even so, I'd risk it.

Steele sits in the seat in front of me. I've put my headphones in, trying to block everything out. I breathe in through my nose and out through my mouth. I force my muscles to relax, and I run through plays in my mind.

We hit a pothole, and I'm jolted out of my thoughts.

"Fuck!" I growl. I rip my headphones out and stand. I lean over the back of the seat next to Steele, putting my face in his. "What the fuck is your problem?"

He smirks. "I like aggravating you. Interesting things happen."

"If we lose—"

"Relax, hotshot. Maybe you'll let Erik score for once."

I snort. "There's a reason you assholes haven't been able to get into the tournament in years. Because Erik is good, but he's not great." *He's not me.*

Just speaking facts.

Steele's gaze hardens.

I sit back, then rise on my knees. Ten rows back, Violet chats with her best friend and a few other girls... and Miles. Jacob has taken Steele's spot, too. I ball my fists and stand. I'm halfway to her before she notices, and then the rest of them do, too.

"What's your problem, man?" Erik glares at me on my way by. "Just chill the fuck out."

Like I'm interrupting Miles' and Jacob's time with the girls? What the fuck?

Fuck, everyone is getting on my nerves, and it's all because she's on this damn bus. Before she can ruin everything and open her mouth, I latch on to her wrist and haul her up. She doesn't offer a word of protest as I drag her up the aisle.

Similar to what I did to Steele, but a bit more gentle.

Just a hair.

I sit and pull her down on my lap. She lets out a little squeak and tries to stand, but I grip her tight. Her back rests against the window, her legs toward the aisle. I don't know how comfortable it is, and I don't give a shit.

This isn't about her.

"Just fucking sit still," I grunt. I pull out my headphones and replace them in my ears. I hit play on my music, a special curated playlist to repeat the same few songs. They always help me get in the zone, and I know them so well I can recite all the lyrics.

She goes quiet. Her hands fall to her lap, and she tips her head back against the window.

Then shifts.

I should close my eyes, but I'm watching her try not to squirm.

I think she's more curious than anything. I shift, and her weight moves toward me. She's looking toward Roake, who has his head buried in a book. He won't look up until we get there—that's guaranteed. When she realizes that for herself, she relaxes the slightest bit.

So it isn't me—it's what others will think.

Interesting.

I slouch in the chair, making it easier for her to fall into me. And eventually, she does. She seems resigned when she puts her head down on my shoulder. Every breath she exhales hits my throat.

But I'd rather deal with this, and the goosebumps, and the way my blood rushes to my cock, than jealousy.

She reaches up and takes one of my earbuds out. I almost protest, but I keep my mouth shut. She slips it into her ear and closes her eyes, her hand landing on my forearm. And then she goes still, and the rest of the world fades away, too.

Finally, *finally*, I can focus on what I need to do. The plays. The ice. I envision the stick in my hand, my blades gliding across the ice. The soft scrape as I dig in and fling myself forward. The weight of the puck as I push it forward.

All at once, loathing constricts my chest.

I shouldn't have to go fetch Violet to get back in the zone. I'm pissed that this even had to be an option. That my teammates would mess with me—and worse, that Violet would put me in this position.

Without thinking, I slip my hand into her jeans.

She tenses, but she doesn't move. I glance to my left and find Knox has gone elsewhere. There's no one in our row. And no one else can see—not that I'd mind if someone saw my hand down her pants, but I think she'd try to get me to stop.

And that sort of fight doesn't go over well in public.

I touch her clit. She's wet, and she lets out a harsh breath when I rub slowly, back and forth. She doesn't lift her head from my shoulder. My lips brush her ear.

"Remember the last game you went to, Violet? Remember what happened to us?"

Me and her. Caught in a loop.

She nods, her lips parting.

I reach farther, sliding two fingers inside her. Her pussy clenches at me, and I stroke inside her. Then out, back to her clit. And repeat. She shifts her hips, trying to get more from me.

"If we win this time, what will you give me?"

She opens her mouth wider, then closes it. She doesn't know what the fuck I want from her—I don't even know. I wonder if her cut has scabbed over and begun to heal. I wonder if she'd let me slice her open again.

My cock is rock-hard, caught between us.

This sort of energy will get me through the game.

"What do you want?" she finally asks.

The song changes. Something a little faster. I rub her clit to the beat, aware that the music pounds in both of our ears. I want so many fucking things from her. I want everything.

"I don't think I'm going to tell you," I say. I move my fingers harder, and she shudders.

A tell. Another fucking tell.

"Maybe it'll involve my team. Maybe I'll let Steele watch me fuck you, so he'll know there's no way he can do better than me..." I catch her earlobe with my teeth. She's more turned on now than she was a minute ago. *Bingo*. She's just as depraved as I am. "You like that? Do you like the thought of other eyes on you?"

"In your dreams," she replies.

I bite harder on her ear. Her breathing is coming quicker now, her hips moving just a bit. It's causing agony across my groin.

"In my dreams and your fantasies, I think. It's okay, baby. You can be just as twisted as I am, and I won't judge you for it."

She turns her face more into my shoulder, and she comes on my fingers. I relish the spasm of her muscles. That her release is tied to whatever fucked-up madness is running through my head just makes it ten times better.

I pull my hand out of her jeans. My fingers glisten.

She lifts her head and watches me lick my fingers clean. Her taste is sweet, unlike anything I've sampled before. I don't know why she's like a drug to me.

"Good girl," I murmur in her ear.

We'll return to normal tomorrow afternoon. And Monday, what I told the publicist will go live. Our destruction is imminent.

26

VIOLET

Willow gets me to Dr. Michaels' office five minutes before my appointment time. Mia Germain rises from her seat in the waiting room and strides toward me. She looks the same, if not a tiny bit older. Time marches on for all of us, after all.

I hold my breath when she gets closer, convinced she's going to make a comment on my physique.

Instead, she just spreads her arms and wraps me in a giant hug.

Her dark hair is streaked through with random strands of silver, giving it a tinsel appearance. It's twisted into a bun on top of her head. Her oversized sweater makes her seem smaller.

"I'm so glad you made it," she says, withdrawing.

I grin. "Me, too. This is my best friend, Willow Reed."

"My parents are hippies," she says, trying to explain away her name as she shakes Mia's hand. "I've heard a lot about you."

Mia chuckles. "I wasn't going to comment. I've known

some extraordinarily talented young girls and boys who have the most eccentric names."

Willow cracks a smile. "I'd have fit right in, then. Darn."

"I can give Violet a ride home," Mia says to Willow. "These appointments can take some time."

My best friend nods. "Sounds good. See you back at the hotel."

I follow Mia down a hall and into an appointment room. Dr. Michaels comes in a few minutes later, introducing himself with the sort of charm I expect from Greyson. The-world-is-my-oyster type.

Oddly enough, it puts me at ease.

If someone has to be the smartest in the room, I'd prefer it be the doctor with my career in his hands.

He leads Mia and I back into his office. On the wall behind him are two x-rays. He flicks the light box they're clipped to, then takes a seat. He motions for both of us to sit, too, at the front of his desk.

"You got these x-rays done last week, correct?"

I nod. I had slipped away to have them done midweek. It feels like a lifetime ago. They sent them to Dr. Michaels.

"The good news is, the fractures healed well. The bones realigned perfectly, and the surgeon used minimal hardware." He gestures to a spot halfway up my leg. "When we talk about *shattered* bones, it usually means a comminuted fracture—that means it's broken into several pieces and needs to be reset. I'm not seeing evidence of that here—or you've healed spectacularly well."

"Good news," I echo. First time I've heard those words...

Mia squeezes my hand. "So, what's next?"

"We're going to test mobility, see where the pain might be, and strength tests. It's going to be a long appointment, Violet, and it will get uncomfortable at times." His expression turns sympathetic. "We see many dancers come through our clinic after injuries. Before we begin, are you sure you want this?"

Am I sure? I've never felt so sure in my life. "I've been waiting for this opportunity for months."

He smiles. "All right. Let's begin."

The rest of the appointment is a blur. He has me change into athletic shorts and hop up onto a table. He runs his hands down either side of my leg, his eyes narrowed in concentration. He spends a lot of time prodding it, feeling the bone through my muscles.

Then we move to a different room, where Mia guides me through warm-up exercises. She gradually increases the level of each skill. When I step out of the last one, the pain buckles my knee.

I hit the floor.

Dr. Michaels helps me up, bracing under my elbow. "What did you feel?"

I want to shrug it off—but I can't keep collapsing after exercises if I want to go on stage. No one would cast me.

"I get a shooting pain occasionally," I mumble.

"Occasionally?" Mia raises her eyebrows.

"Usually daily," I amend.

Fuck. Fuck. Fuck.

"I thought it would go away. It will—"

"It's most likely nerve damage," Dr. Michaels says. "Muscular issues would have a more immediate pain and its own set of limitations."

He helps me back down the hall to his office. After a few steps, I'm able to mask the lessening pain. It's still sharp but getting better. Mia trails us, and I feel her gaze on my back. We sit again. I bounce my right leg. I'm not usually an anxious person. Dance was my outlet for stress for such a long time, I used it to get more confident. But now I'm slowly disintegrating into a wreck.

"Have you experienced this pain for a while?"

I bite my lip, unable to answer. The doctors thought nerve pain would be the culprit of me not returning to dance. I was just hoping he'd have a different theory.

"I want to get an MRI to look for things we may have missed. Stress fractures could also be causing the pain, and they're best picked up with more intense imaging." He shuffles papers, and it's clear that our appointment is coming to an end. Which is good, because we've been here forever.

I could have *stress* fractures. Girls in the company would get them on occasion, especially before an audition. The added classes worked us all ragged, because we wanted to be the best. There was do or fail, with no middle ground.

Did running through the woods from Greyson make my pain worse?

Did my exercising do this?

Mia pats my knee. "This isn't the outcome we wanted, but it's okay, Violet."

It's so far from okay, it isn't even funny.

"For now, my assistant will call for a prescription to help with the pain—"

"It doesn't hurt," I blurt out. "I might've moved it wrong, so today isn't accurate—"

"Violet." Dr. Michaels takes off his glasses. "I'm so sorry. But as of right now, dancing isn't an option."

That hope inside me? It grew and grew and grew, and now it *pops*. The pain is sharp, like being stabbed with a hot poker. Every beat of my heart seems painfully hard.

I stand. My leg doesn't hurt like he says it should. Not really.

"I can dance," I tell Mia. I grab her hands. "Please."

"Violet," she says softly.

Dr. Michaels clears his throat. "I'm going to recommend aquatic therapy. It's been known to have great success with patients with nerve pain. Then we should see you to reassess."

I swallow. Water therapy, basically. Swimming and whatever nonsense they'd have me do in a pool.

"Oh, and Violet," he adds. "Please stop by the receptionist's office on your way out. She'll schedule your next appointment and get your insurance on file."

Uh-oh. "Insurance?"

He gives me a measured look. "If you have it. Otherwise, we'll bill you. Or your mother?"

Why the *fuck* didn't I think about money? My mom is well-off, sure, but she's not... pay-for-a-random-doctor-visit rich. And she's definitely going to get the bill. I'm on her insurance for now. Until I can do my own thing.

Suddenly, I hate that I don't have that figured out.

And there's no way in hell I'm letting Mom find out about this. Any of it.

Which means... this isn't happening. It can't.

I nod and leave Mia and Dr. Michaels behind. I stop at the receptionist desk and tell her that I don't have insurance, that she can bill me directly for the visit. She tuts, sympathetic, when she passes me the invoice.

"I'll just need to take a day... I'll pay it soon." I swallow, my shame eating me alive. "I'll call to schedule the MRI back in Crown Point."

That's a lie.

My finances haven't been an issue because I have a fund my dad set up. He put money into it to pay for everything I could need to get me through college. Mom put some of the money from his life insurance into it, too. But with my junior year coming to an end, I can't pay thousands of dollars—what I'm imagining this will cost without insurance—without a job to back it up.

I've always been sensible about money, and this feels largely out of my scope of knowledge.

I need to get out of here. I can't breathe. The walls of his office press in close. My fingers go numb. I want more than anything to run away—so I do. I manage a quick apology and bolt out of the office.

I might be ruining my relationship with Mia. Not that it fucking matters anyway.

I burst through the doors and onto the sidewalk, my chest heaving. I brace my forearms on my thighs, head bowed, and focus on sucking in deep breaths. My lungs are in a vice. I rasp with every inhale, like my throat has actually seized up on me.

Minutes later, my chest loosens. I take deeper inhales, counting to five on each exhale. But that doesn't negate the need to get out of here. I take two steps when the doors open behind me.

"Violet," Mia calls. She slings her purse over her shoulder and catches up to me. "I told you I would give you a ride."

I wrestle my emotions under control. *Fuck*, it's really hard not to burst into tears. I mean, I felt like a crazy person two seconds ago, but sobbing my eyes out would make it worse. I think. Money and nerve pain and more tests. It's all going down the drain.

Even this bill will set me back. *Stupid* for it to not even dawn on me that I'd pay for this myself.

I imagine my mother walking away from me, leaving bits and pieces in her wake. I'm the thing she keeps trying to leave behind, and something keeps picking me up and returning me to her. Only to be set down again.

It's okay—I can take her hint. She doesn't return my phone calls, she only calls or texts me when she absolutely has to. Like with Mia. And the newspaper article.

"Besides," Mia adds, "walking would suck."

I choke on my laugh. She's got a point. She gestures to her car, and I slip into the passenger seat. She pulls away from the curb, and we're well on our way before she glances over at me.

"You know I broke my ankle?"

I start. "What? When?"

"My prima ballerina years. I was nineteen and voracious. At a particularly brutal rehearsal—in which I was chasing my dreams and cast as principal—I took a bad leap. I landed wrong, and the thing snapped under my weight." She goes quiet.

We've all heard horror stories of that happening, but I didn't realize it had happened to her.

"I was out for a year." She peeks at me. "I wanted it so badly. I went through three surgeries before my ankle was able to hold up. Now, I'm not advising that. I'm just saying, it might be a no for now—but because of something that could get better. Not because of the accident that broke your leg."

I nod once and fix my gaze on the side window. Vermont is very pretty. There's more snow covering the ground here, and most of the pine trees are lush, dark green. I can see why, of all the places, a specialist orthopedic surgeon chose to come here.

"It'll be okay," Mia says again. "You looked nervous about the insurance. Are you?"

"Mom and I aren't in the best place right now." I sigh.

"If she finds out, then it'll be a nightmare. And since I'm on her insurance..."

"You're doing this yourself."

"Yes."

She nods, then glances at the folded paper in my grip. "I got you this appointment, and I didn't realize your situation with your mother. Let me take care of this one. I can't do the rest—I have limited funding for the ballet—but this? For you? No question."

She holds out her hand for the bill.

I stare at her. "You don't have to do that."

"I want to. I want you to dance again, Violet. I think it would be a damn shame if the world never saw you on a stage again. Think about telling your mother about the water therapy. Get the nerve pain under control. I'm sure some of it would be covered by her insurance."

An ache fills my chest. So tight, I don't know what to say for a long moment. But slowly, I extend the paper toward her. She takes it, reads the total, and nods to herself. She stashes it in her cupholder.

"Promise me one more thing." She grins. "When you're back on your feet, call me."

I nod and climb out of the car in front of the hotel. I lean down once I'm out and meet her gaze. "Thank you for everything."

She frowns. "This feels like a goodbye."

"It is for the next six weeks. Maybe more. Who knows if I'll be good enough by then. Maybe I'll need another six, or eight, or twelve to get back in dancing shape."

Bitter. I'm so fucking bitter, I taste it on my tongue like ash.

"We'll get you there," she says.

I close her door and turn away. The damn lump is back

in my throat, cutting off my words, and the backs of my eyes burn. I make it into the hotel, get my key card after giving the receptionist my name, and trudge upstairs.

The game started fifteen minutes ago, which means I should be alone. Thankfully. I swipe the card and trudge inside. The room is nicer than I thought it would be. Two queen beds, the drapes pulled back to reveal a beautiful view of the ski mountain.

I text Willow to let her know I'm back and contemplating crashing.

Willow: There's a sky bridge on the third floor that will take you to the stadium. Paris is taking attendance and has already asked where you are.

I groan and turn right back around.

Five minutes later, I'm in the stadium. Luckily, Willow waits for me right on the other side of the booths, and she hands the guy my ticket. I smile at her as he allows me through.

"How was it?" she asks. "Did he tell you anything good?"

My smile wobbles. I don't know whether to feel hopeful or defeated. Right now, the two emotions are warring in my head—and defeat is winning.

"Oh, no." She stops us. "Do you need a hug? Or a distraction? Or—"

"Distraction," I manage. "Definitely a distraction."

She nods. "Okay, well, let's go watch the Hawks kick some Knights' ass, right?" She lets out a loud whoop, drawing some stares.

The Knights are red and white, and the attendees all wear those colors. We work our way around the outside of the stadium, passing kiosks selling popcorn, beer, ice cream.

"Wow," I mutter. "We got the good view in our room, huh?"

She shakes her head. "This town is crazy for hockey."

I don't bother to acknowledge that Crown Point is, too. We just hide our crazy a little better.

We find our seats, and I catch Paris rotating back to count heads. I wiggle my fingers in her direction, and she scowls.

"She takes her job seriously, huh?"

Willow snickers. "The girls have been pushing back on her as dance captain, so she's gotta get her kicks somewhere."

"How is that anyway?"

"Dance?" She seems taken aback. We've been going by the policy of *let's just not talk about it.* In the beginning, I wanted to know everything. The new routines, the new people. Even though I wasn't in Crown Point, I felt like I had to keep being a part of it. And then, further into my recovery, I realized that things weren't going my way.

Obviously, I have no problem continuing my friendship with half the girls on the team. When you're in it, you eat and breathe and sleep dance team. They're my circle of friends. And somehow, they've managed to make me feel like the same girl who showed up to practice with them every day without ever talking about it.

Maybe they conferred with Willow before I came back. My best friend is astute and a good judge of character—unless a guy is involved—so she probably would've been able to toss anyone negative out.

"There you are," Amanda greets me. "You haven't missed much. Just a lot of blustering."

Six rows down, the hockey players whizz past our seats. I try to spot Greyson, but I don't see him immediately. It takes a minute for me to orient myself with their royal-blue jerseys, striped with silver, versus the mostly white jerseys of the Knights, accented with red lettering. At home games, the Hawks wear their light-colored uniforms.

Miles is in the net. Steele and Jacob skate in front of him, coming out to defend against the Knights' offensive line. One of their players has the puck, and he speeds toward our side. Jacob intercepts him, and the two collide. They both go down.

A whistle blows.

Immediately, the Knights player hops up. He seems steaming mad, his teeth gritted, and he shoves Jacob. Our defenseman slides backward, then narrows his eyes and rushes forward. Jacob grabs the Knight by the front of his jersey and yanks his helmet off—and uses it to smash the guy in the face.

I lean forward in my seat. Chaos breaks out.

I catch a glimpse of the blue jersey with *Devereux* on the back rushing into the fray.

The refs blast their whistles and dive into the middle of the fight. After a few painstaking seconds, the players are all separated. Jacob lost his helmet, too, and grins at the Knights with a bloody smile.

"Oh, shit," Jess mumbles.

The referee waves his hand, sending everyone to their benches. He skates to the center of the rink to confer with the others, and finally announce that the Hawks will be penalized. A two-minute power play for the Knights.

There are screams and chants from the crowd—except our section. Even I'm outraged enough to know that we didn't start that fight. We're just being penalized for finishing it.

Greyson skates by the glass, his gaze searching the

crowd. I don't know if he finds me, if he's even looking for me, before he's back at the center line.

Knox and a Knight square off. Jacob is noticeably absent, stuck in the penalty box for the duration of the power play—or until the Knights score.

I suck my lower lip between my teeth. I suck at watching hockey, mainly because the rules are foggy. It's exciting, sure, and I like actively *watching* it. But understanding it is the main struggle.

I'm stuck wondering if Greyson was involved. Did he land a hit? Did he *get* hit?

The ref drops the puck and skates out of the way as the Knight center takes control. His team quickly sweeps forward, taking advantage of the shortened defense. Steele covers the best he can, shooting it out of range before another Knight wing brings it back.

Within a minute, they score.

The crowd erupts.

The white-and-red players do a mini victory lap, clapping each other on the backs and smiling broadly behind their masks. Greyson skates to the bench and takes a seat. I watch him across the rink as he picks up a water bottle and sends a stream of liquid into his open mouth.

He swallows, his head tilted back, then refocuses on the game.

They need to win. Jess explained on the bus, before Greyson dragged me away like a Neanderthal, that they had to win this one and their last game of the season if they want to advance.

It's stressful.

My phone vibrates, and I yank it out of my pocket.

Greyson: You seem worried. Don't be.

Me: I'm not worried about you.

Greyson: Whatever helps you sleep at night...

Egomaniac.

Me: Why aren't you on the ice?

Greyson: Because I've been playing straight through since the game started. Why did you miss half of the first period?

Damn him for noticing—and for bringing up memories I'm trying to leave behind right now.

Me: Tell you what...

Me: Winning is a team effort. If you want my secrets, I need you to prove you deserve them.

His little typing bubble pops up, then disappears. Again. I watch it, ignoring the rest of the game. Hell, ignoring the rest of the world. Then it comes through.

Greyson: Do you have something in mind?

I can feel his intrigue from here. I bite my lip. I know immediately what I want to ask for, but I hesitate for a split second. My fingers hover over the screen. Should I? Shouldn't I? I waver, then go for it.

Me: Get your hands bloody next time.

It's a dare I shouldn't make. I shouldn't ask for his violence. But I look up and find him staring at me. Helmet off, hair a mess. It stands straight up, like he ran his fingers through it a few times. His expression is... wonder.

Or horror.

It's hard to tell from this angle.

He didn't expect this. And why would he? Why would he expect a level of bloodthirstiness from me? But I'm beginning to discover that I like the dark side of him. That it's oddly attractive—but I want to see him pitted against someone else. I want to see how far he'll go.

He leans over and says something to his coach, who waves him off.

I glance at the scoreboard, at the seconds ticking down to end the first period. The Knights are winning, one to zero. The buzzer sounds. The game stops.

I sit back. Will he take the challenge?

And the bigger question: will I give him my secrets if he does?

27

GREYSON

Coach taps my arm, and I hop up onto the wall dividing the rink from our bench. My replacement, a junior named Finch, skates toward me and practically dives over. A split second later, my blades touch the ice and I'm off.

I move into position, my muscles stretching and warming back up. I've had precious few breaks—all the starters have been rotated out, giving us a chance to breathe, but then we're right back in. The other team is faring no better.

This game is testing us. The Knights haven't been fighting fair, and I have the sneaking suspicion the refs aren't on our side. Because of that, I've played the second period with my head screwed on right. Sweat soaks down my back.

Still, I love this sport. My blood sings, adrenaline pumps, and the roar of the crowd just makes me fight harder for it.

I catch a glimpse of Violet out of the corner of my eye. Her friends are all preoccupied, and she looks lost.

The right wing from the Knights skates past and pushes his stick in front of me. I don't see it until I'm right on top of it, and it hooks around my ankle.

I go sprawling across the ice.

My anger flashes, boiling through me, and I push myself back up. Now's my chance.

"HEY!" I yell, chasing after the guy who tripped me.

Normally, it would be a flag. A power play for us, a trip to the penalty box for the son of a bitch who did it. But the refs aren't paying attention, even as I skate full-speed into the Knight. I crash into him and immediately grab the front of his jersey. I curl my fingers under the edge of his helmet and pull until it pops off his head.

He shoves back at me, a sneer curling his lips.

Fucking prick.

I'm not going to lie—I see red. I get in two hits to his face before the rest of our teams swarm us. I'm vaguely aware of Knox beside me, pushing at some asshole on the other team. Our limbs tangle. Pain shoots across my knuckles. I feel a crack, but I keep fucking going.

Finally, someone rips me off the guy.

I didn't even realize he and I had fallen and I was on top of him.

Someone locks my arms up, their hands pressing to the back of my head.

"Chill the fuck out, Devereux." It's Coach in my ear. Coach dragging me away.

I thrash for a second, then go still. I let him pull me clear and then right myself. I've never seen him on the ice before. Not during a game—not even when the fights break out. He doesn't like to get his suit ruffled.

"Get to the bench," he orders.

I collect my forgotten stick and take a seat. My cheek

throbs. Somewhere along the way, I lost my helmet, too. Knox arrives, dropping down beside me, and hands me my helmet. I take it and shake my head.

"Don't start," I grumble.

"The asswipe tripped you, and the refs did nothing." Knox shrugs. "The whole team deserved the beatdown."

I glance at him. His eyebrow is split open, blood dripping down his temple.

Everyone has cleared off the ice except the refs and the two coaches. There seems to be some arguing going on.

"Here," one of the assistant coaches says, coming down the line behind us. He hands Knox and me a pack of gauze.

I avert my eyes.

Well, I fucking got my hands bloody. Like Violet wanted.

Violet... more like Violent. Who knew under such an angelic face lived a monster as sadistic as me?

A knuckle on my left hand is hot to the touch. My skin is split open on both hands, but that one feels the worst.

Broken, maybe.

Fucking hell.

The assistant coach shuffles back down behind us and moves Knox over. He takes my hands and presses on my knuckles. When I hiss, he tuts. I should've kept my damn mouth shut, because now he's glaring at me like I'm never going to play again. Dramatic asshole.

I'm ready to pick a fight with anyone and everyone.

"It's fine," I grit out.

My ring finger is tingling.

The assistant coach, fresh out of college himself, scoffs. "Yeah, right."

He wraps my hand in gauze, interweaving around my

fingers to keep them immobile. He gestures to the gauze in my lap. "Use that to take care of your other hand."

He moves away. Knox and I exchange a glance. I don't know what to fucking say—the guy tripped me. What resulted should be on the Knights, not us. I lean forward to look down the line. A few seem in bad shape—Miles has blood on his jersey, and his smile is bloody. He's got his helmet off, too, sitting there right as rain—and hungry for more blood.

Good.

We're down by a goal. We'll need the bloodthirstiness to keep going, to push harder. We're only two minutes into the third period.

Coach Roake, the Knights' coach, and the referees finally break their little huddle. Roake strides across the ice in his fucking dress shoes like it's concrete, stepping up out of the rink. He's pissed.

"Devereux," Coach says. His voice carries down to us. "Penalty box. Five minutes. But after that, you're out."

I stand. "Coach," I protest. "Out?"

He points at me. "A fucking five-minute power play because you couldn't keep your shit together. Do you think your teammates want to pick up your slack?"

Fucking hell.

I hop over the wall and skate to the penalty box. It kills me when the rest of the starters take their positions. At least the defense is strong. Miles flashes me a grin as he goes by. The suited guy sitting next to me, to make sure I actually stay in for the allotted time and no one else replaces me on the ice, ignores me.

I take a seat on the short bench and tap my stick against the mat. Even when I get out of here, I'm apparently replaced.

The game restarts. I force myself to watch every move they make, hunting for weakness. My hands pinch with pain from how hard I'm gripping my stick. It's killing me to be locked up for so long.

This is Violet's fault.

Would I have gone as crazy as I did if she hadn't put the thought into my head?

No. I'm always calm, cool, collected. I'm the skater coaches dream of having on their roster. I don't start fights, but sometimes I finish them.

Tonight, I threw the first punch.

The refs wouldn't throw me out of the game for that. Fighting is technically allowed. It's a brutal sport, after all. No, this is Roake's decision.

I grumble to myself, leaning forward and bracing my elbows on my knees.

Somehow, we manage to hold them off. No one scores.

When the man opens the door for me, I burst out onto the ice and charge forward. Coach yells my name, and I ignore him. He's going to give me shit for this. I catch a glimpse of my replacement sitting on the wall, waiting for me to get over there.

Knox skates up beside me. "You good?"

"Peachy."

"You're going to get your ass reamed."

I grunt. Worth it if we win.

The puck comes back up to us, a shot long by Steele. I cradle it and shoot forward, dodging around an incoming Knight player. It's not the same jackass who tripped me—I think he might be out, too, to tend to his face. I pass to Knox, who keeps it for a moment before sending it right back to me.

Erik, on the other side of the rink, races toward the goal.

I clench my teeth and snap the puck to him.

He fakes a shot, making the goalie react, but it flies back to me instead. I flip the puck above the goalie's outstretched glove, and it soars into the net.

Tied game.

I clap Erik on the shoulder. He does the same to me, his lips widening into a grin behind his mouth guard.

"DEVEREUX," Coach screams.

I wince. Erik is quiet, which is unusual. He always has a half-assed comment when one of us gets yelled at. I skate to the wall and grind to a stop before I crash into it.

Coach grabs the front of my jersey. "You think this is funny?"

I shake my head. "No, sir."

"You think you can just make your own decisions?"

Um… well, it worked out in our favor. Not that there's a chance in hell I'd say that out loud. I know Coach is good for an ass beating if we deserve it. Or a verbal lashing—each are unpleasant, in my experience.

"Sit," Coach orders. "Don't move a fucking muscle the rest of the game. If you get up, if you so much as shift, you're off the team."

Chills sweep down my spine.

He's not messing around.

I hop over the wall and give him a wide berth. I find a seat on the back row, against a wall, and sit heavily. I pull my helmet off and set it beside me. Then gloves, which didn't do shit for my knuckles. I lean my stick against the wall.

And then I watch my team fight like hell to win.

But, eventually, my gaze scans the crowd.

I find Violet again, as much as I shouldn't.

I want to know what she's thinking. Her eyes move,

seemingly at random, to mine. We stare at each other, ignoring the world, and my stomach knots. Another thing to fault her for.

Another thing to punish her for.

I'm looking forward to it.

28

VIOLET

Greyson: Stay after the game.

      Greyson: In your seat.

      Me: Why?

Greyson: Because I fucking said so.

Me: Sounds dangerous.

Greyson: When have you not liked danger?

Greyson: Admit it—there's a thrill going through you right now. Maybe you're squeezing your hand into a fist trying to fight it, or you're clamping your thighs together. The thought of us alone... in this stadium?

I shiver and don't answer him.

I can't.

Because he's right, his words do something to me. Something uncomfortable, that I'm not willing to admit. Not even to myself.

Knox scores with ten seconds left, officially breaking the tie. Willow—and the rest of the girls—jump up from their chairs, screaming and cheering. My own reaction is delayed, my phone clenched in my hand. I force myself to be happy, to clap and holler along with my friends.

There's one more play, the ref dropping the puck, and then the buzzer sounds.

Game over.

The Hawks won—barely. By the skin of their teeth, with Greyson benched for the second half of the final period. Both teams look like they went through a war, but our blue-and-silver-clad team rushes out onto the ice in celebration.

"Come on," Willow says, tugging on my hand. "We're going out to celebrate."

I smile and stay seated. "I'll be right behind you."

Her gaze sweeps my face, and she eventually nods. "Text me if you want me to come back to the hotel room. Even if it's only ten minutes from now. Got it?"

My breath hitches, and I force another smile. "Got it. Thanks, Willow."

She leaves with Jess and Amanda. It takes some time for everyone in the section to go. Paris doesn't so much as look at me as she sweeps by, but I hear her mention Greyson. Maybe she thinks this is her own version of a power play. Doing what she does best, flirting with him in a crowd full of people.

I swallow.

Slowly, slowly, the whole stadium empties. A Zamboni drives out onto the ice, the driver old and weathered. He maps a crawling path around the rink, and the ice returns to a smooth, blank slate. I track him with my eyes, unable to do anything else.

My nerves are shot.

Eventually, he finishes and rumbles through the opening. Silence reigns.

It forces me to concentrate on my heartbeat. My body. The dull ache in my leg.

Nerve pain.

I don't want to think about how long my body has betrayed me. I want... something more than a distraction. Something worse.

And then a door from the players' bench swings open, and Greyson steps out onto the ice. He's shed his pads, the uniform. He wears a form-fitting black sweater and jeans. His skates are laced over them. His hair is wet.

He glides to me and presses his hands to the glass.

We stare at each other, and then, with deliberation, he tips his head to the gate left open by the Zamboni. Do I want to go out onto the ice? Not particularly.

Still, I rise and find my way down there. It takes several painstaking minutes, and then I'm in a mat-covered hallway. I spot the Zamboni first, parked against a wall, and then the opening.

Greyson waits for me there.

His hands are wrapped, his left thicker than the right. It doesn't stop him from extending them toward me, and it doesn't stop me from taking them. He steadies me as I take my first step onto the ice.

My boots aren't made for this. I slip a little, and he chuckles. He's taller in skates. Whereas our height difference used to be manageable—annoying, but manageable—now he towers over me.

Without warning, he swings me up into his arms. One arm under my knees, the other against my back. His fingers curl on my ribcage.

I shriek and latch on to his shoulders. Some part of me is convinced he's going to drop me in the center of the ice and watch me try to make my way back to the edge.

He grins. "You okay, Violent?"

I narrow my eyes.

"New nickname." He skates away from the opening. His

motions are fluid, easy. Like he was born skating, not walking. The air whistles past us as he picks up speed. "Do you like it?"

"Violent? Not particularly."

"It suits you." He flexes his left hand, just visible under my knees. "I blame you for this."

"You would've done it regardless," I argue.

He skids to a halt in the center and sets me down.

Shit.

See? I knew this was going to happen.

I hold on to his forearms once I'm upright, although I don't expect to stay standing for very long. He spins me in a slow circle, rotating around me on his skates. My boots make my movement easy—as in, unable to stop myself from going wherever the hell he wants.

"You put the idea in my head." He tips forward, putting his face in front of mine. "You fuck with me every chance you get."

I laugh. It's mean and coarse, even to my own ears. "I do? You're one to talk."

I release him and step back.

Bad idea.

My arms pinwheel, and I manage to latch on to him. Too late, my feet slip out from under me. I hit the ice hard on my ass, my legs between Greyson's. His upper half is dragged down with me, doubling him over, but he manages to stay upright.

"This is going well," I mumble.

He hums and traces his finger over my collarbone. "What's wrong?"

I cringe. "Nothing."

"Uh-huh."

He lifts me again, this time urging me to wrap my legs around his waist. He grips just under my ass, on the backs of my thighs. I hang on to his shoulders and lock my ankles behind him. I feel oddly secure like this. Less like he's going to drop me anyway. It helps that he's steady. I lean back slightly to stare into his eyes. He's not being nasty—which is a first.

I open my mouth to ask him about it.

First the bus, in which he sat me on his lap... and made me orgasm. Now we're here.

"I don't want you to be nice," I whisper.

He shrugs and skates. Instead of going for the wall, or the opening, he goes in a wide circle. His hand slides up my back, pressing me closer.

It should be weird for him to skate with me clinging on to him like this, but he doesn't say a word. In fact, he seems to enjoy it. His blades leave trails in the ice, and he goes in a wide circle. The only sound seems to be the way his skates carve the ice and our breathing.

"I love fresh ice," he says in my ear. "I love that there aren't any other marks to catch my blade. There's something about the perfection of it that gets me."

"How often do you get to skate on fresh ice?"

He shifts me slightly, readjusting his grip. "Depends on the day. Sometimes I sneak into the rink at Crown Point just to carve it up before anyone else can."

"So you like to take away the opportunity from others," I retort.

Greyson's laugh is husky. "Yeah, sure. If they wanted it, they'd get up early like I do."

Hmm.

I glance over my shoulder to see where we're going when he suddenly changes direction. He's heading for his team's bench. He sets me down on the wall and glides backward.

I watch him go.

He throws his arms out wide and takes off. It's almost like he's running on the ice, full speed toward the opposite end. It's impressive. Captivating.

I have the insane desire to let him see me dance—and then it's immediately squashed.

Anger surges through me at the diagnosis Dr. Michaels gave me. Stupid. It's so fucking stupid how one thing can happen, and then another, and *another* on top of that.

The lights shut off, and I let out a short shriek as we're plunged into darkness.

The rasping sound of skates is the only thing that tells me Greyson is incoming.

He stops just before touching me, showering ice shavings against the wall. A second later, his fingers slip up my knee.

"We might get locked in here." His fingers are still traveling upward.

Meanwhile, my heart is going a hundred miles per minute. And then I realize: he reacts best to my fear. He likes it. He wants it.

My fear is blood in the air, and he's the wolf following the scent.

He tugs at my jeans, his deft fingers unbuttoning and unzipping them before I can protest. He gets them down around my ankles. The cold air pricks at my skin. My eyes aren't adjusting fast enough. One sense down, I'm operating blind.

But my ears pick up a second zipper, and a rustle. And then his cock is pressing against my slit. His skates put him at the perfect height for this. To thrust into me.

He grips my hips and presses into me, so freaking slowly I think I might die.

"I've been waiting to sink into you all day." He inches forward more.

My head falls back. He feels too good, and after the day I've had? I need this more than I'm willing to admit. My muscles are tense until he touches them. My brain whirls until his lips find mine in the darkness.

I pull him closer.

His lips trail away from mine, down my cheek, to my jaw. Then the sensitive skin just under my ear. I let out a moan when his teeth scrape my throat. I find the hem of his shirt and force it up, sliding my hands up his abs.

Yep, I was right earlier—they're defined enough to have their own zip code. I pinch his nipple, and he lets out a hoarse laugh.

"Naughty." He drives harder into me, enough that my body scoots back on the chipped, painted wood. He pulls me right back into him, and his hands start wandering. He gets under my shirt, then my bra, and palms my breasts. "So fucking perfect. Your tits are fantastic."

He lowers his head and shoves my shirt up the rest of the way, forcing me to lean back. He bites my flesh.

"God, more," I groan. I tense around him.

I need this pain to ground me.

"Grey. Harder. Fuck." Every word is on a pant. I just want more viciousness from him. I put my hands over his wrapped ones and press down. His body ripples, answering the involuntary spike of pain, and he growls.

He picks me up in one move and lays me down on the ice.

Cold seeps into me, almost burning, and I arch away from the sensation. But he's right there, already between my legs and driving back into me. Pushing me into the ice. The sensation is like needles stabbing into me everywhere it touches. My ass, my shoulders, my head. My hair is fanned out, and the sweat that collects on the nape of my neck immediately induces chills.

But after a minute, all I can focus on is Greyson.

The feel of *him*, hot against my cold body. The friction of his cock going in and out, his lips on my skin. Always moving. Breast, throat, collarbone. He trails kisses, soft in contrast to the hardness of the ice. His forearms are braced on either side of me, his hands curled in my shirt.

He shifts to the side and slips his hand between us. He touches my clit, soft at first, then harder. He tweaks it, and I almost scream.

"I want to hear you," he says in my ear. "I want anyone who lingers here to know exactly who's fucking you."

I'm silent.

He twists, a new angle, a new punishment. Harder *and* faster. "Say my name."

"Fuck off." I squeeze my eyes shut.

His hand leaves my clit, and I'm left gasping for air. His orgasm comes swiftly, out of nowhere, and he stills. Buried in me.

In the back of my head, I know I should be worried. Birth control doesn't protect me against everything.

He lifts his head, and I slowly open my eyes. My vision has adjusted. Moonlight comes in through skylights and high windows. There are faint emergency lights outside the rink, just barely visible from here.

The cold hits me, and I shiver.

He slips out of me and scoots back on his knees. He grips my knees and widens my legs as far as they can go.

My ankles are still trapped together by my jeans, stuck on my boots.

When he runs his finger from my slit up to my clit, my lips part.

"Here's a little challenge for you, Violent." He toys with my clit again, analyzing my reaction.

I squirm. I want to get off, I'm *right there*, on the edge, but he pulls away before I can get there. Again. And again. We go through this for fucking eternity, until I'm desperate enough to do it myself.

So I do.

I touch myself while he watches, while I shiver and moan and try not to let him see all of me. I fucking hate it. Where did my self-control go? Where did my will? But his gaze combats the cold, and I know just how to take myself there.

In seconds, I'm floating.

He thrusts two fingers inside me, and I gasp at the additional sensation. I clench around him, startled, but my orgasm keeps coming. He strokes deep inside me. I shudder. I keep shuddering. My vision flickers.

"Your cunt looks like it was made to hold my cum," he says eventually.

He hauls me up before I'm fully ready, setting me on my feet. He slides my jeans back up my legs, making sure to touch my cold, red skin on the way.

Did we really just fuck on the ice?

My face heats with shame.

I'm close enough to the wall that I make it there on my own, sliding and fumbling until I reach the opening. Once I'm back on solid footing, I pick my way past the benches and into the hallway that leads to the locker rooms.

Yeah, not going back there.

Greyson is behind me.

He catches my wrist. I haven't made it very far, spinning me around. It's a little lighter out here, emergency lights on the wall giving us a yellowed glow.

His gaze roams my body again. "Forgot to say earlier, but I enjoy your school spirit. I'll see you soon, Vi."

And then he releases me and steps back. I stand there until he disappears around the corner.

29

VIOLET

I hurry back to the room and change my clothes. I need to get the smell of him off my skin. I need a hot shower, too, but that isn't happening.

My phone has blown up with texts from Willow, Jess, and Amanda. They're getting progressively drunker.

I comb out my hair and paint on a new line of mascara, winging it out. It's a slightly edgier look than I'm used to, but I feel like I'm ready to just... let go.

Who do I have to impress anyway?

All my life, I've been the happy one. I loved ballet, I loved dance class, I loved my friends. My mom was good enough for me to get by. My dad... well, whatever. Growing up without a dad wasn't the worst thing that could've happened to me.

Although sometimes I do think about him and what he would say if he could see me now. He'd either be proud or disappointed, and I can't figure out which one. Mom was no help when I wanted answers about him. What kind of person he was. What kind of *father* he was.

He died when I was seven.

Seven is a weird age.

I can remember him in the vaguest of memories. Like my mind has taken those days, those weeks, those *years*, and turned them into watercolor paintings. The edges are blurry, the colors run together.

Beautiful, nonetheless.

I sit heavily on one of the beds. My leg is on fucking fire, with pain shooting up into my hip. Tears fill my eyes, and I have to stare at the ceiling, blinking rapidly, to get them to recede.

It's okay, I tell myself. *I just need to get out of here.*

Willow sent me the address of the bar that the team and half the party bus has found. She sent a picture of a stage with two pianos on it, the floor in front of it packed with people. I grab my coat and get down to the first floor, asking for directions to get there.

The front desk agent guides me the right way with a smirk. I find it relatively easy and pay the cover, then step inside. Immediately, my senses are assaulted.

It's dark and loud. Bright flashes of colored lights sweep over the room from the stage, which is lit up with two glittering pianos. Dueling pianos, I guess, judging from the way the two performers are going back and forth.

I wiggle my way toward the oval bar in the center of the large room, then decide to bypass it in favor of finding Willow. Or Jess. Or anyone with blue-and-silver clothing.

I do find Miles and Jacob in the corner, holding their version of court. Paris' friend, Madison, is sitting almost on top of Jacob. He sees me and raises his cup in a silent cheers.

I nod back and keep going.

"Violet!" Steele comes up beside me and runs his hand down my arm. "Hey, there you are! We've been looking for you."

"We?" I crane around him, but there's no one else. Just him, staring at me. "Have you seen Willow?"

He shifts. "Can we go somewhere and talk?"

I raise my eyebrow but then nod. I shoot off a text to Willow, telling her that I'm here but going to chat with Steele, and then stow my phone back in my pocket. He leads me through the crowd. He's broad-shouldered and easily moves people aside.

When I tried to make my way through earlier—without anyone acting as a human plow—I had to push and slip and shove to get anywhere.

This is a lot easier.

I've known Steele since I started at Crown Point University. We ran in the same circles, especially when I started dating Jack. He doesn't have a crush on me. I know this absolutely, because he's been lusting over Amanda for years. Since they had a one-night stand and she blew him off immediately after.

There's pain and attraction there, and that's way more than anything I've offered him.

Except that forced blow job.

My stomach twists. Is he going to bring it up? Try and get me to do something like that again? I consider slamming on the brakes and going back the other way, but I don't. I go with my gut, following him down a hallway that's empty of people. There are bathrooms at the end, and a coat closet.

I pull my jacket tighter around me.

"What's up?" I keep my tone light. At least Willow knows who I'm with in case he goes all crazy on me.

He rubs his face, then meets my eyes. "I just..."

I tip my head back. "Spit it out, Steele."

"Look, I just wanted to apologize. For forcing you—"

I wince and hold my hand up. "Stop."

"Violet—"

"Stop, Steele." I can't believe I'm about to defend Greyson, but here it goes. "Greyson and I have a... thing. It's kind of fucked up. But I assume he told you." *Lie.* "I haven't said anything because I figured you were cool with it. You know."

He narrows his eyes. "You have a thing with Greyson."

"Yep." I'm going to kill myself for this later. "We like messing with each other..."

He steps back and chuckles, but it's nervous. "Oh, so... okay. You knew? Because you seemed pretty distraught."

Well... Fuck. Yeah, I think I tried to beg and plead my way out of it. To no avail. Greyson is hard and unyielding when he wants to be. He's a monster. Not that anyone needs to know it. I always assumed that, on some level, his teammates knew. And were okay with it.

I guess there's a thin line between being a demon on the ice and off of it.

"There's no girl you'd go so crazy over, you'd do terrible things for? To?"

He has the decency to flush.

So there is someone.

I let my curiosity burn through me, quick and instant, and then shove it away. Whether or not it's Amanda, or some other girl who has the misfortune of catching his eye? I don't want to know. Talk about a can of worms.

"It was a punishment," I say softly, closing in on Steele. "But I've got it handled. Okay?"

He scratches at the back of his neck. "Yeah, if you say so, Violet."

"I do."

He nods and moves past me. He leaves me alone in the

hallway, and I lean against the wall. Have pigs flown? Did I really just make up an excuse for Greyson?

"Feeling guilty, are you?"

I glance over and find Greyson at the top of the hall.

"How much did you hear?"

He shrugs.

I narrow my eyes. "Was it a setup?"

He smiles.

Shit. That could've been another trap I walked right into. Imagine that.

I shiver, and he strides toward me. I don't move from where I'm leaned against the wall, because I'm curious. Sue me, but I want to see what he's going to do. A small part of me hopes he wraps his hand around my throat and pushes me to my knees.

But he doesn't. He stops just shy of touching me at all.

And then his question hits me again, and I squint at him. "Why would I feel guilty?"

He lifts one shoulder. "I'm just imagining you didn't sell me out this time because you hate that you sold me out last time." He does lean in now, his breath fanning across my face.

I bet he tastes like whiskey. Didn't realize it was the kind of night that required getting drunk fast, but here we are.

"You're delusional."

"Am I?" He laughs. "Doesn't matter how hard I fuck you, baby. I still hate your guts."

My chest tightens, and my eyes burn. Again.

Shit.

Why the hell am I having such an emotional response? I don't want to care about what he says. It would appear to be his own special brand of brutality. He makes me obsessed with him and then *this*. He tears the rug out from under me.

I push him away and slip past him. It doesn't take me long to find Willow, Jess, and Amanda. They're dancing with some other girls, drinks in hand. Willow hugs me tightly when I appear at her shoulder, and she doesn't object when I reach for her drink and take a few gulps of the vodka tonic.

"I'll buy your next one," I say, handing it back.

I don't want to get blackout drunk—just enough to dull the razor edge I'm straddling.

One of the other girls grabs my arm and leans in. "You look like you could use a pick-me-up, not a downer. I've got something for that, if you're interested..."

I raise my eyebrows. "Yeah?"

She extends her hand, fingers uncurling to reveal an innocuous white pill.

"Molly," she says.

"Violet."

She giggles. "No, the drug. Well, it's a cocktail pill. It'll pick you up like ecstasy and set you down gently when it's done..." She winks. "I'm Sav."

I take it from her and put it on my tongue, swallowing it dry. Willow watches me with wide eyes, then laughs. She hooks her arm around my neck and plants a kiss on my cheek.

Ah, maybe she's already taken one, too.

"How long for it to kick in?" I ask the girl, but she's already spinning away.

I shake it off and drag Willow back to where Jess and Amanda are dancing. The pianists are playing a Lady Gaga song, but there's a beat behind it. A thundering baseline that keeps the song moving—and keeps us dancing.

"You find our special friend?" Amanda asks. "Jess is being the responsible one. She'll get us home."

Oh, well, that's a brilliant plan.

"I need a drink," I call.

They wave me off.

I stand at the bar, silent for a moment, then carefully tug my shirt lower. I don't have a ton of cleavage, but I guess it does the trick. Seconds later, the bartender pauses in front of me. His gaze goes down, then back to my face.

"You got a boyfriend, sweetheart?"

I smile sweetly. "Nope, but I do hope I can get a screwdriver. And a vodka tonic for my friend."

He smirks. "I can do that for you."

"Thanks." My cheeks heat at the insinuation.

He hands me a glass filled to the brim with orange juice and vodka. I slide him cash and wait for my change, then take a sip. The taste of vodka gets stuck in my nose, but I ignore it.

I've stayed away from drugs my whole life. I was the good girl. The one who tried to do no wrong, because I thought that was what would save me in the end.

Newsflash—that's a fucking joke.

When I rejoin the girls, handing Willow her fresh drink, they absorb me into their circle. I let the music flow through me, and I sip my drink and sway. The others are crazier. They hop around and wave their hands, screaming along to the lyrics.

The green, red, and yellow lights strobe across Willow's face. I lucked out with a best friend like her. She's as loyal as they come. Even now, she slides her hand down my wrist to clutch my fingers, keeping her with me as we move closer to the stage.

The dueling pianists have been replaced with a DJ who

stands in front of a podium between the huge instruments. He calls something, and the tone echoes through my skin. I wear his words for a moment.

Are you ready to party?

Then they drop off, scattering to the floor.

I grin and twirl. My body is lighter than it's been in months. My leg doesn't hurt.

Oh god, my *leg* doesn't hurt.

What a miracle.

I hop up and down and sing along to the music. I follow the lights around the room with my eyes, my face, my whole body. Like I'm just trying to tag along on its adventure.

"Hey, hey," someone says, gripping my biceps.

I stumble back. "I'm good."

"You don't look so good."

My gaze lifts, lifts, lifts.

Grey. Paris. Well, the former holds my arms. I knock them away, and he replaces his arm around Paris's shoulder. Her arm is around his waist.

They're twisted together like snakes.

Yes, they're snakes. Evil, slippery, horrible things.

I giggle and slap my hand over my mouth to suppress the sound. It doesn't matter, the music overshadows it anyway. There's no way I can cut through it.

Grey takes a step closer to me. His brows are scrunched down and together. Doesn't change the fact that she's still clinging to him like he belongs to her.

"You're a good-looking couple." I step forward and pat Paris' cheek. "I know what his cock tastes like. I know you do, too. Obviously. But I'm just saying... I think he likes my mouth better."

She reels back, her mouth dropping open.

I turn. My legs aren't working right, but I make quick work getting the fuck out of dodge.

Jess is gone, and so is Willow. Amanda finds me, though, and she's with the girl who gave me the pill. We dance and dance until I don't think I can move anymore. My thoughts go blissfully blank. No more Greyson, no more Paris, no more ballet. Just music and my heartbeat and the lights dancing across our skin.

They keep catching my attention. The lights, that is. They remind me of the ones we use for the shows. *Used*, I guess, since I'm not part of that world anymore. Standing under the spotlights on stage was warm. Hot, even. Add in pointe shoes and difficult choreography... It was a lot, and I miss it.

And then I'm airborne.

30
VIOLET

I'm lifted and flipped around, thrown over a shoulder. An arm bands the back of my thighs to my assailant's chest. I raise my head, but I don't see Paris or her lackey, or the snake she was tangling with. Until I inhale his scent, and understanding dawns.

Ah.

Grey carries me outside and down the block. He doesn't set me down, and I don't fight it. The world is tilting, and I'd rather tumble headfirst into traffic than let him assist me. Right now, he's just taking charge.

Nothing I can do about that.

"Your girlfriend already get you off? Is that why you came back for me?" I ask the concrete.

"She's not my girlfriend."

"Does she suck your dick like I do?"

He groans. "You said that really fucking loud back there, you know."

I roll my eyes and relax further. His steps aren't headache-inducing. It's kind of nice actually, to be off my feet. I let myself sway with his movements.

"Hey. You pass out?" He jostles me.

I yelp and grab his waist. "Easy, asshole. What do I look like? A sack of potatoes?" I consider that, then frown. "Don't answer that."

He chuckles. "We're almost back."

"I don't have my key," I lie.

"It's not in your pocket?"

It's weird, having a conversation with him while my ass is right next to his face. He doesn't seem bothered by it, though. In fact, his pace is slowing. And then he sets me down, and the world flips again.

"Whoa." I squeeze my eyes shut. "I didn't sign up for this ride."

"You've been dancing for hours." He moves my arm to loop around his waist, then puts his around my shoulders.

"Hours?" I shake my head, and my stomach heaves. "More like minutes. I just got there."

He laughs and shows me his phone. Three o'clock in the morning. The game ended forever ago...

I groan and close my eyes, but he just shakes my arm.

"Keep your eyes open, Vi. We've got to get you inside."

I exhale. "I don't want to go inside."

He pauses and sets me against the wall outside the hotel. Its sign glows above the door, feet away. "Why not?"

I rub my hand under my nose. "Because inside, everything becomes real. And I just really don't want to live in the real world for a little while longer."

He stares at me. He's a starer. I don't know if he realizes it, because he doesn't stare at anyone else. Just me. And it's kind of creepy, sometimes. But other times, it feels like he's trying to carve out a spot in my soul for him, and that does seem nice. Like he wants room inside me for him.

What he doesn't know is that he's been digging his

grave in my chest for weeks, and me in his. We're going to trade one day. My heart for his. An even exchange.

"Are you going to have your wicked way with me, Mr. Devereux?" I run my finger down his chest.

He steps closer, between my legs.

Boy, does this feel familiar. I'm not mad about it.

No matter how hard I fuck you, I'll still hate your guts.

I've got to wonder if there's room for hate and love in the same space. In us. I don't know if I want to consider it. Leaning into the hate seems a lot less scary.

But wouldn't I still be in the same predicament with or without the accident? With the possibility of stress fractures knocking me out of the game? Indefinitely, maybe.

I'm twenty. How much longer would I be able to sustain this career?

That was always the nightmare floating over my head. That my body would give out well before I was ready to retire. It led me to CPU. It led to the business degree I don't care about, because a backup plan is better than nothing. Dance classes came first, and fitting my regular college classes around that schedule was always my priority.

Except, now? The only thought rattling through my head is that I *shouldn't* have had a backup plan. I should've gritted my teeth and worked through the break, through the pain, and come out stronger on the other side because I had no other options.

Did a backup plan make me weak?

Too many questions and no answers for me.

"Violet," Greyson says softly. "You're in no shape for that."

"I'm as good as I'm going to get." I let out a harsh laugh. One that scrapes my vocal cords. "Newsflash, Grey. I'm the broken girl."

He looks down at his hand, then back at me. "Tell me what's on your mind."

I sneer. I should be happy from the Molly, I should be floating still. I miss that experience. I miss the euphoria of it.

Instead, I'm leaning against a cold brick wall with an even colder man at my front. And I'm burning hot for him.

So instead of answering, I fist the front of his shirt like I'd seen him do to an opponent before he decked them. I don't go for the hit, though. I yank him down and rise at the same time, slamming my lips to his.

They slide against mine, and I take that as a comfort. I take. It's what I do.

I take and take and take.

The people in my life who know me best, they know I take and don't give back. My mother, for instance, always leaving those pieces of herself behind. I collect them because the alternative is worse. I kept them to remind myself of her, because even when we're standing in front of each other, she's not there. She lives in baubles and forgotten bits.

My father? I harbor the watercolor memories of him.

Willow? I steal her generosity, I leech her comfort.

Greyson.

I'll suck the anger clean out of his body, because I think he can live without it—while I need it to keep going.

His lips move against mine, giving me exactly what I need, and I open my mouth. I take his tongue. I palm his dick through his jeans, tug at his waistband to get him closer. Fuck public indecency. I bite his lip, then flick at it with the tip of my tongue. His blood is metallic and hot.

We dig at each other. Teeth and nails and pain, until we're both breathing hard.

He's the one who pulls away first.

He's the one who steadies both of us, his gaze searing into me. I'd keep taking until I couldn't take anymore, I think.

"Come on." He leads me inside, brushing his thumb over his lower lip.

His arm is warm over my shoulders, and I twist my fingers in his shirt while we walk. My nail traces an indistinguishable pattern across the skin I can reach, and he shivers against me.

On my floor, he helps me off and leads me to the door. He swipes a key and pushes the door open.

There's my stuff on one of the beds, the familiar room I used to get ready, but no Willow.

I rotate slowly and stop when he closes the door behind him.

"What are you doing?"

He opens the closet and reveals...

His stuff.

My heart skips. "Grey?"

"I changed your room." He admits it so casually.

I can't respond for a long moment. My mouth just gapes open. He changed my room? Where is Willow? How the hell did he manage to do that?

"Knox put Willow on his room reservation. I put you on mine. You two checked in separately..." He shrugs. "It was rather easy. We canceled your other room."

I shake my head, which has started to throb. "Bet you had a whole sexy night planned, huh? And then what happened? You decided to fuck me on the ice instead, then asked Steele to try and set me up again." I nod, my anger spiking. Not high. It hits a threshold I'm not prepared for. My brain seems to mellow before my face can get red or my hands shake. I just feel the anger circulating under my skin, pulsing and then fading. "Is she back with him?"

"They left the club an hour before I took you."

I circle around to my clothes, the assortment I had laid out on the bed when I changed, and shove them back into my bag.

"What room?"

He shakes his head, leaning against the wall. Casually blocking me from the door. "No."

"What. Room." I glower. "Fine. I'll just text her."

I pat my pockets.

My empty pockets.

"Looking for this?" He holds up my phone.

"Pickpocketing now? You just love to push what you can get away with."

He shrugs. "Prove it in a court of law, Ms. Reece."

I lunge for it, and my left leg gives out. I fall hard, narrowly avoiding smacking my face on the edge of the bed frame.

Greyson drops down beside me. "What happened?"

I put my weight on my hip, bringing my leg around. I watch his gaze go from it to my face and back again, and his jaw tenses.

"Why won't you tell me?"

My mouth opens and closes. I can't tell him. I can't speak it into existence. And also... I have this giant fear that he's going to laugh in my face.

"Vi," he tries.

"Do you ever want to say something so fucking bad," I whisper, my attention fixed on my shoes, "but you know that no one will give as big a fuck about it as you?"

He nods slowly, then reaches out and pulls the lace of

my boot. I watch in silence as he completely undoes it and gently slides it off my foot. Then my sock.

My feet are... dancer feet. They've improved since I haven't been training, but the remnants are there. My toenails are chipped and short. My toes are crooked from years in pointe shoes. My feet and ankles are still flexible. I stretch every morning and crack my joints. My foot is still pretty by ballet standards, but to the naked, untrained eye...

I pull my leg in, but he grasps my ankle.

"Stop." I know the power it holds, and I say it anyway.

He stills.

It's the word. The magic word that ends everything between us. A wall slams down into place—that wall is his guard and my own defense against him. It's going to save both of us.

I exhale. I can deal with him choking me, chasing me through a forest, fucking me into a different stratosphere, bullying me—but I can't bear this kindness.

Not when I don't believe it to be true.

"If we're sharing a room, fine. I can live with that," I tell him. "But I'm not doing... whatever you were about to do." I rise and snatch my toiletries. "I need a shower."

And he'd better believe I'm locking the door behind me.

31
GREYSON

I consider Violet Reece. *Before*. The girl who seemed to have everything together.

Outward appearances can be deceiving. I know that better than anyone.

While she hides in the bathroom, I pull up a video of the Crown Point Ballet. One of their shows that stars my girl as the lead. I keep the screen close to my face, trying to analyze her every expression when she dances.

There's another video in the suggested list on the side —an interview with Mia Germain and Violet. I don't know who Mia is, but I'm curious to *see* Violet. Not just dancing, but her demeanor.

It's different in front of a camera, that much is immediately obvious. Her and an older woman sit in cushioned chairs side by side. Violet on screen is thinner than she is now. She wears a t-shirt, leggings, and a wraparound cardigan cinched tight to her waist. It gapes at the top. Her hair is slicked back in a bun. Even her face has a sharpness to it that isn't present nowadays.

The date on the video is from a year ago.

I hit play.

"Mia," an off-camera woman says, "you've created a stunning company, and this latest show is probably your best work to date. Was it a hard decision choosing your next ballet?"

Mia Germain, director. Her name and title appear under her in blocky letters, hovering there for a moment and then vanishing. I skip through her answer.

"And Violet," the interviewer says. "You're nineteen, with the world ahead of you, and you've just been cast as the principal in Mia's upcoming production of *Swan Lake*. Can you tell us what went through your head when you found out?"

Violet rubs her hands together and leans forward. Her smile is enigmatic. "It's a dream come true. Mia called me and told me just a few days ago, actually. There were some tears... After this show wraps up, we're beginning rehearsals for it. I couldn't be more thankful to Mia for giving me this opportunity."

"Violet has enormous potential," Mia interjects, patting Violet's leg. "She has a unique ability to portray both the innocence of the white swan and the darker side of our black swan."

"Did you draw inspiration from any other ballerinas, Violet?"

"Turn that off."

I drop my phone. It falls off the bed and across the floor, coming to a stop under the desk. It still plays as I stare at the real Violet. The girl in the flesh.

How different she is now. Her skin flushes, her hair is shiny. She's got a body that I don't think I'm going to break when I sink into her.

I stand and make my way to her. She backs up until the

wall catches her. She's got a ragged, holey t-shirt on and shorts. No bra. Her nipples stiffen under my gaze, standing out under the cotton.

Behind me, the tinny voice of the old Violet is talking about whoever she consulted.

I've seen *Black Swan*, but that's about as far as my knowledge of ballet goes. I know that sort of role could drive someone crazy. And that's what they were talking about. *That's* the show Violet was invested in...

"You were going to be the swan when I hit you." I haven't seen any performances of her as it—does that mean that it was ripped away from her before she could be the lead?

She flinches like I'm hitting her now.

"I don't want to talk about this," she repeats. "You forced me to share a room with you, and then you act like an asshole." She moves past me, ignoring her body's reaction.

I roll my eyes and strip off my shirt. I drop it on the floor and follow her away from the steamy bathroom to the beds. I should've asked for a king, but it's not my tab. Coach definitely would've had questions.

When she turns back around, her breath stutters.

"You know what I want, Violet?"

She lifts one shoulder an inch, then lets it fall. I can see the war within her, strong as a hurricane. She doesn't know what to make of me. Cruel, brutal, kind, gentle. I'm giving both of us whiplash.

Well, she's doing the same fucking thing.

"No," she answers. "But you're going to tell me."

I scoff. "I want a truce. Just for the remainder of this trip. Until we get back to Crown Point."

Her eyes narrow. "A truce," she repeats. Skeptical little thing.

"Just believe that I'm actually being nice." I scoff. "It's not completely foreign to me."

"It is to me," she says under her breath.

Still, she seems intrigued.

The clock is ticking. It's almost three-thirty, and my alarm is set for nine. The bus leaves at noon, and we'll be back by mid-afternoon. It's not a lot of time. It's doable.

"Come on," I press.

She finally nods.

I stride forward and wrap my arms around her.

The action surprises her, but whatever. I have a feeling she needs a hug. The seconds tick by, and I almost doubt myself. But then her arms come up around me, and she grips me tightly. I realize I'm shirtless at the same time she does. When her cheek touches my bare chest and her fingers dig into my skin.

Doesn't matter. Her body heaves, and she bursts into tears.

Oh.

Well.

I make a shushing noise and rub her back. I have no fucking idea how to handle crying women, but she doesn't object to my terrible soothing. I keep going, up and down, and slowly steer us to one of the beds. At least the video on my phone has stopped.

She takes a deep, shuddering breath, then steps back.

"Thanks," she murmurs. Embarrassment heats her face. The red creeps down her neck, where the hickeys I gave her begin their trail south. Bet she had fun discovering those.

I flip the covers back and retrieve my phone. I plug mine in and hers beside it. Hers is open to a message thread with

her mother. There are a bunch from Violet—at least five—
over the course of three days that have gone unanswered.

I grit my teeth and put it screen-down, then flick it onto
silent.

Her mother might be on par with my dad for biggest
asshole.

When I turn back around, Violet's in bed. I click the
light off and climb in beside her, earning a surprised yelp.

"What?"

"What are you doing?" Her voice is guarded again. "You
have your own bed."

"This is a truce." I get closer, adjusting my pillow, and
hook my arm around her waist. "Get comfortable."

"This is embarrassing," she says. "What if I fart?"

I snort. "Good thing I'm fully aware that females have
bodily functions."

She shifts.

Bad idea.

Her ass shifts against my groin, waking up my cock. I
shut my eyes and try to think of something else, but it
doesn't work. She moves again, and instantly I'm hard.

I've never met an aphrodisiac that has the same effect
as her body. And as much as I want to sink into her warmth
again, I'm not going to do it. I am fucking exhausted—
mentally and physically.

She makes a noise, but I shush her.

"Ignore my hard-on. It'll go away."

Her laugh is breathy, and she rolls into me. Something I
wasn't expecting for someone who wasn't sure she wanted
me in her bed a minute ago. Now we're face to face, and it
strikes me that I haven't *slept* with anyone before.
Overnight.

There was no use for that.

I wish she would tell me what's bothering her. If I pry now, she might actually tell me. But instead of opening my mouth, I lean forward and kiss her.

When's the last time I've done this? Just kiss someone for the sake of their lips on mine?

I don't like that Violet is pulling my strings—and soon enough, the charade we're building is going to crash down around us. But for now, I grip her side and kiss her while her hands roam my upper body. Every touch seems to light me up inside, until I'm burning.

And then, eventually, we break apart.

We breathe in the silence.

Sleep comes not long after that.

32
GREYSON

I rise before Violet. I quietly brush my teeth and pull on different clothes, then sit on the unused bed. I grab her phone from the charger and open it, still sort of miffed that she hasn't thought to put a password on it.

Some people are far too trusting.

Like Violet, asleep in my bed. I glance back at her and take in her hair scattered across her face, her full lips, parted as she takes in long, deep breaths. Her eyelids twitch, like her eyes are moving in a dream, and her fingers are curled into her pillow.

Other than her tense grip, she seems relaxed.

My hand aches, but I'll deal with that later. Both hands are still wrapped. People kept commenting on them last night when I was trying to keep one eye on Violet. The normal rush from being at the center of attention didn't come, because *she* wasn't paying attention to me.

When the hell did my brain flip to only giving a shit about her?

I don't like it.

I go to her texts, and a conversation with Mia Germain

catches my eye. The director of her last show, from the video online. If she's done with ballet, why is she talking to her? Then I see the appointment time, the doctor's name, and my throat gets tight. I look back farther, but that seems to be her only correspondence.

I Google Dr. Michaels. He's in Vermont. This town actually, which might explain Violet's weird mood... and why she came along on this trip in the first place. Did Mia Germain infuse some hope in her, then the doctor—an orthopedic surgeon who specializes in working with athletes—took it away?

Well, I guess that solves some of the mystery. I erase my search history and move on. I click onto her social media and follow myself across the various platforms. I snoop through her emails, which proves to be slightly more fruitful.

Her academic advisor has sent her the form to graduate. My thumb hovers over the delete button, and then I glance back up at Violet again. She rolls away from me, burying her head in the pillow.

I go back to her texts.

The ex-boyfriend has sent a slew that has me grinding my teeth. There are a lot from immediately after the accident: *I'm so excited to see you when you get back* and *we're going to have an awesome junior year* and then a few weeks later: *Fuck, Violet, I miss you. I don't care about your leg, just take me back. I'm sorry.* Then they stop up until her return to school. A big gap.

I delete his thread and block his number.

What did he say to her? The line that he crossed to make her end things with him? For a second, I envision holding him down and cutting off his tongue. The imagery is satisfying, if a bit violent.

Like her.

I set aside her phone and circle around to the other side of the bed. I peel the blankets off her, letting them all slide to the floor. Sheets, comforter. Until all that's left is her. I crouch beside it, level with her knees, and inspect her left leg more thoroughly. The scar is silver and straight down the front of her shin. I reach out and brush my finger over it.

How long was she in surgery?

When did they tell her she wouldn't dance again?

I carefully lift her leg, shifting her weight, until she rolls onto her back. I wait a handful of seconds, but she doesn't stir.

Whatever she took last night has done its job. First the high, then the crash.

So she doesn't move when I pull her panties down either, exposing her pink pussy. The hair is trimmed and neat. She's already wet—dreaming about me, I hope. I touch one of her outer lips, tracing the hot skin down and back up on the other side.

I lick my lips and lean forward, crawling between her legs. Her face is still angelic, peaceful. Relaxed. I rarely see her without some sort of pinched, exasperated expression. Even when she comes, she holds back.

It's irritating.

On some surface level, I get it. We don't trust each other. We can barely tolerate each other most times. But then there are times when all I want to do is get close enough to her to climb into her skin.

I don't understand it.

I press a kiss to the inside of her thigh. Her legs are open, and she doesn't react to my touch. Not yet. I slide a finger inside her, my gaze going from her cunt to her face. Over and over. I thrust in and out, curling the finger when it's in her. Then add another one. She shifts at that, as my digits stretch her a bit.

I add another, then lean forward and taste her. She's sweet. A hint of salt, of sweat. I lick her, then focus on her clit. My hand doesn't stop moving. I nibble on her clit and keep the pressure. My focus is on her body, her face.

She squirms, and her muscles clench at my fingers.

When she comes, it's beautiful.

Her mouth opens. Her back arches off the bed, pushing her breasts up. Her nipples are hard and pebbled, poking through the thin shirt.

Violet lets out a whimper, and she shivers. The orgasm overwhelms her.

I hope she's having a good dream.

I slowly pull my fingers out, but my cock is rock-hard. Without thinking, I climb up, kick my shorts off, and thrust into her.

Hard.

Her eyes fly open, her expression transforming from sleepy to surprised. I don't think she recognizes me. It's still a little dark in the room, not quite sunrise, and she shoves at my chest.

I capture her wrists and pin them beside her head.

"Easy," I say in her ear. "Just me."

"Grey," she groans. "Get off me."

"Get *out* of you?" I roll my hips, eliciting another groan from her pretty mouth. "Really?"

She wriggles beneath me, and I hold her wrists harder. I start again, because her cunt squeezing my cock is going to make me lose control too soon. When I move, she stops. She blinks rapidly and stares up at me, squinting.

"Did you have a good dream?" I smirk at her.

Her pulse is quick under my fingertips. The hickeys on her neck are darker now.

There's no hiding what I did.

"You—"

"I taste like you, if you don't believe me." I kiss her. I don't give her a choice.

None of this is her choice—but it doesn't stop either of us from chasing the feeling.

I pry her lips open and sweep my tongue into her mouth. Her morning breath isn't too bad, surprisingly. I guess I always assumed that everyone woke up with dragon breath. I brushed mine before I snooped through her phone.

But no... I kind of like it.

Did Jack kiss her with morning breath? Or did she insist on rushing to the bathroom before they had any sort of intimacy?

My dick gets even harder at the thought that I'm experiencing Violet unmasked. Our kiss turns fierce. I bite her lip, drag my teeth down her flesh. She jerks her wrists against my hold and puts up a fight for a second. A minute.

Fire burns between us. She tears her lips from mine and twists her head to the side, kissing down my neck. The touch is electric jolts going up and down my spine. She marks me the same way I've marked her. Savage, then soft. Until I can't take it anymore.

My balls tighten, and I slam inside her one more time. I still, coming hard, and a few moments later, I relax.

I loosen my grip on her wrists.

She rubs her face. "You can't do that."

"What?" I stay inside her. I like the feeling too much. Not that she's in any real hurry to get me off her. She's practically molded into the mattress. "I can't make you come? Or I can't...?"

"You can't not use a condom."

I smirk. "Why not?"

"Because you could have an STI—"

"I don't." I frown. "I get tested. I'm not a Neanderthal."

"Uh-huh." She reaches out and runs her hand along my jaw. "I have the worst headache."

"Lucky for you, I have something for that." I slip out of her and stand, but I get caught in another trance. Her pussy is fucking captivating, I'll say that much. And the way my cum seeps out... I go back to her and push two fingers inside her.

She rises on her elbows and watches me.

I look up and rub her clit again.

"I'm sore." She tries to push my hand away.

"Too fucking bad." Her body is an instrument I'm quickly learning how to play. And I'm enjoying the ride. The way her thighs quiver and her hands grip the sheets. There's a slight sheen of sweat on her collarbone.

I push her shirt up with my free hand and cup her tit. I pinch her nipple—not hard, just enough to make it stand even more at attention.

"Grey," she pants. "I can't—"

"You will. Twice now, I think." I nod, emphatic. Something happens to me when she shortens my name like that, but I ignore the warm feeling in my chest. A few more orgasms will do her good—and then the painkillers to take away her headache. She probably needs to drink water, too. Coach is always after us about hydrating. Keeping our bodies like temples.

She twists away from me. The motion knocks my hands

away, and I watch her shimmy toward the opposite side of the bed. On her belly.

Her ass is perfect. A little rounded, pale.

I climb back up and straddle her legs. I smack her ass cheek hard. The pain whips through my hand—especially my fucking knuckles. I'll probably have to spend the week icing it to get ready for the next game. Never mind practices.

Fuck, I'm getting distracted.

A red print rises on Violet's skin.

She didn't make a noise the first time—and her face is pressed into a pillow now.

I narrow my eyes. "Vi."

She doesn't respond. She's turned into a statue under me.

A foreign emotion winds through me, forming a weird pain in my throat. Concern? *More* concern than I've felt for anyone, I think, compounding on worry.

It's such an abnormal reaction for her, I don't know what to do for a minute.

Then I get the fuck off her and flip her over, her body so stiff she moves like a board. There are tears leaking out from under her closed eyes, streaking down her cheeks.

What caused this?

"Violet. What just happened?"

"Nothing." She covers her face.

I pull her hands away and sit her up. Her shirt falls back into place.

"Spit it out."

She tips forward and presses her forehead to my shoulder. "I just don't like… that. It brings up bad memories."

I narrow my eyes. Someone else did that to her?

Spanked her in a way that left a lasting, negative impression?

She takes my hand and sniffs, then sits up straighter. Her expression is granite when she looks me in the eye. "Is it so bad that I draw a line with that?"

"Yes," I say. Simple. "You don't draw lines with me."

Violet narrows her eyes. I like making her mad—and this seems to be a touchy subject for her.

"Why?" I question, letting more of my weight down on top of her. "More reason for me to banish whatever is making you feel like this is bad."

"It's dirty." She pushes at my shoulder. "Let me go."

"Not until you tell me more."

"My dance teacher used to spank us when we messed up." Her face gets even redder, and she averts her eyes.

I quirk my lips. "Naked?"

"No!"

"Sexually?"

"Greyson."

"Grey," I automatically correct.

She narrows her eyes.

I shrug, going for nonchalance. "Violet and Grey? Makes sense to me."

Luckily, she drops it. And with that, I slide off her. I'll bring this back around another day, but I'm mollified by the few questions I asked. A monstrous dance teacher who spanked his students for punishment—not pleasure.

Shame. The two should always go hand in hand.

But definitely not when she was... "How old were you?"

She covers her face again. "Ten."

I make a face. Definitely *not* for pleasure then. My mom had her own brand of punishment, but it came in varied, unexpected ways. It was meant to knock me off-kilter, I think, rather than hurt. Dad just went for the pain as a reminder not to fuck up.

After she has her Advil, she slips into the bathroom. She has a slight limp, but it's barely noticeable. The only reason I notice it at all is because I watch her ass as she passes, and there's an unevenness to the sway of her hips.

My phone chirps.

Rebecca (Publicist): All set to publish. Roake approved it.

I swallow and cast a glance toward the closed bathroom door.

No going back now.

33

VIOLET

The trip organizers rented out one of the conference rooms for breakfast. There's a congregation of CPU students in the room, spread out across tables, at the buffet line. I ignore them all, though, in my hunt for Willow.

I never ended up texting her last night, and I feel a pang of guilt. It eases slightly, though, when I see her sandwiched between Knox and Amanda.

Grey stops beside me. Hearing that I've used a nickname he likes—especially coming from me, I guess—does weird things to me. Good things. Strange things. It's a step in a direction I wasn't expecting. Like our truce. Like pretending not to hate each other.

I'm pretty sure I have frostbite on my ass, though.

"Hungry?"

I glance up at him. "A bit."

He smiles. "Go sit. I'll grab us something."

"No, it's okay." I head toward the buffet.

He snags my wrist. "Vi."

"Grey." I narrow my eyes. "I have a weird relationship with food, okay? Don't fight me on this."

He appraises me, understanding lighting his expression. He finally nods and releases me, but he stalks close behind. I get the sense that he's taking notes of what I take, what I waver over, and what I pass by without hesitation.

"Are you trying to dance again?"

I stiffen. "What?"

"If it's off the table, you could theoretically eat whatever you want." He looks pointedly at my plate. "Instead, you're eating the breakfast equivalent of rabbit food."

I grunt. Aquatic therapy is probably a shot in the dark, and it'll put me in debt. But damn it, I'm still going to try. And I'm not going to let myself waste away—or slack. Sometime in the middle of the night, I came to that decision. That I'd rather open a few credit cards than not dance again. Screw the consequences.

"I'm not losing hope," I tell him.

He makes a noise in the back of his throat.

I stop and look at him again. His dark-blond hair is still damp. It's longer on top, short on the sides, and a few locks curl down over his forehead. Blue eyes. Full lips. Killer jaw. And right now, he gives off the vibe that he's homing in on something.

What that is, I don't know.

"You gonna tell me?" he asks again.

I shake my head. I meant what I said yesterday—I'm not going to tell someone my most intimate fear, and new discovery, when I know they won't care. Deep down, I know Grey doesn't. He's incapable of it.

We're enemies.

This truce is exactly what he called it yesterday: temporary. It'll burst the moment we arrive back on campus.

So why should I get deep in the trenches with him now? When I know he can twist it around to hurt me later?

I finish filling my plate and head toward Willow. My headache is receding, but my muscles ache. I feel strangely awake, too. Like I'm buzzed without coffee.

That could be from Greyson making you come before you woke up.

He asked if I had a good dream. Sarcastic, sure, but I did. Come to find out my body's very visceral reaction was from him.

Although I can't say I hated to be woken up that way...

It's a little invasive. But let's be honest. *Greyson* is a little invasive.

As a human.

"Good morning!" Willow's singsong voice precedes her shit-eating grin. "Sleep well?"

I grimace. "You abandoned me."

She laughs and leans across the table. "I was dancing, and suddenly you were gone. I think you abandoned me."

I squint at her. Huh. My memory of last night is foggy, so I'll have to take her word for it. But anyway, that's not what I was referring to—I was talking about the hotel room. I look across the room, to where Greyson is filling his plate. He was too focused on what I was grabbing to take care of his own.

He fishes his phone out of his pocket, sets the food aside, and strides out of the room.

"Earth to Violet," Amanda says.

I jerk back around, my face heating. "Sorry. What?"

"Are you okay?"

"I'm fine." I'm good at suppressing pain. I'm good at minimizing my emotions. So I do just that, shoving everything down, and slowly eat my breakfast. My stomach roils.

Steele comes over and takes the seat beside me. He grins at me. "Hey, Violet."

Oh, yeah. I'm mad at him for going along with Greyson's stupid ploy to try and make things worse for me. If that was even a thing. Maybe Steele actually *was* apologizing, and Grey just decided to twist it.

Unsure, I eat in silence and ignore Steele. I ignore everyone, then dump my plate. I grab a coffee from the in-hotel café and return to the room. Greyson isn't here, and my head still hurts.

I pop another painkiller and set my drink and phone on the nightstand, then flop onto the bed that we didn't sleep on. My phone immediately buzzes, rattling in place. I reach for it and sigh. A blocked number.

Either a telemarketer or my mother, I'd be willing to bet.

"Hello?"

There's a second of silence.

"Hello?" I repeat.

"Violet Reece?" A woman. I don't recognize her voice, but she sounds rather professional. Not in a sell-you-something way or the *trying to contact you about your car's extended warranty* way.

"This is her," I say carefully. "Who am I speaking with?"

"Martha Sanders," she says. "I'm Senator Devereux's assistant."

I sit up so abruptly, the room tilts. I squeeze my eyes shut and try not to lose my breakfast in my lap. What the hell does he want with me?

"Um... Okay," I reply weakly. "How can I help you?"

"Greyson has informed us that you're attending Crown Point University."

I bite my lip, then force myself to release it. I can't help my tone when I reply, "Yes. And I've been here since I was a freshman."

She's quiet for a moment. "You see, we didn't expect to run into this... complication."

I don't answer. What the fuck am I supposed to say to that? How is it my fault that they sent Greyson to the same school I attend...?

"Here's the thing, Violet. We believe that Greyson would do better without distractions. He's working toward the NHL, did he tell you that?"

"No," I whisper.

She tuts. "Well. There are rumors that the two of you are romantically involved. Now, I'm sure you know how damaging rumors are. Especially since things on the internet never disappear forever. Right, dear?"

I *do* know that things on the internet never disappear forever. I do know that there's a video out there of me giving Jack a blow job. There's an article smearing Greyson's name, with mine attached. There's another article, from six months ago, that *didn't* come from me—but it could've. The media ran with that for a full twenty-four hours before it was locked down and brushed off. Senator's son drives drunk, crashes, gets away with it. The paper released an apology shortly after, and I was silenced, but the internet is forever.

There was a lot going on in those days. A lot of trauma. I was half out of my mind on pain medication, my leg in a cast, my future over. Greyson was released from jail before I had even come out of surgery. How fucked up was that?

I was glad he was getting burned from it.

I was happy *someone* was paying attention to what happened to me.

But it bit me in the ass, and it seems to have left a continual sting.

"What do you want?" My voice is lead.

Martha clears her throat. "It's come to our attention that you might be able to dance again. Is that true?"

I freeze. My hand, almost of its own accord, slides down my leg. I wrap my fingers around my calf, holding it tight.

"I don't know," I answer. "Maybe."

"Insurance is fickle about these things," she continues. "And if it's more physical therapy, or surgery... we're willing to help you out. Your mom isn't made of money, is she?" She pauses. "Consider this a donation to your future."

I stare at the wall. My eyes burn. They'd pay for what I need? To dance again. The MRI, the aquatic therapy. My nerve pain might go away. I might *dance* again.

Where is Grey?

"Help me out," I repeat, my brain working to catch her subtle meaning. "Like..."

"Like we did before."

Huh? "Wait—"

"Violet," Martha interrupts. "Here's the thing. You and Greyson just need to keep away from each other. We don't care how you do it. He's getting distracted. Even his coach thinks so. That fight yesterday wasn't like him, and you're the only new factor in his life. His future is important."

I dared him to do it. A tear leaks out, rolling down my cheek. She's right—I'm a distraction to him. And there's my dreams, being dangled like a carrot on a stick in front of my face.

His future is important. It is—and so is mine.

"Fine." I say it because if I don't, I'll never forgive myself. If I don't chase ballet as far as I can go, I'll combust. "I'll send you the fucking bills."

"Good choice." The line goes dead.

And I'm left wondering what the hell kind of deal I just made with the devil.

I toss my phone aside.

A moment later, the door opens, and Greyson appears around the corner. He sees me on the bed and smirks. "Get naked."

My lips part. "We're leaving soon."

"The bus leaves in an hour. That's plenty of time." He wiggles his eyebrows. "Come on, Vi. Temporary truce and all... this is the nicest side of me you're going to get."

I swallow. *That's true.* He just doesn't know it yet. So it isn't too much of a hassle to push my pants down and kick them off. He stands at the end of the bed and watches my little show. I sit up and strip off my shirt, then unclasp my bra and pull it down. The cool air touches my nipples, and they instantly pebble.

I lean back again, raising my arms above my head. My legs open.

His expression darkens, and he tears off his clothes. His cock is already hard, bobbing in front of him as he crawls toward me. He hovers above me, waiting for a moment, then sinks inside me with one hard thrust.

My back arches, my chest brushing his. He drops his weight on me and wraps his arms tight around me. He crushes us together.

I hook my legs around his hips, crossing my ankles, and hold on to his neck.

This *feels* like a goodbye.

From playful to serious in a fucking heartbeat.

Regret burns through me, but I shove it aside and catch Grey's lips. I love the feel of him sliding in and out of me, his skin pressed to mine. The weight of him grounds me.

It shouldn't, but here we are.

Our tongues touch, exploring our mouths. He tastes like orange juice.

I don't expect to come like this. I've never come without stimulation on my clit. But suddenly it washes through me, and I tighten my grip on him. My muscles clench. He pumps twice more and stills inside me. He lets out a growl that reverberates through both of us.

My heart beats out of control.

He tears his lips from mine and tucks his head into my shoulder. Maybe it was the phone call, or today, or whatever happened yesterday, but it hurts. Everything hurts. My skin, my thoughts, my bones, my heart.

I hold on to him longer. Until our phones go off, alarms set to tell us that we have five minutes before the bus leaves. He releases me, climbs off the bed, and disappears into the bathroom. I lie still, wondering if I can still move after that.

It wasn't intense physically, but emotionally?

How much can we convey without speaking?

He returns with a washcloth in his hand. He sits next to my hip, and I start when he runs the damp fabric across my core.

"It's fine," I say quietly.

I rise and slip into the bathroom. Our stuff is packed and waiting by the door, so once we're clean and dressed, we both head out.

He doesn't say anything, and neither do I.

Willow leads me toward the party bus. Away from Greyson and the hockey team's bus.

And you know what? At this point, I'm okay with it. I'm ashamed to say I've grown attached to him. I like his asshole behavior. I like when he pushes my buttons—and when I push his. We're fixated on each other. We've *been* fixated, but now...

Per his father's orders, we're going to be putting distance between us—why not start now?

34
VIOLET

Willow rushes me after my first class. She almost crashes into me, skidding to a halt inches away, and drags me into the bathroom. She checks each of the stalls and then locks the main door.

"What the hell, Violet?"

I jerk back. "What?"

"What. The. Hell. Violet." She glares at me. "You should give a girl some more warning before you go off script."

I drop my backpack and shrug, helpless and more than a bit confused. "I have no idea what you're talking about. You going to tell me or just keep scolding me?"

"This." She pulls her phone out and shoves it at me.

It's a blog for the CPU Hawks. All sorts of athletic team write-ups, reports, and coverage of the games... plus notices put out by the publicist. Rebecca Dumont.

"We met with the publicist the other day," I say slowly.

I click on the most recent post that went live twenty minutes ago.

Didn't take long for Willow to find it—and then me. I'm not sure what I'm expecting to find. I told Rebecca that the previous article posted in the newspaper was a complete fabrication. There was nothing to tie Greyson and I together except that photo.

Seems like now, their official angle is that the article is *my* fault. Again.

Just when it had been swept under the rug, they have to drag it right back out into the limelight.

She has quotes from Greyson and me—more from him, of course. And a few from his coach. Even Steele and Knox. They all conclude that I've been obsessing over Greyson and his rise to fame since coming to Crown Point University. That, yes, I have a history with him. We knew each other from growing up in the same town. And the accident that took away my career has made me bitter.

Me.

Bitter.

I stare at the words from Steele, and it's just another confirmation that he and Greyson were messing with me. Figures.

I choke on a laugh. "This has to be a joke. Right?"

They say I supplied the story to the journalist. That someone close to me took the picture in Greyson's house.

Everything tied up in a neat bow. My fault, my bitterness, my regret.

Well, *he's* going to regret getting under my skin.

"It probably won't be seen by many people," Willow tries.

I shake my head and toss her phone back. I got backlash for the article that came out and was subsequently pulled. This is going to spread like wildfire... and there's no one to take the heat off my head.

The only people who were able to smother the other

articles had a stake in it. The Devereux name. This is all on *me*, put there by Greyson. And his coach. His teammates.

Fuck.

"Let's get out of here," I eventually say.

She unlocks the bathroom door and walks beside me all the way to my second class. I'm getting more attention by the second, and I hate it. Everyone stares. A guy steps in front of me and looks me up and down, then laughs. Like he's judged me in two seconds and found me lacking.

I wince.

Willow grabs my hand and keeps pulling me along. "Ignore it."

Easy for her to say. We part ways a half hour later, and I feel... marginally better. But the rest of the day is hell.

I slink into the library after my last class, intent on just getting through my work before going home. The only good thing is that most people don't have my new number, and it's been blissfully silent.

Greyson had to know this was going to happen. I'd be naïve to think he didn't play a part in this. He spoke with the publicist after I left the room. He got his teammates to back him up.

Fucking hockey team.

I force myself to leave the dance girls alone. I don't want to drag them down with me. In fact, they should all just pretend I don't exist until it blows over.

Greyson wins this one.

"No one wants you here."

I glance up from my laptop. A guy on the football team stands at the edge of my desk, his brow lowered in anger.

"You all take opinion as gospel, huh?"

He steps closer. "Are you calling me dumb?"

No, but you probably are. I smile sweetly at him, hiding my grinding teeth. "Never."

He leans down in my space, forcing me to scoot back in my chair to put some distance between our faces. "You fuck with the team, you fuck with the whole school. Got it?"

"You should really get better lines." I roll my eyes. "Go away."

He sneers. "Just wait. Whore."

He doesn't see my flinch. He's already turned away, striding down the stacks to get back to the main room. Stupid me, I shouldn't have chosen an isolated desk. I was looking to get a reprieve from the stares.

Of course, I get accosted instead.

I finish my work quickly, but I can't shake the unsettled feeling.

Whore. I never solved the mystery of who trashed my room. I thought it was the same person who was in my room the second time, but the more I think about it, the less it makes sense.

I flip my notebook open to a new page and start a list.

Greyson and I discovered that we were at school together my first night back. Before the semester had even officially begun. That same night, he gets a video of me drunkenly giving Jack a blow job.

Total mistake, by the way. I barely remember doing it. I think I would, because I like the thrills that go along with something like that. Almost getting caught. Well, obviously we did get caught. Did Jack notice them? Did he see Greyson film and not say anything?

Then, someone breaks into my apartment and trashes my room. They leave Willow's room—and the rest of the place—alone. They write *whore* across my wall of pictures. Most of my clothes were destroyed.

I suspected Greyson, but he never said anything about it. At all. He'd have found a way to rub it in my face by now.

The locker room incident was next, followed immediately by the second break-in.

Not long after that, an article comes out that included a picture I was sure I had on my wall. It was of my mom and I in front of the hospital, but we weren't happy. Not the one on my Instagram, where we faked our smiles. I remember that giving me pause.

The article, featured in print and online, was taken down. I don't know if the print copies were destroyed, but I do know that they were removed from campus. And maybe other places, too.

I tap my lips.

Since the article, of course other shit has happened between Greyson and me. But beyond that... I've felt like I was being watched.

I brushed it off. I foolishly thought Greyson was the one doing the stalking, even when I was with him—or headed to him. I'm a bigger idiot than I give myself credit for. Has someone been watching me?

Did whoever destroy my room have something to do with the article?

By the time the second break-in happened, most of my personal belongings had been tossed. My room is no better than an empty slate at this point. Clothes, some baubles, a few pictures I salvaged and put into frames. If they were looking for more, they didn't find anything useful.

So what's the connection?

I don't have an answer.

Instead, I pack up and head home. The walk home gives me the creeps. I keep my keys between my fingers, hidden in the sleeves of my jacket. My hat is pulled low over my head, covering my ears, and I keep glancing around like someone is going to jump out at me.

Willow has a late dance meeting, so the apartment is dark when I turn up the front walkway.

"Violet."

I almost jump out of my skin, then focus on the person sitting on my porch steps. They're no more than a hunched shadow until they rise and push their hood down.

Jack.

Relief goes through me, and I march toward him. I smack his shoulder. "You scared me half to death."

He chuckles. "Sorry. I tried calling, but it goes straight to voicemail."

I step past him and unlock my door, flicking on the lights as I go. He follows me in and kicks off his shoes. I pause a beat, then shrug off my coat and toe off my boots.

"It hasn't rung," I offer, scrolling through my recent calls. "Not sure what happened."

He runs his hand through his hair. "Well, I just wanted to offer my support. I know that you might not be getting a lot of that right now..."

"That's true." I frown. "One of your football buddies went off on me in the library, actually."

He raises an eyebrow. "What? Who?"

"Wish I knew." I sigh. "Actually, it's probably better that I don't. Who knew people could be so invested in one guy?"

One popular, hot, charming...

Stop it, brain.

"Well, I'm here to make you feel better." He steps forward and runs his hands up and down my arms. "Dinner? Movie?"

I take a breath and find myself nodding, although something twists in my belly. I'm not sure why I don't want to hang out with him—probably because he's not who I really want here. But who I want is a figment of my imagination. The truce Greyson and I bartered for was temporary. It ended the minute we got back to Crown Point.

So I'm not going to delude myself.

"Sounds good," I add belatedly.

He flops on the couch and pats the space beside him. "You know," he says, "if I were you? I'd want to get back at him."

I raise my eyebrow. "How?"

"I don't know. Hit him where it hurts. It was clearly Greyson behind it, right? I've never liked that guy." He pats the space again.

I ignore it and sit on the other end of the couch, wrapping my arms around my legs. "Hit him where it hurts? The guy is practically made of armor."

"You've got a point. Not even a defamatory article could bring him down."

Yeah. That. I think of my list, of the weird things that have been happening since I got back. Maybe it has less to do with Greyson and more to do with me. I'm the vulnerable one.

Either way, I'm not going to solve this mystery tonight.

I settle in and let Jack pick a movie. He orders us food, too, and jumps up to get the door when it arrives. I'm not going to lie... it's nice to have company. I feel better not being alone in the apartment.

Still, the fact that Jack dropped me so fast after that video went out still stings.

And the worry that he might've seen Greyson take the video...

"What's been up with you since...?" I bite my lip and set down my drink. The pizza is mostly gone, the movie is half over. I didn't mean to bring up the video, but here we are. He acted so cold outside the dining hall. Hateful, even. And here I am, sitting on my couch with him like everything is fine. It's not. It's far from fine. "Actually, Jack, I think you owe me an apology."

Regret flashes across his face.

We talked briefly after he lashed out at me. But he pretended the whole thing didn't happen—and now he's sitting on my couch doing the same thing. It's not how I want tonight to go. Especially if he's going to pretend we're okay.

He twists to face me and takes my hands. "You're right. I am truly sorry for how I acted after that video was posted. I knew you didn't have anything to do with it, but Devereux got in my head about it."

I pause. "What does that mean?"

"Just that he was joking about it to his buddies. He had a good laugh at our expense and kind of blamed it on you..." He shifts.

Jack called me a slut. His apology shouldn't erase my memory of it.

I pull my hands from his grip and stand. "I'll be right back."

What the fuck is happening to me? I lock myself in my bathroom and close my eyes. I shouldn't do anything with Jack. I shouldn't even have invited him in... wait, no, I *didn't* invite him in. He just... came.

But he is right about one thing. I should hit Greyson where it hurts.

Strike back.

We can't be together, him and I.

So we may as well be enemies.

The thing is, there's not much Greyson cares about.

Hockey, of course. His friends. Like Willow and me, I doubt they'd be easy to tear apart. But... there is something else.

I splash water on my face and step back into my room. A wave of dizziness washes over me, and I grab the doorjamb.

"You okay?"

My head snaps up. Jack sits on the edge of my bed, his gaze steady on me.

"Just dizzy."

He hums. "Shame."

"What is?"

He tilts his head. "The movie isn't over. But maybe we should get you to bed."

Goosebumps rise on the backs of my arms, and I head for the hall. "It'll pass."

"It'll get worse." He rises and grabs my forearms as I pass. He grips me just under my elbows, and my knees give out.

I blink, and it feels slow. Like they're closed a lot longer than they should be.

When I finally force my eyelids open again, we've moved closer to the bed.

"What did you do?"

He makes a face. "Nothing you don't deserve."

He sets me down on the edge of the bed and waits. The room swims around me, and I brace my hands on my knees. I try to rise again, but my legs aren't working. It's like someone detached my head, and I'm floating up into the ceiling. He swings my legs up, setting my head down on my pillow, and pulls out his phone. I blink again and lose precious seconds.

An alarm goes off in my mind.

His phone flashes, the *click* of the camera loud.

"Hey!" I didn't say that. And neither did Jack.

He whirls toward the voice.

I push myself up, but my muscles can't hold. I catch a glimpse of Greyson storming into my bedroom.

He grabs the phone from Jack and glares down at the screen. "What the fuck do you think you're doing?"

Jack sneers. "You're not the only one who can use her—"

Greyson punches him.

I close my eyes and try to roll on my side. I teeter on the edge of my bed. My legs hit the floor first, and my body follows. I crash hard, my shoulder catching my nightstand. Searing pain bursts down my arm, numbing it. The room keeps going in and out of focus, and my hearing, too. Like I'm floating through a wave. Caught in a riptide. Nausea hits me, and my stomach knots. I can only hear the grunts that I know come from Greyson. They're familiar to me in a way Jack never was.

What was Jack going to do to me?

"Come on," Greyson says, suddenly close. He grips me under my arms and lifts me.

I weakly curl my fingers into his shirt. I force my eyes open and barely see Jack's legs extending past the end of my bed.

Greyson ignores him and swings me up into his arms.

He carries me into the hallway. I can practically feel his mind working. He goes into the hallway bathroom and sets me down in front of the toilet.

"Sorry, Vi," he mutters.

Then he jams his fingers down my throat.

I gag and try to fight him off, but it's fruitless. His two fingers press down on my tongue, and my stomach contracts. I fall toward the toilet as I vomit. I'm vaguely aware of his hand on my back, collecting my hair, and the other one supporting my torso. I sag to the side and close my eyes.

Plastic touches my lips, and then cool water. I open and swallow, and then it's gone.

"One more time," he murmurs.

"No," I whimper.

"He drugged you." Greyson pinches my chin, directing my face back around to him. Doesn't matter that my eyelids are so heavy, I can't keep them open. "The bastard came in here and gave you a fucking date rape drug."

He doesn't need to stick his hand down my throat again —that thought is enough to get me to gag. I cough and choke after, the taste burning my throat. He gives me more water, then scoops me into his arms.

He carries me back to my bed and sets me down on it.

"What—"

"You're safe. Go to sleep. It's okay."

He pulls my jeans off and drags the blankets over my legs. I curl on my side, every part of me aching again. I can't seem to catch a break.

My thoughts are sluggish. I'm vaguely aware of Greyson moving around my room, and then, sometime later, silence.

I'm left with one question.

Why did he come here in the first place?

35

GREYSON

Knox meets me on the sidewalk, his hood over his head and his hands in his pockets. He raises an eyebrow, but we don't speak until he's in my passenger seat and we're well away from the house.

We go toward the point. The cliff that the hockey team jumped off of months ago. I was just out here with my father, at the restaurant that overlooks the lake.

"You gonna loop me in?" he finally asks.

"Jack Michaels."

He turns toward me. "What about him?"

"He tried to rape Violet."

Knox is silent.

I don't know if that's what he would've actually done. If that's how far he would've gone. But I'm assuming it is—after all, why drug her? Why go to those lengths?

My grip tightens on the wheel. "He's in the bed."

Of my truck, I mean.

Knox cranes around, but it's too dark. We're on a road without streetlights. Besides, I hogtied Jack and bound him to a few cinder blocks. A tarp covers him. It won't suffocate him, but he's probably cold.

February hasn't lightened up on us. Weather-wise.

Which works in our favor tonight.

"What's the play?"

I smile. "We're going to make him regret ever coming to Crown Point."

He nods slowly. "Sending mixed messages, aren't you?"

"Because of that press release?" I glance over, then back to the road. "She's mine. That hasn't changed. It's just public perception. A necessary evil, if you ask me."

"Uh-huh."

"We both denied our involvement with each other," I say. Not sure why I have to explain it, but there's a compulsion there. For my friend to understand. "It's not us. It's everyone else who will care. My dad, her mom…"

"Because of your past," Knox guesses.

"Something like that."

"Lot of smoke-and-mirrors shit going on around here." He heaves a sigh. "Whatever. I don't really give a fuck as long as we win our game next week. Which means ensuring Jackie boy here doesn't get us kicked off the team."

I nod. "I know."

"So… I'll ask again, what's the play? The actual plan, Devereux. Don't bullshit me. We going to scare him? We going to blackmail him?"

I lift one shoulder. He'll get the idea when we get there.

We ride the rest of the way in silence. I don't get the vibe that Knox is against this. More like he's anticipating it. He's as bloodthirsty as me. My only regret is that Violet isn't here to witness this. But with the drug in her system, she wouldn't be awake for it.

She wouldn't remember it either.

She might not even remember me being there.

Which is for the best.

The glow of the restaurant is visible, and then we go down a short decline in the road, and it disappears. This is where most people jump from, since technically cliff jumping is against the rules. It's a secret thing here in Crown Point, initiation bundled with the thrill of something illegal-adjacent. You're not going to be arrested, but you will be scolded if they catch you.

To some, that's the same thing.

We park on a gravel shoulder and hop out. I reach into the bed and tap the tarp. Jack flinches under it, then jerks against his binds. A muffled yell comes out of the lump.

Knox, across from me, raises his eyebrows.

I shrug. I pull the tailgate down and flip the tarp off him. He stares at us, completely wide-eyed, and I grin at him. I climb up beside him and flick my knife out. He squirms, trying to get away from me, but the rope and cinder blocks hold him firm.

I slice through the cord that binds his legs and arms to the concrete, then jump down. Knox and I each grab a leg and haul him out. He falls to the gravel in a heap.

"Ready?" I ask Knox.

He meets my eyes, and his brow lowers. I'm asking him to trust me—and in turn, I'm trusting him. We'll be in this together.

After seeming to mull it over, he grins. I knew I read him right.

We lift Jack by his arms. His feet drag between us, still bound, and he makes a few attempts to get free from us. Finally, we reach the edge of the cliff.

We throw him to the ground, and I open my knife again.

I lean down and trace it along his throat. His Adam's apple bobs with his harsh swallow.

The fear is real now. I think he's finally getting it through his thick skull.

It isn't as intoxicating as Violet's fear.

At the thought of Violet, my chest tightens. Rage goes through me when I look at him—at what he almost did to her.

I peel the tape off his mouth. There's blood crusted on the corner of his lip and his nose from where I decked him in Violet's room. He's got a black eye forming, too, and a half-moon-shaped bruise on the bone on the outside of his eye socket.

He spits into the dirt beside him. "What—"

"Shut up," I hiss. "Here's what's going to happen. You're going to tell me—in excruciating detail—what you planned to do to Violet Reece."

He stares at me for a moment. I wonder what she ever saw in him, because all I see is poison.

"And if I don't?"

I let him see how devoid of emotion I truly am. It's easy to let the veil drop sometimes. I let out my demons around Violet—in the gym, in the woods—and on the ice, occasionally. When we're hard-pressed for a win and there's no other options. Becoming something people fear just adds another layer to my personality.

Two parts charm, one part insanity.

And a powerful family name to boot.

I give him a smile. The sort that *feels* crazy—and must look it, by the way his eyes widen. "If you don't, I'll break your fucking legs and make sure you never touch a football again."

He falls backward. "You wouldn't. You—"

"I what?" I grip his throat and yank him toward me, until we're eye to eye. "I'm the worst monster you've ever come across, asshole." I toss my phone to Knox. "Film it."

I release Jack and step back, leaving him lying on the ground. He swallows and pushes himself up. The flashlight comes on, illuminating his face, and he gulps again. His eyes dance around, like he's trying to come up with a good enough lie.

A good enough excuse.

But here's the thing: there is no such thing.

He wanted to take what's mine. He wanted to hurt her in the worst way he could think of. He wanted to *steal* and *take* and *destroy* her. But she has a meaner, scarier, *crazier* stalker.

Me.

And I'll protect her with every breath in my body.

"I went to her apartment after I saw the press release." His eyes lose focus, like he's remembering. Or fabricating.

I glance over at Knox, whose brows are drawn together.

"I have a prescription to help me sleep. I brought some with me and crushed them up to put in her drink. It took a little while for it to hit her. I didn't even have to force her to her bedroom—she walked there on her own two feet." He looks up at me, his eyes dry. Not a speck of remorse. "I was going to fuck her, and I was going to video it and send it to you."

Me.

I narrow my eyes and gesture for him to keep talking.

He does. "I've been dating Violet forever. She's been by my side for the past three years."

I make a face. "Technically, she broke up with you six months ago."

"And then you come crashing into her life," he

continues as if I hadn't interrupted, "and suddenly she wants nothing to do with me." He kicks at the dirt, inching himself backward. "I fucking hate her for that. It's a betrayal. She just *left* me? No."

I tilt my head. "You wanted to win her back?"

He laughs. "I fucking tried to mess with her head like you do. Especially after that video of her blowing me was posted. But instead of reacting like she does to *you*, she just... was done with me."

My lips twist. Of course she was just done with him. She was done with him months ago, it sounds like. He just wasn't ready to face the music.

"You messed with her how?"

Jack's expression turns pained. "Come on, man."

"Did you know she was too drunk to remember when you stuck your dick in her mouth outside Haven?" I clench my fists, then force myself to release them.

He just laughs. "And you bet I saw you filming it, jackass."

I motion to Knox to cut the video. The light dies, shrouding Jack in darkness again. Knox tosses my phone back to me. I watch it through, listening carefully to make sure we get all of his words, and cut off the last part where he mentions my involvement. It's irrelevant, anyway.

"Wait here," I say to Knox.

He inclines his chin.

I stride back to my truck. What I want to do and what I have to do are two very different things. I *want* to tie him to the cinder blocks in the bed of my truck and shove him over the side of the cliff.

I can't do that. Murder is a bit too far, even for me.

Instead, I find the crowbar in my backseat and heft it in my hand. When I return, Jack is pleading with Knox. He's crawled forward again, farther away from the drop-off, and he stares up at Knox like my friend will save him.

He won't.

"This is strictly business," I inform Jack.

His attention switches to me, but it's too late to stop me. Or to get away. I'm set on my mission, the fury under my blood hot and demanding revenge.

I raise the crowbar. The weight is solid in my hand, my grip sure. I swing it up over my head. I relish the expression of horror that crosses his face. And the acknowledgement that he can't stop me. For a perfect moment, we're all frozen. And then I slam it down on his knee.

36
VIOLET

I feel like I've been hit by a truck. I rub my eyes and manage to roll out of bed. My mouth has a sour taste, and I brush my teeth twice to get rid of it. My head pounds. A quick glance at my phone tells me it's midmorning. Later than I would've normally slept... and it's Tuesday. I'm missing classes.

"Shit," I mutter.

I get halfway dressed before I realize that making it to campus isn't going to happen. I stumble out into the living area and glance around. It's neat and organized, like...

Wait.

What happened last night?

I stand in front of the couch and stare down at it, confusion hindering my thought process. There was the press release on the athletic blog, the football player in the library, Jack waiting for me on my front step.

And then... nothing.

Like my memories have corroded. There's nothing left except that taste in my mouth. I don't remember putting myself to bed or what Jack wanted...

Panic surges up my throat. I put my hand over my chest and try to breathe, but getting air in seems to be the problem.

The front door opens, and Willow strides inside. Her voice, calling my name, seems to come from a long way off.

Something crashes, and then she's right in my face. She lowers me to the floor and kneels next to me. She puts my hand on her chest, miming deep breaths.

I squeeze my eyes shut and try to match her. The rise and fall, everything slowing down. There's still panic riding through me, but after a few tries, I manage to catch my breath. I inhale and exhale until my heart rate slows, too.

"You with me?"

I open my eyes. "Sorry," I croak.

Her concern bleeds through her expression. "What happened?"

I frown. "I don't know."

She frowns, too, and sits beside me. We lean against the wall.

"Walk me through it?"

That's the problem. I don't know what happened, and I can't seem to articulate it. So instead, I ask, "What time did you get home?"

"Eleven. Coach had us learning new choreography, and it was taking forever to get to a stopping point." She tuts. "You were asleep by then, though. Did you order out?"

I roll my head toward her. "Did I order out?"

"Yeah." She nudges my shoulder with hers. "There are takeout boxes in the trash. Beer, too. What happened?"

My heart skips, then picks up speed. "I can't remember."

She watches me carefully.

"Willow." Tears fill my eyes. "I walked home, and Jack

was waiting on the front step for me. I remember him coming inside, then... nothing. It's blank."

"Did he...?" Her gaze drops.

I wrap my arms around my abdomen. "What are you saying?"

"The last time he talked to you, he was awful. I'd never want to accuse someone of... that..."

"He didn't." I don't know how I know it, but I do. He didn't rape me. That's the sort of thing I'd be able to feel, right? I'd be sore. Or there would be evidence. Bruising, tearing. All the sort of vicious stuff we hear about in relation to sexual attacks.

Right?

The more I think about it, though, the more suspicious I become. Why don't I remember? I push myself back to my feet and go to the trash. There are two beer bottles nestled against the plastic, along with a pizza box. Not stuff we'd usually throw away.

We like to recycle, for one.

I have that same untethered feeling as when I was high on the Molly. Like I'm lost and might just float away. So I pour myself a tall glass of water and force myself to drink most of it, then refill and repeat.

Worry churns my gut. I can't let it go. Something happened, and it's eluding me. Just out of my grasp. Every muscle in my body is strung tight.

Willow guides me back to bed, and we both jerk to a stop in my room.

My nightstand is tilted, like something crashed into it. My lamp is askew, leaning haphazardly against the clock. It seems like a miracle it didn't fall and break. Everything else that used to be on it, nice and neat, is jostled, too. My book is on the floor.

"Something happened," Willow says in a low voice. "I don't know what, but... we need to find out."

"I agree." I'm afraid, but at the same time, I need to know.

"Do you want to stay in my room instead?"

I shake my head and shuffle over to my bed. I fix the lamp, straighten the rest of it, then sit heavily.

"As soon as this headache goes away, I'll play detective with you," I tell her.

She nods and watches me. Concern creases the outer corners of her eyes, and her lips press together, but she doesn't say anything.

"Go to class," I sigh into my pillow. I wrap my arms around it and bury my face. "I'll be okay."

She hesitates.

"Really, Willow."

"Okay. Under duress. I'll see if..." She shifts, drumming her fingers on my dresser. "Maybe someone knows something. One of our neighbors."

We live across the street from other college students. It's common in this area, really. But if she thinks one of them saw something, I have a feeling she's mistaken.

Still, I don't refute her. I want to know—no, I need to know. The unknown is an itch I can't scratch. My skin crawls, and I can't seem to tear my thoughts away from what *might* have happened to me.

I close my eyes. Willow leaves my door open on her way out, and I don't fault her for that. She's worried. I'm worried.

Her shower kicks on, and I fail to fully relax. Every time I do, something has me tensing. Sleep haunts me. It's right there, then gone. My eyes are sandpaper behind my eyelids. The tears that keep leaking out aren't helping.

I need to know what happened last night.

Which means confronting Jack.

As soon as the front door closes, I force myself back out of bed. I take a shower and dress warmly. A baby-blue sweatshirt over a long-sleeved white shirt with *Crown Point Dance* across the front. I brush out my hair and braid it back, then hunt down a hat. Winter jacket. Jeans. Boots.

Armor.

I swipe on makeup, to disguise how I feel on the inside, and pop a few Advil.

Then I head to campus.

Today, I draw more stares. I'm not really concerned with them—I am on a mission to find Jack. It's almost dinnertime, so the sensible place to find him is in the student center.

And, sure enough, I find him with his football friends in a gathering outside the dining hall. He turns and scans the room, like he can feel me enter, and quickly averts his eyes.

Anger surges through me.

It's the confirmation I need.

I march toward him and stop dead. His leg is in a cast, with crutches leaning on the table beside him. He's pointedly ignoring me at this point, and so are his friends. Although I doubt his friends have even seen me, since I'm still far enough away to not impose. And Jack isn't giving them any clues that he's uncomfortable.

But *something* happened... and I have a feeling I know who might be behind this. The one person with little regard for anyone else. Or the law. And he's possessive enough to strike out at Jack if he somehow knew...

I spin on my heel and get the fuck out of there.

Once I'm away from the student center, I fish out my phone.

Me: What time does practice start?

I wait a moment, then bubbles pop up on the chat.

Steele: Six. Why?

I don't answer. It's almost six now, which means there's a very real chance I could catch Grey before then. I tug the zipper of my jacket higher, burying my chin in it, and hurry to the stadium.

My exposed skin is frozen by the time I make it there. Once inside, I unzip the jacket and rub my hands together. I peer through one of the entrances to the stadium seating.

Jackpot. Only a few people are on the ice, wearing pads and sticks in hand. I hurry to the lower level and watch again, making sure one of them is Greyson. It sickens me that I know him just by the way he moves and the back of his head. The way he skates.

Ah, well.

No time like the present. Except, more people are filing onto the ice from one of the open doors. More players. They skate around, and one of them cocks his head when he sees me.

Still. I step out onto the ice. I'm on a mission, and I feel unstoppable. Unlike the last time Greyson had me on ice, I don't let fear keep me away.

"Hey," someone barks. "You can't be out here."

I ignore them and head straight for Greyson. He turns and watches me approach. Of course he doesn't try to get closer, to help me out. No, he just eyes me from behind his mask with a gleam in his eye.

Answers. I'm here for *answers.*

So when I stop right in front of him and poke his chest, I'm surprised when no words come out.

I hit his chest again, harder.

He just stands there, taller than he should be in his skates.

A lump forms in my throat, and I hit him again. It doesn't make me feel any better.

Why can I voice what I remember to Willow but not here?

"Violet," Greyson says in a low voice. "If you came here just to hit me... you could've waited."

"You're an asshole," I choke out. The words are shreds of glass moving through my throat. I stagger backward.

He raises an eyebrow. "Okay."

"You're fucking with my head. You don't have any idea what I've been through. And then last night—"

He glides forward. Right into my space. He rips his helmet off and leans down, so we're eye to eye. "Nothing happened last night."

I grit my teeth. "No." I try patience, but it's not my strong suit. "No. Something *did* happen—"

"Nothing happened to you. Nothing happened to me." He narrows his eyes. "And nothing happened to Jack."

So it was him.

I don't know why I'm surprised—he's literally the first person I thought of when I saw the cast. But he's *Greyson*. He's the kind of asshole who hits you with his car and puts an innocent passenger in the driver's seat. He doesn't beat up ex-boyfriends for fun.

He doesn't care that much.

"Ms. Reece!" Coach Roake skates toward us. "What the hell are you doing on my ice?"

I face him and wobble. "Um—"

"And I know you're not my newest hockey player," Roake snaps, "because tryouts were three months ago."

My cheeks heat. "Sorry, sir. I'll just..."

I take a step and, wouldn't it be my luck, my heel slips out from under me.

Greyson catches me from behind before I eat it. "Got her, Coach."

I can hear his cheeky smile, even though I can't see his face. He keeps his hands where they are and lifts me back up, my feet barely losing contact with the ice. He speeds us toward the entrance I came through. He doesn't set me down until we're both on the mats.

"We're not done," he warns.

We are, though. I can't just forget about the conversation I had with his dad's secretary. I can't forget about ballet and the help I can get. The resources for my leg.

I got my confirmation that he did something to Jack. Why he was at my apartment is a question I'll just have to live with—especially if I want my future back. It hurts to step away from him again, hurts worse that I won't get my answers. I take a deep breath and exhale my frustration.

"Goodbye, Greyson."

He winces.

I've got to leave it there. It was a mistake to come here in the first place. I've got to focus on my own future, and he has to focus on his.

37
VIOLET

The more I ignore Greyson, the more angry he becomes. Maybe not angry, but more like a toddler throwing a tantrum.

A toddler holding a grenade, but still.

February slips into March. The hockey team win their final game of the season, and they qualify for the national tournament. There are two away games—they win both—and next week is a home game. The whole school is buzzing.

It's also the weekend that kicks off spring break.

To keep myself sane, I've been sneaking into the dance studio at night. Better than the gym, I reason. I got my MRI late one afternoon a few weeks ago, and Dr. Michaels cleared me for aquatic therapy soon after. There was only a little guilt winding through my bones when I mailed the bill to Senator Devereux's office.

Did I call the clinic every day for a week to check on the balance?

Yes.

And who was more surprised than me to find that they *did* pay for it?

The aquatic therapy feels ridiculous at first, and I pull at my one-piece swimsuit self-consciously. The woman who guides me through stretches and exercises is patient and calm. She has one of those voices that brings down my adrenaline and relaxes my muscles.

It's been helping. So much so that I've started taking dance lessons again, too. Slowly getting back into shape, teaching my body how to move again. The instructor yells at me often, but I feel the improvement in my sore muscles.

Willow's not quite in agreement with me on the dancing front. She thinks I'm pushing myself too fast. On the Greyson front, however, she's fully on my side. In solidarity, she's quit seeing Knox. She said she didn't need to be over at their house every night, rubbing it in Greyson's face. I think she'd just rather not see the parade of women he probably has coming and going.

Paris has restarted her attempts to woo him. She sits next to him in the dining hall, casting furtive glances my way. As if she's going to catch me caring. Maybe she thinks she'll spot me weeping into my soup bowl.

Unlikely.

Besides the pull toward the dark cloud that is Greyson Devereux, I'm finally feeling... *happy*. And somewhat back to normal. Even the news about the press release has died down. Jack disappeared into the background noise, nursing his broken leg.

I do my best to put him and that night out of my mind, although my trust in men has officially broken. Either way, I'm moving on.

But, as always, good things have to come to an end.

Greyson finally reaches his limit.

I don't know what it is that sets him off, but it happens after our last class of the week together. For a month, I've sat as far from him as possible. I've studiously concentrated on my textbook, my notebook, the professor. Anything but the burning glares he sent my way.

Part of me has been eager for him to break. He's not used to things not going his way. I wait with bated breath for the grenade to go off. But for so long, all he does is glower from afar.

Unfortunately for both of us, his father is more used to getting *his* way—and that's exactly what's happening. Greyson just doesn't know it.

For the record, I'm minding my own business. As always. My new friend, Stacy, and I have been debating topics for our final projects in environmental economics—one of the classes I share with Greyson. Willow, Jess, and Amanda have a dance class. At least Paris isn't around because of it, too.

Part of my mission over the last month has been to make friends outside of the dance team, for no other reason than they're getting increasingly busy—and I don't want to eat alone every evening. The dance team is gearing up for a big competition that takes place over spring break.

Stacy's eyes widen, and then the chair beside me is yanked out. I know it's him. He has a certain feel to him, like he's projecting raw energy. He sits so he faces me, his knees pressing into my thigh.

I still ignore him.

"Violet."

Nope. This isn't happening.

He grabs my chin and forces my head around. I let out a little gasp at the connection and the way his eyes burn up close. His gaze drops to my lips, then lower. My throat, my heaving chest. Then back up. He smirks when our eyes collide again.

He doesn't seem too worse for wear. There's new stubble on his cheeks. He doesn't bark at my new friend to leave. He doesn't really do anything except stare into my eyes. Does he think that I owe him something?

I don't. I'm grateful, but that's as far as it goes.

His nails dig into my cheek. His thumb swipes across my lip.

So much anger.

His life is going just fine. He's back at the top of his game. Amanda gave me the highlights from the last few games. Greyson has been on fire, leaving everything on the ice. He's been interviewed for the local paper a few times. There's been a feature in the *New York Times*, along with a smiling photo of him and his father, who attended one of them.

"You're not leaving me any choice," he mutters.

My eyebrows hike up, and I open my mouth to retort. He holds my chin fast, his thumb pressing harder on my lips.

"Don't give me your excuses. You're going to get up and come with me. You're going to sit next to me, and you're going to fix your expression so you don't look so shell-shocked."

"I *am* shell-shocked," I say against his thumb. "I don't want anything to do with you."

He laughs. It's low and throaty and it does something to me.

It's been a long month.

"You know what, Violet?" He leans even closer. "I don't fucking believe you."

I don't answer. Can't.

I hardly believe myself.

"Threats work best on you, I suppose." His expression turns contemplative. "Okay, how about this? You come with me, or I'll spread you out on this table and make you come, and then no one will fucking doubt that you're mine."

The blood drains from my face. I can totally see him doing that. I squeeze my thighs together, because... *fucking hell*. He's twisting me. A small part of me wants him to do it. I'm turned on by the thought.

And if I didn't know most of the students—maybe not their names but definitely their faces—I don't even think I'd give a shit.

What does that say about me?

"Dirty girl. You like that?" His gaze drops to my legs, then back up. "Mmm, you do. Tell you what. We'll live out that fantasy one day, if you do what I say. Otherwise, it's happening right now."

I rise. His hand slips from my face, and he quickly stands, too. He follows me so close, he's practically my shadow.

If shadows were hulking, hot, dangerous hockey players.

We arrive at his table. The one I've been avoiding for the last month, give or take. Steele, Knox, Jacob, Miles, Erik. They're all chatting, eating, like nothing is wrong. To them, nothing is.

Paris and Madison are here, too. I suppose their dance class has concluded.

Greyson pulls out a chair for me.

I sit, and he sets my plate in front of me. He scoots his chair so close, his thigh presses against mine again. His arm comes around behind me, on the back of my chair.

"Your expression," he reminds me.

I press my lips together and quickly scan the table. Of the people here, I'm pretty sure Steele, Paris, and Madison don't give a shit about me. Knox probably hates my guts because of Willow. And the rest are neutral. Still, there are a lot of people here. It's peak dining time.

Which is why I shouldn't be surprised when Willow and Amanda come into the dining hall. They're wearing exercise clothes, same as Paris and Madison.

Paris looks at me, and I smile at her. Maybe it isn't so much a smile as a shit-eating grin, but Greyson should really take what he can get. I can't magically rearrange my face any more than he can.

I lean back, bumping his arm, and the heat emanating from him feels... nice. It shouldn't but does.

Another fucked-up thing between us.

"When did you get here, Violet?" Paris asks.

I tilt my head. "What?"

"When. Did. You. Get. Here?"

Greyson snorts. "She's more welcome than you."

You know... when I want him to stick it to her, he doesn't. He lets her climb all over him and sit close and flirt and fawn. And when I'd rather be anywhere but here, he tells her to shove it.

Lovely.

"Grey," she tries.

Oh, hell no. "You did not just call him that."

Her expression darkens. "Why, did you lay claim to that nickname?"

I cross my arms. "As a matter of fact, I did."

Jesus. Who would've thought I'd be arguing about a nickname... this whole night is a mind-fuck. And in the back of my head, I have Senator Devereux's secretary reminding me of my agreement with them. The fact that my aquatic therapy costs hundreds of dollars that I don't have to spare, and they've been footing the bill.

"You're nothing special," Paris snaps at me, flipping her hair over her shoulder.

I roll my eyes. I'm sick of her attitude, but I don't have the energy to deal with it today. "Neither are you, Paris. Pretty sure you've never had an original thought in your head."

She stares at me, then stands. She grabs her drink and marches over.

Absolutely not. I'm not getting another drink dumped over my head.

I start to rise, but Greyson beats me to it. He snatches it out of her hand and slams it on the table, then sinks back into his seat.

"You're an embarrassment," he says to her. "Get the fuck away from us."

Paris freezes.

This would be so fucking gratifying if I wasn't pissed at myself for coming over here.

Then she glitches. That's the only way I can describe it. Her mouth opens and shuts, her eyes twitch. She's motionless in front of us. If she was a computer, she'd be the spinning wheel of death, just thinking over and over.

So I do the only thing I can think of to make her meltdown even worse.

I turn and grab the front of Greyson's shirt, pulling him into me.

Our lips touch.

He lets out a huff of surprise, and then his hands wind around my back. Smugness radiates through him. Whatever element of surprise I had, of control, is quickly lost. He leans into me, bending me into the back of my chair, and pries my mouth open with his tongue. He tastes me and conquers my mouth. I feel thoroughly claimed by the time he's done.

And when he is, when I finally straighten, Paris is gone.

Madison, too.

I just kissed Greyson.

Something I *shouldn't* have done.

I lean back. "Maybe I wasn't clear before."

He cocks his head.

"We're done." I stand, and he mirrors me. He follows when I back away. "There's no us. There's no you and I together at a table, or kissing, or—or looking at each other."

He watches me.

It's not enough to tell him we're done.

I need to go bigger.

He steps forward, and suddenly it becomes a game in his mind. I must give him something. A flash in my eye, a twitch. Something that reminds him that he has the power to put fear into me—and he likes it.

"You don't call the shots, Vi."

I turn and walk briskly away. I make it all the way out of the dining hall before he catches me. He's civil in public— barely. Can't have another defamatory article calling him an abuser, probably. Although Daddy Dearest would get that removed in a flash—and probably sue the paper to boot.

Nothing sticks to Greyson Devereux.

He drags me up the stairs, to a lounge area, and backs me into a corner. There's no one up here. Everyone's down- stairs, heading into or out of the dining hall.

That's probably why he picked here. Right on the edge of being discovered.

He pushes me to my knees and unbuttons his pants.

I rock back on my heels and glare up at him. "Grey—"

"Don't." His hands fall away. "Take my cock out and suck it, Violet."

I look away. Shame fills me. If I make a noise, we'll be caught. If anyone decides to come up here and check this shadowed corner, we'll be caught.

A shiver races up my spine.

"Maybe I'll take a video of this and post it on the school's main page again? Two guys, one semester, one filthy mouth." He grabs my jaw again and forces his thumb into my mouth. He opens it, pressing the pad down on my tongue. "Just say the word. Or..."

I shudder and lower his zipper. I pull his boxers and pants down just far enough to free his cock. It bobs, hardening by the second, at eye level. I reach out and slide my hand down his shaft.

He releases my jaw and winds his fingers in my hair. My control is nonexistent... in that Greyson has me right where he wants me. A fly in his web. He moves my head forward, and I open my mouth wide. He tastes familiar, but he doesn't give me a moment to adjust. His hips rock forward, and the tip hits the back of my throat—then slides farther down.

I gag around him, choking when my breath is cut off.

I forgot he enjoys that aspect. He likes to watch my face redden, my eyes fill with tears. He pulls out, and I suck in a deep breath through my nose before I lose the ability again. I hold his thighs as he fucks my face, one hand on the back of my head and the other braced on the wall behind me.

Someone gasps behind him. Fire erupts through me,

shame and embarrassment turning my whole body into an inferno.

We're caught.

"Get out of here," Greyson growls over his shoulder.

I don't know if they listen. I keep my eyes half-closed until he jerks my head back. I lift my gaze to his and hold it. It's blurry through my tears. My nose runs, too, and I can't do anything about the saliva.

He moves faster, taking and taking and taking.

"You. Don't. Leave. Me."

I hope my eyes translate my thoughts.

Get fucked, Greyson.

His fingers tighten in my hair. The pinpricks of pain have my jaw tensing. My teeth skim his cock, and he shudders. And then he comes. He groans and fills my throat so deep, I don't have a choice but to swallow. His head bows forward, his eyes drinking in my face. I can't breathe like this, and an alarm blares through my system. The need to get free. To take in oxygen.

"How would it feel to die like this?" he asks, reading my mind. "Suffocating on my cock."

He waits another second. Then he pulls out, and I fall backward. Except, now isn't the time for pity or staying huddled in a mess of tears on the floor. I stand quickly, wiping my face with the bottom of my shirt. The hate comes next—that he feels free to use me like this.

You're nothing special. Paris said as much.

So why have I been plucked out of the crowd? Because of one night?

"Would you have done this to Paris if I didn't come along?"

He lifts one shoulder. I don't think his gaze has left me once, and I need to know what he sees in me.

"No. She's the kind of slut who begs for my cock. And if not mine, Knox or Miles or anyone who knows how to play a sport. You're my goal, Violent. You're the one who doesn't let anyone in. Even your bastard ex-boyfriend never got to see the real you." He runs his finger under my eye. "The real you craves this. The *real* you is fucked up in the head, just like me. Isn't that right?"

I jerk away. Even if he's right, I'm never going to admit it.

"Even if you hadn't *come along*, as you said..." He gets even closer. "Even then, we were destined to find each other."

"All we do is hurt each other." I incline my chin and turn my back on him. I need to retrieve my bag and get away from here.

Get away from him—as if that's even a possibility.

He lets me go for now, and once I have my things, I hurry away from campus. He's got evening hockey practice coming up soon. That may be the only thing stopping him from following me.

My pointe shoes are burning a hole in my bag, and I'm itching to put my muscles to good use. Instead, my feet lead me to the sidewalk outside Greyson's house.

I check my watch. It should be empty.

Against my better judgment, I walk right up to the front door and try the handle.

It opens easily under my hand.

They don't lock it? They probably think they're invin- cible—if Knox hadn't already infused that in his starters, I would've been sure Greyson brought it with him. The aura that accompanies people who are used to getting their way.

I hesitate in the doorway and listen. They left the lights on. It smells faintly of booze in here, the aftermath of too many celebrations. When only silence greets me, I close the door and hurry to the stairs.

Greyson's door is closed but not locked either. Not that I would've anticipated it... that would've thrown a wrench in my plans.

His room is as neat as I remember, if a little more lived-in. There's a hamper in the corner that's overflowing with clothes, but that's the only sign that he might be losing it.

My fault?

I run my finger along the edge of his desk and rifle through his papers. There's a printed copy of the research paper due for one of our shared classes, environmental economics. I am actually liking that class a lot more, now that I'm paying better attention.

Turns out, I don't have much of a social life when I take away dance.

I fold up the stapled pages and tuck it in my jacket pocket. Then I head for the true prize.

It sits on the bookcase, slightly pulled out like he's recently looked at it. The photo album he practically begged me not to touch.

This is how I strike back and get Greyson to abandon me once and for all.

I almost feel guilty zipping my jacket around it, keeping it hidden and protected from the elements. It could've gone in my bag, still looped over my shoulder, or I could've kept it tucked in my arms. But part of me wants to treat it as well as Greyson has.

The book is thin and easy to conceal. I can examine it later, but for now I just hurry back to the street. My skin prickles, and I glance around. The street is dark, with illuminated circles from the spread-apart street lamps.

I can't pinpoint why I feel the hair raise on the back of

my neck, so I bolt. I shouldn't run—I'm still trying to get my leg back into better condition, after all—but I can't stop myself. I fly along the sidewalk for a block, then another. The book rubs against my skin. My bag bangs my hip with every step.

Finally, I slow and take a breath.

Back safe in my apartment, I pull it out. Leather-bound, with *Devereux* stamped into it. I want to know more about where it came from and who chose the photos that fill it. I only saw a few, and I have the urge to scan the rest of them.

I can't.

I search the apartment for a hiding place and eventually find one.

Once it's safe, I go back out. To the studio.

To dance my adrenaline away... and prepare for Greyson's next move.

38
GREYSON

Violet, Violet, Violet.

I can smell her sweet, floral scent in my room, like she rubbed herself along my walls, my sheets. There's no imprint. No sign of her at all except for the smell. Something I don't think I could concoct in my imagination.

I sit on my bed and inhale again, not wanting to exhale.

My father calls me. I consider sending it to voicemail, but the last time I did that, he showed up at my game.

Him. At a game.

I haven't seen him witness me play in years, let alone speak to me after the fact. It probably has something to do with our clashing reputations. Can a beloved senator really have a bloodthirsty hockey player for a son?

Since our next game is at home, I don't want to risk that. Coach Roake acted like he walked on water, and I was once again reminded of the complex power my father holds. It goes far beyond his domain of New York.

I don't know if there's a place his influence can't reach.

"Hey, Dad."

"Greyson," he greets me. Brisk and businesslike, even though it's nine o'clock at night. "How was practice?"

"Good." It's a reflex to answer that way. I was distracted, so... not so good.

"Really? Because I got a call tonight, informing me that my son was almost thrown off the ice."

Oh, that. Well, Erik should really keep his fucking trap shut when it comes to Violet. He made some passing comment about her, and I went off the deep end. I'm sure as hell not admitting that to my father, though.

"If it's team trouble, you need to clear that up by the weekend."

Obviously. "We got it sorted," I lie.

Unlike Violet, I actually know how to lie. Well enough to trick my father to his face? Probably not. But the phone is a barrier that makes it easier to pull the wool over his eyes. What he doesn't know won't hurt him.

"That Reece girl is leaving you alone?"

I cringe and almost drop my phone. "Um..."

"I haven't seen the merit of hockey," he continues. "But I have several donors who are following your game closely. We're planning on attending the tournament finals in April —so your team better be there. Roake mentioned that some teams have been scouting you?"

I'm suffering from a case of mental whiplash. From Violet to donors to scouts.

"Yes. A few have come to speak with Coach and me after the games."

He hums. "Good, good."

"Why did you ask about Violet?"

He hesitates.

I stand suddenly, my stomach twisting. Violet. Donors. Scouts. "What did you do, Dad?"

"I'm not talking about this." He harrumphs. "You focus on playing well for Crown Point University, son, because the real world will kick you in the nutsac if you're not ready for it."

Great imagery. "I'm ready."

"Prove it by *focusing* on what's important." He pauses. "Hockey. Your grades. That's it."

He did something. I can feel it in my gut—but he's not going to fess up to it.

"Oh, and Greyson?"

I stop myself from hanging up on him.

"You'll be home next week. Spring break. We're cele-brating." He sounds... pleased with himself. "I'll send a car."

A car to take me on a five-hour drive back to my home-town of Rose Hill. Me and a driver and nothing but awkward silence—and music, if we're lucky. Sometimes they play shitty stuff, or my headphones get stowed in the trunk by accident.

I find myself nodding, wondering what I can do to get out of it. I don't need to go home—it isn't like I live in a dorm that's closing. CPU actually doesn't offer *that* much on-campus housing. I'd bet most of the students will be sticking around for the week-long break.

"Sounds great," I agree, mainly to not suffer an argu-ment. Another one. My gaze swings over my bookcase... and the hole in the neat row of spines. My heart stops. "I've got to go," I manage. "Homework."

"Get to it." The line goes dead before I can hang up. If there's one thing my father is skilled at, it's having the last word.

But that doesn't matter.

I stand and cross to the shelves, running my fingers over

the spines. Books I personally stacked. One in the center leans across a gap, resting on its neighbor.

A missing piece.

And there's only one thing that's worth going missing.

Nausea snakes through me.

I smelled her. I knew she was in here. I knew and I didn't think to inspect every inch of it. I was distracted. But now I'm not. Now I know she was here for one thing, and one thing only: to steal the last memorabilia from my mother.

Dad eradicated her from our lives when she left.

And then she died a year later, alone in a hospital room. She didn't want to tell him about the cancer. And in turn, I never got to say goodbye.

By the time we found out—by the time her family clued us in—she had been dead a week.

We missed the tiny funeral out on Long Island. They spread her ashes into the Atlantic Ocean from a small fishing boat. Dad had already removed evidence of her from his house. He took down the pictures that hung on the wall, donated or tossed the clothes and jewelry she left behind. Without her physically being here. And then she was just... gone. Like she had never even existed at all.

So the photos in that book are the last pieces of her.

Without them, I fear I'll forget her face. Her voice is already a distant memory. Her smile, her fake-serious expression when she caught me doing something I shouldn't, and she was doing her best not to burst into giggles... those stick. Her laugh, too. I hope I never forget them.

I slide my feet back into my shoes and grab my keys. I blow by Knox and Miles and storm outside. I should be tired. Physically. But the photo album missing has given me a second wind, and I pull up my app to find Violet.

Last time I had her phone, I gave myself access to her location.

Good thing, too, because she's not at home. At this hour?

Not on campus either.

I zoom in, but I'm not too familiar with where she is. I don't really give a fuck, though. It doesn't matter where she is—she's going to give me that photo album back. Immediately.

It's close enough to walk, so I do. And I find myself outside an old brick building, her little blue dot on the map showing me that she's still here. The front door, which opens onto a long, narrow hall, is unlocked. I step inside and keep my weight evenly distributed. I move silently. The first door I come to reveals what seems to be a dance studio. It's dark, but the light from the hallway shows the bars along the wall and one full wall of mirrors. There's a piano in the corner, too.

I bypass it for the next.

Light and music spill out of the third and final one.

I stop just shy of it and peer into the opening. Piano music fills the room, and there she is, at the center. Only one row of fluorescent lighting is on, casting the edges of the room in shadow. She wears pointe shoes—I'm pretty sure anyway—and is balanced on one leg, pointed straight into the floor. Impossibly streamlined. Her other is bent, and she spins gracefully around.

Then she bends forward at the waist, and her bent leg comes up behind her. She's still balancing on her toe but comes down slowly. She folds out of that pose and flows into another one. Her gaze is locked on herself in the mirror.

She wears athletic shorts and a cropped top, and it

paints every muscle in sharp relief. The harsh lights and shadows help give her a dangerously fragile appearance. Like that of a bird about to take flight.

The music pauses and loops, the piece beginning again.

Violet seamlessly moves into a dance, and I don't know if she's making it up as she goes or if this is a piece of old choreography that she's clinging on to... either way, I'm ensnared.

Which is the last thing I want to be.

When I blink, I see her in the car again. Broken and bleeding.

Then I blink again, and I see the arc of the crowbar coming down on Jack's knee.

Again, and Violet is up against a tree.

Again, and she's in my car, blood welling up on her thigh.

I shake my head to dislodge those images.

The violence I crave versus the woman dancing before me.

"I see you," she says. Her head whips around with each spin, up on her toe. She turns breathtakingly fast, but she doesn't lose balance.

Not until I step into the room.

Then she falters.

"Afraid?"

She narrows her eyes. "No."

The music loops again.

"What's playing?"

"It's the 'Moonlight Sonata.' The first movement." She tilts her head. "How did you find me?"

I tap my chin, pretending to think while I step closer. I circle to her right, away from the mirrors. She turns, keeping me in her sights. Smart girl, to think that she's in danger right now. I want her against the mirrors, I want her on the floor. I want to rip through the thin fabric of her shorts and make her walk home half-naked.

I want her humiliation and I want her pain.

But most of all, I want to know where my photo album is.

"You took something from me," I say.

She smiles.

Smiles.

Goddamn, she's beautiful.

"I know."

I narrow my eyes. "I suppose you would."

She sinks gracefully to the floor and begins to undo the ribbons around her ankles. "Whatever you want to do to me... I may as well take these off. They're too expensive for you to ruin."

"But your body isn't?" I focus in on her, my lips curling.

Yes, something in the back of my mind hisses. *Ruin her for anyone else.*

"My body will heal." She meets my eyes. "Unless you're planning on breaking me again."

I smile, too. I can't help it. "When I break you, it won't be your leg. Or your ribs. Or your vocal cords. It's your mind I'm after, Violet. Your mind and your soul, because that black heart that beats behind your ribcage? That already belongs to *me*."

I thump my chest.

She starts and rises, newly barefoot. Still graceful, even afraid.

Oh, the adrenaline. Another shot, better than a drug, flows through me. I inhale. She smells the same, floral and sweet, with an undercurrent of sweat. When I catch her, I'll lick it from between her breasts. Between her legs, too.

There's no part of her that's safe from me.

And she knows it, judging from the way she's suddenly trembling.

I raise my eyebrow. "What are you waiting for, Violet? You know this game."

Still, she waits.

For me to give the order? For me to announce which version of the game we're playing?

The one with no safe words. No protection.

It's about time we stripped away those barriers.

I lean against the mirrors and fold my arms over my chest. She's breathing hard, although I'm not sure if she realizes it. Her chest rises and falls rapidly. It's an elixir I didn't know I needed, so I open my mouth and give the only order she'll listen to.

"Run."

There must be something about this time that makes her believe it'll be different, because she doesn't hesitate. She leaves everything behind—her precious pointe shoes, her phone and bag in the corner.

She bolts out the door, and I count to five in my head. I pull my sweatshirt off and drop it to the floor next to her shoes. I crack my neck and roll my shoulders back, taking a deep breath.

Then I chase.

The door to the street is just closing when I hit it. It slams open, loud in the quiet night. I spot her on the sidewalk, booking it away from me, but the noise makes her flinch. I break into a run after her.

I'm faster.

It won't be long before I catch her, unless I toy with my food before I devour her...

She must step on a stone, because she suddenly stumbles. I purposefully slow, letting her feel my hand graze her back. If I had wanted to stop her, I could've. But she lets out a frightened yelp and puts on a burst of speed.

She knows this chase is different.

Last time, she went toward the woods. She wanted to be concealed when I fucked her. This time... this time, I'm not going to take her where I catch her. As much as I want to, I'm not going to ruin this experience for us.

We're at the edge of the neighborhood when I run out of patience. The cat-and-mouse game can only last so long, and I've already suffered through Coach's practice. My hair is still damp from my shower at the stadium.

She's been yards ahead of me, but now it's feet. Then inches.

I don't want to tackle her, so I grab her hair instead. I wind the soft strands through my fingers and guide her into a slower run, easing her back toward me.

She whirls around and shoves me—more fight that I would've expected, sure, but I'm delighted at the turn of events. Doesn't matter what she does, though. If she claws at me, if she goes for my face. I've got one focus: her pretty little throat.

I wrap both hands around it, ignoring the way she pushes and grabs at my wrists. I pull her close to me and squeeze. Not her airway but her pulse. I want to feel it slow under my fingers. I want to know the moment she loses consciousness. We're just outside one of the streetlights. I'm in shadow to her, backlit, but her angel face is crystal clear.

Her mouth opens and closes. Maybe she's trying to tell me that she's done, that I'm pushing too far. There's no stopping this. There's no stopping *me*.

Her fingers slip from my wrists, and her eyes roll back. She goes limp, and I quickly capture her falling body.

She's right: this isn't like before. I'm not going to fuck her until she comes or any such nonsense as that. We're going to get right to the point.

This is an interrogation.

39
VIOLET

"Time to wake up," Greyson says in my ear.

I open my eyes and blink rapidly, trying to make sense of where we are. Not on the sidewalk anymore, that's for sure. The air is warm, absent of a breeze. I'm sitting with my arms over my head. I tug, but they don't move. Something holds firm around my wrists.

A rattling to my right draws my attention. He stands at a wall of windows, pulling a chain to open the vertical blinds. We're in the dance studio, and the lights are off. My eyes catch on myself in the mirror, but it's hard to reconcile what I'm seeing with the truth.

I'm naked to my waist, my wrists tied to the bar just over my head. My skin pricks, goosebumps rising on my flesh. I force my attention away, back to Greyson. He still stands by the large windows, but his attention is now on me. He's got the blinds open. Moonlight streams in.

"What are you doing?" I scoot backward, until I'm as upright as I can be. My back bumps the wall, and I tilt my head back to get a better look at what's binding my hands.

It looks like he's used shoestring. I rotate my hands, trying to see if there's a way for it to come off, but I don't get far.

Greyson stops in front of me.

I pause and look up at him.

"You're not getting free." He nudges my bare foot.

I wince. I move it, bending my knees to draw my legs in close, and a streak of blood follows.

Stepped on something.

My head hurts. My throat, too, when I swallow. Like I've got blades in my vocal cords.

When he gets down on my level, right between my legs, it occurs to me that this isn't a game anymore. I don't know who crossed the line first, but we've blown past it.

I don't bother asking him to stop, to let me go. I know he won't.

So I tip my head back again, letting it rest against the wall.

He narrows his eyes. "You've lost your fear."

"Pointless, isn't it?"

"Yes." He slides his hand up my right leg, starting at my ankle. "Let's get something out of the way. You're not here for pleasure."

My mouth is dry.

"You're here because you took something from me."

It didn't take him long to notice. That's satisfying.

I chose correctly. My assessment of him proved to be accurate.

I lean forward as far as I can. My arms stretch backward, my shoulders straining. I'm flexible, but even this is pushing it.

"Okay." My voice is pitched low. "I know what this is about."

He swallows, and his gaze drops from my eyes to my

lips. He seems caught, for a moment, when I bite my lower lip.

"Tell me where it is." He's swaying closer.

It's just going to make him angrier.

He leans in, stopping shy of my lips. I've been staring at his, too, and now I meet his gaze. He's frigid. Cold enough to freeze straight through.

"You'll never fucking find it," I say. "Because I burned it to ashes."

He stops. Even his chest stops rising and falling. And then he laughs. Hard. He rocks back on his heels and throws his head back, the noise unleashing from him like he's gone mad. He swipes at tears in his eyes and finally exhales, his chuckles subsiding.

Greyson reaches for me, and I've got nowhere to go. I'm not surprised when his hand closes around my throat.

He shoves me against the wall and follows, keeping his face in mine. His breath is hot on my fevered skin, and he smirks. "You're not a good liar, sweetheart."

My heart drops. "I had you for a moment."

"And for a moment, I considered strangling you and leaving your body here."

More lies. Right?

"I'll ask you one more time," he continues. "Last chance for tonight to end... well, not *good*. But better than where it's headed."

I gulp.

"Where is it?"

I imagine the photo album. Who knew a leather-bound book of memories could cause so much trouble? And I know, if I want my life to keep on track *at all*, I'm not going to break. I can't do that to myself.

At the end of the day, I'm the only one who's going to stand up for *me*.

I took it so Greyson would finally hate me enough to leave me alone.

"Go fuck yourself, Devereux," I hiss.

His grip tightens on my throat. My oxygen is cut off, and he watches me until my face is surely beet red. My whole body is hot, burning to the touch. I stare at him, into his eyes, and I thought I would be tough. I thought I could outlast him.

I can't anymore. The need to breathe is too high. I yank at the bindings and struggle to get away from him, simply out of self-preservation.

But there's no escaping it.

Again.

Into the darkness I go.

When I wake up again, I'm in the same position, leaning mostly on the wall. My fingers are tingling and numb from being above my head for so long.

However long *that* has been.

This time, my shorts are gone, too. My legs are open wide. I shift and feel something... *in* me? It's too dark to see.

Then the object buzzes to life.

It's inside me and pressed to my clit. I gasp at the sensation, which keeps growing until it's almost violent. My back arches, and my feet scrabble at the floor for purchase.

And then I spot Greyson, across the room in the shadows, and I come.

Violently.

It doesn't turn off. I draw my legs back together, but I don't know if that makes it better or worse. Worse, probably, because my clit is throbbing under the vibrations. I scream when another orgasm is ripped from me. A wordless cry. My body quakes, and I sag back when it finally switches off.

The only sound in the room is my ragged breathing.

"Where is it?"

I don't answer.

He turns it on again, but low. Not enough to do anything except flutter inside me. I squirm, gripping the bar above my head and pulling myself up again.

"This your worst?" I ask.

He saunters across the room and flicks open a knife. It makes a little *snick* noise, and the moonlight glints across the metal. He pries my legs apart and kneels between my legs. He runs the tip of the knife down my chest, between my breasts.

Then back up, around the underside of my breast and around, spiraling closer to my nipple. Even knowing that if he could maim me in more physical ways, I'm entranced by it.

I'm horrified of my own reaction.

And the vibrator just makes it worse. Or better.

"No, Violet," he says softly. "This isn't my worst. Not by a long shot."

My breathing is coming harder. My heart has kicked it up a notch. And when he finally digs the blade into my skin, dragging it diagonally down my breast, I'm not surprised. The pain, twisting my already sensitive nerves, blends with the pleasure in my pussy.

"I've never gotten to explore this side of myself," he admits.

We're both fixated on the blood welling up on my skin.

"Deeper," I whisper.

He grunts and leans forward, licking the line. His tongue rasps against the slice, collecting my blood.

And then he gives it back to me, catching the nape of my neck and pressing his open mouth to mine. His hand gropes my breast, and his nails dig into the cut.

I come like that. With my blood on our tongues and the intoxicating mix of pain and pleasure.

He strokes himself, then grabs my hips and flips me to my knees, facing away from him. The vibrator shifts, reaching a new depth, and I arch. My only view now is of the wall in front of me. I twist my wrists to grab the bar better, supporting my torso.

"Where is it, Vi?"

He pulls my hips back toward him and palms the toy. It presses more firmly on my clit, and although the setting is still low, my body is strung tight from the multiple orgasms. My muscles ache, but I feel boneless.

I groan, bowing my head. "There's no way in hell I'm telling you. Not until you promise to be done with me."

His laugh his hollow.

And then his wet finger touches my asshole, and I go rigid.

"Has anyone fucked you here?" He presses his finger in, inching deeper.

I don't know if it feels good or not, but it's foreign. And he doesn't seem to care that helpless whimpers are coming out of my throat. He pulls it out and pushes in again, testing me.

"No?"

"No," I say on an exhale.

"Good."

His finger disappears. There's a ripping sound, and then a condom wrapper floats to the floor. "Round two is going in your pussy," he informs me. "Bare."

I swallow.

The tip of his cock rests... *there*. I try to relax, but I'm not sure I can get my muscles to cooperate. He spits on my ass, and I squeeze my eyes shut. I curl my hands around the bar, the laces cutting into my wrists. It hurts when he forces his way in. He's not gentle about it. One minute he's teasing me, touching my thighs, and then next he's got me in a tight grip and has pushed all the way in.

"I can feel the toy vibrating inside you," he tells me.

I bite my lip so hard, blood fills my mouth. I don't want to give him a single sound.

He gives me a second to adjust, then starts to move. My body is on fire. And then, weirdly enough, something flips in my brain.

It doesn't feel bad. Or like an intrusion.

I rock my hips back, and his cock slides deeper. The double penetration makes me feel too full, but it's a unique, shiver-inducing sensation.

"Give it to me," he grunts. "Tell me you like my cock in your ass."

I don't say it. Fuck that.

He reaches around me, his front pressing to my back, and tweaks my nipple. The vibrator goes to a higher level, a pulse, and he groans. He rubs my breast, scraping his nail along the cut he gave me. Fresh blood rolls down my breast and drips to the floor. He alternates between touching the cut and pinching my nipples between his fingers.

He thrusts into me harder, and I let out another whimper.

I can't come again.

But it seems he has other plans, because he doesn't let up. He circles his hips, and my eyes roll back. He pounds into me with wild abandon.

"So fucking tight." He slides his hand between my

chest, down to my abdomen, and holds it there. "You don't know what taking your last virgin hole is doing to me."

He comes with a roar, slamming into me a final time.

It's too much. *Again.*

I let go, and I think I black out as my orgasm overtakes me. My body relaxes all at once, and Greyson grabs me before I take a header into the wall. Still, my eyes close.

When my eyes open, I'm flat on my back. Somehow, we went from there to here, my wrists now untied and resting at my sides. I flex my fingers to get blood circulating in them again, and I move to sit up.

Greyson stops me. "Tell me what my father told you."

I stiffen.

He shakes his head and winds his hand to the back of my neck, helping me rise a little. "Don't fucking lie to me, Vi. What's he giving you in exchange for... avoiding me?" He narrows his eyes. "For having nothing to do with me?"

He knows.

Somehow, he knows.

Dread laces through me, and I grab his wrist. I keep it on my neck. I don't know what to feel—part of me is too exhausted to feel anything at all. But I know that I like Greyson far more than I should.

I know this last month of avoiding him has been hell.

"It's a long story," I hedge.

He sits beside me. His brows furrow. "Then tell it."

I shiver.

He pauses, then goes to get his sweatshirt. He helps me slide my arms through the sleeves, briefly touching my wrists. I put it over my head and immediately sigh. It's not cold in here, but when you're naked...

It smells like him, too.

"I went to Vermont to meet with a specialist, at the behest of Crown Point Ballet's artistic director," I start.

"Mia Germain."

"Uh-huh." I narrow my eyes. "How do you know that?"

He shrugs. "I saw your texting thread with her."

Oh, great. I should really password protect my stupid phone. Willow calls me out for being too trusting, too.

"Anyway." I shift and try to ignore the soreness in my ass. Ugh. "Dr. Michaels said my leg healed okay, and it was physically able to support my dancing, but the nerve pain was holding me back."

"Nerve pain." His gaze drops to my leg, then back up. "How long has that been going on?"

"Since the accident?" I shrug.

"You touch it sometimes. Your leg, I mean. Like it hurts. I just thought it was something that you did as a habit." He winces. "And you've been running—"

"Dr. Michaels ordered an MRI to check for stress fractures and then suggested aquatic therapy for the nerve pain," I say in a rush. "But I wouldn't have been able to afford any of it. My mom and I... I don't know what happened, really, but we don't have a relationship anymore."

Is it her fault or mine that we fell apart?

Whose responsibility is it to keep a family together?

"Vi," Greyson says.

I tap my fingers on his wrist. "Your father's secretary called when we were still in Vermont. She knew..."

"Because I mentioned Dr. Michaels." He rubs his eyes. "Goddammit, I just wanted to know if he had heard anything about the man. I didn't expect him to piece it together—especially since he knew where we were."

"She said, and I'm assuming this was coming straight

from your father, that I was a distraction for you. They had high hopes of you going to the NHL or something." I hate that they were able to twist me like that. They played me like a fiddle. "They took care of my medical bills. The MRI, the water therapy. The place just bills them every time I go."

Shame fills me.

"I don't know what to do. Because ballet is finally within reach again. My leg feels better than it has in months. But..." *You*.

He leans forward and kisses me. Hard. It reopens the nick on my lip from where I bit it earlier, but neither of us care. We're suddenly dying to get closer to each other.

I crawl into his lap, straddling him, and wrap my arms around his neck. We're chest to chest. It's not even a surprise when his cock slides into me again. I rise on my knees and lower myself slightly. My groan gets lost in his mouth.

He pulls away a bit, still flexing his hips up to meet me. "That's it? That's how they're bribing you?"

"That's it," I confirm. "But it feels like a whole lot."

"Violet, I have a trust fund. I've had access to it since I turned twenty-one three months ago." He cups my cheeks. "My father can fuck off. If you need someone to cover that therapy, *I* will."

I shake my head. "I won't ask you to do that—"

"You're not asking." He thrusts into me harder, then brings my face down to him. He plants a kiss on the corner of my lips and sweeps across to my ear. "I'm fucking telling you, Vi. It's you and me. Only us. I'm not letting anyone or anything come between us again. You can count on that."

"Only us," I repeat, clutching him tighter. "Okay."

40

GREYSON

Violet comes home with me.

I don't ask about the photo album—she doesn't seem to believe that I'm serious, and I don't blame her for that. She'll hold on to it until she feels safe again. And for now, I'm okay with that. After her terrible lie about burning it. She was right. For a split second, I believed her. Then my common sense kicked in... and I was able to piece together her intentions.

Everything I told her was the truth. The last month was my most frustrating—and hockey was my outlet. Now I'm flying high on adrenaline and *her*. The smell of her. The taste of her. She lies on her side, her head on my shoulder. She's curled around me, our legs tangled, and I feel... content.

There's another shoe waiting to drop, though.

Secrets I don't think she knows.

She seemed naïve about my father paying her medical bills, because that offer didn't come out of left field.

It's been tried—with great success.

I force my eyes closed. Six months ago, we were

different people. She was hurt, I was angry. Okay, she's still injured and I'm still pissed, but it was *new* to us. We didn't yet know how to live with it. I'd always felt the rage, but what proceeded to happen with her, the media... it turned it into an uncontrolled inferno.

The added complications stemmed from our families.

Would everything be different if it were just her and me?

Yes—I would be rotting in prison. Probably. I don't actually know what they would've charged me with, and I don't know how much time I would've served. Those are mysteries I hope to never know.

Her breathing is even, and it doesn't change when my eyes open and I slowly reach for my phone.

I've got the old article saved.

The one that "broke" the story of me driving drunk, and how easily it was swept under the rug. They included a picture of me leaving the police precinct with a ball cap pulled low, obscuring my face. One of Dad's bodyguards was guiding me toward the car.

My father was fighting to pass a bill, and he was constantly in the news. That's why the paparazzi were at the restaurant that night. They were probably tipped off that a Devereux—the name on the reservation—was dining that evening, and they showed up to find me.

I didn't used to be a heavy hitter in the paper. I didn't sell copies like Dad.

Still don't, if we're being perfectly clear. There are a lot bigger fish to fry in Rose Hill.

There was also a photo of Violet. They didn't give her much print space. She was used more to invoke anger toward the Devereux name. They said her career as a prima ballerina was ripped away. I find that paragraph and read it again.

Violet Reece, a rising star in the ballet scene, had a promising career as a prima ballerina. Unfortunately, she'll never get the chance to dance again. Mr. Devereux's careless driving has ripped that away from her—and he won't face any consequences for his actions.

Something gives in my chest. A sort of pressure releasing.

Well, she *will* have her career.

We're going to make sure that happens.

The first time I read it, I was pissed. It appeared in physical print. Dad tried to squash it, but there wasn't much he could do after it caught fire. Online media outlets picked it up and ran with it, and all eyes were on me.

And then... it fizzled. Like all things eventually do.

Once that happened, it was easy to get it removed from searches and from people's memories. There's always something new and flashy that comes along and diverts attention.

I've reread it a few times since, if only to remind myself of what can happen if I'm not careful.

But then my eye catches on the second to last paragraph, and I pause.

Though the world will soon forget Greyson Devereux's role as the antagonist of Ms. Reece's life, she has supporters who won't. The ballet community stands behind her.

No shit.

I squint at the screen and contemplate jostling her awake. She seems peaceful, though. And it's late.

Hunches and theories can wait until the morning.

My mind spins, though. Does she have supporters who

would bring my past out of the woodwork? Does she have superfans who would... do anything for her?

And how mad would they be that she's with me?

I hug her tighter to my side.

I'm worrying for nothing... or so I hope.

41

VIOLET

Something is wrong. I reach for Grey—he's reverted back to that in my mind, seemingly overnight—but his side of the bed is cold. There's a dent in his pillow where his head was, but he's gone.

Instead of just assuming he went to the bathroom, I sit up. My stomach somersaults. I grab one of his t-shirts and slide his sweatpants over my hips, because if I'm going searching for him, I sure as hell don't want to run into one of his roommates half-naked.

So... dressing in his clothes seemed like the better option.

I quickly scrub at my teeth with my finger and tooth-paste in the hall bathroom, then follow the sounds to the kitchen. I pause on the last step and try to hear what two voices are saying.

"I think she has a stalker," Greyson says.

My eyebrows shoot up.

"Maybe you're blowing this a little out of proportion." Knox, I'd guess. Maybe Miles.

The two brothers have similar tones.

"I'm not. Look."

I really wish I knew what he was showing *him* and not *me*. Especially if I'm the one with a stalker? Really? It's ridiculous.

I stride into the kitchen. "The only one stalking me is you," I inform him.

Grey's gaze lands on me. He meets my eyes, then sweeps down my body. Back up.

Miles leans on the kitchen counter, arms crossed. His attention bounces between the two of us. "Kissed and made up, then?"

I smile tightly and don't answer.

"Yep," Grey says. "Can you give us a minute?"

Miles rolls his eyes. He grabs the mug that sat next to his elbow and shuffles out of the room. I step aside to let him pass, still feeling that weird, *off* sensation. It's not him, but it's... maybe it's being here. In this house.

"A stalker?" I question.

He comes to me and takes my hands, easily pulling me into him. My arms automatically wrap around his waist, and he hugs me tightly. I rest my head on his chest. His heart is going crazy, but outwardly he seems calm. His lips touch the top of my head.

"I've realized something," he says in my hair.

"Please, do share."

"We're on the same side."

Oh.

Oh.

I pull back and meet his gaze again. He seems one hundred percent serious, and I... I don't know what to do with that. He just *decided* that we're on the same side? After the last few months of hell...

"Vi, listen." He walks me over to the counter and lifts

me so I'm sitting on it. He pours me a cup of coffee and adds a pretty decent amount of hazelnut creamer from the fridge. Just the way I like it. When he brings it back and curls my fingers around the mug, he just smiles. "I pay attention."

"And that's how you've deduced that I have a stalker who isn't you."

"Yep." He inclines his chin. "But let's be honest with each other. For real."

I swallow at the lump in my throat. "Okay," I whisper.

"I'm going to tell my father to fuck off the first chance I get." His palms land on my thighs, spreading them to step even closer. "I'll take care of the therapy. It's... it's the least I can do for you."

My eyes are fucking burning. I set aside the coffee and grip his neck with both hands. I don't know how to convey my gratitude... and shame that he has to offer in the first place.

"You're going to tell me everything that happened around the accident," he says. "The hospital, who visited you, the doctors—all of it."

And then he'll know about his father coming and forcing me to sign the NDA. It was right after that article came out. I wanted to sue the Devereuxes for personal injury, since Greyson was allowed to walk away so easily. Instead, I was threatened with a countersuit for defamation.

The senator would've wanted a whole lot more money than my mom or I had. It could've bankrupted us. But instead, he offered me a nice little deal... sign an NDA, drop the suit, and everyone will go their separate ways.

Needless to say, I dropped it and signed the nondisclosure agreement.

Grey knows I signed one, obviously. He's held that over my head since I got to school. But does he realize how far his father went?

He's tracing a pattern on my leg, and I realize I haven't given him an answer. I should tell him to clear the air. I should just tell him in general, even if he already knows.

"I will," I say on a sigh. "But I'd like to hear your stalker theory first."

Diverting. Again.

He nods. "Right. I saved this."

He pulls out his phone and brings something up on the screen. I peer over it, upside down, and catch the all-too-familiar headline that haunted us for months. He swipes, and I realize they must be screenshots.

Smart.

He gets to the end and turns the phone around. I scan the page, and my eyes catch on the second to last paragraph. When I was hurt and angry and scared, I read those words and thought it was a blessing. I also thought, *YES, he took away my career. Someone else gives a shit.* But now, with suspicion—and a heavy dose of reality—it's chilling.

Though the world will soon forget Greyson Devereux's role as the antagonist of Ms. Reece's life, she has supporters who won't. The ballet community stands behind her.

"Who are these so-called supporters who won't forget what you did?" I look up. "I was dancing in Crown Point when I got injured. It was a fluke that I was in Rose Hill at all."

He presses his lips together.

I've connected the dots, though. It means whoever is angry enough about this—whoever *was*, I should say—is in Crown Point. They have to be. Maybe not one of the dancers, because we're cutthroat about roles. But in the community maybe?

And how did they hear about my accident that happened hours away?

"CPB is ruthless," I whisper. "If this person was in it, they'd know my spot would've been filled in a minute. Mia sought me out because she's known me forever and cares about me. That's the only reason I'm coming back."

I cover my mouth with my hand.

Obviously, it isn't Mia. She's the artistic director with far too much to lose—and my injury doesn't significantly impact her *or* the company.

But... is she tied to it?

Could she know who wrote that?

"That article is six months old," Grey points out. He gently pulls my hand from my face. "Maybe I'm wrong—"

"Someone broke into my room," I blurt out.

He gives me a weird look. "I know."

"Before that." My face heats. "They trashed my room. I had a wall of photos, and they wrote *whore* across it in paint. Everything was destroyed."

He freezes. I see the moment it sinks in, because it hits me, too.

This is happening. What started as a simple break-in and the feeling of being watched—that I blamed on Greyson— seems to be exploding.

He pulls me down from the counter. "You and Willow aren't safe in that apartment," he declares. He taps a message on his phone, then stows it. "You're going to get your things. Right now."

"And...?"

"And move in with me."

I shake my head. "Absolutely not."

Is he nuts? We literally *just* made up, and it was rather violent. I've still got bruises in a ring around my neck. The cut on my breast is scabbing over slightly. There are more bruises on my wrists, too, from the laces he used to tie me up.

There's still *evidence* of our anger and hatred clashing together—and my body has suffered the consequences.

His phone chimes, and I peek over his shoulder again.

Knox: On it.

"What is he on?" I ask, suspicious.

He just smiles. "Don't worry, Vi. You and Willow can still be roommates."

I shake my head and stride away from him. "I need a shower. And my own clothes before class."

This can't be happening.

All of it.

Any of it.

I go back into his room and find my bag on his desk. He tossed it there haphazardly last night, not bothered when it knocked everything askew. I rummage through it for the first time. My pointe shoes are there, the ribbons carefully wrapped so they don't get tangled. I certainly didn't do it, and a warm, gooey feeling swims through me.

Who are we?

We should be enemies.

We were, until he decided that we weren't.

I think, in a way, he knew the outcome of last night before he even arrived at the dance studio. As much as he rolls with the punches—sometimes literally—he's better when he has a plan. Like in hockey, there are plays. A rule book. Sometimes they go off-script, but he shines when he knows where to put his feet.

That's my interpretation anyway.

His father must've given himself away.

Somehow.

I don't have many clothes. He stashed my underwear in here, too. I grab them and my jeans. In his closet, I find a folded towel and take it with me.

Hopefully there's shampoo and conditioner in the bathroom—but part of me doesn't want to count on it. Guys can be heathens about taking care of their skin and hair.

I lock the door and immediately flip on the water to hot. There *is* a small bottle of conditioner under the sink, and I silently cheer at whoever slept with a smart girl. I strip out of Greyson's clothes and step under the blast.

A minute or several later, the door opens and closes. My eyes, which had been closed as I massaged shampoo through my hair, fly open.

Then the curtain pulls back, and Grey steps in with me. Naked, of course. His abs are out of this world. I reach out and touch them before I can stop myself, then let my hand fall away. His cock is hard, bobbing between us.

He's beautiful, and I kind of hate it. His beauty is what lets him get away with almost everything. Maybe *anything*.

He smirks. "You think a lock can stop me?"

I roll my eyes.

He motions for me to turn around. I do carefully, giving him my back. Water pounds into my chest. His fingers massaging my temples is too good. I lean into his hands. He lets it go on for another few minutes—probably longer than my hair needs—then gently turns me around. I face him again and keep eye contact as I step back under the water.

Once the soap is out, we trade places. I squirt conditioner into my palm and run it through the strands. He grabs the shampoo and does his own hair, until I stop him. I let out a tsk and inch closer.

We're doing this.

I reach up and slide my hands into his hair. He watches me carefully. I drag my nails lightly against his scalp, and he hums.

"I might get used to this," he murmurs.

"Don't."

"Why not?"

"I like to shower alone," I retort. I'm already getting cold from being out of the water. Jack was a water hog. I put a quick end to showering with him.

"You thinking about another guy when I'm right here?" His eyes are dark.

"No," I lie.

He scoffs and tips his head back, rinsing it without comment.

For a moment, I think that's the end of it. He'll get pissed and leave—which should've been my end goal.

But then he guides me back under the hot spray. He reaches over me and turns the shower head, aiming it at the wall. His hands slide down my sides, over my hips, my ass. Then he lifts me without warning, slamming me against the now-warm tile.

He thinks of everything.

I wrap my legs around his hips.

"You think of anyone else other than me, and I've got no choice but to eradicate them." He raises an eyebrow. "Best decision I made was blocking Jack's number from your phone."

I stare at him. "Are you—"

He thrusts inside me, cutting off my ability to speak. "Am I possessive?" He ducks forward and kisses my throat.

"Am I not going to let anything—or anyone—come between us?" His teeth graze my skin, followed by his tongue. "Am I *serious*?"

I tilt my head, giving him more access. "Any of those."

"The answer is yes." He runs his nose up my throat. "To all of the above."

I snort. "Of course I'm dating a psychopath."

He goes still.

Hell, *I* go still. Open mouth, insert foot. "We, um, I didn't mean—"

"Dating is a bit casual," he finally says.

"Casual? Dating is a big step." My muscles automatically clench around his cock, still buried inside me.

He smirks. "Let's see... You're never getting away from me. What do we call that? Certainly not *dating*." His hand cups my jaw, then slides down. Over my breast, down my stomach. He pauses there. "You're on birth control."

My jaw drops. "You're just now thinking about that?"

He shrugs. "I saw the pills in your bathroom once. But I'm not worried."

"Why not?"

"If you get pregnant, that's just another thing keeping us together."

I shove him—it doesn't do much, but it's the thought that counts. "If I get pregnant, my dance career goes up in flames. So, no thanks."

He chuckles. "Okay, okay. Not now, but someday."

I eye him. Maybe not. He can't win *every* argument.

"Now..." He resumes moving, sliding out of me almost all the way then thrusting back in. His hand is on my ass, going between my cheeks. His finger pushes into my back entrance.

I gasp.

"Did you like last night, Violent?" He kisses my throat. "Did you like coming with me and a toy inside you?"

He pushes his finger deeper, and I squirm against him.

"One day I'll let you in on my biggest fantasy," he adds.

I'm panting by the time he finally picks up the pace. I lean forward and kiss him again, keeping my lips on his. Somehow, I come like that. As he fucks me with his cock and finger-fucks my ass. My breasts slide against his chest.

Everything tenses as I come.

He follows a moment later, groaning and spilling into me.

He withdraws slowly, holding my hips until my toes find purchase on the wet floor. I've still got conditioner in my hair. The room is full of steam, so thick it's like a damn sauna.

The door swings open. "Hurry the fuck up," one of the guys says.

Grey growls, and the door slams before he can respond.

I rinse my hair, and he takes the opportunity to squirt bodywash into his hands. He takes his time running his sudsy hands up and down my body, touching everywhere. He cups between my legs, and I automatically widen my stance.

"Eager for more, Violent?"

I hum. So what if I am?

"I think I'm addicted to you." I slick the water out of my eyes and rotate, rinsing away the soap.

"Here's a secret." He winds his arms around me, pulling me against his chest. "I'm addicted to you, too."

42
VIOLET

Willow glowers at me. She was forcibly kidnapped from our apartment by a grumpy Knox this afternoon. I guess neither of them are thrilled with the situation that Grey and I have put them in, but they're stuck.

Grey doesn't want anything bad to happen to me, and I'm not staying here without her.

We sit on the couch. I attended all my classes, and I actually found myself paying better attention now that we've worked through our issues.

That's what I tell myself anyway.

And now, I've finished explaining everything to my best friend.

"Why hasn't this stalker made himself known?" She twitches. "I mean, I know you've felt like you were being watched, but I assumed Greyson."

"I did, too. So I brushed it off. And I thought the break-ins were related to the article. An overzealous journalist or something."

"An overzealous journalist destroying your room?" She

bites her lip, her expression twisting. "What if it's the other way around?"

"What do you mean?"

"Everyone focused on Greyson in the article. Both times, right? First, right after the accident. And then the one that came out here. But what if it wasn't so much about him but *you*?"

"That still doesn't answer why they would go to such extremes. Calling me a whore, trashing everything I own..."

She shrugs. "What happened right before that?"

"The video of me and Jack." I wince. "Worst decision ever. I don't even like blow jobs."

She snorts. "Sure."

"Okay, fine." I shift. "The video that painted me as a slut was posted—and taken down." Except, something bothers me about that. Things on the internet tend to live forever, don't they? That's what Greyson's dad's secretary said, in a sort of offhand way.

"Then that article comes out," Willow says.

"That was almost immediately after..." I exhale. "That incident."

She narrows her eyes. "Remind me which incident? There seems to be many."

"Greyson had her blow me," Steele says from behind her.

She whirls around, then makes a face at me.

"It was hot," Steele says.

I glare at him until he raises his hands in surrender. "And never to be repeated," he hastily adds. "I'll leave you girls to it..."

He disappears around the corner, and Willow gapes at me. She switches seats and plops down next to me.

"You could've told me Greyson had gone off the deep end."

"That was just the start," I whisper. "But I think I'm just as fucked up, because I enjoy what he comes up with."

She laughs. "Okay, fair enough. Match made in Heaven."

"Or Hell."

"Did he tell someone? Or Steele maybe? It could've been a tipping point."

I don't know. But now that I think about it, anyone could've seen me go into the locker room. They would've seen Steele leave, then Greyson. Then me, much less put together than when I went in.

Thinking back, I doubt I even looked around. I just got out of there as fast as I could.

"The photo they used was taken from my room," I point out.

She frowns.

"What're you guys doing?" Greyson enters the room, dropping his gym bag on the floor by the doorway. He flops on the couch on my other side.

"Creating a theory," Willow says carefully.

"Don't let me stop you." He takes my hand and kisses my knuckles.

The move is unexpectedly sweet, and butterflies flutter in my chest.

Willow sniggers when he keeps my hand. "Okay, so. Someone's been following Violet's ballet career. Enter: Greyson Devereux and the car crash." She side-eyes him. "Violet is taken to the hospital, presumably, and Greyson goes on his merry way—"

"Until he's arrested," Greyson grumbles.

"Until he's arrested," Willow agrees. "Let's say whoever

was following her career was already interested in her personal life. Maybe Violet posts something on social media about being in the hospital, or an accident. *Something.*"

"I did," I pipe up.

Greyson makes a noise of contention. "Did you delete it? I don't remember seeing it on your Instagram."

My face heats. "Actually, yeah. It was pretty negative. I think I was still coming down off the anesthesia when I posted... I was really upset."

I grab my phone and scroll through my archive of private posts. I find it relatively quickly—there are just a few that I've been annoyed with and taken off my public feed.

The picture is black and white. It's clear I took it myself. It's just of my leg, in a cast and propped up on pillows, in my hospital bed. My other leg is under the blankets.

I wrote: *I will probably never dance again. Pray for my leg. And let's not even talk about the shape my car is in...*

Greyson reads it and winces. He passes the phone to Willow, who frowns.

"Yeah, I remember that. You called me right after it." She shakes her head. "I don't know. Has anyone stood out over the years? Since you joined Crown Point Ballet?"

I shake my head.

"Continue with your theory," Greyson says to Willow.

She raises her eyebrows. "You care what I think, Devereux?"

"I'm curious about your take on it," he retorts.

Not the *best* comeback...

Still, my best friend accepts it. "Fine. Violet posts that, and whoever follows her career decided to look into it further. They find out you were responsible and were released without being charged.

"*Then*, just a few months later, you come to Crown Point and join the hockey team. You rise to infamy yet again."

He snorts. "Sure."

"Whoever leaked your story to the media obviously knows your name," she points out.

"Wait." I hold up my hands.

They both look at me.

"Who wrote the article? Those last lines felt personal, you know?"

Greyson pulls up the screenshots and shows me the name. Marcus Vindicta. The name isn't at all familiar to me.

A quick search online doesn't bring up anything else for his name either. Like, *nothing*. We search just the last name, and I immediately freeze. It's Latin for *revenge*. At least, that's what the online translation page says.

"A fake name?" I shiver. "This is getting creepy."

"Let's just assume that whoever wrote it was able to convince the editor to put it under a pen name," Willow says. "I hate assuming, but we don't have much to go off of right now. Whoever it is then witnesses Violet's return. And your... interactions."

"And they react poorly against both of us," I finish. "God, now that you put it out there..."

I've got goosebumps. And without any idea of who to trust, everyone feels like an enemy. How am I supposed to go about my business after this?

I hop up and spin to face them. "I almost forgot!"

They both wait.

"I have an audition," I blurt out. "For *Sleeping Beauty*. CPB is doing that next, and they're casting in a few weeks. It's perfect timing for me." I can't believe I forgot about it. In all the bustle of Knox and Willow moving her stuff in, and classes... Mia called me this morning to let me know I had a spot for an audition if I wanted it. Which would mean potentially re-signing with Crown Point Ballet for a year contract.

Those are a big deal. It's security. It's basically a full-time job that could launch my career. I had that—and I lost it in the snap of my fingers. Easy to go, hard to get back. So, yeah, a big fucking deal. A terrifying opportunity.

Greyson stands and cups my face. He kisses me soundly, his tongue sliding along the seam of my lips. Too soon, he pulls back slightly. "Fight for it, Vi."

Willow practically shoves him out of the way and hugs me. "I'm so fucking proud of you."

I hug her back. "Thank you."

"And you're coming to finals, right?"

"For the dance team?" I scoff. "I wouldn't miss it."

We're only halfway through the semester, and it feels like our junior year is coming to a rapid end.

Knox breezes in and freezes when he sees Willow and me embracing. "Did I miss something?"

"Nope," she says smoothly, releasing me and stepping away. "I don't suppose you have a bedroom for me to stay in, Whiteshaw? Or are you taking the couch while I take your room...?"

She strides toward the stairs.

He gapes for a moment, then gives chase.

Greyson grabs my hips and pulls me close. "Promise me something," he says in my ear.

"What?"

"That you won't do anything stupid."

I sigh. "I don't think anything I do is stupid. But, sure, if you need that promise from me..."

"I do."

I face him and loop mine around his neck. "I won't do anything stupid."

He grins. "We have a game tomorrow. Will you meet me in the locker room afterward?"

I mirror his expression. I feel... *happy*. Even with a stalker, who has yet to be found. Like everything is finally going right between Greyson and me. I tap his hand, which has slipped under the hem of my shirt to press against my bare back. His knuckles healed just fine after the last fight. No breaks, just a sprain that healed rather fast.

So I don't feel particularly bad for saying, "Only if you get your knuckles bloody."

43

GREYSON

Today's the day I get to tell my father to fuck off.

Never thought *that* would happen.

It's also game day.

There's a certain magic that happens to the school on Friday nights when the hockey team is playing at our home stadium. There's a buzz in the air that's infectious. It keeps me light all day, instead of worried. Instead of plotting the ways this could all go wrong.

Because it could go wrong in a shit ton of ways.

I don't think my father can take *away* the trust fund. Not since it's currently in my possession. I even checked with a lawyer yesterday who told me what I needed to hear. If I wanted, I could move the money into a separate account without his name on it.

That's exactly what I did.

Whether or not Dad's accountant will catch it in time to ask me about it today is another matter. This could come up on Monday, or a month from now...

Anyway. I lace up my skates and join Jacob and Erik on the ice. They're warming up, stretching their legs by doing a few laps around the outside perimeter. I come up behind them and fall in line.

We've got this morning's practice, then we're required to show up at five o'clock for a pregame warm up and check-in. We'll go over the plays, make sure all our equipment is set.

We're joined by the rest of the team, then break into different warmups. Using cones, pucks. Miles has his full pads and mask on, and he takes up his spot in the net after skating through some of the drills.

Coach Roake is standing at the half-wall with a clipboard in his hand.

"Devereux," he barks out.

I skate to him and stop just before running into the boards.

"Tell me why I'm getting a phone call from your father's office telling me to pull you from the team?" He glowers at me. "And this better be good."

"He what?" I stare at him. Does this have to do with the phone call Coach made to *him*? My muscles clench, and I struggle to contain my emotions. In all the excitement with Violet, I had forgotten the conversation with Dad the other night.

Fuck.

Now I look at my coach with a new lens... of distrust. And the last thing I want to do is lose faith in him. But maybe he's been talking to my father behind my back, reporting on me. It would certainly explain why Dad took such a dislike to Violet.

I clear my throat. "Trust me, Coach, I'd never ask him to do that. He and I haven't discussed this."

"This is the biggest fucking game of the season, so he's

nuts if he thinks I'm pulling one of my best skaters." Under his breath, he adds, "Fucking senators."

"Um... did he say anything else?"

Roake pauses. "Nothing that concerns skating. Get back out there."

So he did figure out I moved my trust fund out of the joint account. I wonder if he knows why, or if he thinks I'm trying to finally separate myself from him. It would be an accurate assumption—but he couldn't possibly understand my motivation.

I shove that thought away and get back to business.

I skate to the back of the line, gripping my stick tightly in both hands. We're doing a simple puck-control drill, navigating through a pattern of cones before shooting at the goal. There's another line on the other end of the ice doing something similar, with the replacement goalie in the net.

As soon as our short practice is over, I grab my phone from my locker and call my father.

This is ridiculous.

He answers on the fourth ring, right before I would've probably been dumped into his voicemail. "Greyson," he greets me.

"Hey, Dad. Why are you telling Coach to pull me?" May as well just get it right out there.

There's silence. Then, "What?"

"He got a phone call from you." I growl my frustration. "Said you wanted me off the team. After our conversation the other night, it seemed to have come out of the blue."

"That's bullshit." He sounds pissed. "I know what this means to you—in fact, this is exactly why I didn't want you to have any distractions. We just talked about this."

"I'll be there tonight," he adds. "I think it'll be good for the scouts to see a united family unit."

Right. Better to tell him to fuck off to his face. That was my plan all along.

"Coach wants us there early," I tell him. "So, we'll chat after?"

"Yes. I've got to go. I have an appointment." There's a click, and he's gone.

I scowl at my phone for a second, then stash it. Luckily, Coach already said he isn't going to listen to my father—so whether he was just trying to mess with me or he really didn't interfere...

Was it Violet's stalker?

I don't know how familiar Roake is with my father's voice. How much of a stretch would it be to call and say you're Senator Devereux? That type of power forces people to accept what you say, no questions asked.

I throw my helmet into my locker and swear.

Knox pokes his head around the corner. "You good?"

"Fucking peachy," I growl. "Where are the girls?"

He shrugs. "Class, probably."

I pull my phone out. Violet doesn't have class on Fridays. Her little dot on the map shows her at the large Crown Point Ballet building. It's a few blocks from the dance studio she's been using to practice.

Why would she go there?

Is she trying to find her stalker? Lure him out?

I stow my phone and clench my teeth. I'm so fucking pissed, I can't even see straight. What I should be doing is keeping calm, focusing on the game tonight. We're getting closer and closer to the finals. We can't afford to lose a single game.

Spring break starts today, technically, as well.

We'll have a week with no class.

My phone buzzes.

Vi: Party?

Me: If you want to go to one, I'd gladly get you drunk.

Vi: Apparently you don't have a choice.

Vi: There's one happening at your house tonight.

I sigh. "Erik?"

He comes around the corner, grinning like an asshole. "Yeah?"

"How many people did you invite over?"

He shrugs. "I don't know. I told Maddie and Paris to handle it."

Great. So, a fuck ton. I make a mental note to lock my door—and give Violet a key. People at parties can be weirdly invasive. They think it's okay to go into any room, touch people's stuff, fuck on their beds... no thanks.

"You've never minded," he says.

I lift one shoulder. I didn't, back when a party was a guaranteed way to get laid. Now, I don't need it to get Violet naked. It's a good excuse for it, though. And it might salvage my mood once I actually confront my father about her.

"You good?" he asks.

I nod sharply. "Never better."

"You know, no one asked me if your girlfriend could move in." He sticks his hands in his pockets. "And her roommate, too. I would've appreciated a heads-up."

Girlfriend, huh? I like the sound of that... although I'd like to call her something more permanent. I'll have to think on that.

Part of me wants to flip him off and be done with it— but he's right. It's his house, too. And we've gotten along amicably for most of the year. It really would be a shame to piss it away in the final semester.

"Yeah," I finally say. "Sorry. It's not forever."

He nods. "Yeah, man, I know."

I watch him retreat, then finish getting changed. I've got one class, then a paper that I need to work on. But I'm also itching to blow it off and make sure Violet's safe.

Me: I just heard. You good?

Vi: Yeah, just got out of a meeting with Mia. She wanted my clean bill of health from Dr. Michaels. Just had to sign a release, then got chatting with her.

I frown.

Her typing bubble pops up, then disappears. I clench my phone tightly, watching it come up again. My heart is going crazy—this stalker has my blood pressure rising.

It's stupid how much I want Violet all to myself. And maybe that's something akin to caring about her. I want her so badly, it hurts when I'm not near her. But is that possessiveness or something else? Do I want her because of everything we've been through, and everything she means, or because of *her*?

I've never loved anyone.

I don't know what it feels like or if I'm feeling it *right*. All I know is what my father has taught me. And my mother... she tried, but she taught me that sometimes even love isn't enough. She left us, and then she died.

It takes dedication on top of the love. It takes a willingness to fight to stay together.

And that's exactly what I want. I want to get so close to Violet, I inhabit her skin. I want to wear her scent on my clothes. I want to lock her away so no man ever fucking looks at her again.

Vi: Want to make a bet?

Me: You've got me intrigued, Reece.

Vi: You ever score a hat trick?

Look at her, learning all these fancy hockey terms. Have I personally scored a hat trick? Well, it was definitely easier when I was younger, up against less experienced teams. Nowadays, it's few and far between. And in the tournament? Up against a well-known team?

Me: A few times...

Vi: Do that tonight, and I'll do whatever you want... until midnight.

My cock stirs.

Fuck.

Me: And if I don't?

Vi: Well, I guess we could try celibacy...

I laugh. Loudly. I'm pretty sure I'm the last one lingering in the locker room, because no one bothers me. I shake my head at my phone.

Me: You'll pay for that.

Vi: Will I?

Saucy thing.

Me: Yes. When I win this bet, I'll fuck you on the table in front of the team.

I say it because I know she likes the thrill of being watched. Well, I don't *know*, but it's a good fucking hunch. Sure enough, she types and erases twice more. Poor Violet is flustered, and now I can't get the thought of her spread open for me out of my head.

Vi: You wouldn't...

She's curious, though. I don't respond—I'd rather just prove to her what I would or wouldn't do. After I score a hat trick—three goals—against one of the best teams in the national fucking tournament.

But for her, I'm not sure there's anything I wouldn't do.

44
VIOLET

The hairs on the back of my neck stand up.

This time, I don't brush off the sensation. I stop, my shoulders inching higher. I can't relax enough to lower them, to pretend that everything is normal. I glance down at my phone, wondering what to do. Text Greyson? Video while I rotate in a circle?

I scan the street, but I don't see anything out of the ordinary. No one obviously watching me anyway. My gaze lifts to the windows of the shops and the apartments above them. Still nothing. It's as quiet as can be expected on Friday, mid-afternoon.

Yes, there are people around. But no one pays me any attention.

After a moment, I continue on. My gait is a little faster, my stride stretching. I don't want to panic. Not yet. And once I round a corner, I'm suddenly able to breathe again.

I shake it off and continue to campus. I walk into the student center and find the spot Willow has holed up in with Amanda and Jess. They've got their textbooks and laptops open, notebooks on their laps.

"Hey," I say, sinking down into the empty chair.

"How was it?" Willow asks.

"How was what?" Amanda scoots toward me. "You holding out on us, Reece?"

I laugh. "Yeah, I guess I am. I have an audition with Crown Point Ballet in two weeks."

Her eyes widen, and her mouth drops open. She chucks her notebook to the floor and bolts to her feet. "No fucking way!"

She grabs my hands and pulls me up, hopping around me. "You're a fucking rockstar!"

"Easy, easy." I hold on to her forearms, steadying her. "It's just an audition."

"Up until recently, you never thought you'd dance again." She leans in. "It's a big deal, okay?"

"Let us celebrate with you," Willow adds. "It's the least we can do."

"We will celebrate," I allow. "At the party."

Jess perks up. "We're going?"

We've been avoiding parties at the hockey house for the last month. I didn't ask them to, but they did it out of solidarity. Willow and I weren't comfortable being around Knox and Greyson. Actually, I'm not quite sure they've made up...

"Did you make Knox sleep on the couch?" I ask Willow.

I saw him folding sheets this morning, seeming annoyed.

She smirks. "Yep."

"I wouldn't have thought you could make that man do anything he didn't want to do," Jess says, awe in her voice.

Willow shrugs. "I told him he could risk it if he trusted me..."

I wince. I see that look in her eye. She was hurt by it,

too, as much as she's putting on a brave face now. "Well, we'll get plastered and we'll forget about him," I advise.

"Perfect solution," Amanda agrees. "We're going to need it to drown out Paris and Madison."

I snort. That's the fucking truth.

"Hey, what did your mom say about the audition?" That comes from Jess, whose brows are drawing together. She has an over-the-top mother, too. The pinch of concern is warranted.

But it reminds me... "I actually need to break the news to her." I rise. "I'm going to call her now."

I step away from them, going to another quiet corner and taking out my phone. When I open her contact information, it shows me all the attempts to reach her that have gone unanswered. And again, I'm reminded that I'm just one of those things that has been left behind.

I dial her number, not hoping for much. I'll leave a voicemail. One that explains everything, so she can decide. Because I can't keep putting myself out like this, over and over, for her to ignore me.

Because it hurts. Each call that doesn't connect with her *hurts*.

"You've reached Leigh Reece," her recorded message says. "I'm not available at the moment. Please leave a message!"

She doesn't promise to get back to me, I note. Whose benefit is that for? When calls go unreturned, she can say, *I never said I'd call you back, Violet.*

"*We're sorry. The mailbox is full. Goodbye.*" There's a beep, and the line cuts out.

I stare at my phone screen for a second in disbelief.

Really?

I try again and get the same message. Has she not been

checking them? Has she not seen my voicemails building up? With no inclination to listen to them—or delete?

I call her again, the hysteria climbing my throat.

This time, it doesn't even ring. It just goes straight to that message.

Funny. I thought... I thought I'd have her if I truly needed her. Like if I was hurt and needed help, I could ask her to come back. And I thought she would. It's a lie, though. A fabrication I created to make myself feel better.

A noise rips out of me. It comes out in a screech, like nails on a chalkboard. The sound cuts my throat, but I can't stop it from bursting out. I don't know what possesses me.

"Violet," Willow says, shaking my shoulders. "Violet, *stop*."

I close my mouth.

The sound is still building behind my teeth. I press my tongue to the roof of my mouth, trying to seal it out. Agony lances through me, and if she wasn't holding on to me, I would fall to the floor. My vision swims.

"Breathe." Willow looks over her shoulder. "She's not breathing. Someone—fucking hell."

White spots dance in my eyes, and I try to focus on her —I do. I really try. But there's so much going on in my body. My skin is on fire. My lungs burn. My mind is going a thousand miles a second, racing toward the inevitable conclusion.

That my mother just doesn't. Fucking. Care.

Willow releases me and steps back. I grasp at her, but then someone else steps in.

Greyson.

A sob bursts out of me, and I fold in half in front of him. I just know, somewhere deep in my heart, that he'd come for me even when all else failed.

But he's the last one who should suffer through my public meltdown.

Maybe he feels differently, because his arm slides under my knees and behind my back. He scoops me up like I'm weightless and cradles me to his chest. My mouth is open, desperate for air, but nothing comes.

I'm not weightless. I've got a thousand pounds on my chest.

He carries me into a bathroom and sets me on the counter. He's between my knees now, holding my face in both his hands. His lips touch mine, and I don't know what to do with that. My mind shorts out.

I grip his shirt and anchor myself to him.

He kisses me through my tears and mess, pushing air into my lungs.

It isn't so much a kiss as a resuscitation.

His breath fills my chest.

I exhale in a rush, through my nose.

We repeat, and I don't have time to think. My mind stutters to a stop, just aware of his fingers splayed across my face, and his lips on mine. I tug at his shirt, inching closer. Until I can wrap my legs around his hips and fully press my torso to his.

He pulls away, just slightly, and looks me over. He swipes his thumbs under my eyes, catching tears and probably no shortage of running mascara.

"You always see me at my worst," I murmur, a lump forming in my throat again. I'm too greedy taking deep gulps of air to say more. I feel like I just starved myself of oxygen for too long. The dizziness is still there, pushing at the edges of my consciousness.

"I want to see you at your worst," he replies. "And your best. And everything in between."

I don't know how to respond.

"Tell me."

"My mother." I close my eyes.

More tears. They leak out, and he catches them with the pads of his fingers. He collects them like memorabilia, savoring them before they disappear.

"I think she's finally set me aside for good." I force myself to look at his face, to absorb his reaction. "She does that, you know. She forgets things, leaves them behind. I didn't think she'd do that to me... but I haven't talked to her in months. *Actually* talked to her."

He scowls. "Parents are overrated."

I touch his cheek. Of course he thinks that. His mom... he has happy memories of her, but she's gone. And his father is the authority in his life. The loveless, political, power-hungry authority.

My mom did love me, but my father dying changed her. It ripped her up on the inside.

How do I compete with a broken heart?

"You and me, Vi," he swears. "Okay? That's all we need."

I nod carefully. "That, and your teammates, and my friends. They're our support system, too. Deep down, I think you love them just as much as I love Willow, Jess, and Amanda."

He hesitates.

"If you didn't trust Steele, you wouldn't have had him in the locker room with you," I point out. "And if you did something to Jack, I think you would've had someone with you for that, too. Or did you fly solo?"

I hold my breath. I never got concrete confirmation that he did anything to Jack. And while I don't *want* to know what almost happened to me, I think I deserve the truth.

He sees my determination and sighs. He opens a video on his phone.

Jack is in the frame, hunched on the ground with the cliffs of the point behind him and the lake glistening in the moonlight in the distance. He's looks like he went through a battering ram. His face is bruised and bleeding. He glares at someone off camera.

Greyson watches me. "Are you sure you want to know? You just... I just found you on the floor, Vi. Maybe wait a day."

I shake my head and hit play.

"I went to her apartment after I saw the press release. I have a prescription to help me sleep. I brought some with me and crushed them up to put in her drink. It took a little while for it to hit her. I didn't even have to force her to her bedroom—she walked there on her own two feet. I was going to fuck her, and I was going to video it and send it to you."

Jack pauses.

"I've been dating Violet forever. She's been by my side for the past three years. And then you come crashing into her life, and suddenly she wants nothing to do with me."

He shuffles backwards a little.

"I fucking hate her for that. It's a betrayal. She just left me? No."

From off camera, Greyson asks, "You wanted to win her back?"

He laughs. "I fucking tried to mess with her head like you do. Especially after that video of her blowing me was posted. But instead of reacting like she does to you, she just... was done with me."

It ends. The camera goes black.

At least it sort of confirms that Greyson didn't take on Jack alone—but still, hearing those disgusting words come out of Jack's mouth is something I *wasn't* prepared for. I shudder.

"Why did you come to my apartment that night?"

He scowls and looks away. "A fucking fluke. I wanted to see up close and personal how you were handling the press release."

"Asshole," I mutter.

"You don't remember what happened that night?"

I shrug. "No. I remember Jack waiting for me when I got home, and the next thing I know, I woke up feeling like garbage. Willow and I pieced together that something happened, but..."

"I came into your room to find him..." Greyson's jaw tics, and he visibly has to wrestle himself under control. "He was about to make a choice that would've ended a lot differently for him if I had arrived five minutes later."

I shudder.

"I knocked him out, put you to bed, and took him to the point. He needed to know that touching you would have consequences."

"And you broke his knee?"

He sneers. "He got off easy."

"After hearing that? Yeah, he did."

He steals a kiss from my lips. It's quick, there and then gone, but his smile is back. "See? You're as bloodthirsty as me. Another reason why I love you."

I freeze. "Love?" I choke out.

He grimaces. "Not romantic enough? Fine. I'll tell you in other ways... tonight. After my hat trick." He puts his lips next to my ear. "I'm looking forward to seeing you naked on our kitchen table."

45
VIOLET

Here's the thing about hockey: it's fucking brutal. Fights are legal, for the most part. As in, unless it's extreme, you're not going to get kicked out of the game. Brawls are an integral part of it.

So when we take our seats in the stadium, the energy is... intense. More so than the regular season games. It thrums through my system like a cranked-up stereo is pressed to my skin. Grey gave the four of us—Willow, Jess, Amanda, and me—better seats. We're at center ice, right up at the glass. Directly to our left is the penalty box and the Hawks' bench. If I stand and lean back, I can see the broad-shouldered players.

We're in the third period, just the start of it, with eighteen minutes left on the clock. The score is two to three, with the other team in the lead. Greyson has scored once, and my heart is in my throat. Two more, and I'll be at his mercy. Until midnight anyway.

But I think I'll be at his mercy anyway.

My phone vibrates, and I glance at the screen.

Mom: We need to talk.

I scowl.

Higher above us, Senator Devereux is in attendance with an entourage. They've taken over one of the suites. I've avoided looking up there—avoided turning around in general, for fear that he'll see me and the ruse—the one where I stay away from his son—will burst.

My phone goes off again.

Mom: Violet, please. I'm outside the stadium.

She's... what?

I nudge Willow and show her the two messages.

"You've got to be kidding me." She scoffs. "No. Just pretend you didn't see them."

"Oh my god!" Amanda screeches, grabbing my arm.

Greyson has the puck, and he charges across the ice. He's a force to be reckoned with. He passes it to Knox and darts around one of the defenders. Knox passes it to Erik, who gives it right back to Grey.

He shoots and scores, and the Hawks come barreling toward him in celebration. We all jump to our feet, cheering and screaming as his teammates skate around him and clap his back.

Three to four.

He skates past and points at me. He grins, holding eye contact, and then raises his index finger up. *One more to go.*

I blush and grin back. It's hard to beat back the team spirit. The dance team embedded that in me, if nothing else. I want our school to win—to go all the way to the finals, even. And I definitely want to know what Grey is going to do to me after he makes another goal...

My phone buzzes, more insistent.

Mom's calling me now.

"I've got to take this," I say to Willow.

She grimaces. "Do you want me to go with you?"

I pause and meet her eyes. "Really?"

"Of course." She's decked out in blue and silver, just like me. We sprayed some blue glitter in our hair, and some of it has flaked off on our skin.

I'm about to tell her not to bother, that I'll be okay, when she rises.

"Not going to give you a choice," she says. "Let's go."

We slip out of the row and hurry up the steps. I make the mistake of glancing up as we're about to go through the tunnel out into the hallway. Senator Devereux stands at the glass, his gaze on me.

Fuck.

Greyson was planning on talking to him tonight.

Willow pulls me away, and I take a deep breath as soon as we're out of sight. He freaks me out more than Greyson ever did.

We exit the stadium and step onto the sidewalk. I check both ways, trying to find my mother. I finally spot her across the street, pacing in front of a sleek black car.

"Violet!" she calls. She waves her hands.

Willow and I cross the street together, but I make the last few steps alone.

Even though time has passed, she appears... the same. People always said we looked similar. Like you could see us and tell we were related. Sisters, people often said, because Mom's skin is smooth. Her hair is perfectly coifed, golden blonde. The features we share are those she can't alter with Botox. The shape of our eyes, our noses, lips. The heart-shaped face.

Where I try to keep myself lean for ballet, she has curves. Hips and an ass that used to catch all the guys' attention, her breasts—well, those are fake, at any rate. Not that anyone cares.

I don't know what I expected. New wrinkles at the corners of her eyes maybe, or streaks of gray in her hair.

Whatever I think I might see... I don't.

"What's up?" I internally cringe at the question.

She twists her hands together, then sticks them in her pockets. "What's been going on with you, Violet?"

I let out a choked laugh. "Excuse me?"

"You're not this girl." She steps closer, and her eyes dart over my shoulder. "You know the agreement we made."

"I signed the NDA. What more is there?" My skin prickles. I sense there *is* more. The senator's secretary let something slip that had me wondering—but this confirms it. "What did you do, Mom?"

She straightens. Her expression turns stony. "Come with me."

She grabs my arm and tows me back toward the stadium. I stumble along with her, glancing over my shoulder. Willow trails us, her brows drawn down in confusion.

We get inside, and she drags me up the stairs. My stomach is in knots. We go around the corner, heading for the row of suites. I have a feeling I know exactly where we're going. And yet, I can't seem to slam on the brakes.

I need to know what kind of deal with the devil she made.

This moment is inevitable. It has been inevitable since my mother pushed me to file a lawsuit. Brought in the shiny, expensive attorney who sat next to my hospital bed and took notes, took pictures. It was invasive. The whole thing made me sick to my stomach... but I did it because I trusted her.

Somewhere along the line, my trust in her broke.

Maybe it was when she dropped me off at CPU and didn't look back. Maybe it was earlier than that, when the light in her eyes dimmed when she watched me. Like *I* was the failure because my dance career shattered worse than my leg.

Either way, this distrust gnaws at me.

All the way to the senator's suite.

She pushes the door open and goes inside. No hesitation. I keep my focus on her quick, short stride. Her body is tense. She raises her hand to fiddle with her hair, then drops it before touching a strand. Her mouth is pulled into a wide, fake smile.

My muscles tremble.

Willow is stopped at the door. I don't realize it until a suited man moves in my peripheral, shutting the door with a quiet *click* right in her face.

I'm on my own.

Ahead of us and to the left are rows of chairs for viewing the game. A long table with white tablecloths is set against the right wall with a buffet-style assortment of finger foods. Behind us, against the wall, is a mini bar. So the rich don't have to travel far for their liquor.

The senator is holding a mini conference toward the front, right by the glass. He and his friends don't notice us enter. Their conversation continues, loud and boisterous. Below, the game continues. The clock ticks down. The Hawks are in the lead by one.

Something must've happened, because there's a Knight in the penalty box.

Mom pinches the inside of my arm, and I snap back to attention.

"Senator," she calls, guiding me with her.

Her arm is wrapped around mine now, and her nails are lodged in my skin. She gives me another pinch when I put up the slightest resistance. The pain is localized, but it still *hurts*.

Grey's dad turns our way. His expression shuts down.

Not good.

I can't tell if it's me or my mother who causes it, and I swallow past a thick lump in my throat. I don't like him. For six months—seven, now, actually—he's been the boogieman in my mind. The one who has the power to ruin me. Financially, socially. I have no doubt that he could make it so no ballet company gave me a contract.

He's got the reach and the incentive.

"Ms. Reece," the senator replies.

His gaze lands on me, and shame bleeds through me. I wonder if he's silently calling me out on my relationship with his son.

The son who loves you, I remind myself. I'm not sure why that's a comfort, but it is. It soothes some of the turmoil inside me.

Mom thinks he's talking to her, and she steps forward with renewed vigor. Like this warm welcome, if we can call it that, is exactly the sign she was looking for that things would work out in her favor.

Whichever way *that* is.

"James," she greets him.

I bristle.

Why the hell is she on a first-name basis with him?

His gaze goes from her to me, then to the hand wrapped around my wrist. His lips quirk, and he turns to his friends. "Could you excuse us for a moment?"

They nod and eye us curiously, but they stride away. I watch them regroup at the bar.

"Leigh." His eyebrow raises. "I thought you and I had an understanding."

"I thought so, too," she hisses.

"Ah." He smiles. "Well, it seems your daughter didn't get the memo."

"What..." I glance between them, then settle on him. "What did she do?"

He grins. His forehead doesn't wrinkle, his brows don't furrow, but his eyes gleam. Another chess piece conquered, he must think. Another family divided.

Secrets will do that.

"Honey—"

"Your mother," the senator interrupts, "has been getting paid to keep her mouth shut."

I jerk out of her grip and stagger away.

But Mom is fast. She reacts like a snake, striking out and latching onto my shoulder. She hauls me into her. "Now is not the time to cause a scene, dear."

"What did you do?" I whisper at her.

She shakes me slightly, then glances over her shoulder at the senator's friends. She forces another smile. Like all is okay.

It's not.

It's far from okay.

"Except the payments stopped, did they not?" Senator Devereux tilts his head. "It was a decent sum altogether. It's a pity that our agreement has come to an end."

Her mouth drops open. "Excuse me?"

"These articles you keep writing." He sighs and glances out toward the ice. Just a cursory glance, as if to keep up appearances. Faking his way through interest in his son's life. "It's getting tiresome, Leigh. Your desperate attempts to extort more money from my coffers."

"I have done no such thing," she snaps. "And—"

"And your daughter seems to be unable to keep away

from Greyson." He inclines his chin again, looking down his nose at us. Grey must've got his height from him. There are some other similarities, too. But even when he was at his cruelest, he didn't have *this* sneer. "My son was part of the agreement, do you remember?"

She turns to me. "Tell me that isn't true."

It's my turn to snort. "Tell me how I'm supposed to keep an agreement I wasn't part of?"

"You agreed to keep away from my son," the senator snaps. His composure is on the verge of breaking.

"Someone should've told him that," I mumble.

What happened to my mother? She had a job, she had a house and a social life. *Friends.* A husband. Me. Then her husband died, and I didn't realize how much that must've shattered her. She just couldn't keep it together anymore.

I grab her hand, pulling her back a few steps. "Come on, Mom. You don't need his money."

She laughs. Loudly. It draws the attention of the guys at the bar, and the senator shakes his head.

"She's high." He doesn't bother to lower his voice either. "She took my money and used it to buy more of those pills they gave you in the hospital. Or, perhaps you didn't realize the bottles always ran out faster than they should've?"

I flinch.

"I never took those," I whisper. I stare at her, trying to figure out if he's telling the truth. I had a bad reaction to the opioids. I couldn't eat, couldn't walk. The room was constantly spinning.

But now I'm remembering how Mom told me we could just wean me off them. That I didn't have to concern my doctor with it.

Did she keep filling a prescription for me?

Did she *take* them?

The shame in her eyes is confirmation. I stumble away from her, pushing off her attempts to keep me next to her. Her hands grasp at me.

"Stop her," the senator says on a sigh.

Someone steps in front of the door. The man who opened it for us. A bodyguard of some sort? Either way, he doesn't move for me.

Dread flushes through me, and I whirl back around. "What are you doing?"

Senator Devereux comes closer. He puts his hand on my back, steering me to the glass. His gaze lifts to the friends, pointedly ignoring us now, then back to me. "You and your mother are going to sit. Watch the last few minutes of the game. Celebrate when the Hawks claim their victory. And then we'll chat."

He shoves me down into one of the chairs. Mom comes over and practically falls into the chair beside me. She immediately slings her arm over the back of mine. She sends a glare his way, but he's already heading back toward his friends. No doubt to placate them.

I focus on the ice. On the *game*.

They're tied. It was three-two in favor of the other team when Willow and I left. Was it Greyson who scored again? Completing his hat trick? I lean forward, trying to see my friends at the glass. I see Amanda and Jess, but no Willow.

And then I try to find Greyson, but I can't seem to focus. The players skate harder. The Hawk that has the puck—Erik?—gets slammed into the wall, and the Knight takes off with it. My heart is in my throat, both at where I am and the game.

I glance behind me. The group of men have drifted back toward the windows, drinks in hand. The bodyguard at the door gives me a cold look when my attention turns his way. I whip back around.

Someone skates by, head turned out toward the crowd. *Devereux.*

My throat closes. He seems to be searching for me.

A Knight catches him off guard and crashes into him. They both hit the glass hard, and Greyson shoves at the other player. Instead of a fight, they part and go in separate directions.

The buzzer sounds.

Overtime.

I swallow. The skaters leave the ice, and the announcer gives a rundown of what's about to happen. A three-on-three sudden death. The first team to score in the next five minutes wins.

Mom leans toward me. "You have to believe that I did this in our best interests."

Our best interests? I scoff. "I don't have to believe anything."

She bites her lower lip, and she can't meet my eyes. My phone buzzes in my pocket.

Grey: Where are you?

I type a reply, but a large hand snatches my phone before I can hit send. I twist around, shocked. The bodyguard tucks my phone in his pocket, then looks pointedly down at my mother. With a quiet sigh, she pulls hers from her purse and hands it over.

This is so fucked up.

"You have to fix this," I say under my breath. "Mom. Please."

"Quiet," the guy snaps.

I face forward again.

'That's my boy," Senator Devereux says to his

colleagues. "Coach Roake made a smart move sending him out to clinch the deal."

There's a general consensus. Agreements about his son's talent, the coach, the team. I twist my fingers together. My palms are sweating. Even up here, in our glass box, I can sense the crowd's energy. Their excitement. But it doesn't touch us.

My nerves are rioting, and it takes everything in me to sit still.

Knox and Steele join Grey. Miles takes his place in front of the goal. They begin, and I hold my breath when Grey gets the puck. He's checked by a Knight and goes sprawling.

The senator grumbles. Just as quick, though, Grey is back up and charging after the puck. He wins a battle for it and takes it all the way into the Knights' territory. He flicks the puck toward the upper-left corner of the goal.

The goalie is quick to snatch it out of the air. He tosses it back to one of his teammates. And they're off again. Miles blocks one, two, three shots from their opponents.

My heart remains in my throat until there's only precious seconds left. In the end, it's Knox who scores the final goal. He fakes a shot, which the Knights goalie falls for, and then sails it easily between his open legs.

The stadium erupts. The ice is immediately swarmed with Hawks players, closing in fast on Knox and Miles. They're jumping up and down, celebrating their much-needed win. I lean forward and see the senator accepting congratulations like *he* won. He mentions something about scouts and his son getting recruited, then waves his hand toward the door.

They all leave, and his bodyguard follows. The door swings shut, and there's a heavy *snick* of a deadbolt sliding home. They've locked my mother and me in.

46

GREYSON

"Devereux," Coach calls.

I stop mid-stride and turn back toward him. I was on my way to find Violet. She disappeared partway through the third period, and she never returned to her seat.

Neither did Willow.

Knox, just behind me, makes a face. But he keeps moving toward the doors.

I sigh. On my own.

Except... *not*. Coach slaps my arm and gestures for me to follow him. We get in the elevator and ride it in silence, getting off on the publicist's floor.

He glances at me. "You've got natural charm," he says. "Use it."

I nod. I don't have time for this, but it's my future. There must be a scout looking to speak to me... and Coach is acting like it's a big fucking deal.

So I staunch my worries about Violet and follow him down the hall to the publicist's office. She's there, pouring a cup of coffee from her side table. She turns and brings it further inside and hands it to...

My father.

I grimace but quickly smother it. No need to show my disgust. Our phone call this morning was rather abrupt, and I had planned on telling him to fuck off. That was part of the plan. No, the *main* part of my plan. And then Violet and I were going to ride off into the sunset together and pretend none of this shit ever happened.

Wishful thinking.

"Ah, Greyson." Dad draws attention to me. He's standing beside a man I can only assume is an NHL scout. He wouldn't waste his time on anyone less. "Good game, son."

"Thanks," I reply, forcing a smile.

The charm came easier before I knew what sort of demons he keeps close. Still, I straighten my spine and step farther into the room with Coach Roake at my back.

"Yes, most impressive," the scout says. "Tim Monroe, with the Boston Bruins."

I almost choke. *Almost.* Not just a scout—the fucking coach of one of the best teams in the league. "Pleasure to meet you, sir."

He smirks. "A hat trick at this level? You're going to go places... but only if your record remains clear."

He eyes me, and I eye him back. He's the guy who coaches the *Bruins*. He's got a thick head of light-blond hair, smooth skin. His beard is trimmed and neat. I wonder how many other players he's personally visited...

Coach Roake nudges my foot. A subtle prod to stop being so fucking starstruck and *respond*.

"My record will be clean," I promise.

He nods. "Good." We shake hands, and then he turns to

my coach. "A word?"

The publicist looks back and forth between us and murmurs something about stepping outside. The door shuts softly behind her, leaving me alone with my father.

Dad's face contorts.

"Are you fucking new at this?" he growls.

I raise my eyebrow. "Excuse me?"

"You're supposed to be getting yourself into the NHL, and when an opportunity comes along, you clam up. Is that the man I raised you to be?"

Wow.

I guess that's how he sees it. One chance and then it might be gone forever. That's how it was for him, after all. One chance with my mother, and he had to nail her down or she would've left him before ever stepping foot in a church. That didn't matter so much in the end, though. She found a way to leave us both. One chance for his political career, snatching the opportunity that came sailing his way.

But I'm a junior. I have another year to impress scouts —and it isn't like Tim Monroe is going to recruit me *now*. If anything, he'll wait. See how I mature... and if I can keep my face out of the newspapers for reasons that don't revolve around hockey.

Then I'll face the draft.

If not him, maybe someone else will want me.

Dad sneers at me. "You're a disgrace. But you'll learn how to be a real man soon enough."

A chill sweeps down my back. "What does that mean?"

"Play the part, and I'll show you." He inclines his chin just as the two coaches step back inside.

I run my hand down my face, trying to wipe away the emotions my father always seems to inflict, and smile at them. Tim Monroe offers us some pleasantries, shakes my hand and then my father's, and departs. The publicist follows him out.

Coach Roake looks back and forth between the two of us, finally landing on my father. "Let me get one thing straight with you, Senator."

My father's eyebrow raises. I don't know the last time someone talked to him like he's done something wrong—besides me anyway. And my mother. He's become overwhelming with his power, surrounding himself with people who only ever agree with him.

"I respect your authority, but you will not tell me how to run my team. And asking me to pull my best player before one of the most important games—"

"Respectfully, Roake? I have no idea what you're talking about." Dad scowls. "I told Greyson this morning after he took a similar approach."

Coach Roake glowers at him. "Then you've got a problem, Senator, because someone called me pretending to be you."

I swallow. Could that be Violet's stalker? They would've seen with their own eyes that Violet's no longer at her apartment—she's no longer as accessible as she was. And maybe he's trying to lash out. Him, confirmed, thanks to this. Unless it was a masterful trick on the stalker's end to disguise their voice.

"A problem, indeed," my father responds. He sends a quick text message, then stows his phone back in his breast pocket. "I'll have my people look into it."

"Great." Coach glances at me and nods. "Enjoy your weekend."

I follow my father out the door, curious and somewhat sick. I'm not sure what he's planning or what he's already done. We stand in silence in the elevator and exit on the floor with the suites. I saw him watching me with his friends during the game, but I was more interested in Violet.

Violet, who has pulled a disappearing act.

Worry squirms in my stomach.

And yet, I'm not entirely surprised when we arrive at my father's suite, and the man who had been posted outside the door steps aside to reveal Violet and another woman.

Her mother?

Violet sits in the corner, her legs drawn up to her chest. And the other woman, identity to be confirmed, paces in front of the glass. On the ice, the Zamboni is making slow passes. There are still people lingering in the seats, taking their time filing out. The last dregs, it would seem.

My teammates are long gone.

At our entrance, the woman stops moving. Violet shoots to her feet.

"You're bringing him into this?" the woman spits.

My father doesn't react. He just watches her for a moment, then nods to his guard who followed him in. He's one of the newer bodyguards, unlike some of the others my father employs who have been around since I was a kid. I don't even know this one's name.

This one doesn't seem to have a moral compass, because he marches over to the woman and grips her forearm, hauling her toward us.

"It's about time he learned the family secrets, don't you think?" He shakes his head at her, then gestures to the woman. "This is Leigh Reece, Greyson. Violet's mother."

As I suspected.

When I don't react, Dad faces her. "I'll get to you in a

moment. Let's have a little chat about your daughter."

My shoulders inch higher. He better not have his guard manhandle her like he did to her mother, or I'll go fucking mental.

"Violet." There's a new chill in Dad's voice, laced with something like... disappointment?

She cringes, still sitting in the far corner. She seems so fucking small like that, and I clench every muscle in my body to stop myself from reacting. I need to know what my father is planning—and that means he has to reveal a few more cards before I can act.

He doesn't wait for her to stand. He sends his fucking guard over there with a look, and I ball my hands into fists to stop myself from reacting when he bodily lifts her out of the chair and marches her over to us. She lets out a squeak, and her gaze cuts to me.

I can stop him, she's thinking. And she's wondering what keeps me immobile two steps behind him.

When the bodyguard releases her next to her mother, she takes a quick step back. My father pins her with a glower, and she goes still.

"You and I had an agreement, young lady."

She swallows. Her throat moves, and she brings her hands in front of her. Her fingers tangle together. I hate her nerves and that she ended up here. How did she even get up here? Was she caught by my father's guard like a fish in a net... or something worse? Led here by her mother? Or perhaps she came up here simply because he asked.

But this is the confirmation I needed that he did do something. And this is the last time he's going to see Violet. I'm going to make sure of that.

My dad glances at me. "She was going to stay away from you."

How did my father turn into this?

I have so many questions, and I know I won't get the answers I want.

"Her physical therapy is expensive, and little Violet Reece hopes to be a ballerina again one day. Since you took that away from her, I assumed it wouldn't be a hardship on her to just stay away." Dad narrows his eyes at her. "But she couldn't do it, could she?"

Her mother gasps. "Physical therapy?"

"No," Violet says. Her voice is steady, her expression bland. She ignores her mother and instead tells me directly. No, she's not going to put up with this. And I can tell she's trusting me to catch her, since she's abandoning any chance of lying.

"Our agreement is null and void," he snips. He waves a hand, and that guard-turned-lackey retrieves a folder from Dad's briefcase across the room. When the pages settle into Dad's hand, he flips through it. "Four thousand, four hundred sixty-three dollars and fifty-two cents," he says slowly. "You can write a check... or I'll take cash."

He holds it out for her.

I step forward and take the folder from his hand, opening it to the first page. An invoice.

"Well, this is fascinating." I run my finger down the list of itemized charges, which of course included her therapy bills, but also include service charges, labor, and tax. It's laughable. And completely ridiculous. The labor and service charges are almost forty percent of this invoice.

Leave it to my father to try and bury her for this.

"Greyson." Dad snaps his fingers at me.

Of all things.

I can't fake my way through this anymore.

"Fuck off, Dad."

Wow. That felt better than I thought it would.

"Fuck you and your pretentious ideology, and fuck the way you think you can bully the woman in my life." I hold out my hand to Violet, and she practically leaps forward. As soon as her palm connects with mine, a weight lifts off my shoulder. I pull her into my side and wrap my arm around her shoulder.

I throw the folder down at his feet. "And fuck this inflated bullshit you have going on here," I add. "You can't just meddle in my life like this anymore. I'm done."

Silence.

My father laughs.

Laughs.

My face gets hot. My body flushes. I'm so fucking sick of him, I can barely see straight.

"Grey," Violet whispers. "It's not worth it."

I grimace... and then I notice my father's expression. He doesn't like to lose control—and he's lost control of the most important thing: *me*. And the room. Violet's mother has resumed pacing, casting glances at us like we're about to start fist fighting. She keeps gnawing at her fingernails, too. Violet's hand slips under the hem of my shirt, pressing against the small of my back. She's grounding me.

I look down at her, and my resolve hardens.

She's *mine*. Not something to be manipulated by my father. Not a pawn or a toy or leverage.

When Dad's laughter has subsided, the mirth falls from his expression. His tolerance for disobedience is low at best. Something tells me that I should've held out longer. That he still has a trump card to play.

And sure enough, he seems smug when he says, "This girl you're championing has been stealing from our family for months."

47
VIOLET

S*tealing from our family for months.*
That's why we're here, right? Because my mother's been getting paid by Senator Devereux, and she's developed a drug addiction, and it's on me. It's my fault that the payments have stopped and her way of life is disrupted.

Her flightiness makes sense now. I can fill in a million motives for her absence, for the way she hasn't returned my calls. The loneliness I felt, the *abandonment*. Maybe she's always been addicted to something, and the opioids just provided another level of escape for her. But at the end of the day, she stopped talking to me because of the drugs.

No other reason is necessary.

I haven't been stealing from the senator. That's a nice little twist on an ugly truth: that he's been giving her the cash to get high. And who knows what she moved onto after my prescription ran out. Who knows what sort of people she's been with, and in what sort of situations... drug dealers aren't exactly known to be safe people.

I hate that for her. I really do.

And the guilt follows me a second later, because now I'm left to wonder if I should've seen the signs. Could I have prevented this?

How, though? With no idea that she went behind my back to get my medical bills paid for, and then took it a step further to blackmail the Devereuxes. I thought insurance took care of my hospital expenses and that she had a job she liked.

And Grey? Does he believe this? Because right now, the senator is painting a picture for his son, and I'm the villain. I'm the leech, the gold digger. The one who wanted payback on their family and continually lashed out.

His father would like that, wouldn't he? Just to have everything neat in a bow.

Maybe I should just cut and run now.

I risk a glance at Greyson, and his arm tightens on my shoulders, as if he senses where my thoughts are going. I have a desperate need to flee, but there's a man guarding the door. My biceps ache from where he grabbed me earlier —and he still has my phone.

"Elaborate," Greyson says stiffly, unmoving.

I want to scream at him that it's not true. That this final manipulation is an effort of his father to break us apart once and for all.

Why? I haven't done anything to them.

Grey's father steps closer to him. "It was Violet's idea to file a lawsuit. She wanted to ruin us."

"I wanted my medical bills covered," I say quietly. "Because my career was over."

His upper lip curls. "And then you leaked your story to the press. But threatening a countersuit wasn't enough, was it? I'll admit, it was my mistake not to have your mother sign the nondisclosure agreement. And once I realized, it was too late."

"I was just trying to get what I was due," my mother spits. She jabs her finger at the senator. "Your boy destroyed us."

I flinch. How did I not see this? Was I that blind to her fury? Right now, she's trembling and red and the angriest I've ever seen her. Maybe she hid this from me while I was recovering, and living with her as I relearned how to walk correctly, when I was navigating around in a boot. Between now and then, though, her façade broke.

"How did it destroy you?" Grey asks. His tone is stoic. Uncaring. Not even curious. More like he's trying to poke holes in their stories, one question at a time. More will come, I'm sure.

Mom stiffens. "You took—"

"Violet's career," he interrupts. "Which we're rectifying. But you... *you* had a daughter who needed your support, and instead you extorted us for money?"

She throws her head back and cackles. I shiver. I've never seen her like this. Angry, sure, but also unhinged.

Senator Devereux raises his eyebrow at his son. "This is what you're inheriting," he says. "By cutting ties with me, I'm wiping my hands clean of this problem. You'll deal with the fallout of her threats, if they come to pass."

I snort.

All our focus comes back to me.

"Sorry, Senator, but she's your problem. Unless you'd like to explain to your voters how you funded a drug addict for the last six months?" I shake my head. "I'm sure any article that comes out about you would be national news. Right, Mom?"

My mother's eyes light up. She knows a cash cow when

she sees one—and right now, the senator is in her grip. There's nothing Senator Devereux can say to that either. He knows I'm right, but he was probably hoping we'd miss it. That would've been a solid deal, passing off two problems —my mother and me—onto his unruly son.

I take Grey's free hand and tug at it. "I think we're done here, don't you?"

"I do," he murmurs.

We leave them in silence, and I pause in front of the bodyguard. I glance at Greyson. "He has my phone."

Grey's expression darkens.

The guy lifts his hand to his breast pocket, retrieving my phone and holding it out to me. As soon as it's in my grip, I take a step back.

Grey has other ideas. He lunges at him and snaps his fist forward. His knuckles smash into the guy's face, skating across his cheekbone and nose. The guard stumbles backward, covering his face, but Greyson follows him. He fists the front of his shirt and shoves him into the wall.

"Don't you ever fucking lay a hand on her," he says in the bodyguard's face.

He holds out his hand to me again, and I take it. He squeezes twice, and we walk out the door. As soon as we're in the hall, I let out a breath. But he doesn't slow. He tows me down the stairs and around the corner, out of sight.

Good. I don't want to even *think* about seeing them again.

"Holy fucking shit," Grey breathes. He pulls me into an alcove and spins me against the wall.

My back touches the concrete, and I tip my head back.

My heart is going a million miles a minute.

"That was crazy." I run my hands up his arms. "I mean... yeah, no. Crazy is all I've got."

"I was going to go out of my mind when he put his hands on you," Grey admits. He pushes my sweater off my shoulders, his fingertips grazing my upper arms. Like he's searching for bruises or signs that he hurt me. "But I swear to you, Violet, no one is going to hurt you again."

My chest tightens, and I hold his wrists. "But..."

"Don't say I can't protect you. Because I will. God, I'm so fucking furious at my father. He locked you in his suite while he came up to schmooze, and then so casually threatened you. Absolutely fucking not."

Yeah. And it felt like an eternity, too, with my antsy mother. It felt like I was waiting on the edge of a cliff, unsure if someone was going to push me off.

"Thank you," I say. "For coming to rescue me. But... what if I want you to hurt me?" My voice drops. "What if I want you to make me scream..."

His gaze falls to my chest, which is suddenly heaving. He plays with my bra strap, then slowly pushes it down. I lean more of my weight on the wall and tug him forward by his waistband. He steps between my legs and leans down. His lips touch my collarbone, and I close my eyes. He works his way up my shoulder, the crook of my neck. He nips my neck, and I tilt my head to the side to give him better access.

His teeth skim my throat. His tongue samples me.

I'm breathless when I ask, "Kiss me, would you?"

He chuckles. "I will. But I'm too busy imagining all of the demons that live under your skin, and how I'm going to make every single one of their dreams come true. You're just as twisted as I am. Excuse me for taking a minute to compose myself... or else I'll rip your clothes off right here and show you how much I appreciate that sentiment."

I shudder. I meant what I said, though. The quiet,

terrible things I can admit to him and only him. I like when he brings out his knife. I like the little sparks of pain that prelude the pleasure and intertwine with it. I like knowing that he can—and will—take me to that edge.

I want it—and I know he wants that, too.

"You should." I tug at his pants again, then slide my hand into his waistband. I wrap my fingers around his cock. He's hard and waiting for me, and he doesn't object when I push his pants off his hips. His erection appears, and my mouth waters.

Before I can go down on my knees, he shoves my leggings down to my ankles and spreads my legs. He lifts me by my thighs, slamming my back harder against the wall. I can't wrap my legs around him like this, with my ankles essentially bound. I'm at his mercy, and his grip on my thighs makes me squirm. He takes a breath, looking between us. There's no foreplay, no waiting. He runs the tip of his cock through my wetness, as if testing, then thrusts hard into me.

I arch my back, my lips parting. He fills me completely, and I realize how much I needed this. He pauses for a moment, taking it in, until I squirm again. He pulls out slowly, then pushes back in. He hits a deep spot inside me, and stars burst in front of my eyelids.

Soon, he's increased his speed. I tighten my hold on his shoulders and let him go at a punishing pace. The only noise between us is the slap of skin and our harsh breaths. The hallway just to my left is silent, the stadium beyond us dark. I could believe that it's just us in the whole damn building.

"Touch yourself," he orders, his eyes boring into mine.

I obey without question, slipping my hand between us and rubbing quick circles on my clit. My cunt clenches around him at the sudden wave of new sensation. It isn't enough, though. I crave the connection—all of it. He wants to unchain my demons? I want to climb inside his skin and stay there forever.

What do I do when even this close isn't enough?

"Kiss me," I beg.

He finally obliges, leaning down and capturing my mouth. His tongue sweeps along my teeth, tasting every inch of me. I crave the invasion. I want him to fill me up completely, because I'm not sure I am even a person anymore. I don't know who I am or who I'm supposed to be, and part of me needs him to guide me there.

We keep up the furious pace until an orgasm crashes through me. I tense again, whimpering his name against his mouth, and it knocks him over the edge, too. He comes with his lips on mine.

He pulls out of me and lowers my feet to the floor, but immediately his hand is between my legs. He thrusts two fingers inside me, pressing his body to mine. Keeping me pinned to the wall. "I can't fucking wait for the day you have a baby in your belly," he says in my ear. "And even though you're on birth control, and you have a dance career ahead of you, I want you to picture our future every time I come inside you. Every time I push my cum back into your pussy."

Ugh. What a fucking turn-on.

"Come on," he says suddenly, pulling away from me.

I let out a groan, the loss of him sudden, and yank my pants back into place. He chuckles and offers his hand again.

"I scored a hat trick," he informs me. "And we have a party to attend."

48

VIOLET

I'm buzzing by the time we get back to Grey's house. My skin is electric. I feel like I keep lighting up where he touches me—which is everywhere. His hands are on me constantly, roaming my body. The possessiveness in him has me panting for more.

I don't let myself think about how fucked up this is.

For once, I go with what *I* want.

We maneuver together through the crowd. His hand is on the back of my neck, guiding me along with him. And telling every other guy in this place that I'm *his*.

I shiver, and he catches it. He gives me a wicked grin, and I smile back. I don't know what to do with the anticipation riding through me. It's eating me up inside.

We end up in the kitchen, where Erik mans a long row of liquor bottles. He gestures to us. "Want something special? On the house for the man of the hour."

Grey smirks. "I live here. And I chipped in for the booze, asswipe."

Erik laughs and pours him a drink. Grey takes a sip and passes it to me.

"What is it?" I peer into the cup. It's an orange-ish opaque color, and it smells sweet. I take a sip—and don't taste the familiar burn of alcohol. It's not bad, actually. "You know what? Don't tell me."

Grey laughs. "Give me tequila. Straight up."

"Yes, sir." Erik mock salutes, then grabs a bottle and gives Grey a hefty pour.

Grey knocks his red cup against mine and takes a swig. I mimic him, swallowing another mouthful of the sweet drink. He leans forward and tips up the bottom of my cup, keeping it raised until I've drunk the whole thing. Then he tosses my cup into the sink, finishes his tequila, and grins at me.

"Dancing," he says.

Heat unfurls through my chest. I don't argue when he leads me into the living room, my hand gripping his tightly. The music is louder in here, the lights dimmer. There are strands of red LED lights strung along the ceiling, casting everyone in an eerie glow. I shake out my hair. Grey spins me into him, catching me carefully at my waist. The room tilts, and I blink rapidly. It gives me a strobe light effect, slicing the dancing couples around me into still frames.

I giggle and slide my hands up his chest.

We move to the beat—it's hard not to with it pounding through us—and inch closer. He doesn't go for my lips, though. I hold the back of his neck as he lowers his lips to my throat. Every stinging bite sends more lust crashing through my bloodstream. I dig my nails into his skin when he goes lower, pushing my shirt out of the way.

He kisses my collarbone, the tops of my breasts. His hands keep me upright.

I don't fucking care that we're not alone.

He grinds his hips against mine. His erection digs into

my abdomen. I slip my hand down and cup him through his jeans. He groans and lifts his head. His fingers thread around the back of my neck, into my hair. He holds my head carefully, although his gaze is fucking heavy.

It conveys everything he wants to say—but doesn't.

Every fucking promise.

I look pointedly at my watch.

It's eleven.

Only one hour left until his prize expires.

"Patience," he mouths.

I run my nail along his skin at the top of his jeans. Just an exposed little sliver. But he shakes his head at me, silently reprimanding me. I want to drag him into the bathroom and tell him to fuck me. I want a million orgasms, and I want to see the expression on his face when *he* comes. Once wasn't enough.

I need more.

But demanding Grey to do anything has never worked in my favor.

So I bite my lower lip and let him sweep me along for the ride. Whatever he has planned.

———

We dance until my legs are numb. I drink another cupful of the juice, not caring that it's getting harder to open my eyes. The floating sensation doesn't go away.

Midnight comes and goes, but I don't think Grey has to worry. I'm still going to do whatever the fuck he wants.

What he *has* done is tease me. Repeatedly. Every dance, every shift of his thigh, which has inched between my legs and settled against my core, has me on edge. I'm a sweaty mess by the time he finally stops moving. Our dancing was erotic, bordering on dry humping, but no one cares.

And the party has filtered down to a more... intimate setting.

Maybe that's what he was waiting for.

Goosebumps prick along the backs of my arms, and I swing my head around. It's hard to focus on any one person. They're all in their own little spheres. Willow's around, dancing with someone I don't recognize. Not Knox, that's for sure.

Greyson leans down and catches my mouth, dragging my focus back to him. I relish the way his tongue sweeps into my mouth and the taste of tequila on his lips. He backs me up until my ass bumps into something, but he only lifts me and sets me on top of it.

"Do you think they know you're mine?" he asks me.

I raise my eyebrows. "Maybe you should prove it. Just in case."

He glances over his shoulder, then back to me. "Okay, baby."

Without warning, he pulls my leggings down past my knees. I gasp and grip the edge of the table, looking around the dark room. We're in our own little bubble... just like everyone else. And if we get a few glances, who cares?

Grey's finger slips under the edge of my panties and pushes into me. I arch my back, closing my eyes as he curls his finger inside me.

"Eyes on me," he orders.

I'm vaguely aware of a chair at the table being pulled away, dragged back against the wall. Someone sitting, watching. And yet, with the way Greyson leans over me, I don't think the viewer can actually *see* anything.

It's more about the feel anyway.

And right now, all I feel is *good*.

"You're drunk," he says in my ear. "Like that will protect you."

I snicker. "It was never about protecting myself."

He cocks his head. He moves his hips, and I groan at the sensation between my legs. His finger still moves, slowly pumping in and out of me.

It makes me wonder if his cum is still there, evidence of our earlier tryst.

"What's it about, then?"

"Trusting you." Simple as that. "I hope you're going to fuck me now."

"She's delirious?"

I roll my head to the side, focusing on Steele. My gaze narrows. "You like to watch, O'Brien?"

He leans forward in his seat, steepling his fingers. "Sometimes. Other times I like to participate."

My eyebrow tics up. Grey grips my chin, directing my face back to him. His fingers tighten just a bit when he leans in, placing an open-mouthed kiss on me. When he pulls back, I sway with him.

He presses down on my chin, opening my mouth wider. My tongue comes out, sweeping along my lower lip. He spits into my mouth, and I make a noise in the back of my throat. Belated shock, but mainly... turned on. By all of it.

"You're putting on a show," someone says over Greyson's shoulder.

Another hockey player.

"She's mine, and you fuckers need to know it." He looks back at me. "Aren't you, baby?"

I swallow, tasting his saliva mix with mine, and nod.

Jacob moves around his friend, leaning against the wall. Another pair of eyes on us. I run my hands up Grey's front, pushing his shirt up and exposing his chest. I lean forward and kiss his pec. My mouth moves lower, my tongue flicking his nipple, and he grabs me by the throat. He guides my head back up, straightening my spine.

I meet his mouth again, and this time when he squeezes hard enough to cut off my air, his lips are *right there*. And then his cock is slipping down, nudging my entrance. I'm ready to beg him to fuck me, but the words won't come.

The oxygen won't come either.

White spots flicker in my vision, and he releases my throat at the same time he thrusts into me.

I suck in air and grab his shoulders, trying not to slide across the table. He doesn't seem to give a shit that his friends are watching. He traces his finger down my throat when my head falls back, then kisses it. As if to soothe the marks that are undoubtedly forming on my skin.

Unnecessary but sweet.

"Fuck," I groan when he brushes my clit. He moves at an indecently slow pace, driving me mad. His finger, too. I'm panting. Putty in his hands. "Please go faster," I beg.

He smirks.

My gaze lifts, going over his shoulder. Willow's gone, which is a relief. Most of the dance team girls are. On the couch in the other room, a girl grinds on top of Miles. Erik has another pressed against the wall.

I look at Steele and Jacob, their attention fixated on us. Steele mindlessly palms his hard-on through his jeans.

"I need to get laid," Jacob says suddenly, rising. His cock is stiff against his pants, too, but he ignores it and leaves the room.

"How about it, Steele?" I whisper, my voice husky. "You need to get laid, too?"

"You're trouble, Violet," he answers. "Talking to me when your man is inside you."

My muscles clench around Grey. I pinch my knees into his hips and let my head fall back again. Grey runs his hands through my hair, scratching my scalp. I wait for him to grip it, to force me one way or another. He doesn't, though. He just lets me lean back against his hand, all the way down until my back rests on the table.

Then he moves his hands, pushing my shirt up to expose my bra. He pinches my nipples through the fabric, and I arch up into him. I'm floating again. If I close my eyes, I'll just drift away.

"If anyone touches her, I'll break your face open," Grey says to someone. "Got it?"

When I open my eyes, we're alone. The couples are still in the other room, but the chair Steele sat in is empty.

"You want to come, Vi?"

I blink at Grey and nod.

He pulls out and steps back, taking me with him. My feet touch the floor, and he immediately spins me around. He nudges my legs wider and thrusts inside me from behind. His grip tightens on my throat for a moment, stealing my breath, until the fight comes back into me. I like being manhandled—but I think I like to fight more.

And maybe that's the only way he'll let me come.

I claw at his hand, shoving myself backward. He lets me take a gulp of air just as more white spots flicker in my peripheral vision. The room is swimming, alcohol dulling my senses—and my timing. If he really wanted to hurt me, he could. Easily.

He pins me facedown on the table, and I gasp when my face hits the wood. I grip the edge of the table and push back, meeting every fucking thrust. He's picked up his pace, and our skin slaps together.

"You know what keeps me up at night?" he asks in my ear.

I don't answer.

"The thought of your cunt pulsing with the need to come. And you, lying in bed, tortured by it but unable to take yourself there." He groans, and his pace quickens. "Because I think you like to be told what to do. And if I say you can't fucking touch yourself, you won't."

Shame burns through me that he's absolutely right.

He chuckles. His breath fans along my neck, raising goosebumps in its wake. "Be a good girl and answer the goddamn question out loud."

"You're right." I whimper.

His hand slips around my leg. He rubs my clit in rough circles, and I can't tell if I fucking hate him or love the sensation. It's different.

He's letting his demons out. Showing me that I can bare mine, too. He works me right up to the edge, and then he goes still inside me. His fingers stop moving, too. He just lightly presses on my clit, capturing the trembling that racks through me.

His forehead touches my shoulder, and he comes harshly. His breath hits my skin, raising goosebumps. I'm stuck where I am, my fingers frozen around the table. My cunt clenches around him, but what he gave me isn't enough to give me relief.

"When I do finally let you come, it'll be the best orgasm you've ever had." He pulls out and immediately pulls my leggings back up over my ass. "But until then... enjoy every sensation like it's your last."

Well, fuck me sideways.

49

GREYSON

I wake up to Violet grinding on me in her sleep.

At least, I think she's asleep. Her eyes are closed, her leg thrown over mine, but her hips rock into my thigh. Her lips are parted, her hair all askew.

Naughty girl.

I twist toward her and gently push her shoulders until she's flat on her back. Her face twists at the loss of contact, and I smile. She's feeling the effects of not coming. I pushed her to the edge again... and again... and again. It wasn't planned. I *was* going to give her the best orgasm of her life —as I told her—last night.

But something twisted.

Nothing she did. It was me. The perverse side of *me* that enjoyed her trying to make me get her off. Like she's got a choice in the matter.

I part her legs and scoot down, resting between her thighs. Her cunt is a beauty. She trims with deadly accuracy. She smells intoxicating. I lean into her and inhale, then flick my tongue out. Just a little taste.

She shudders, and I slide my arms under her thighs. I lift her ass slightly, giving myself a better angle.

May as well give the girl what she wants.

I lick her again and find her clit with my tongue. I suck it into my mouth, then move lower. I explore her, taking note of what gets a subtle reaction. When her thighs tense, when she squirms in an effort to avoid the pressure. I thrust two fingers inside her and press on her G-spot. In and out.

Fascinating.

I want to spend the rest of my life pulling Violet apart piece by piece, inspecting how she works, how she was made, and then putting her back together again.

Her first orgasm is a big one. As I predicted. She comes with my lips around her clit and my fingers in her pussy. Her thighs squeeze together, and her back arches off the bed. I glance up, taking in her expression. Her eyes still shut, her mouth parted. Maybe this just goes along with the dream she's having.

I reach up and palm her breast, brushing my thumb over her stiff nipple. And then I dive back into her.

God, I couldn't have predicted how obsessed I'd be with her. How much I'd enjoy all of what she gives me. Even the irritating parts.

I meant it when I said I loved her, but it's terrifying, too. I felt, in that moment, like I was offering my heart out for her to do with what she pleased.

But she didn't stomp on it. She looked scared, and I can fucking relate to that. I didn't want to tell her I'm *terrified*. My only example of love is my parents, and we all know how that ended. In a word: badly.

It just took me a little while to realize that their marriage didn't contain love. They might've started out that way, but it became about appearances. That's why my mom left, why Dad probably didn't let her even think about taking me with her.

The Single Dad trope hits hard with the voters.

Destitute father left by mother *and* son? Not so much.

After meeting Violet's mom, I have to wonder how much love Violet was shown. Between her shitty mom and her dead father.

We're both part of the dead parent society. That club no one talks about that fucking sucks, but it's also a bit of a comfort.

She comes again before she wakes up. And when she does finally open those pretty eyes, shifting and trying to roll away from me, I don't let up. She gasps and pushes at my head, but I'm dug in. My fingers pump in and out of her, I've got her taste in my mouth, and I want another climax.

Vi shudders, moaning something unintelligible at me.

Is this how it's going to be for the rest of our lives? This addiction? This feeling in my chest like I'm inflated with helium?

"Grey," she murmurs. "What are you—*ah, God*—"

I grin and move my tongue harder against her clit. Her third wipes her out. I relish the feel of her pussy clenching at my fingers, and then she relaxes. I climb up her body, hovering over her, and kiss her throat.

"You're my favorite person on this planet, Violet Reece." My confession meets her pulse point. "And we're going to wake up next to each other for the rest of our fucking lives."

She wraps her arms around my neck and her legs around my hips.

I don't need much more prompting to slide inside her wet cunt.

Perks of sleeping naked.

She frowns at me, her eyes no more than slits. "What time is it?"

"Time to fuck, darling." I roll my hips.

"It's five in the morning." She glances at the clock, then back at me. "I think I'm still drunk."

I laugh and kiss her. I still feel it, too. The haze of liquor on my mind. Maybe that's what's driving this melancholy.

Oh, no. It was Violet humping me that woke me up. I smile against her lips, and she automatically mirrors me. I lick her lip, then suck it into my mouth. My teeth nibble her flesh, wanting a taste of their own. I bite harder, until the familiar metallic taste of blood drops on my tongue.

She kisses me harder. She presses into me, nipping my lips. If I didn't know better, I'd think she was trying to climb into my skin. The prick of pain of *her* breaking open my skin is refreshing.

We mix our blood and saliva and love together.

Maybe she doesn't know about the last, but I do.

I feel it in the way she touches me and how she looks at me. She brushes my hair off my forehead and examines my face. She's got a bead of blood on her lip that I lean down and lick away. Her eyes soften, and she cups my cheeks. Kisses me again, even after everything that once ran rampant between us.

Violet Reece is totally in love with me.

50
VIOLET

"How are you feeling?"

I glance up from my position on the floor. When I see Mia in my rented studio, I shoot to my feet. "Good." I clear my throat. "Fine. Thank you."

She chuckles and runs her hand down one of the bars. "Sorry to drop in unannounced."

I try not to fidget as she appraises me. Hair in a braid over my shoulder, a loose cardigan over my gray leotard and black, stretchy shorts. I had a dance class an hour ago and have been working through the choreography for my audition.

Grey is sitting in the corner, his homework forgotten and his gaze on me.

"What's up?" I grab my water bottle.

"Laramie told me you requested additional studio space after your lesson, so I figured I'd swing by and see how preparation is going."

I shoot her a smile. "It's going."

She snorts. "Want to show me?"

"Is that biased?" I lift one shoulder and take a swig of

the cool water. Surely she's the one deciding who gets the part. But then again, she's the one who pulled me out of retirement. That may have been the biggest tell of all.

"It may be." She crosses to the speaker connected to my phone and hits play.

The familiar piece fills the room, an orchestral work from the original *Sleeping Beauty*. I want the lead role of Princess Aurora. Whether I can achieve her sweetness and grace is anyone's guess. This particular part is a variation in the first act. She's celebrating her sixteenth birthday, on the cusp of being cursed to a hundred-year sleep, and dancing alone before meeting four suitors.

I take my position in front of the mirrors, cue my entrance, and begin.

There are pieces we're still working on, movements I wanted to perfect, but my body feels good. My leg is solid, almost entirely painless while I dance. It's strong again. That alone is enough to bring a burn to the backs of my eyes.

The aquatic therapy helped—and I almost couldn't do it because of money.

I turn my mind back to Aurora. I don't believe her parents told her about the curse. If they did, she wouldn't be tempted later in the act to inspect the spindle. She wouldn't have been so curious as to reach out and prick her finger on it.

Would I have been so curious about Greyson if I knew all that my mother had done—and was doing?

Before I know it, the music has moved on, and I hover in my final pose. I come out of it and meet Mia's eyes in the mirror, shocked that she has a huge smile on her face.

"It's like you never left," she says softly.

I beam.

"Truly beautiful. Work on those parts that weren't as seamless, but other than that?" She shakes her head. "You know, I would've loved to see you in *Swan Lake*."

The role I had.

"Maybe I'll dance as the white and black swans one day." I lift a shoulder.

She frowns. "It's unlikely Crown Point Ballet will do it again."

I tilt my head. It would be unusual for me to stay with the same company for the entire length of my career. But I don't answer—it wouldn't really do either of us any good for me to tell her I plan on leaving CPB one day. In fact, I have a feeling it would hinder me.

Mia nods again. "I just wanted to stop by and give you some more information about *Sleeping Beauty*, if you have time?"

I check my watch. I have the studio for the rest of the evening, and I'm curious about why she stopped by. I nod to Mia and leave Greyson in the room. We go down the hall to a darkened studio. She picks the one Grey and I had our... um... moment. My face heats, and I squash those memories.

"Crown Point Ballet is using *Sleeping Beauty* to hold open auditions for the company," Mia says. That's a way to get new blood into the company. Most hold open auditions maybe once a year, gearing up for the season. "We have a new choreographer for this ballet, but I think you know him. Shawn Meridian?"

I raise my eyebrows. Shock echoes through me—chased by *excitement*. Do I know him? Sort of. Do I want to dance his choreography? Abso-fucking-lutely. "I had the pleasure of meeting him once. My mom wrangled me an introduction when we went to see one of his ballets. I was in high school. Pretty sure I made a fool of myself and gave him a tape of me dancing. How did you know that?"

She chuckles. "Believe it or not, there was a time when you wouldn't shut up about it."

"That makes sense." Especially around the other girls. There's a competitive edge amongst dancers. We're friends, but we also all want to come out on top. Bragging is normal.

"We're hosting a summer intensive," she adds. "Which I think you'd excel at. Get your stamina back. And then we've got a home season and jump into national touring from there."

I nod along. I don't bother to tell her that I already know this. I toured with the company as part of the ensemble and later a soloist. My chance at principal prima ballerina—the coveted spot—was ripped away before our season started. Before I had danced in front of *one* audience.

"Anyway, I just wanted to give you a heads-up about Shawn and the open audition. I'm looking forward to seeing you bring your A game."

Because I'm competitive. That's why she really told me. Letting me know I'm not just up against Crown Point Ballet for the lead spot—while that's not *easy*, I know most of the girls. I'll be up against anyone. Everyone.

"Thanks," I murmur.

She nods and leaves me standing in the empty room. We never even turned on the lights.

"Interesting meeting." Grey leans against the doorframe, his hands in his pockets.

"Mia," I say faintly. "Yeah, she's an interesting person."

"Seems like she's looking out for you, yeah?"

I shrug it off. "Is she? Or does she just want someone..." Familiar? Safe? I don't want to be either of those options. I want to be the one who everyone gravitates toward. The one all the choreographers want to work with. "Either way, I guess it's a good thing."

He shrugs, then straightens up. "Are you hungry? I'm going to go grab something to eat. I can bring you back whatever you want."

I perk up. "A turkey wrap from that place on the corner? And fries. And a Gatorade." I stop right in front of him, reaching out to play with the bottom of his shirt. "You remember this room?"

The cuts he gave me were barely deep enough to scab over—they probably won't even scar. And it'll be sad to see them go.

He cups my jaw, tilting my face up to kiss me. I lean into him. Each kiss goes through me like electricity, and I don't know how he does that. How he makes every touch important. His tongue dips between my parted lips, tasting me, and he hums when he leans back.

"I'll be right back," he promises. "Once you're done dancing, we can come back to *this* room..."

I smile.

We go in separate directions—him to the exit, me to the studio I rented. I cross to the speaker and hit play on my music, but it isn't the piece I've been rehearsing to that comes out. It's the faint notes of a solo from a different ballet.

I read the words on the screen, the title of the piece, but my mind is stuttering. It's familiar in a dream-like way. My body knows what to do—and I'm certain I've never performed this. I don't know that I've even seen more than snippets of this ballet. *Giselle.* It's tragic in a way. The orchestra pulls at my heart.

Without really knowing why, I rise from my position

next to the speaker. I restart the song and move to the middle of the room, staring at myself in the mirror for a moment. Then I close my eyes and let muscle memory take over. I move through choreography I don't remember learning.

The tempo picks up, and I fly across the room. For a moment, I feel the weight of my future lift off my shoulders. But my pointe shoe catches on something—or perhaps it's my leg that fails—and I stumble.

Suddenly Grey is there, catching me before I crash.

"Oh," I gasp, clutching at his arms. "Sorry."

He tilts his head. "That's not the piece you've been working on all day."

"No, it isn't." I straighten and step back. "I'm not sure where that came from."

"Interesting." His arms fall back to his sides.

"It was queued up on my phone," I explain. "Must've been on shuffle after the *Sleeping Beauty* one. In a playlist for ballet music."

"Right." He watches me, his expression curious.

I have the distinct impression that I'm fumbling my way through this. That I should feel flustered by what I just did. And I *am* flustered, because I don't remember learning that choreography. Maybe I made it up. An imaginary dance to go along with moving music.

"What ballet is it from?"

I glance over his shoulder. "What happened to food?"

"Decided to just get it delivered," he says. "I called the place. Someone's bringing it over soon."

I grunt.

"Vi. The ballet?"

"*Giselle*," I say. I venture in closer to him. "A romantic tragedy."

"How's that?"

I run my hand up his arm. "A trusting commoner falls in love with a disguised nobleman. He tricks her, making her think that he's like her. But he isn't."

Grey's eyes narrow. "Vi."

"His ruse is uncovered," I continue. "And poor Giselle dies."

His brows furrow. "She dies?"

"That's just act one, baby." I shake my head and turn away. "She turns into a forest apparition, one of many that lure men into the forest to dance until they die. But when the nobleman is lured into the forest, she dances with him... and she chooses to keep him alive. Do you think that's love?"

"I don't know."

I grimace. "As I said. It's a tragedy."

"But you didn't explain how you knew it."

"I made it up." I cross to the music, which has looped again to repeat the song. I put the *Sleeping Beauty* one back on and take up my position in the middle of the room. "I'm sure I did."

51
GREYSON

Violet makes every movement seem effortless. Even when she's straining, her muscles trembling, an easy expression remains glued on her face. She follows through. Her leotard gets damp with sweat, her hair stuck to her head.

Eventually, our food arrives, and she takes a break.

Stamina, she explained. Professional dancers have to have the stamina to keep dancing. If she stops for a day, the next she'll feel a bit sore. If she stops for a few days, her next practice will be tiring. And if she stops for longer than that, her muscles will feel the effects.

I understand it well. It's why I train hard during the summer, keeping myself in peak fitness. Because coming back is harder when you let yourself go on the *off* season.

Violet's had seven months of being *off*. I understand her drive.

We don't have classes this week. Crown Point University is basically a ghost town. Not that it matters, since she's been staying with me. Willow went home to spend time with her sister and probably to escape Knox.

I finish off my sandwich and eye Violet again. I don't care if she catches me staring. She already knows how I feel about her.

Obsessed. In love.

Sometimes I think they might be the same thing.

She's stronger, though. Her muscles are more defined. She's eating better. For a while, I was worried that she was going to perish on lettuce alone. But it seems the intense workouts have resurfaced her appetite.

When she's done eating, she flops backward on the polished wood floor. I take my cue and crawl over her, lowering my body until we're flush.

"Hi," she says.

I take her wrists one at a time, stretching them up over her head. She smirks at me and shifts but keeps her arms up there. Her fingers twist together. I lift slightly and run my hand down her arm, her throat, her chest. I palm her breast, and she exhales. Sometime between Mia Germain's visit and now, she removed the cardigan that shielded her breasts from me. Her nipple is visible through her sports bra and the tight leotard. I brush my thumb over it, waiting for another movement by her.

I'll take a million moments like these to learn her body.

She spreads her legs wider, hooking them around my hips. She uses her legs to pull me down, and I give her what she wants. I grind my cock on her core, separated by too many layers of fabric. Her shorts, the leotard, my pants and boxers.

"Promise you'll stay with me forever," I say in her ear.

"Is that what you want?"

I nip her skin, if only to hear her hitched breath. To feel her chest hit mine. I sit up suddenly, rocking back on my knees. She stays exactly where she is, her arms over her head, her legs spread. Her gaze is decidedly lustful. I shift aside, peel her shorts off, and toss them away. Then I resume my position between her legs. I eye the thin strip of fabric of the leotard hiding her cunt from me.

She squirms.

"What do you need, baby?"

Her eyes lock on mine. "I want to come. And then I want to go back to work."

I laugh. If it was me, and she was standing in my way of hockey practice? Yeah, I'd probably have a similar feeling. She wants to get down to business. No objections from me.

We can take our time later.

I move her leotard to the side and run my finger through her wetness. She squirms again, already impatient. Part of me wants to draw it out just because I *like* her annoyance and the way her brow is drawing down because I'm not going fast enough.

She's cute when she's annoyed.

"Grey—"

"I've got you," I promise. "Relax."

She pushes up on her elbows and watches me thrust a finger inside her. Her lips part, and we both watch me finger-fuck her with one, then two. I use my other hand to hold the fabric aside and brush her clit. I touch her just the way she likes. The fastest way to an orgasm for her—direct pressure. Unwavering stimulation.

Her head falls back. The combination is too much for her, and she comes in record time.

Not that I'm keeping track or anything.

Her muscles pulse around my fingers. I withdraw slowly once her body stops trembling. She eyes me— perhaps waiting for me to pull out my dick and fuck her— but I just lick my fingers. I love the taste of her.

So even though I'm rock-hard, I scoot back and give her room to get up.

"What are you doing?"

"Letting you go back to work," I say with a shrug.

Her eyes narrow.

"What?" I gesture to the room. "I'd expect nothing less from you if I had to go."

She crawls toward me. "Yeah, right," she murmurs. She pushes me back, then unbuttons my jeans. I suck in a breath when she pulls the front of my pants and boxers down enough for my cock to emerge, and the air escapes in a ragged exhale when her pretty head descends over it.

Her mouth is hot and wet on me. I groan and suppress the urge to grab her hair and take over. This is her show... for now. My willpower will only go so far. She takes more of me in her mouth, and my abdomen tightens. She has a magic tongue, I think.

The tip of my cock touches the back of her throat, and she gags.

Fuck me twice.

"My self-control is dwindling," I warn her.

She grips the base of my dick and uses it to help her mouth. Her hand slides down, cupping my balls, and I swear. My hips jerk, and I hit the back of her throat again. Then deeper.

Fucking fuck.

"Vi," I mutter.

She ignores me and continues, sucking hard and flicking her tongue against the underside of the head. My balls tighten as her assault continues, and I watch in absolute fascination. She bobs up and down.

I wind my fingers through her hair, freeing it from the hair tie. I love her hair and the way it fans around her shoulders. It's silky, too, against my skin. I press her deeper, and her throat works around me.

"Fuck, Vi."

I pull out just enough for me to be in her mouth, not down her throat. I want her to taste me the way I taste her. On her tongue, overwhelming her senses. And when I do come, I hold her head steady. Bliss rocks through me, and I fight the urge to close my eyes. I need to see her. All of it.

She swallows. Her throat works, and she kisses the tip of my dick when she straightens back up. She's definitely the first person to do *that*. I choke on my laugh. My cock has stopped throbbing, but I have a feeling I could be hard again in minutes. There's just something about her that demands more, and my body wants to respond to it.

"That was hot," she whispers, wiping her lower lip with her thumb.

"I'm going to fuck you into oblivion later," I promise. I stand and help her to her feet, then tuck myself back in my pants. She straightens her leotard and collects her shorts. "But for now, I'm going to give you space to work."

She smiles. "Thanks for hanging out with me today."

I kiss her, then collect my things.

It's surprisingly difficult to walk away from her. I make it all the way down the block before I cave and open my phone. I look up the ballet. *Giselle*. There are some recent videos from other ballet companies performing it on stage. One of the more popular videos is from just a month ago, and it's a solo.

I click on it and wait for it to load. My annoyance picks up the longer it takes—hell, I don't even know if I'm on the right path here. I'm completely winging it.

When it does load, the music is immediately familiar.

And what might be even worse? The dance is familiar.

Especially when the music switches, the frenzy of the song picking up. It's the same moves, as far as I can tell. The same choreography.

Where would she have learned that?

There is where she stumbled. Just at the end.

Something isn't adding up here. Choreography she doesn't have a reason to know, muscle memory. How long does it take for that sort of thing to stick? How many hours of practice would she have needed to do to cement it in her memory?

Even if her *memory* isn't there.

I let out a ragged sigh and rub my face. I believe her when she says she doesn't know how she knew it. But now it's a mystery that will nag at me—so I'll figure it out for both of us.

And I have a feeling that means digging more into her past than she'd want.

Whatever. I'm going to do it anyway.

5²

VIOLET

Today is the day. I know it before I even open my eyes.

I barely slept last night. The anticipation was almost too great. Grey didn't seem to mind that I kept rolling over, tossing and turning like my sleep problem was pillow-related. He was as awake as me, I think, holding me until I found a comfortable position.

Which lasted only an hour before I was shifting again.

At one point, probably close to three in the morning, he slid inside me and fucked me into a dream-like state. We both slept after that. But now, as I twist toward him and stretch out, reaching, I realize I'm alone.

His side of the bed is cold.

I sit up and press the blanket to my bare chest. His bedroom door is open.

Silence reigns through the house, but I still wait a moment, then slip out from under the covers. I find a Hawks sweatshirt, my panties and shorts, and pull every-thing on before I wander into the hall. Still nothing.

I brush my teeth, take care of business, and shake out

my limbs. The nerves return with a crackle—not that they ever left. Grey's disappearance just temporarily distracted me.

Crown Point Ballet is holding company auditions at nine o'clock. It means I'll probably be there all day. But there will be plenty of time to stress about that... after I eat breakfast.

At this point, it feels like this house is partially more like home. We've been here for a while, and the guys have adjusted. They cleared out a cabinet in the kitchen for us and space in the fridge. They stock our preferred liquor. Knox and Willow are still going back and forth like a seesaw, but I told her I wouldn't interfere. They'll work it out.

There's a piece of paper in the kitchen, a handwritten note from Greyson. *Went for a run. See you soon. -G*

I smile and turn away. There's already coffee in the pot. I make myself a cup and slink into the living room, curling up in a ball. I should've grabbed my phone when I was upstairs, to run through the music, but I'm so tired.

I just woke up and it feels like I've been awake for a year.

My eyes close, and I sink deeper into the cushions.

Before I know it, someone is brushing my hair out of my face. I blink up at Willow, who just shakes her head at me. "I was going to leave you here, but I heard some guys are coming over to watch a hockey game."

I make a face. "Yeah, probably don't want to be caught sleeping by any of them."

"You okay?" She sits next to me, stealing some of the blanket.

I sip my coffee. "Just nerves. I didn't sleep well."

"About that..."

"About what?"

"Sleeping." She rolls her eyes. "Knox and Greyson share a wall. So when you guys get it on at three in the morning, I can, you know..."

My face heats. "Oh my god. Why didn't you say anything?"

She snorts. "I was trying various ways to drown it out, until..."

"Until...?" Understanding dawns on me. She hasn't wanted to live here *ever*. It was only because my issues put her in danger. But she was probably never in danger to begin with, and with me out of the house, the problem is solved. So, she doesn't have to say it. She's going back to our apartment. And I can't even blame her. I set my mug down and throw my arms around her. "I'm sorry."

She hugs me back. "Don't even apologize, Violet. It's not your fault."

I roll my eyes. "Yeah, right. Pretty sure it is."

She pulls back and glowers at me. "It is *not* your fault some wacko decided to obsess about you."

"You girls talking about me?" Grey strides into the room, pausing next to the couch. "I mean, I wouldn't call myself a wacko but I'm definitely obsessed with you."

My face gets hotter, and I don't answer him.

Is it weird to be attracted to his sweat? His shirt is soaked, his cheeks red. His hair is damp and pushed back off his face. It just makes me want to jump his bones.

"I'm uncomfortable," Willow deadpans. "So on that note... I'm gonna head back to the apartment. See if there's any damage. I'll see you guys later."

Later. *Right*. We're going to Grey's hockey game together. It's a pretty big game, the quarterfinals for the national tournament. Their bus leaves at two, and Willow and I are driving down with Amanda after my audition, which should end by two or three.

Grey doesn't look away from me, but he nods at her words. As soon as she's out of the room, he braces his hands on either side of me and leans down. He gives me a quick kiss. Before he can pull back, though, I grab the front of his shirt and yank him down more forcefully. He takes my coffee cup and tosses it behind him. It crashes, coffee probably going everywhere, but we don't even flinch. He's immediately pushing the blanket aside and sliding his hands up under the sweatshirt.

"I like when you wear my shit," he murmurs against my lips. "And when you still have that just-fucked look, even though we haven't done it in a few hours."

I bite his lower lip and pull, eliciting a groan from him. He cups my breasts, pinching my nipples. I gasp, arching into his hands.

"Are you using sex to distract yourself from the audition?" He's inches away, and I feel like he's trying to see into my soul.

I frown. He doesn't stop touching me, though. He just wants me to admit it.

"Because if it's a distraction you want... I can make that happen."

I close my eyes.

"Vi," he murmurs. "Tell me."

"I want the distraction," I finally say. "Of a violent variety."

He leans back slightly, and I wonder what he sees on my face. I crack my eyes to see his expression, and it's dark. Intrigued.

"Did you have something in mind?"

I sit up, forcing him back a little. "Actually, yes."

More intrigue. A small smile crosses his face, and he stands. Holds out his hands for me. There's coffee and broken ceramic that we pick our way through, but he doesn't seem bothered by it. He's the one who tossed it, after all.

He follows me upstairs, into his bedroom, and lets me close us in. I go to his dresser and pick up the pocket knife he carries around sometimes and flick it open.

"Sometimes I think we'll never be close enough," I admit softly. "Is that strange?"

He tilts his head and stays silent.

I press the tip into my thumb. There's a tiny bit of pain, and then a drop of blood rises to the surface. My gaze fixates on it, until I stick my thumb in my mouth and lick the blood away.

"What do you want me to do, Violet?"

"Sit on the floor," I whisper.

He does, leaning his back against the wall. I turn away from him and pull the sweatshirt off slowly, revealing my bare back. I don't know why—he's seen me naked. But there's something erotic about stripping on purpose.

When I drop it, I bend forward, arching my back. My thumbs hook in my shorts, and I drag those down my legs. When they get to my ankles, I kick them away. I face him in just my panties and the knife in my grip. I motion to his shirt, which he quickly shucks. Then he shimmies out of his running shorts, leaving him in just tight black briefs. They do nothing to hide his erection.

I lower myself to my knees, straddling his lap. I inch closer, until only a breath of space separates our chests.

"What's your plan, Violent?"

I smile at his nickname for me. It is a little violent. And violating. But he doesn't stop me when I raise the knife and press the blade to his throat. I hold it there lightly, watching his face.

Doesn't change.

He doesn't flinch.

I move it lower, to his chest. One of his pecs. And then I just do it.

I cut him.

He lets out a small hiss, maybe of surprise? Or shock? But his cock twitches, getting even harder. I palm it and lean forward, kissing the edge of the cut. Blood wells up, little beads at first, but it's deep. In seconds, the blood drips down his skin. I flick my tongue, catching it and letting the metallic flavor burst across my tastebuds.

Then I withdraw, meeting his eyes again.

He takes the knife from my hand and mirrors my movement, holding the blade first to my throat, then trailing it lower. Between my breasts, all the way to my navel, then back up. I shiver.

"Will they see it? With your leotard?"

I push his hand down my breast, until he's only an inch or two above my nipple. "Don't worry about it."

He cuts me with the same ruthlessness. There's a prick of pain, followed by a pulse that seems to shoot straight to my core. It stings, and we both watch it bleed.

"I think I know what you want," he says. "You want my blood and yours. Together."

Yes. I almost say it out loud. I want another thing binding us together. And what's better than blood? I love that he knows it automatically. That he followed my line of thinking all the way through my fucked-up mind and ended up with the same conclusion.

He scoops me up and rises, turning and slamming my back to the wall. Our chests press together. He spares one hand to shove his briefs down, then slices through my panties. He folds the knife and tosses it away. It clatters to the floor.

I wrap my legs around his hips. The pain and blood are all I can focus on. Mirror cuts—my right and his left. When he thrusts into me, my mouth falls open. He takes advantage of that. His hand cups the back of my head and guides my face toward his. Our chests smash together as we move, the cuts rubbing.

Every inch of me is a live wire right now. Every point where we touch—our chests, arms, mouths, between my legs—is extra sensitive. He drills into me, each thrust knocking me harder against the wall. I wrap my arms around his shoulders and hold on to him. Our tongues war in our mouths, twisting and tasting each other. I hope he tastes his blood on my lips as I taste mine on his.

"You're so fucking perfect for me," he says, tearing his lips away and moving down my throat. I tip my head to the side and let him suck and bite my neck, knowing full well it'll take extra time to cover *those* marks. But it's so worth it.

He grips my ass and fucks me like he's feral.

And maybe he is.

Maybe *I* am.

Because he doesn't even have to touch my clit this time. I'm just knocked over the edge of a cliff, and my climax comes hard. I see stars when it crashes into me, and I dig my nails into his back.

"That's it," he urges. His hand slips between us, and his fingers on my clit bring me right back up before I've had a chance to come back down to earth. There's too much sensation. I move his head away and lean down, sinking my teeth into his shoulder.

"Ah, fuck," he growls. He rolls his hips. His fingers don't stop.

I'm falling apart around him again when he quickens, then stops buried fully inside me.

My heart slams against my ribcage, and I twist my fingers through his short hair. He comes, and I press my lips to his, swallowing the noise. His heartbeat is as frantic as mine.

"Wow," he murmurs.

Our fronts are covered in blood. Not a lot—the cuts weren't *that* deep—but we're streaked with dark brownish-red.

"Shower," we say at the same time.

He doesn't even put me down. He adjusts his grip and carries me to the bathroom. Only when we're locked inside does he set me on the counter.

"When you spit in my mouth?" I say suddenly, gripping the edge.

He glances over his shoulder at me. "Yes?"

"I, um, liked that." I cough to hide my smile. "Just saying."

He raises an eyebrow. "Oh?"

"Yeah, so, feel free to do that again. When the mood strikes you."

Grey crosses back to me and steps between my legs. One hand cups my pussy, and the other grips my chin. He pulls my mouth open and leans in.

"What do you like more?" he asks, flicking my clit. "When I touch you here, or... *here?*" His hand slides lower, and suddenly his finger is pushing into my asshole.

I try to wriggle away from him, but he keeps a tight grip on my face.

"Maybe my spit would be better used to wet my cock

before I fuck your ass," he muses. "Have to keep my girl on her toes."

He kisses me again, then backs away. He's smirking at me as he goes.

Fucker.

53
VIOLET

I stride into the Crown Point Ballet building. I've been coming here for years, but this time feels more significant. There's a new energy in the halls. People I don't know—men and women auditioning, hoping to be signed on for the performance season.

The familiar faces, though. They smile when they see me. Hug me, say they've missed me. I'm not sure I believe them. I got a lot of condolences when I was in the hospital. No one knew why I had driven back to Rose Hill—my hometown—that day. I asked them because my memory was... blank.

I remember being in Crown Point the day before. We were preparing for the home performances, and then the touring would begin after that. There were interviews and clips of rehearsals to be filmed, costume fittings, classes.

Being back here reminds me that I never did find out why I went back.

At the time, I assumed it was for my mother. I never asked her, and she never said. I guess she thought I'd know.

"Violet," Sylvie, Mia's assistant, calls out. "This way."

I follow her into one of the large studios. It's set up for a barre class. A handful of dancers are already here. They've claimed spots and are slowly warming up.

"You'll be auditioning with everyone else," she says when I reach her side. "Mia wanted me to apologize—"

"It's okay," I say. "I get it." Expected it, even. She can't give me preferential treatment just because she likes me.

She leaves me there, and I drop my bag next to one of the bars. I sink to the floor and unzip my bag. The first thing in it surprises me. I half pull it out, rubbing my fingers through the soft blue material. *Devereux*, it says in white letters. He put his jersey in my bag.

I allow a small smile, then lean down and press my nose to the fabric.

It smells like him, too.

Focus, Violet.

I stow it away and get ready, putting my earbud in to replay the audition music. It reminds me a bit of Grey, listening to music to get in the zone. We're similar in that regard. I stretch, slip on my pointe shoes, and secure the ribbons. My body is ready, and my mind is there, too. Ready to work.

I block everything out until the ballet master arrives. The room is full, my muscles are warm, and I feel... decent, actually. I stow my earbuds and put my bag against the wall, then get back into position. It's been a while since I've been in a group class, but I ignore that twinge of nerves and focus on the ballet master.

She strides around, correcting various positions, technique, and calls out changing positions. She also brings our attention to those who are doing well—and some who could be doing better.

"If I tap your shoulder, you are dismissed," she calls.

She arrives next to me and watches for a moment, then offers a small smile. "I'm glad to see you back, Ms. Reece. It looks like you've even managed to improve."

"Thank you," I manage.

She moves on without a backward glance.

When her class ends an hour later, she's halved the room. We put the barres away and return to the center. Mia enters, followed by the choreographer, Shawn, and her assistant. The ballet master stamps her cane into the floor, catching our attention.

"Mia Germain," she introduces. "Artistic director for the Crown Point Ballet."

Mia dips her head. "Thank you. Welcome," she greets us. "We're so pleased to be offering spots in our company to talented dancers. As most of you are probably aware, our upcoming season will be focusing on *Sleeping Beauty*. The wonderful Shawn Meridian is our guest choreographer, splitting his time between here and the American Ballet Theatre in New York City. He's joining us today to offer his input as we not only hope to offer contracts but to also cast our Aurora."

We applaud until Shawn steps forward and raises his hands.

He's easily recognizable as one of the most talented choreographers of this decade. I still remember being awestruck by him in high school—although that feels like forever ago now. He definitely doesn't remember me.

Although, Mia was right. I sure did talk about it a lot when I got to Crown Point Ballet. I was giddy at the prospect of giving him a CD of me dancing. Even though it led nowhere.

He appraises the room, then motions to the doorway.

Annabelle, another principal dancer at CPB, comes into the room. She smiles at him, then us.

"Annabelle is going to run through the audition piece," Shawn says. His voice is deeper and raspier than I remember. "Ready?"

The pianist strikes up the singular melody of the piece I learned. In a way, it's more haunting with just one instrument. Not as joyful.

Giselle was joyful before she turned to tragedy, too.

Annabelle dances it well. Her turns are perfect, her extensions... she's a beautiful dancer. But maybe she lacks the passion because she's never been in love. Or because she thinks she's not being judged right now.

A mistake. We're all being judged.

She finishes in a flourish, posing with her arms uplifted, her knee bent, her head thrown back. A wide smile on her face.

"Thank you," the ballet master says to her.

We don't immediately proceed into that, though. There's still more to come. Leaping, turning. We line up and cross the room, showing our lines and movement, our turnout. We pair up and show how we do with partner work.

I get lucky and end up with a dancer who already belongs to the company. He and I have danced together for a few years, and he winks when he steps up beside me.

Finally, we break. We'll do the audition solo one at a time—those who want it anyway. Mia, Shawn, and the ballet master have already further whittled our numbers down.

Annabelle dances again. Then another principal dancer, and another. I swallow.

"Lydia Parker," the girl beside me introduces, offering her hand.

I shake it. "Violet Reece."

"I was a principal dancer in Arizona. The heat was killer." She leans in. "Are you familiar with Mia?"

"A bit." I glance at her. She's a few inches shorter than me, with dark hair wrapped in a neat bun. Minimal makeup. Pretty, though. Ideal casting. "Why?"

"I've just heard rumors, is all. That she's a good person to dance for."

I nod. "I've heard that, too."

"Violet," Mia calls.

I smile at Lydia and step forward. The music starts. Even though it's a little different, it *feels* the same. I let myself radiate the joy of a birthday party—that's what the dance is about anyway. Aurora arrives at her sixteenth birthday party. The solo ends before she meets the four suitors, and before she pricks her finger on the spindle. But this part is freedom. Happiness.

My smile only widens during the more difficult bits of choreography, and I end in the same pose as Annabelle.

There's a smattering of applause, and I make eye contact with Shawn Meridian. His brow is furrowed, confusion etched across his face.

I don't know what to make of it, so I back away and rejoin the girls against the wall. Lydia goes next. And another, another, another. I sit and stretch and try to keep nimble in case something else is needed, but by the end, it's almost two o'clock.

"Thank you, ladies," Mia says. "We will be contacting those we are offering contracts, and then the cast list will be posted on our website later this month."

We collect our things. My leg is sore, a phantom pain

tracing up my thigh and into my hip. I try not to let it worry me. Just more water therapy, more strength training… and maybe I'll have to live with it forever.

It's not too heavy of a price to pay to dance again.

"Violet."

I've made it to the hallway, but I turn back to see the choreographer coming toward me. I'm surprised he remembers my name, and I try to hide it. He stops in front of me, then glances over his shoulder.

We're alone.

I hitch my bag higher on my shoulder and wait.

"I'll admit, I'm confused to see you here."

I stare at him. "What?"

"Um…" He shifts. "Sorry. Do you not want to talk about this here?"

What the hell is going on? "I just think you might have the wrong person," I say slowly.

He motions for me to follow him. Against my better judgment, I do. Even knowing I have a stalker, my curiosity is greater than my fear. He leads me into an empty office and closes the door.

His gaze drops to my leg, and he winces. "Do you remember what happened the day of your accident?"

I hate the word accident. For the longest time, it didn't feel like it was an accident. It was more than that. But then I register his expression, and his question, and a chill creeps up my spine.

"Have we met? In the last few years?" I take an involuntary step backward. There's no way a man like him would recall a teenager giving him an audition tape. I was in high school, and he was a big hotshot choreographer. This feels like more than that.

Shawn frowns. "That answers that question."

Oh my god. Is Shawn my stalker? Did he have something to do with that day—and everything that happened after?

Maybe he finally revealed himself. He's muscular. Tall. He could be the same build as the person who broke into my apartment.

"I'm leaving," I say quietly. I head toward the door, but he blocks my path.

"Just wait, please."

I skid to a halt. "Get out of my way."

He raises his hands. "Two minutes. That's all I ask."

He's not threatening to kill me... yet. That's a good sign, right? If I can get him talking, then maybe he'll just let me go. Or I can figure out a way to get him away from the door... I look around the room and circle behind the desk, putting it between us. I drop my bag on it and press my back against the wall.

"You and I met that day in Rose Hill," he says. "It was out of the blue, yes, but you drove down. You seemed excited about it."

"Why?" I demand.

"Because I was trying to recruit you."

I rear back. "For what?"

He gives me a look. One that says: *you should know*. But even if I have a theory—and one is beginning to form—I don't trust him. I don't believe him.

"I wanted you to dance for the American Ballet Theatre," he says carefully. "And that might sound crazy, but I was given the chance to handpick some dancers for their upcoming touring season. I chose—"

"*Giselle*." I cover my mouth. My mind is going a hundred miles a minute. "So I met with you that day?"

He nods. "We went over choreography. You were going

to be in touch later in the week to come and dance for the board of directors."

This doesn't make any fucking sense.

"I was Odette." My brow furrows. "I was the principal dancer for *Swan Lake*."

He scoffs. "You think Crown Point Ballet can stand up to what ABT can offer you? You and I both know that they're leagues apart. I was giving you a chance."

"But then I broke my leg. My memory of that day was just..." I snap my fingers. "It was gone. How can I believe you?" I squint at him. "How do I know you're not lying?"

"What about your phone? We had conversations. I left you a voicemail, you called me back."

I'm already shaking my head. "Smashed in the accident. I lost data from a week prior, since my last cloud backup."

He sighs. He's right to sigh—the signs of the truth are there. In the dance I somehow knew, in the spaces of my memory. But it doesn't stop him from opening his phone and setting it on the desk.

A video plays. He stands in a studio that looks awfully familiar, and I face the mirror. Someone else holds the phone for him, filming me dance. Poor Violet back then, she had no idea what was about to happen. When I finish, I turn and beam at Shawn.

It goes black, and I step back. I let out a shaky breath.

"What time was that?"

He looks at the time stamp on the video and wordlessly points. Seven-zero-five p.m. Greyson hit my car closer to eleven.

"Did I leave after that?"

Shawn narrows his eyes. "Yeah, Violet. You got a call and left."

I swing my bag back over my shoulder. "It's been two

minutes," I say stiffly. "And it doesn't really seem to matter much, since you've probably chosen for ABT. That was months ago. Besides, we're both here."

Shawn reads my stiffening posture, and he immediately raises his hands again. Like he's not a threat to me. "I'm sorry. I was just surprised, is all. I didn't mean to make you uncomfortable. I thought you knew me."

He steps aside, and I rush out the door.

My mind is a mess. He wanted me to dance for him at the American Ballet Theatre? One of the best ballet companies in the US? I'd only just debuted as a principal. Hadn't had a chance to dance a lead in front of an audience before it was ripped away from me.

I wipe at a tear that rolls down my cheek. Then another.

"Fuck," I mutter, turning the corner.

I almost crash into Mia.

She grabs my shoulders and lets out a laugh. "Violet! I thought you had left already. Oh—what happened? Are you okay?"

I sniffle and step back. Her hands fall back to her sides.

"I'm okay, thanks. And thank you again for the opportunity. It was nice dancing in a company again—even if it was just for today."

Mia rolls her eyes. "None of that pessimistic bullshit. You were excellent." She hooks her arm through mine and continues with me toward the door. "Between you and me, I think you have an outstanding chance of being cast as Aurora."

"Thank you." I turn toward her. "And thank you for... all of it, I guess. Helping me get back into it, setting up the initial appointment with Dr. Michaels. You've done a lot for me."

She pats my hand. "You know what? I think I need to buy you a drink."

It's only two o'clock. Willow will expect a phone call by three, which gives us plenty of time. I nod and let her lead me to her car. This part is familiar. I can't begin to count how many times she's given me a ride home or spent extra time with me in and out of the studio.

She stepped in to be a mother figure when mine was being chaotic.

I toss my bag in the trunk and climb in the passenger seat. She joins me, pulling out onto the road moments later. We head away from downtown Crown Point.

"Where did you have in mind?" I ask.

Mia glances at me, then back to the road. She doesn't answer.

"Mia?"

Her lips press together.

"Where are we going?" My voice is as level as can be expected, I think. There's not a trace of panic in it— although that panic is wrapping itself around my throat. Maybe I'm just working myself up over nothing. I've known Mia for years and years—she's never had anything but good intentions.

"Hush," she finally says. "You trust me, don't you?"

"Of course."

"I just need to swing by my house. I forgot my credit card at home this morning."

I nod along with her words. With her story.

Watch. In ten minutes, we'll have grabbed her credit card then moved on to a local bar. She'll buy me a drink, we'll celebrate a successful audition, and I'll meet Willow and Amanda. I'm overreacting.

Except... I'm not.

Because we get to a road that goes from pavement to gravel, and the driveways get farther apart. And then we're just on a little one-lane dirt road. Minutes later, we arrive at a log cabin. There's a dog on a chain out front, and the porch light glows dimly.

"You live here?"

Mia exhales. "Only when I want to get away," she says. "Come on, I'll give you a tour."

"Oh, no—"

"Get out of the car, Violet." She meets my gaze for a second, then turns away to open her door. She climbs out, leaving me alone.

The dog can't quite reach the porch. It strains toward Mia, still barking. Its tail wags, though. I swiftly hop out and follow her, skirting the dog. Spit flies from its mouth with each bark, and I find myself flinching each time, too.

I hurry into the cabin, and the door slams behind me.

I spin around.

Mia stands in the shadows, her arms folded over her chest. "Had a good little chat with Shawn, did you?"

"What?"

"After all I've done for you, Violet? You were going to leave me?" She steps forward.

I glance around the room. It's completely not her style —an old, colorful blanket tossed over a worn leather couch, a thick rug, and wood coffee table. Dark wood everywhere. The heavy curtains are pulled shut over the windows, blocking out most of the sunlight.

"Sit down," she hisses at me.

"I think I'd rather go," I tell her.

She shakes her head. "No."

"Mia, I wasn't going to leave you." I step back and bump into a side table. The lamp on it wobbles, and I grab at it.

Turning my back on her is a mistake.

She wraps her arm around my neck, yanking me into her. I lose my balance and grab at her, and that's when she tightens her grip. It doesn't matter how much I struggle, or scratch at her, or try to kick. She just doesn't let go.

Until white spots dance in front of my eyes.

This is where Grey would release me.

But she doesn't. Not until a cold darkness reaches up and drags me down.

And maybe not even then.

54
GREYSON

We're preparing our equipment when my phone goes off.

Willow: Call me ASAP.

I frown and glance at Knox, who's busy wrapping his hockey stick, and then call her. We only arrived a few minutes ago. The bus ride was somber, everyone lost in their own thoughts before this game. If we lose it, we're out.

"I can't find Violet," Willow says, not bothering with a greeting. "She didn't hitch a ride with you, did she?"

"What the fuck do you mean, you can't find her?" I stand, abandoning my shit and leaving the locker room altogether. I love my teammates, but they're nosy as hell. "What happened?"

"I don't know. I called her, and it goes straight to voice-mail. When I showed up at the CPB building, Mia's assistant was the only one there. Said everyone was done already and she wasn't sure..." Willow hesitates. "She said she thought she saw Violet talking to a new choreographer after the auditions."

My lungs aren't working. I can't believe this is happening.

Her stalker finally acted? Took her?

"You checked all the usual spots? She didn't just go home instead of calling you immediately?" I pace the hallway, in desperate need to hit something.

Of course it happens now. When I'm an hour away.

"Willow," I snap.

"Jesus, Greyson," she yells. "I checked everywhere I could think before I called you. Do you think I'm an idiot?"

She hangs up on me.

I swear and call her back but get no response.

"Devereux," Coach calls, poking his head out of the locker room. "What the fuck are you doing?"

I pinch the bridge of my nose and try to bring rationality back. Either that, or I'm going to lose my shit on Roake. I'd bet neither of us would enjoy the consequences of that. So... I've got one option.

I look over at him. "I need your help."

55

VIOLET

My head pounds. When I work up the nerve to crack my eyes open, I find myself in a bedroom. The bed is made underneath me, a small nightstand next to my head. There are no windows, just a single lamp on a dresser on the opposite wall. There's one exit, the wood door closed, and a rocking chair takes up the additional space. It makes everything a bit cramped, like this room wasn't supposed to exist.

It immediately gives me the creeps.

I sit up slowly, eyeing the glass of water on the nightstand. A clinking draws my attention to my ankle.

A padded cuff is locked on my leg, a chain snaking from it down over the foot of the bed. It rattles when I move, the links knocking against each other.

I'm so fucked.

I touch my head, convinced I must be cut open or have a lump the size of Alabama from the way it aches and pulses. But there's nothing. Just a lack of oxygen to thank, I guess. I swing my legs over the bed, my toes touching a scratchy rug, and the chain falls to the floor.

I flinch.

Footsteps immediately pound overhead. I count out the seconds and make it to twelve before the door opens.

Mia steps into the space, looking around, then at me. She seems angry for some reason. I open my mouth, but she strides forward and smacks me. Her palm collides with my cheek, and my head whips to the side.

Blood fills my mouth.

I grab the cup of water and spit into it. A glob of saliva and blood immediately dissipates, turning the water pink.

"You disrespectful slut," Mia says, leaning into me. She grabs me by my hair, cranking my head back. "After all I've done for you?"

I don't answer. Can't, really.

She releases me and backs up quickly, then goes to the dresser. She pulls items out, setting them on top of it. Her body blocks them.

"Get dressed," she finally says, then leaves. The door slams behind her.

I rise and see what she's given me, and my heart drops.

Pointe shoes, a black leotard. That's it.

She can't be serious.

Not with this chain around my leg anyway.

And then I notice the small key sitting beside the pointe shoes. I go for that first, fitting it into the padlock hole. It fits perfectly and clicks when I twist it. The padlock opens, and I yank the cuff off. I toss it in the corner and tuck the key in my sports bra... just in case.

Not sure a detail like that would get past her, but I've got to try. Right?

Right.

Anyway, currently I'm just trying to survive... and I think that means I need to go along with what she says. I check the door just to be sure, but it rattles in place. *Locked*.

So I quickly shed my clothes and pull on the leotard. It fits like a glove, softer than any of mine. Better quality maybe? And twice as expensive. Then the pointe shoes... which appear to be *mine*. The ones I painstakingly prepared a week ago, that I've been rehearsing in for *Sleeping Beauty*. They're almost at the end of their life, but still have another few days in them.

My best guess anyway.

I sit back on the bed with my pointe shoes in my lap. I don't relish the thought of trying to escape while wearing these. If it came to it, though, it would be better than barefoot.

I shudder. Cutting up the bottom of my feet is low on the list of things I want to endure. Although, that opinion might change when I find out what Mia wants from me.

The footsteps over my head sound again, and then my door unlocks. It swings inward, and Mia looks at the shoes in my lap. She makes a face. "Put them on."

We stare at each other. She seems... the same. Her face, her hair, her posture. She hasn't suddenly transformed into the wicked witch or an obsessive stalker. She just holds her tension in her mouth and jaw. Her lips press together, the muscles tense. Tendons stand out in her neck.

"How long have you thought about this?"

She motions to the shoes.

I slip one on, adjusting the ribbons.

"I thought we had gotten over our hump," she finally says. "So I wasn't planning on doing this at all..."

I put on the other shoe.

"Come with me," she says.

I rise and follow her into the small, narrow hallway.

There's a tight spiral staircase that she scales quickly. I go up more slowly, carefully. I don't have it in me to be frightened. I'm just tired and wary and disappointed in myself.

Why didn't I see this in her?

I have no problem seeing Greyson's demons—so why not hers?

There's a trap door in the kitchen floor that's been flipped open. As soon as I'm out, Mia closes it and slides a rug back into place. If she wanted to hide me down there from someone, *anyone*, I don't think they'd find me.

"I inherited this cabin from my great-uncle. He bragged that he was involved in the underground railroad. My father always thought his uncle was a crackpot and he really kept women down there." Mia shrugs. "He drank a lot. Smoked even more. So who knows what the truth is?"

Chills skate down my back.

"I wanted to take this time to work on your technique," she continues. She gestures to the living room; the center is now cleared of most of the furniture. The couch is shoved up against the wall, the side tables piled on top of it. The coffee table is knocked over, belly up, and the thick rug rolled on top of it.

"Fifth position."

I raise my eyebrow. "You want me to... dance...?"

"Yes," she says, impatient. "Go on. Take your position."

I fold my arms over my chest. "And if I don't want to dance?"

Her eyebrow tics, then smooths. "Then I'll make sure you never dance for anyone. Ever again." Her gaze goes to the corner, where a rubber mallet leans against the wall.

"You'd break my leg?"

She lifts her shoulder. "I don't want to resort to that,

Violet. But you either dance for CPB or you dance for no one."

I shudder and inch forward.

She nods and pushes a button on a stereo on the floor, up against a wall. The music that comes out isn't *Sleeping Beauty*—it's *Giselle*.

I cringe.

"Oh, did you think you were going to get off easy? Dance a piece you know so well?" She glowers at me. "I know you snuck away to learn this with Shawn Meridian, Violet. I know you are transfixed by his work. That's why I brought him to you." She comes forward and grabs my hands, both of them, pulling me toward her.

It's the last place I want to be.

Her grip is tight, though. "That was my gift. But you still want to leave me."

"I already told you—that wasn't going to happen."

"*Lies!*" she shrieks, throwing my hands back at me.

I curl them into my stomach and stagger away.

She marches over to the wall and snatches the mallet, hefting it over her shoulder. "Don't fucking *lie* to me, Violet."

"I don't remember what happened," I snap at her, sick of this. "Okay? I don't know what happened that day."

She shakes her head and restarts the music. "*Dance.*"

Reluctantly, I take my place in the center of the room. I begin. It's not as fresh in my head, even though Shawn showed me the video earlier. Even though muscle memory guided me through it so recently. My mind has warped some of his choreography. Muscle memory can get things wrong, especially since I only learned it once.

She slams the bottom of the mallet into the floor like a

metronome. The wood is rough when I rise onto pointe. It grabs at my shoes, slows down my spins.

"Stop," Mia says. "There. Your hip."

She comes forward, and I repeat the move. She puts her hand on my thigh, adjusting it. I ignore the way my skin crawls, her palm on my bare leg.

Then she steps back. "Okay, good. Again."

On and on. She dissects every little part, until sweat rolls down my back and I'm panting for breath. Hours, it feels like. I don't know how long we actually go.

Inevitably, I stumble and fall. I hit the floor hard and stay there, trying to catch my breath. Mia has taken a seat on a kitchen chair she dragged in, and she doesn't try to get me to stand or continue on. Although I fear she will.

"When were you going to tell me you were leaving CPB?"

"I've got questions, too, you know." I twist to sit more comfortably, pulling my leg up to my chest and wrapping my arms around it.

"Ask." She reaches in her pocket and pulls out a pack of cigarettes. I've never known her to smoke, but I don't say anything as she plucks one out and sticks it between her lips. She lights it, then exhales smoke. "Go on, Violet, ask me."

"Have you been following me?"

She tilts her head, eyes narrowing. "After you decided to take me up on my offer to see the Vermont doctor, of course I followed you. I had to be sure you weren't doing more harm than good."

"And the break-ins?"

"No. Although I do suspect your ex, Jack. He's an odd duck, is he not? Possessive, angry." She laughs. "Funny, seeing as how you're currently dating someone a step above."

Two people. Her following me. Him trying to actively ruin my life.

"You didn't have anything to do with those articles?"

"The first one, I did." She lifts a shoulder. "Your mother called me in a panic at the hospital. It was when you were in surgery. She told me the whole fucking story. And then the senator's boy just walked? After hurting you—and potentially ending your career? He's lucky he didn't do more lasting damage. He *should've* been arrested."

Mia taps ash from the end of her cigarette, letting it fall to the floor. There were too many loopholes in the case against Greyson. There was time between him leaving the scene—where no one saw him except me and his passenger —and the police showing up at his house.

There was no solid proof that he was drunk driving.

"I meant what I said, though. That you had a community behind you. I hoped they would've added more, but... oh, well. Nothing I could do about it without getting my hands dirty."

"They're dirty now," I say.

She frowns. "Yes, I suppose so."

"Where do we go from here?"

"You tell me what you learned that would make you want to leave CPB. Leave *me*. And then we'll discuss what our options are." She leans forward, staring down at me. "Think about it, Violet. Your memory can't be that hazy. You only lost a day. But you lost the night *I've* most wanted to forget."

"I think you already know." I raise my eyebrow. "I think you know a lot more than you're saying. I've tried to remember, but it's gone. So please, tell me."

Suddenly Mia is in front of me, brushing my hair away from my forehead. I don't move, can't even breathe, as her fingertips probe my scar.

Greyson makes me forget I even have one. His gaze doesn't stray up to it, he doesn't pay it extra attention, or any at all. He thinks I'm beautiful. But he's not here, and Mia is.

"Did Shawn have you convinced?" she whispers, pressing her nose to my hairline. "Did he give you a two-minute spiel and offer to whisk you away? You can't fall for his bullshit, Violet. Not this time."

Giselle is a tragedy. *Sleeping Beauty* almost is, too. Two girls tricked by people who think they know better. Giselle dies because of it. Aurora falls asleep for a hundred years and wakes up in a new world.

Who pays a lesser price?

Which of them is better off?

"He didn't convince me of anything," I say. "What happened that night?"

Giselle danced with the man she fell in love with and saved him from dying. What's more powerful than that? Being kissed awake by a prince?

"You confronted me," she moans. "I don't know what he said to you, or if he said it again. He knew you weren't going to be cast as Giselle. But he didn't see your talent like I did. Didn't think it was something that could just burst out of you. You told me he said you needed *time*."

I try not to rear back, but I must make some motion, because she twitches. She twists my hair between her fingers. Not pulling, just staring at the blonde strands.

"I came to Rose Hill to see you," she says faintly. "I waited outside the studio. And you yelled... I've never seen you so mad. So hurt. At *me*. But was I so delusional to think that you'd make it so far, so fast? True, raw talent like yours is rare. I had to nurture it. And you! I nurtured you, made you into who you were. And you just wanted to leave me to go be one of his soloists." She scoffs, pounding her chest with her fist. "I make prima ballerinas. *Not* him."

"You scared me," I guess. "That night? Was I frightened?"

By the way she sucks in a breath, I know I'm right. I can almost see it, too. What a reality check. To be told by a choreographer that I so admired that my director was leading me astray. Filling my head with fantasies, when all I needed was to *work harder*. I know how angry I'd be at Mia.

If I'm only good enough to be a principal dancer at Crown Point Ballet, of course I would never leave her. I'd never get a contract as a principal anywhere else. And a few years of being the best, of getting the roles I wanted... Yeah, I can see how she could've manipulated me.

It hits my ego, too.

I can't help but begrudge the fact that I have to learn this twice.

"You ran to your car. Sped out into the road, and that stupid boy hit you," she spits. Her eyes are wild.

This is escalating. I scramble for something to ease her —and give her what she wants.

"I'm going to stay with you." My stomach turns. I take her hand and thread my fingers with hers. "Please don't make me dance as Giselle again. I want to be Aurora for you."

A tear rolls down Mia's cheek. It falls off her jaw and lands on my chest. "You don't know how much it means to me to hear you say that."

It's all a lie.

She releases me and straightens, dragging the chair

with her back into the kitchen. I watch her from the floor as she opens the fridge and pulls out containers, pours a glass of water. I *see* her take a vial from her pocket and let a few drops fall into the water. She mixes it with her finger, then comes back to me.

Is it a test?

She offers me the water first, her eyes large as I bring it to my mouth.

I don't think I can get out of drinking this.

"Is that food?" I ask, lowering the glass slightly.

She nods. "But you're dehydrated. Drink up."

I close my eyes and nod, then take a sip. It doesn't taste any different. There's just a hint of sweet aftertaste. She hands me the container second. Cut up chicken, broccoli, and yellow rice with a plastic spoon shoved into it. I eat quickly, practically shoveling it into my mouth. Any faster and I'll be sick... but maybe the food can slow whatever drug she gave me.

Might be wishful thinking.

My stomach turns, and I brace my hand on the floor. "What was in the water?"

"Something to help you sleep," she says. "It's late. You need rest."

I nod. My inhibitions are fading like I've drank too much liquor. My tongue feels thick, my eyes sluggish.

"Oh, and Violet? If you tell anyone what happened, I'm going to gut your senator's son boyfriend and paint your skin with his blood. Okay?"

It's the last thing I hear.

56

GREYSON

I'm going to lose my mind.

Coach made me play the first ten minutes of the game. He said we had to keep up appearances for the scouts. For my future. I felt sick every second I was on the ice. When he finally switched me out, I left. I hired a car and got back to Crown Point as fast as I could.

Willow met me outside my house. I went inside and checked every room, even the basement. Just in case. Her phone has been off, rendering her location tracker I gave myself access to ineffective.

There was no sign of Violet. No sign that she came back from her audition.

So we kept looking. I kept in touch with Willow as we searched. The hockey team got back and joined in, and eventually, the sky started to lighten.

All night, and nothing.

We meet back at my house. Willow is distraught, her eyes red and watery. I don't have the patience for that. For any of it. I just want Violet back—safe and in one piece.

I punch the wall, and Willow makes a tiny peep of

surprise. It's the only sound she's made since she followed me into the living room, her mouth pinched with worry.

Violet was transparent with her about everything.

Maybe she can figure out who her best friend's stalker is. And I just haven't pushed hard enough to jog her memory.

I wheel toward her, uncaring at the flash of fear that crosses her face. She's never had a reason to *fear* me, but here we are. "Tell me what you know."

"I know what you know," she snaps. "She went to Crown Point Ballet. She's been paranoid about someone following her for months, but no one did anything. We couldn't prove it."

I growl. "This isn't helping."

"You're the obsessive one," she argues. "Don't you have some way of finding her? You're psychotic enough to plant a tracker under her skin. Didn't think of that, did you?"

Well, there's a fucking thought. An idea I should've had already.

"I'll track her phone again." Even as I say it, I'm doubtful it'll work. I last checked less than an hour ago. In fact, I've repeatedly checked when I felt my mind fraying.

Willow creeps closer as I pull up the app and try to ping Violet's location.

Sure enough, a blue dot appears in the middle of fucking nowhere. Her location shows as having only just updated twenty minutes ago. At four o'clock in the morning.

"Oh my god," Willow breathes.

I glance at her. "You recognize where this is?"

"On the edge of a state park. There's just one road in or out."

Good. "Call the cops," I order her. I storm out the door,

my keys clenched in my hand. I don't know that I've ever been so strung up, the need to get to her so badly. Not even when I realized she was with my father.

I get all the way to my truck when I realize it's a little tilted to one side. I circle it, and my heart stops. Two of my tires are cut, the front and back on the passenger side. Flat all the way down to the rim.

Someone cut them, but I don't have time to throw a fit about it.

I go back inside and lift Erik's keys off one of the hooks by the door. He's still out searching with Jacob, the two of them checking the library—again—while Knox and Steele are checking her and Willow's apartment.

Erik will be mad as hell that I took his car, but I can deal with that later. Before I get in, I grab the crowbar out of the back of mine. My heart is beating out of my chest by the time I make it out onto the road. I grip my phone in one hand, the steering wheel in the other.

Twenty minutes later, I'm bumping down a narrow dirt lane. My headlights swing wildly against the trees pressing in, and I spare a thought about turning them off. To sneak. It doesn't really matter—the sun has risen, casting the forest in streams of golden light.

Plus, I've never snuck up on anything—and I'm not about to start now. As bull-headed as it may be, I don't give a fuck.

Violet's stalker has nothing on me.

The road finally dead ends at a log cabin. There's a porch light on, and a dog immediately rises to attention from its spot on the porch. It snarls at me, drool dripping from its mouth. No car, though. Nothing to indicate anyone is actually here.

Maybe it's a dead end.

But I recheck the tracker on her phone, and it has mine practically on top of hers. Sure enough, I spot the slim phone on the porch step. Like it was waiting for me.

I eye the dog, but it doesn't move when I climb the steps up onto the leaning porch. The boards are loose under my feet. The dog seems to be chained to the house far enough away as to not impede the people coming and going.

Vicious thing. The growl that comes out of it is steady and low, a warning that doesn't explode until I grasp the handle.

I shove the door open and raise the crowbar, ready to attack. Not sure what I'm going to find—and terrified that I'm going to see Violet dead. Or hurt.

The room is a mess. All the furniture has been shoved aside, leaving an empty expanse in the middle. There's a lingering smell of rot, like stagnant water and mold under a heavy artificial pine scent.

I keep the crowbar up and step farther inside. The door creaks as it drifts closed behind me.

Then I see her.

She's curled on the floor off to the side, next to a stereo speaker. Someone draped an ugly blanket over her, obscuring her form.

I rush to her side and fling the blanket off, running my hands over her body. Checking for damage, I guess. I don't know.

She's still breathing. And she moans when I shake her shoulder.

Blue and red lights slip in through the partially open door, and the dog barks in earnest. I drop the crowbar and tip my head back, letting out a disbelieving laugh. I fucking hate the police. The last time I saw their lights, I was arrested.

Of course, I deserved it back then.

I cup the back of Violet's neck and pull her halfway into my lap. "Wake up, baby," I urge.

She blinks up at me, her expression going from sleep to surprise in an instant. She reaches for me, and I curl my hand around hers.

"I've got you."

Then the police swarm inside.

57

VIOLET

"The cabin has been abandoned for almost thirty years," the police detective says. He's sitting in the chair beside my hospital bed, a pen poised over his notepad. "And you're saying your captor never showed their face?"

I look away. I've been claiming memory loss due to the drugs, but it's officially all out of my system. I've been in the hospital for two days, for no other reason than Grey is *worried* and demanded the best care for me.

But this detective, a guy named Samuel Beck, is persistent.

"We found a trapdoor in the kitchen," he says. "And a hidden room where we found *your* clothes. A cuff and chain attached to the wall. There's no doubt someone was holding you against your will, Ms. Reece. We just need you to give us a name."

I open my mouth and close it. My chest constricts, and my heart rate on the monitor picks up speed. I catch the increasing numbers out of the corner of my eye as my body reacts to the panic.

I can't tell him. Mia will kill Grey. I don't doubt it.

It was too easy. Grey found me from my phone, which Mia had left on the porch like a freaking beacon.

Maybe she knew that help would be on the way and she didn't want to be caught with me. Her warning rings in my ears, her voice loud and grating. If I tell anyone it was her, she'll kill Greyson.

After Grey was let off the hook so easily, I find it hard to believe Mia will go to prison and stay there. Not if she has the right people on her side.

"Violet," Beck tries, drawing my focus back to him. "We can protect you."

Someone knocks on the door to my room, and the detective jumps to his feet.

"Give us a minute, Sam." Senator Devereux steps inside. He shoots him a bland smile.

My stomach turns. Greyson had to go to class. School has resumed, spring break officially over. I've got a doctor's note to miss another week, and the professors all sent messages that they'd help me catch up when I return.

So it's just me.

The senator takes a look around the room and plucks a card off one of the flower arrangements. "From Shawn Meridian," he reads. "He choreographs for ballet companies, no?"

I don't answer.

He sighs and sets it aside, then stops next to my bed. "How are you feeling?"

"You care?" My brows furrow.

"I had a conversation with my son that has led me here," he says. "Do I *care?* About you? Not particularly. I don't care about much except my own flesh and blood."

I scoff.

He frowns. "I don't think I'll ever be okay with Greyson choosing you over his future."

"Great. Then get out." I point to the door.

"I could," he allows, but he pulls a chair closer and takes a seat instead. "Or I could tell you why I bothered to show up in the first place. I've got a busy schedule, Ms. Reece. Doing charity work isn't usually part of it."

"Maybe you'd get more votes if you did charity work," I retort. I sit up straighter. "But, sure. Call me curious."

"I know that detective outside is pressing you for information you don't want to give. And you've had no recollection, so you say, of who took you." He raises an eyebrow. He's so manicured, it's almost comical. Gray hair, smooth face. His forehead doesn't even crease with the expression, and his skin has that spray-tanned color. His teeth are so white.

Maybe all politicians look like that, and I've just never noticed.

"That's what you know," I say. "But what did Grey say?"

He smiles down at his shoes, then meets my gaze. "His mother used to call him that. She'd carry him around the house singing to him. He was her little raincloud. Always crying, always thunderous in his emotions. He lets you call him that?"

A lump forms in my throat. "He loved her a lot, you know."

"Yes, of course he did. She was his mother."

I swallow, ignoring the burn behind my eyes. I need to return that photo album to him. I've been holding back—and holding out—because I was worried he was just using me. But he found me, even after Mia took me. He left one of the most important games to come save *me*. I believe him when he says he loves me. It just took a little while...

"My son understands you." He appraises me. "He says you're afraid to name your abductor because of what they've threatened. Did they say they'd come back and kill you? Harm you? Perhaps your view of our justice system is tainted because of *our* history."

I keep my eyes on my lap. "Maybe it wasn't me who was threatened, Senator, but your son. If it was me, I could live with that. I would've given up a name by now. But him? Never."

He leans forward, bracing his hands on the side of the bed. "Listen to me, Violet."

I lift my gaze and meet his eyes.

"For this, I'm willing to make the system work in our favor. Do you understand?"

"She can't be allowed to walk free." A tear slips down my face, and I quickly brush it away. God, I hope he's telling the truth.

"She?"

"Mia Germain," I whisper. How easily I'm folding. I can only pray he has good intentions. That he cares about his son enough to put her away forever. His face remains blank, not recognizing the name. How funny, when she's been such a big presence in my life. I add, "The artistic director of Crown Point Ballet. She's been following me. She took me against my will and then she drugged me."

He rises. "Thank you, Violet. I'll take care of it."

When he's gone, I sag back against the pillows. And the tears flow for real.

58

VIOLET

"Do you want to deal?" Willow shuffles the cards, leaning back against the footboard of my bed.

I hold out my hand for the stack and shuffle again. I'm being discharged today, after the doctor checks out my most recent blood panel and gives the okay. Then I'll have to wait for paperwork, but everyone who works here tells me it shouldn't be later than three o'clock. Ish.

Sometimes things run slowly.

Willow's been a comfort. She arrived early, right after the morning rounds, armed with iced lattes and breakfast sandwiches. And games. Something else, too, that I only briefly looked at before tucking it away again.

I relayed what happened with the senator. She's less surprised than Grey was, but I think she has a better handle on how things work. Tricky relationships between parents and children, money and agendas.

"Knock, knock." Grey leans into the room. "You have a visitor."

"You knew Willow was going to be here, didn't you?"

Willow rolls her eyes.

"Not her. Or me." He comes farther into the room, and worry creases the corners of his eyes. "Just say the word, and I'll have security toss her out."

I swallow.

A second later, my mother inches into the room. Her gaze darts around, from the bag of saline over my head to the window, to the monitors, to the needle taped to my arm. Everywhere except me, right in front of her.

Willow slides off the bed, taking the cards from my hand. "I'll be outside."

Grey takes up a position against the wall. Maybe out of her sight, or out of her focus, but certainly not out of mine.

"I was so worried," Mom finally says.

I don't answer.

What the hell am I supposed to say to that?

She clears her throat. Shuffles. "Violet, please."

"Are you here hoping I'll be prescribed more opiates?"

My mother flinches.

I sit up. "I'm going to tell you something. And I need you to hear it, okay?"

She nods and approaches, stopping at the foot of the bed. She grips the plastic.

"You traded in being my mother for drugs." I keep my eyes glued on hers, and she doesn't look away. "You brought me to his father's suite, at one of Grey's biggest games, because you wanted *money* from him."

"I'm sorry," she whispers.

I close my eyes for a moment, then force myself to meet her gaze. "I think it's best if we go our separate ways. I love you, but..." A lump forms in my throat. *I love you, but*—the phrase has been haunting both of us for a while. My mother and I just don't fit together.

Still, she doesn't move. "I only ever did this for us—"

"Don't lie to her," Grey snaps.

"I'm sorry," she repeats. "I'm so sorry."

I let out a breath when she slinks away.

Grey sits on the edge of the bed, then pulls my arms away from my chest. He interlocks our fingers. "You okay?"

"I'll be fine." I look down at our hands—and then I remember what Willow brought. I release him to lean over the edge, grabbing her bag from the floor. "I got you something."

His eyebrow raises. "Oh, yeah?"

I set the bag on my lap and pull out the photo album. It was kept safe in the attic crawl space in our apartment.

He looks at it for a moment, presented in my hands, like he's second-guessing whether it's what he thinks it is. He flips open the first page and glances down at it. Has it only been a few months since he took me up into his room and snapped at me to put this down?

I'm glad I didn't.

And then he starts to talk. I settle back against my pillow, and he adjusts to sit next to me. He tells me about the photos, pointing out people, and my heart aches for him.

I rest my head on his shoulder as he weaves another picture entirely about the family he lost. And for most of it, I hardly dare breathe in fear that he'll stop.

———

Grey offers me his hand.

I wave him away and step out of his truck, then look around. We're not in front of his hockey house. Not near my apartment either. I expected one or the other after we left the restaurant that served us a huge brunch.

We're in a nice neighborhood a few blocks from campus, close to the stadium.

"I rented this for us," he says in my ear, wrapping his arms around me from behind.

I eye the white house he directs my attention to, filling with suspicion. It's *nice*. Manicured lawn, a covered porch with two rocking chairs on it. The backyard is fenced, from what I can tell.

He opens his hand in front of me, revealing a set of keys.

I take them and let him guide me up the concrete walkway. I unlock the front door and step through, poking around. Still suspicious, maybe, that something's going to jump out and ruin everything.

It's been a week since I was released from the hospital. I've been hiding away in Greyson's room at the hockey house, only emerging when he returns from practice to coax me into the kitchen for food. He's accompanied me to the rented studio, too, although I've been dancing without my pointe shoes.

They're evidence, I guess. Not that I would want them back.

Mia made me dance until my toenails cracked and bled. When the nurse gently slid the shoes off my feet, she cringed. Dried blood stained the satin.

I have to go back to class tomorrow. And next week, the Hawks play in the national tournament finals. They beat the team in the quarter finals, then won again on Friday. Saturday, we head to Boston to face a team they've already played —the Pac North Wolves. One of the first games I went to, actually. Greyson says they've had a major improvement over the season and they'll be harder to beat than they were.

Anyway, this is real life, and I need to get back to it.

Mia was arrested. She's sitting in county jail, and Grey's dad has told us that they're transferring her to Virginia—where she was born and raised, I guess. He kept his word and pulled some strings. He also told the judge of her threat against his son, and the judge was more than happy to withhold bail.

I will have to testify at some point. Face her again.

"You with me?" Grey asks.

I refocus on him and force a smile. "Yep."

He holds out his hand. I take it and let him show me the house. It's small, a perfect size for just the two of us. A kitchen with a window into a living and dining room. A bedroom and bathroom tucked out of the way. Stairs lead up to a big bedroom and bathroom on the second floor. It's bright and airy.

"Do you like it?"

I nod, releasing him to run my hands over the kitchen counters, the walls. I turn on the faucet just for the hell of it, wetting my fingers before I shut it off and wipe them dry on my pants. I let out a laugh.

"You mean we don't have to worry about anyone over-hearing us?" I ask.

He smirks.

My smile slowly fades. "I have something to ask you."

His expression turns serious, too. "You can ask. You don't have to preface it with a warning."

"Okay."

He waits. When I remain silent, he stalks forward and smoothly lifts me onto the counter. I part my knees, letting him get closer, and loop my arms around his neck.

"Vi," he urges. "I might die of curiosity."

He knows that Mia threatened his life. He knows his

father came to the hospital and his guarantee of her prosecution was the only reason I confessed.

But he doesn't know what Mia told me.

"Jack's the one who broke into my room," I admit. "And I think he had something to do with the articles about you. Or at least my portion of them."

Grey's gaze shutters, and then he meets my eyes again. "That's not a question."

I grip the back of his neck. "I know you took care of it last time."

"Still not a question."

"I figure you might strike back again. With this new information. And... I want to be there. Will you let me?"

"You're asking to come along with me?" The corner of his lips turn up. "You want to watch me break his other leg, Violent? Or maybe you want to break it yourself?"

He doesn't wait for an answer. He presses his lips to mine.

My eyes close, and I hold him tightly. I let my mind go with his kiss, wiping the slate clean. His hand moves up my front, his index finger finding the scabbed cut on my breast. He pulls my shirt down and breaks the kiss to look down at it.

"We're connected, you and I. There's nothing I wouldn't do for you."

I nod.

"If Mia Germain ever gets out, I'm going to kill her." He catches my lips again, nipping me before retreating again. "That's a fucking promise."

"I believe you."

He brightens. "Good. Now, let me show you how I really feel about you..."

59

GREYSON

We win by one. *My* one.

The buzzer sounds, and suddenly my teammates are rushing onto the ice. They slam into me, jumping up and down. Celebrating. It echoes in my ears, mixing with the roar of approval from the crowd.

I automatically search the crowd and find Violet pressed against the glass with a huge smile. She's surrounded by a sea of blue and silver. I point at her, and she pretends to catch it. I'm pulled away before our exchange can continue.

The next hour is a blur. There's an award ceremony, where the national tournament officials bring out a trophy. And then Coach Roake names me most valuable player. I stare at him, a little bit in disbelief, until Knox prods me forward to accept it.

The crowd is still cheering, the lights dim, and a spotlight is on us.

Insane.

It's one of those dream-come-true things.

"And we're only juniors," Knox says, hooking his arm around my neck. "Just think about next year's potential."

I grin at him. Knox, Steele, and I will be seniors next year. Miles will be a junior. Jacob and Erik are moving on, but I'll be honest—I'm not close enough with them to care. It feels right to be here, to solidify this as my family.

The place I belong.

We go into the locker room, still riding a high, and Erik calls out that we're celebrating at a club. Apparently, he has connections in Boston, and the owner is letting us in—even though we're not all twenty-one.

I change into my street clothes, the button-down shirt and slacks we all arrived in, and stuff the rest of my shit into my duffle bag. We drop off our bags in our hotel rooms. We spill out of the elevator into the lobby. We crammed too many of us in there, but none of us gave a shit.

My phone goes off.

Vi: I see you

I whip around, trying to find her. There's too many people, but then she stands out. My eyes are drawn to her like magnets. She comes through the crowd in my jersey, and my cock instantly twitches at the sight of her. An image of fucking her in that jersey and nothing else comes to mind, and I have to banish that thought before I ignore the club and drag her back upstairs.

A quickie wouldn't be the worst thing in the world.

"Hey, MVP," she greets me.

I wrap my arms around her, pressing my body to hers. Her eyes widen slightly at the feel of my erection, and I laugh. I feel... I don't know. Lighter than a fucking feather.

I have her, I have hockey. I have another year at Crown Point University with her.

"You in my jersey is doing things to me," I tell her.

She smirks. "I can tell. I didn't get a chance to wear it when you first gave it to me, so..."

I kiss her. I can't not kiss her. She lifts up on her toes, and her tongue slips along the seam of my lips. I open for her, letting her deepen it. She tastes like popcorn and beer. I cup the back of her head.

This isn't helping my erection.

She finally settles back flat on her feet and gives me a wicked smile. "Maybe we should take a detour," she offers. "The bathroom is over there."

I find myself nodding before she even finishes talking. She leads me through the crowd, slipping past groups of people easily. I try not to get stuck, people tossing out congratulations for the MVP award, for the game, and Violet's grip on my hand is unrelenting.

Nothing's stopping her.

She pushes into the hotel lobby bathroom and goes straight to the handicapped stall. I raise my eyebrows as she locks us inside and shoves her leggings down.

I don't need much more prompting than that. I undo my pants and push them down just far enough.

"Turn around," I order. "Hands on the wall."

My voice is fucking hoarse, but she does what I say. I grip her hips and kick her legs a little wider, then slide my hand down to feel how wet she is. My cock is harder than granite, but I ignore it for a second. Her cunt is wet for me, and she bites back a sigh when I brush her clit.

"Fuck me," she demands.

I adjust my hold on her hips and slide into her. I grunt as her muscles clench at me. *Fuck.* I'm not going to last long at all. I've been looking forward to this since we left our bed this morning. I probably think about sex with her too much. I'm obsessive.

But I'm pretty sure she's just as obsessed with me.

I lean forward and bite her shoulder through the jersey. She arches, tensing, and swears. It's only then that I begin to move, thrusting in and out of her with powerful strokes. She lets out little gasps, trying not to make much noise.

The bathroom door opens. The sounds of everyone in the lobby slip through, then dull again when the door swings shut. Someone enters, going into one of the other stalls.

Violet looks at me over her shoulder, her expression... still fucking hungry.

I wink at her, but I don't stop. She's holding her breath, I think. Her face is turning red. My hand goes around her front, sliding down into her wetness to flick her clit. I rub it hard, just the way she likes it.

Her fingers grip the tile wall, her knuckles turning white. Her head falls back, and her mouth opens.

She's going to break and say something. Gasp, whimper, moan. Anything.

The girl in the other stall is carrying on her business. Maybe she can hear us and is mortified. It's a quiet bathroom, after all. Just the sound of her piss, and then the flush.

Violet uses that noise to cover her own sounds.

The water turns on at the sink. She takes a fucking eon to wash her hands. I increase my speed, both my finger on her clit and my cock pounding in her. I'm gonna fucking come before this chick leaves.

But then the door opens, the noise seeping back in, and swings shut.

Fucking *finally*.

It seems Violet was holding out for that moment, too, because her orgasm hits her a second later. I groan, her cunt squeezing around my dick enough to send me over the edge, too. I stop fully inside her. She pushes back against me, her ass meeting my hips, and we both stay like that for a minute.

I cup her jaw and turn her face. I kiss her fiercely, then pull out of her.

She lets out another little whimper that sets my heart on fire.

"That was fun," I say.

Violet snorts. Her cheeks are pink. I hand her a wad of toilet paper, then take care of my own mess. When we're both presentable, she unlocks the door and steps out. Washes her hands, presses her palms to her cheeks. She meets my eyes in the mirror.

"Do you think she heard?"

"Baby, don't know if anyone would've been able to miss it."

She freezes, then shakes her head. Can't tell if I'm joking or not, I guess.

We catch up with everyone on the sidewalk. Steele gives me a subtle fist bump, and I grin. Violet ignores it—or misses it. Her friends swarm around her, walking ahead of us.

There's just one last thing to deal with...

And he's in Boston tonight.

Knox knows the plan. So does Steele. We decided to let Miles keep his innocence another year, but this is going to bond the three of us harder than any hockey game.

We've all agreed.

So we follow the girls to the club. We dance and nurse our beers, waving away offers for another round. Until my watch vibrates on my wrist at eleven o'clock. There are so many people in this place. It's three stories of dancing bodies. But I clock Knox and Steele moving through the crowd.

I give them fifteen minutes, then I tap Violet's hand and motion for her to follow me.

She's not as drunk as she probably expected to be either. I've been running interference on her drinks. Her eyes narrow, but she doesn't object when I turn and bulldoze a path toward the door.

We go down the block, back to the hotel, and into the elevator.

She grips my hand tightly, confusion all over her face. "Are you going to tell me what this is about?"

I tilt my head. "No. You'll see for yourself in a minute."

Violet goes quiet, her mind clearly spinning. We get out on the top floor, and I lead her to the stairs that go up to the roof. She hesitates but nods slowly to herself. Steeling her nerves, perhaps. She trusts me.

When she pushes through the door, a cool spring wind tugs at her clothes.

Knox and Steele are there with a figure on the floor between them. He's got a hood over his head and a walking boot on his leg. His wrists are bound behind him.

Violet stiffens.

I glance at her, then stride up to Jack and yank his hood off. He blinks up at me, first shock and then outrage crossing his expression.

"You fucking bastard—" His attention swings past me to Violet, and his outrage explodes into fury. He struggles, trying to get to his feet.

Knox and Steele grab him, forcing him back down.

"I'm going to kill you," he seethes at her.

I punch him.

His head whips to the side, and pain flares through my

knuckles and up my arm. I hit him again, and again, until blood pours down his face. His nose might be broken.

Knox and Steele remain passive, although their jaws are tense.

They like Violet. Jack threatening her threatens all of us.

My girl approaches carefully, stopping just shy of me. Not quite courageous enough to cross that line and put herself in danger.

"Did you sneak into my room, Jack?" she asks.

He spits at her. The glob of saliva and blood lands just shy of her shoes.

I circle around and kneel behind him, gripping his hair and forcing him to face Violet. I put my face close to his. "Look at her, Jackie boy. You didn't break her. You don't scare her. But you will answer her goddamn questions."

Jack scowls, but he does answer her question. "I did," he confirms. "Many times."

Her brows draw together. "What?"

"Any fucking chance I got." He laughs. "You caught me once. I made sure you knew I was there another time. But I loved slipping into your room and jacking off with your panties in my hand. I memorized every fucking picture on your wall, your scent, your makeup."

"That's creepy," Knox mutters.

Violet shudders. "Why go through the trouble?"

Jack jerks, but my grip on his hair is solid. He's let it grow in his off-season. Shame on him.

"Why?" he yells. "Because you're fucking *mine*, Violet. We're soulmates."

I laugh. In a flash, my knife is out of my pocket and at his throat.

I could do it.

He goes silent and still, his eyes flashing with fear for

the first time. Maybe he didn't think we were *serious*. That I wouldn't kill for her.

"You're not her soulmate, asshole."

His eyes roll, finding my face. "I swear to God—"

"You better hope God is on your side." I lean in, making sure he can see just how fucking dark I'll go. "Because the Devil's on mine."

He flinches.

He sees it.

"Here's what's going to happen, Jackie boy." I look up at Violet. "We're going to take that video of your confession and turn it in to the police. Along with you. I don't fucking care what you tell them, but you *will* make sure you go to prison."

His nostrils flare. "Why the fuck would I do that?"

I tap his walking boot, and he cringes again. He's used to pain from me. Expects it.

Good.

"This was just a little taste of what I can do. And if you don't put bars between us to keep you safe, well... maybe we'll take you out on my father's boat. Maybe there will be an accident, and you'll fall overboard. Or maybe you'll slip on your way to a new club tonight, fall into the subway tracks. Electrocute yourself." I hum. "There are so many possibilities."

"You should take prison, Jack," Violet says. "Sounds like the lesser of two evils." She dusts off her pants. Just to give herself something to do maybe. She doesn't wait to see what he decides. She leaves us, the door to the stairwell swishing shut behind her.

I drop his head and step away. There's a great view of the city from up here. And when I inhale, there isn't much of that city smell. I do detect the ocean, though. A faint saltiness.

"Well?" I ask without turning around.

"Take me to the police station," he says.

"Take yourself," I snap.

Knox and Steele cut him loose. He stands between them, wary, and then leaves.

"Follow him," I tell them. "I've got a girl to comfort."

They nod.

It's just me, then. I take a deep breath, then leave the roof. Mia and Jack were loose ends. My father has issued a temporary truce. Her mother is gone... for now maybe. Hopefully.

I unlock the door to the room Violet and I are sharing, and I've barely made it inside when she throws herself at me.

"I love you. I don't think I've ever said it out loud, but I do." She cups my face. "I love you, I love you—"

I kiss her, swallowing the words. Something in my chest unlocks. Not fear, like I expected, but acceptance. I can love her, and I won't lose her. I'm not a child, afraid of my parents disappearing if I cared too hard. Warmth follows a second later, and I wrap her in my arms.

We're going to be together forever.

VIOLET

TWO YEARS LATER

"Ready?" the stage manager asks me.

I nod. The curtain falls to thunderous applause, and my heart soars. The corps de ballet flood past me. The curtain rises, sweeping upward, and the lights come on full force. The dancers separate by scenes, going down stage for their final bows.

They soak in the applause, the *appreciation*, then turn and take their positions farther back. Making room for others.

Across the way, in the opposite wing, is my partner.

"You deserve this," the stage manager says. "Go ahead."

I take a deep breath and raise my arms. I walk gracefully out onto the stage, meeting my partner in the center. His hand comes around my waist, and his other cradles my outstretched hand. He motions to me, stepping back, and I curtsey. Then he bows. We come together and repeat, then glide backward.

It's only then that I can focus on the audience.

And how they're all standing.

Tears burn the backs of my eyes. This is my first show as a principal dancer with the Boston Ballet. Months of hard work, summer intensives, training. Struggling to balance the last year of school with my role in Crown Point Ballet.

Due to Mia's abrupt exit, CPB ended up withdrawing from doing a national tour and just produced a home season with *Sleeping Beauty*. It turned out, there was a lot more going on under the surface. She was abusing funds, adjusting the books. With her rotting in prison, there was a lot of things the board of directors had to fix.

I signed a contract as a soloist and danced through the season... and then I was done. I joined Boston Ballet the following season as a soloist and then was promoted to principal this year.

The curtain closes, and we all come forward. We'll do one final bow, and then it'll be time to celebrate.

Well. Even as I say that, I'm aware that I'm lying to myself. Grey had an away game with the Bruins, so I'll be returning to our empty apartment after a drink at the local bar.

When the curtain reopens, the audience is still on their feet. We all take a final bow.

A murmur sweeps through the room. I crane my head to see where it's coming from, and my heart skips a beat.

Grey walks up the stairs with a bouquet in his arms. He smiles, his gaze locked on me, as he comes down the stage and stops before me.

"Really?" I murmur, leaning in to kiss him.

He winks. "You think I was going to miss your first performance as lead? Absolutely not. Plus..." He hands the bouquet off and pulls something even better from his pocket.

In front of everyone, he goes down on one knee.

"Violet Reece, will you marry me?" He tilts his head. "This is the only time I'll make it a question, love."

Those tears that had been burning behind my eyes spill out. Of all the places, he chooses here. Cementing this memory even more impressively in my mind.

A night I'll never forget.

"Vi?"

"Yes, yes." I grin and give him my hand.

He slips the ring on my finger—a perfect fit, of course—and rises. I throw my arms around his neck and press my lips to his.

We got our dreams *and* each other.

Perfect, right?

THE END

Get ready for more Crown Point University hockey boys in 2023!
Pre-order Devious Obsession:

https://mybook.to/deviousobsession

But if you're not ready to let go of Greyson and his hockey boys just yet, check out their group chat here:

http://smassery.com/brutal-obsession-bonus

ACKNOWLEDGMENTS

The way this story came about is wild, and I don't think a book ever coalesced so perfectly for me as an author.

Greyson and Violet were born from the lovely members of my Facebook group, SMassery Squad. That sounds a little weird, but bear with me.

Almost a year ago, I made a slight little mention of Caleb (from *Fallen Royals*) getting some competition in the form of an even darker, college bully. From that point on, well... Greyson took over. Before I even knew his name, he was in my head.

But because my readers had been there cheering for him since the beginning, I wanted to involve them at the inception level.

I created a series of polls. I thought it would be a refreshing twist to let my readers pick my characters' first names, some major tropes and sub tropes. (Did someone say spit kink? Helloooo, my new friend! Although this wasn't actually voted on, it just... happened. Whoops.)

Let me just say: Best. Idea. Ever.

I love getting readers involved. I loved seeing what *they* wanted in a story from me, and the ideas it invoked from what they were excited about. And, quite meanly, I wrote the dang thing and then kept it a secret for 9 months.

My bad.

Another fun little tidbit: in the book, the CPU Hawks play the Pac North Wolves. That's a real fictional team from my friend Daniela Romero's *The Savage*. She let me include them because I was sitting beside her when I was writing that scene. Thanks, Danielle!

This book was so much fun to write, and I just want to say a sincere thank you to everyone who has been so enthusiastic since I briefly mentioned the possibility of this book existing back in the beginning of January.

Greyson is for you.

So, thank you so much for allowing me the space to create someone so freaking depraved. I had a blast writing it, and I hope you had fun reading it. ;)

Stay tuned for more Crown Point University hockey players and the women that ensnare them, coming in 2023!

ALSO BY S. MASSERY

Dark Bully Romance

Fallen Royals

#1 Wicked Dreams

#2 Wicked Games

#3 Wicked Promises

#4 Vicious Desire

#5 Cruel Abandon

#6 Wild Fury

Crown Point University

Brutal Obsession

Devious Obsession

Twisted Obsession

TBA

TBA

TBA

Dark Reverse Harem

Sterling Falls

(Greek Mythology vibes, anyone?)

#1 THIEF

#2 FIGHTER

#3 REBEL

Mafia Romance

DeSantis Mafia

#1 Ruthless Saint

#2 Savage Prince

#3 Stolen Crown

Romantic Suspense

Broken Mercenaries

#1 Blood Sky

#2 Angel of Death

#3 Morning Star

ABOUT THE AUTHOR

S. Massery is a dark romance author who loves injecting a good dose of suspense into her stories. She lives in Western Massachusetts with her dog, Alice.

Before adventuring into the world of writing, she went to college in Boston and held a wide variety of jobs—including working on a dude ranch in Wyoming (a personal highlight). She has a love affair with coffee and chocolate. When S. Massery isn't writing, she can be found devouring books, playing outside with her dog, or trying to make people smile.

Join her newsletter to stay up to date on new releases: http://smassery.com/newsletter